"Deeply honest, **wholly compassionate**,
and desperately needed."
—Meredith Adamo, author of *Not Like Other Girls*

"Nothing short of **a modern masterpiece**."
—Amber Smith, *New York Times*
bestselling author of *The Way I Used to Be*

"Inspiring, hopeful, and very necessary."
—Josh Silver, author of *HappyHead*

BY KATHLEEN GLASGOW

Girl in Pieces

How to Make Friends with the Dark

You'd Be Home Now

BY KATHLEEN GLASGOW AND LIZ LAWSON

The Agathas

The Night in Question

THE GLASS GIRL

KATHLEEN GLASGOW

DELACORTE PRESS

Wherever you are
However dark the journey seems
Come back
Someone's left the light on for you

Delacorte Press
An imprint of Random House Children's Books
A division of Penguin Random House LLC
1745 Broadway, New York, NY 10019
penguinrandomhouse.com
GetUnderlined.com

The Library of Congress has cataloged the hardcover edition of this work as follows:
Names: Glasgow, Kathleen, author.
Title: The glass girl / Kathleen Glasgow.
Description: First edition. | New York: Delacorte Press, 2024. | Audience: Ages 14+ |
Summary: When fifteen-year-old Bella's latest blackout lands her in the hospital, she enters rehab to confront her addiction to alcohol.
Identifiers: LCCN 2023051553 (print) | LCCN 2023051554 (ebook) |
ISBN 978-0-525-70808-7 (trade) | ISBN 978-0-525-70809-4 (lib. bdg.) |
ISBN 978-0-525-70810-0 (ebook) | ISBN 978-0-525-70811-7 (pbk.)
Subjects: CYAC: Alcoholism—Fiction. | Rehabilitation—Fiction. | Family life—Fiction.
Classification: LCC PZ7.1.G587 Gl 2024 (print) | LCC PZ7.1.G587 (ebook) | DDC [Fic]—dc23

Originally published in hardcover by Delacorte Press, New York, in 2024.

Manufactured in the United States of America
4th Printing

The authorized representative in the EU for product safety and compliance is Penguin Random House Ireland, Morrison Chambers, 32 Nassau Street, Dublin D02 YH68, Ireland, https://eu-contact.penguin.ie.

The branches dug into her palms
She didn't mind the blood there
She kept going
Higher and higher
Leaves in her hair
Tears in her jeans
She didn't mind the blood there
Some fire in her heart
Pushing her higher
Away from the shouting
Away from the stares
Away from the world
Strong feet, bare on the branches
She didn't mind the blood there
At the top
In the sky
Able to breathe
The shouting gone
The stares gone
Leaned her cheek on the tree
Closed her eyes
Took it all in
Washed it all away, away, away
Such a beautiful world

When she dulled it all down
Smoothed its jagged edges
Filed it all to ash
And watched it drift between her fingers
And then
A snap, a crack, and she fell
And fell
And fell
And fell
The shards of her nesting in the blood there

EVERY MORNING WHEN I wake up, I don't think I'm going to make it. Or maybe I think that I don't want to make it. I'm heavy with what I did the night before and I'm heavy with everything inside me and sometimes it is just too goddamn much to carry around. I am the kind of tired that makes your bones feel skeletal and clacky. I am the kind of tired that is cement in your shoes, X-ray vest on your chest, bricks tied to your wrists. But I get up. I drag myself out of bed and plant my cement feet on the floor and start the stupidity of routine because that's what it is to be fifteen: your mother will yell at you if you're going to be late for school; your dad will yell at you that he'll be late to work if you don't get a move on. Your teacher will embarrass you in class because you weren't paying attention. Anyone and everyone knocks into you in the hallway, sending you tumbling against the wall, and it isn't even on purpose. It's worse. They just don't even see you. You don't exist. You are not the tiniest blip on their radar of humanity. You'll see that person who took your heart and cleaved it in half and stuffed it in their mouth and swallowed and you want it back and you think you'll never get it and who can live like that? Or you'll remember your grandmother is dead and that's a giant black hole hungry for you, too. And who can live like that? Maybe there will be a shooter drill today and you'll have to huddle under the windows in art. Or maybe it will be real this time and not a drill. The penguins in Antarctica have plastic in their blood. Fire. Floods. It's hot where you live in the desert and every year it gets hotter. But you have to get up because you're fifteen and that's what you do. Put on baggy jeans. Put on baggy T-shirt. Baggy hoodie. Baggy everything because you need to leave room for your pain to grow. Protect yourself. You've perfected a mask of powder and black eyeliner and a face for people to look at on the outside and maybe it's not really who you are on the inside, but who wants to see that? That part is too much and not enough. That part is all hollows and a gray, dying heart. Everyone says it will get better after all this. When you're older. Like it's a sentence you have to serve. Like it will toughen you up if you can make it. Like it will all be worthwhile. And maybe that's true, but it seems a long way away and a long time to carry that weight and the only reason you can get through the day is because you know what you can do at the end of it to make it worthwhile for a little bit before that comforting wave takes you away and drowns everything else out.

ONE

Ten, ten, ten, ten for everything
Everything, everything, everything

—Violent Femmes, "Kiss Off"

FRIDAY

IT'S LIKE WE'RE PLAYING spin the bottle, but without the actual bottle. I know exactly how it will go. The imaginary bottle will spin among us in a dizzying way and then slow, eventually pointing to me.

Cherie doesn't want to be the one. She says she's not good at it, even though she's only done it twice. She says she doesn't like the way people look at her.

Amber says forget it. Since she's the only one with a car and a license, she drives and says that's enough. If she has to stay sober, she shouldn't be the one. *I'm the ferry captain,* she says. *I'm navigating this drunken ship, so not me.* She doesn't like drinking, anyway. She tried it once and everything seemed okay; she was giggling along with the rest of us in Kristen's room as we passed Dixie cups of crème de menthe around, but then she vomited in her lap. We had to undress her and put her in the shower, me volunteering to stand in there with her so she wouldn't fall. I shampooed the chunks of vomit from the ends of her long hair as she cried. It's a good thing Kristen's mom was at her boyfriend's for the night. We found the crème de menthe on the very top shelf of a kitchen cabinet, the bottle dusty from neglect. It looked and smelled candyish, so we tried it. We were thirteen; what kid doesn't like candy? Anyway, that was the first and only time for Amber.

Kristen is pressed against the car door, pigtails with red bows fluttering in the wind drifting in the half-open window.

"Bella, you do it. You're the best. You don't care," she says, waving her vape pen.

"That's so disgusting," Amber tells her. "Sincerely gross."

"Everything is gross when you think about it," Kristen replies. "Who cares?"

In the back seat, next to Cherie, I sigh.

The bottle has landed on me. What Kristen said is what everyone always says to me, for everything, in various versions:

Bella, you do it.

Bella, tell your sister it's time to get off her tablet and come to dinner.

Bella, tell your father he's late with the check again.

Bella, find out if that guy thinks I'm hot.

Bella, I didn't read the book, tell me what happened so I can write this stupid friggin' paper.

Bella, Bella, Bella.

I close my eyes. I wish I was alone, but I'm not allowed to be alone, after Dylan, and I know I should be grateful my friends are trying to take care of me, but sometimes I just want some peace and quiet, no noise, nothing. Just . . . nothing.

Sometimes it feels like I live in a pinball machine and I'm the scratched-up ball, being knocked from one nook to the next, lights blaring, bells ringing. I can never stop the game because I *am* the game.

Amber pulls up to the curb around the block from the store. Some of the red letters on the sign above the store have gone dark, so it reads L_ C_Y L_Q_ _R.

Lucky Liquor. Some of the older guys at school call it Lucy Licker. *Me and Lucy Licker hung out last night.* Explaining away puffy eyes, bad breath, as if anyone would actually care they were hungover. Honestly, no one ever cares what guys do. Only what girls do.

Everyone in the car is quiet, waiting for me.

I make them wait a few minutes longer, like I always do. This is our routine. It never changes.

If Kristen drives, she says she can't do it. If Amber isn't driving, she says it makes her feel weird and she doesn't really like drinking anyway, so everyone forgives her. Cherie never does it anymore because a gross dude once grabbed the pocket of her hoodie and ripped it off. It's round and round, all the time, spin the bottle. It doesn't matter what we play: the pebble of our booze hopscotch always lands on me.

It lands on me because they know I'll do it.

Bella is always up for adventure. Bella will do it. Bella is good at it. Bella will come through. Bella, come on.

Kristen and Cherie hold out their money and I listen to them breathe. Amber's eyes are turned to the left, toward the darkness outside the driver's-side window, so I can't see them in the rearview. I think she's mad, but she won't say it out loud.

Fine, I say. *Fine, you cowards.* I snatch the money, warm and wrinkled, from their hands.

Bella, they say. *Bella, you're the best.*

I'm not the best. I'm the worst. But it doesn't matter. All I want right now is to dull the sharpness inside me. The stuff that no one can see. The stuff poking me and making me bleed.

I open the car door and get out.

There are rules you have to follow, things you have to remember.

Like waiting a little bit, but not too long, and not too close to the store or somebody might get suspicious. An older lady in a Lexus, pulling into the store, pretending she's there just for Arizona Iced Tea and Altoids. Those ladies are righteously judgmental and need to be avoided, even though they'll come out with plastic bags of wine they'll probably finish in a couple of hours. I mean, come *on.* The reason they're at this crappy liquor store in a crappy neighborhood is so nobody they know sees them buying all that wine in their *own* neighborhood. Because they drink *a lot* and don't want anyone to know how much. And there's always some old suit heading inside, frowning at the girl on the sidewalk (me) pretending to check her phone. *You need something?* he might say, his bald head shining. *You lost?* Even though that's not really what he's asking. You can tell because they always look you up and down. You can't pick them. They'll want to walk you back to the car, "make sure you're safe," check out your friends, be pervy. They probably have daughters and would die if they knew their daughters did this. We are all someone's daughter.

You have to choose carefully. It can never be a lady unless she's slightly disheveled and kind of dumpy (flannel shirt, cigs in pocket, flip-flops), which signifies she doesn't give a damn. She might do it, say, *You be careful with your party, now,* as she hands over the bag. *Don't get into any trouble.*

It can be a guy in his twenties, maybe, but not too cool, not too slick, maybe lonely-looking (taped eyeglasses, T-shirt with inscrutable cultural reference, dirty sneakers), but you can't let him think he can walk back to the car with you, or get your number, and you can't talk to him too long or it turns into a *thing,* which did actually happen once and ended with Kristen literally catching the guy's fingers in the car window as she furiously rolled it up, him calling us names, and Amber hitting the gas. We screamed hysterically in the car, everyone's voices blending together in a high pitch, but soon enough we were buzzed (not Amber) and laughing hysterically. That's the kind of nice thing about drinking: what seemed to be one thing becomes an entirely different thing once you're drunk.

That can also be bad but I'm trying to stay away from bad stuff and thoughts. Like Dylan. Which was definitely a situation where one thing became another, and not in a good way. That was the night I had what Kristen refers to as Bella's Extremely Unfortunate Public Downfall.

Anyway, you need a person who doesn't care. A person going into the store for their own reasons. You want a person who doesn't even bat an eye, just listens to you and takes the money and comes back with their bag and gives you yours and takes the change and goes back to their car or walks down the sidewalk into the night without even saying *goodbye* or *where you partying* or *be safe,* because they've got to get on with the night, too. You need to scope out who is absolutely here for alcohol, who has to have it *now,* like you, and doesn't mind making an extra ten for their trouble.

You have to make it quick and clean. Blunt. I've learned a lot just from the few times we've done it this way.

Hey, will you buy me a fifth of vodka? You can keep the change.

You want a guy. Oldish, hair messy, ball cap, band T-shirt under a sports jacket, shuffling along in his low-rise Converse, smelling like cigarettes. Like one of my dad's friends, actually: used to be in a band "or something" and on the wrong side of cool now. Maybe thought he'd be a rock star, but now he's cubicle-bound during the day, dreams dead and gone in a blur of Excel spreadsheets. All he's got comes from this store.

On the sidewalk, I jiggle my toes inside my sneakers, pretending to scroll on my phone but peeking up furtively every few seconds to scope out the situation. If I'm being honest, I don't actually mind doing this, because I know where I'll end up: feeling better. And a tiny part of me gets a little thrill from it.

Then I see him.

I can tell; he'll do it. This guy doesn't give a damn. Eyes on the sidewalk; doesn't care if I'm cute or hot or not. He doesn't give a crap about me. He's here for the same thing I am: to get drunk.

Right when he's about to pass me by, out it comes.

"Hey, could you buy me some vodka? You can keep the extra money." I make sure my voice is neutral my face expressionless. "A fifth. Not the little bottle."

He doesn't stop to stare at me. Look me up and down like the guys in suits. He's got things to do.

He barely stops. Nods. His hands have ink on them and his skin is dry as he takes the money and says, "Yeah, sure."

There's always that moment when my heart beats too quickly and my hairline prickles with sweat. Will he come out and take off in the opposite direction? I can't chase someone down. Will he come back and walk right by me, give me an evil grin, and say *Stupid kid* as he taps the bags and keeps going? That's happened a couple of times.

I track his progress through the barred glass windows of the store. Chips aisle, Gatorade, beer cooler, liquor aisle, then the counter, his lips moving, his nod to the cashier, the bottles being bagged up, my heart still racing, my palms a little wet.

I text Kristen. *All good.*

She texts back. *Hero.*

The gentle *bing-bong* bell of the door as he pushes it open and walks across the parking lot to the back edge, where I'm standing on the sidewalk, half hidden by a shrub.

He's got the bag in one hand and a case of beer in the other, the Gatorade shoved in his jacket pocket, its weight making the fabric sag.

"Cheers," he says, and that's that, he's gone, shuffling down the sidewalk.

When I'm back inside the car, Kristen and Cherie cheer, but Amber stays silent.

"Bella!" they shout. "Bella, our queen!"

"First one's mine," I say, cracking the bottle and pouring as much as I think I can get away with into my half-empty bottle of Sprite.

It always is.

Amber is looking at me in the rearview mirror, her eyes darkening slightly.

"Jesus, take it easy," she murmurs.

"It's Friday," I tell her. "Just *chill.*"

Kristen's fingers tremble as she scrolls on her phone. The nights are getting colder and she's not even wearing a hoodie or anything, just a thin tank top and jeans with holes in the knees. The tips of her ponytails brush against her bony shoulders. "People are hanging at Cole's," she says.

At the exact same time, Amber and Cherie say *"No"* and point to me.

Kristen sighs, shoving her phone in the back pocket of her jeans and jumping up and down to keep warm.

We're sitting on a picnic bench in the park, just four girls with bottles of Sprite and a bag of cheese popcorn on a Friday night. Innocence and fun. We won't be able to stay here long. The park closes at ten, and there are some sketchy-looking people drifting around.

But for now we're okay. I take a long sip of my drink, the vodka spreading in my body like a rush of warm water. The feeling I've wanted all day.

"You guys are like hobos, you know, boozing it up in the park," Amber says.

One by one, we giggle.

"What else are we supposed to do, Amber?" Cherie asks. "There's nothing to *do.*"

It seems like such a long time ago that we just stayed in, watching movies, practicing cat's-eye makeup with YouTube videos, falling asleep in heaps of blankets and pajamas and messy ponytails, and now here we are. This is what we do. The park or parties or someone's garage. It's what everybody does.

How did it change, and where and when? This is just kind of life now. There was a life before, and sometimes it seems like one day I woke up and everything was different.

I don't really like to think about it, how things changed so suddenly, because then I'd have to think about Laurel, and thinking of her feels like being squeezed by a very large, mean person. So tight that I can't get away and I can't breathe.

"How long is she going to be on social probation anyway? This is getting old." Kristen turns to me. "Can you *just* get over him, already?"

I raise my head and take a long drink of my Sprodka, as Cherie calls it. The combination of sweet and strong feels good as it goes down. I start to loosen.

Sometimes I'm so wound up I think my body is going to crack in a million pieces.

Okay, not sometimes. All the time.

"I'm totally over him," I say, keeping my voice smooth and light. "I've loved and lost and learned my lesson."

"Liar," Amber says, scrolling on her phone.

"Agree," Cherie says. "I saw you staring at him yesterday in the courtyard. You totally looked ready to cry." Her hand on my back is gentle.

The tiniest pain races through my heart when she does that, so I take another sip and move slightly to make her hand fall away.

"You can't go to any parties until we're sure you won't flip out again," Amber says, looking up from her phone. "That last time was bad."

"It was kind of funny, in retrospect," Kristen says. "Bella's Extremely Unfortunate Public Downfall." She takes out her vape pen.

"Can we not talk about that, please?" I say, my stomach tightening. The memory of Luis's party is still hazy. I can only remember blurry patches: The heat of too many kids in too small a house. Music from tiny speakers. The keg in the galley kitchen. Then seeing Dylan, in that sweater of his that I loved, the old green one we found at Tucson Thrift, the one that felt so soft when I leaned my head against it. His hands in his pockets, bending close to that girl, Willow, and the way her hair fell against her cheek as she leaned in to hear what he was saying.

Standing there, kids bumping me, sloshing drinks and yelling, I remembered what Dylan said when he broke up with me in the parking lot of our high school, his eyes traveling anywhere but at *me,* the way he said, "You're just . . . too much."

At Luis's party, I watched as Dylan's fingers tugged the ends of Willow's hair, gently. Something splintered inside me.

After, things got weird.

Amber touches my hand. "Hey," she says. "We're just looking out for you."

I nod, breathe in deeply. Take another drink.

"Don't point that toward me," Cherie tells Kristen, waving her hands in front of her face. "My mother will kill me if she smells anything weird. I'm already going to have to Febreze the hell out of this jacket."

Kristen makes a face. "Just take me to Cole's, pleeeasssse," she begs Amber. "I'll get a ride home. Love you, Bella, but we shouldn't have to suffer just because of your broken heart."

"Thanks for the support," I say sarcastically, giving her a thumbs-up.

"Fine," Amber says. "But Bella stays with me."

We watch Kristen weave up the drive to Cole's house. He lives in the foothills, a fancy, sprawling place with huge windows and a glossy, heated pool out back. That might make him sound like some popular rich kid, but only the rich part is right. He's just a kid whose parents don't care if he parties. They buy the alcohol and then they leave for the night, and at that point, it really doesn't matter who you are at school. If you have the drinks and an empty house, people will converge. I don't even know most of the people at these things and I supposedly go to school with them.

I can't help it, but my eyes scan the packs of kids outside the house for Dylan.

Cherie says, "Sorry, but I don't want to waste this night, either," and jumps out of the car, running after Kristen. My heart drops when I see our bottle of vodka in her hand. I check my Sprodka. Not enough.

I climb into the passenger seat.

Amber looks at me.

“It’s cool,” I say. “If you want to stay. I’ll behave. I will.”

Part of me hopes she’ll say yes so I can look for Dylan.

She shakes her head. “Nah, you’re not ready. I gotta get home anyway. My mom needs the car for her shift tonight and I’m on Lily duty. You can stay over if you want. We can Couch.”

Couch means hanging out in her living room, watching movies and YouTube, eating junky snacks, but no drinking. That’s not allowed at Amber’s house.

“Not tonight,” I say. “I should probably just go home, hang out with my mom. I have to work tomorrow.”

“Okay.”

It takes about twenty minutes to get from the foothills back to midtown. We’re on River Road, which is curvy, like a beautiful roller coaster. Amber is a careful driver, and the car’s headlights illuminate the prickly pears on the side of the road, each one an eerie, spiky green ghost. It feels almost like we’re floating in a dreamworld, a weightless, half-glowing thing.

I sip my Sprodka slowly, savoring it, being careful. I can’t have too much in front of Amber or she’ll get weirded out. She’s being quiet right now, and it’s peaceful.

I feel like if I could just stay in the car with Amber forever, slightly buzzed, feeling warm and safe, not lost, that would be perfect.

But I can’t.

Amber turns down my street.

My brain says: *Lie to her.*

My heart says: *Oh, Bella.*

Casually, I say, "Actually, can you just drop me at Laurel's? I forgot my mom asked me to check on the house."

"You want me to wait and take you home? I can come in. I love Laurel's house. I miss it. I miss her."

That last part she kind of whispers.

All my friends loved Laurel. Who wouldn't? She was semi-famous in a way that they didn't fully understand but that seemed cool. She took us to the mall and bought us earrings at Claire's and makeup at Sephora and laughed at all the horny things in Spencer's with us. She asked to listen to our playlists and she actually *did.*

They were all really nice to me after it happened. Of course they were, because they're my friends, but after a bit, it kind of felt like they moved on, and I was somehow still standing in the barn at Agnes's staring at my beautiful, cool grandmother in a black-and-white photograph on a table surrounded by candles and incense and sage and cameras and postcards and Polaroids and flower petals, my little sister's hand tight in mine as our parents argued in the corner.

Those Polaroids. I took them from the barn. People sent them to us from around the world when they heard about Laurel. The test shots she'd do before a session, for lighting, angle, to get people loose.

I have a whole stack of photos of complete strangers in my dresser drawer. Some people wrote on the white borders. *Laurel captured my soul. Laurel saw beauty in me when I saw none.* Some of these people are incredibly famous, or were, and some people are just people, but Laurel made them seem like more than that.

The squeezing is starting and I hold my breath, shove my Sprodka bottle in my backpack so I don't have to see Amber's concerned eyes.

"No, I'll be fine. Text me later? Tell me what you're watching?" Am I slurring? I don't think so. I bite my lip a little too hard. The sharpness helps me focus.

"Okay," she says. "Hey, you know what?"

"What?"

"We should look at the map again soon, go over our savings. I've got fifteen hundred now. You?"

The trip. The map on Amber's wall in her tiny room: red pins for weird attractions, like the World's Largest Tin Family in North Dakota, constructed entirely out of empty oil drums; blue pins for natural landmarks, like the Grand Canyon, which neither of us has ever seen, even though we only live six hours away. We've been planning this since we were eleven and everything was locked down, like maybe someday when we could go out in the world again, we'd really make it worth it. Buy a car together when we were old enough, spend the summer after graduation driving around, sleeping in hostels and camping in tents, seeing weird things and beautiful things and meeting weird people and beautiful people, maybe people who are beautiful because they're weird, just two girls in a car out in the world, before whatever comes after high school happens. Amber walks the dogs in her neighborhood to make money, scooping poop into bags while holding the leashes of barky terriers and lustrous retrievers. I bus tables at a place whose signature dish is a hamburger with three patties, six varieties of cheese, ten pickles, three habanero peppers, and a crunchy layer of batter-fried onions on top, and if you finish it, you get a bumper sticker that says *I Ate the Pepper Patty at Patty's Place and Survived.*

I hesitate. "I had a setback. Laptop went haywire. I just have eight hundred now, but I'm being careful with tips, so I'll make it back. I will."

That laptop is hidden under a pile of old clothes in my closet at my mom's house, the screen shattered, half the keys missing. My mom refused to buy me a new one, so I used some of the tips I'd saved and went out and got a refurbished one, since it was cheaper.

It was a bad night, the night of Luis's party. Like I said, the details are a little muddled. When I try to catch distinct memories of what happened, they float away from me, like fluff on a dandelion after you blow it. Usually, I remember everything. Well, almost everything; sometimes the memories are like a book with pages missing. But the night at Luis's was different. It kind of felt like I had tipped over into a bottomless well, just falling, falling, falling, and no place to land. And then things just . . . disappeared at some point.

The laptop was a casualty. Obviously, I threw it or something, or hit it, and that's what made my mother wake up and come to my room. The noise. And then she found me and that was that. I was too messed up to pretend I wasn't messed up. So not only are Amber and my other friends keeping me on a tight leash, so is my mom.

Amber smiles. "No worries. We've got plenty of time. Hey, I found another cool place. It's called Bubblegum Alley, and people have been sticking their gum there for *years,* can you imagine? It's in California. It's, like, fifty feet long!"

"That's disgusting and somehow fantastic at the same time," I say. "Excellent addition. Good find."

I step out of the car carefully.

"Bella!" Amber calls.

I turn back, lean down through the open passenger window.

"It'll be okay. The Dylan stuff. You just need some time. Remember how long it took me to get over Caleb?"

I remember. There was a lot of crying, and Couching, and eventually Amber became Amber again: positive, clear-headed, focused.

But the big difference between Amber and Caleb and me and Dylan is that Amber broke up with Caleb. He didn't dump her. She dumped *him.* She didn't have to stand in a parking lot in front of half the high school while he told her she was *too much,* his friends flanked behind him, like a giant collective, protective squid.

Oh, shit, she's crying.

Dude, we gotta get out of here.

Dylan, man, chill, it's done, let's go before she loses it.

Dylan's Squid Squad had their phones out just in case, though, because there's nothing better than posting a breakup meltdown. I had to stand there and take it, or my freak-out would be posted everywhere within seconds. I had to pretend I was nothing, a ghost, no feelings, no expression, just . . . *Whatever okay be cool Dylan you know whatever have a nice life.*

As I walked away, he said, "Take care of yourself, Bella," unaware that inside, I was disintegrating, shattered by the casual tone in his voice.

"Yeah," I tell Amber, trying to smile, biting my lip again to make sure I don't slur or anything. "I know. I'm good. It's cool."

She hesitates. "Maybe take it easy tonight, okay?"

She means the Sprodka. *Did* I slur?

"Oh, for sure," I say quickly, because the best thing to do here is just to get into Laurel's as fast as possible. "I'm gonna ditch this inside and then head home."

"Love you, B," she says.

"Love you, too, A."

* * *

There's a part of the bricked walkway leading up to my grandmother's house that I always avoid. I've learned to count how many steps it is to her front door. On the fifteenth, I know to swerve off the path and return only when I know it's time for step eighteen.

A little part of me always blanks out at step fifteen and comes back to life at step eighteen. I know nothing will happen if my sneakers land on those particular bricks, but it still seems wrong.

It hurts knowing what happened there.

I exhale deeply as I unlock and open her front door, a blast of warmth hitting me. It's November in Tucson, so the nights dip down to the fifties and the stars hang crisply against the dark blue night sky. My mother still hasn't turned off the gas, or the electricity, or changed anything. Laurel's house is still Laurel's house, five doors down from ours, just like she left it. Like she's going to come back any minute from a trip she forgot to tell us she was going to take.

She's not coming back.

Every time my dad tells my mom it's time to put the house on the market, her face turns ugly with a mix of sadness and anger. *You don't get it,* she tells him. *You just want the money. Haven't you taken enough from me?*

And then my dad shuts down. And then my mom shuts down. And then Ricci amps up and starts hitting, or yelling, or kicking the dishwasher, and then

Bella, calm your sister.

Bella, tell your father it's time to leave.

Bella, tell your mother I'm out of here.

I unlock the front door and walk straight through Laurel's living room, past her pretty vintage robin's-egg-blue velvet couch, past all the pristinely framed black-and-white photographs of my mother as a child that first made Laurel famous, the ones I usually like to stop and look at for a long time, my mother frozen at four, seven, ten, her skin luminous and ethereal in the woods of upstate New York, her body like some sort of marbled girl ghost.

Sometimes I look at my mom now and try to find that girl in the photographs, the one whose eyes stared out fiercely, who seemed not just a girl but an otherworldly entity, brave and powerful even in her smallness.

I'm not sure I see her now in my mom's matted, hastily pulled-back hair, in her eyes, which have seemed so sad for years and even more now that Laurel, her mother, is gone.

I wish I could find her. I feel like we could have been friends, that girl and me.

I head straight to the kitchen, to the pantry, which is also still the same: boxes of tea, cans of soup, bags of rice and pinto beans, canisters of incense and flour.

And the endless bottles of gin and vodka and vermouth and brandy and schnapps.

We don't *have* to go out and shoulder-tap at Lucy Licker. We could come here. My mother never comes here. But I don't want them here. I love Cherie and Kristen, but they'd get loud after a while. Messy. Something about them being here would ruin it, maybe. The stillness.

It's my place.

* * *

I never sit in the living room because that makes me lonely, seeing her empty lounger and the tray table where she'd set her dinner while she watched television. Plus, once, Mrs. Rabinowitz saw the lights on and came over and knocked on the door to see if everything was okay and I had to stand there for like ten hours listening to her yammer about her cat and her bad back, praying the whole time she wouldn't notice I was a little drunk.

"Such a nice girl to watch over her house. She loved you so much." Mrs. Rabinowitz had tiny, kind eyes behind her giant glasses. One hand stroked the thick white braid resting on her shoulder, and when I saw the tears starting, I almost lost it, so I told her I heard my phone ringing and shut the door practically in her face.

You'd think an old lady would like cozy romances or historical stuff, but Laurel liked murder, especially true crime. I feel like after she stopped being a photographer, she should have had a second life as a detective, really, because she could solve half the stuff on *Forensic Files* within the first fifteen minutes. "All people," she used to say, nibbling cheese and crackers, her delicate hands shaking like they always did, "have a darkness inside them. You just need to dig a little."

I pass the hallway leading to the bathroom and the bedrooms. One was Laurel's bedroom, one was for me and Ricci if we stayed over, and the other is where she stored her photo archives. I don't think she liked to go in there much on her own anymore, but sometimes she'd let me look through her files, which I could do for hours. She made a lot of money at one point photographing actors and rock stars. Sometimes she'd tell me little stories about the famous people she met.

I walk to the kitchen to sit at the long, old-fashioned

wooden lab table she found at 22nd Street Antique Mall, her favorite place to wander for hours before driving got hard and she couldn't get there. She and I would play Scrabble on this table, or backgammon or Go Fish.

"Just a bit," she'd say, pouring me some schnapps. "Something sweet for my best girl."

She never gave me too much. Just enough to send prickles of pleasure down my spine. Enough to make me somehow feel *better.*

Our last game of Scrabble is still on the table.

I get a glass, some ice, and pour myself some vodka, add some Sprite from a can, sit at the table, look at our leftover words.

Apothecary. Hidden. You. Hush.

I pull my phone from my jacket pocket.

My mother's texted me three times. I ignore her.

Kristen and Cherie are posting from the party. Hazy lights behind them, glossy faces. I zoom in. Is Dylan there in the background? I don't see him.

I check his Stories, my heart pounding.

Nothing.

Once, he told me I was the coolest girl he'd ever known. Pressed me against the lockers at school and kissed me. Didn't drop my hand when his friends came around.

I told Laurel about Dylan before my mom even knew. She shifted letters on her tile holder and looked at me.

"Romantic love is dizzying and wonderful and frightening and lovely, but don't let it obscure you." Her sea-blue eyes were serious; the charcoal eyeliner lopsided at the corners. It was hard for her to apply with her hands so shaky, but she was determined to do it, every day.

My grandmother was an artist; everything she said was fascinating and strange to me. I didn't understand what she meant then, and I'm not sure I do now. Maybe I will when I'm older.

My stomach tightens. I wish she was here at this table with me right now. I wish I'd never—

I close my eyes and drink.

Move letters around on my Scrabble tile holder. I could spell *douse.*

Once, I asked Laurel about my mother's father and who he was and where he was and she just said, "Sometimes you can't take people to the places you need to go."

I wonder if Laurel was ever *too much.*

She always liked me just as I was.

I drink drink drink.

It's so quiet here. It's the only quiet place I know in my world of noise.

I brush my teeth before I leave, careful to rinse off the toothbrush. I wash the glass, dry it, put it back in the kitchen cabinet. I pop three mints just in case. Pinch my cheeks to feel more alert and less woozy. Fill up my Sprodka bottle again, shove it in my backpack. Make sure the lights are off and the door is locked and everything is just so. Outside, the cool air feels good on my skin, sobering me up a little.

When I'm two houses from ours, I can already hear Ricci, long whines and cries of "*Nooo.* I don't want to."

I take a deep breath as I open the front door. I'm so glad I have something inside me to blunt all this, just a little.

My mother is standing in the living room, her face exasperated and pink, hands on hips, as my little sister rolls around on the floor, clutching her tablet.

I close the door. Mom swivels toward me. "Where were you? I texted you."

The house smells like overcooked noodles. Macaroni and cheese is the only thing Ricci will eat right now, and she likes the noodles so soft they practically dissolve on her fork.

"With Amber. I told you this morning."

She sniffs the air. "What is that smell? Were you smoking?"

I drop my backpack on the ground.

My brain says: *Tell her it was Kristen. She doesn't like Kristen anyway.*

"Kristen vapes. I don't. You know that."

"Was there drinking? We made a deal, Bella."

Ah yes, the deal after Luis's party: no drinking, no parties.

"Nope. Want to smell my breath?" I open my mouth.

My mother considers me.

If you want to pretend nothing is amiss, pretend nothing is amiss. Like you have nothing to hide. I'm a good girl. I get good grades. I do a lot around the house. I have a job. I keep everything together. I've survived death and divorce. I had a little blip with my Unfortunate Public Breakdown, that's all.

I keep my eyes on my mother's face as I say, "Mom, come on. Honestly?"

"You know how I feel about Kristen."

I shrug. I'm safe. My mother's dislike of Kristen will override any suspicion of me. Also, she's too frustrated with Ricci right now.

Her shoulders sag. "I need help here. She only lasted half the day at school today and I have a deadline. I can't miss it. Can you . . ."

My mother is a writer for a weird daily radio show based in another state. In seven years, she's never even met her boss in person, just exchanged emails and phone calls and Zooms with the producer. They send her ideas for stories, like about aliens in Roswell, or how a famous Hollywood actor has cryogenically preserved his mother in his mansion. She researches all the theories and news stories and then writes up the content, and the radio host, some guy named A. W. Stryker, does shows about them. I like listening to it—it's a trip. He gets dozens of calls for every episode, and believe me, like Laurel said, people really do have darkness in them. And a lot of time on their hands. It's a very popular show, but the host is weird and sometimes switches up the topics at the last minute, leaving my mom to work and write late at night. I know she wants to do something else, like what she'll sometimes call "real writing," but it's the only job that lets her deal with Ricci.

Ricci is a lot of work.

"Ricci!" I shout, standing above my sister. "Ten hut."

She stops rolling and pops up, standing at attention, tablet wedged under one arm.

"Sergeant Sister, are you ready for bed."

"No, ma'am, no."

"Sergeant Sister, will you be ready for bed after thirty minutes of cat videos and three Oreos and one glass of milk? Major Mom is on work detail and must be released or it's the stockade for her. Do we want that to happen to Major Mom?"

"No, we don't."

"Do we understand each other, Sergeant Sister? This is your captain speaking."

My sister straightens her shoulders. "I am ready, Captain."

"Then forward, one two, one two." I make marching steps, pointing down the hall to her bedroom.

My sister, blond ponytail swinging, Olaf pajamas sagging around her butt, one-twos down the hall. I follow her.

"Ricci, did you fake being sick at school again so you could come home?" I ask softly, once we're in her room. "You know Mom needs time to work."

"Sorry," she says, rubbing her face.

Ricci has a hard time at school. My parents moved her to a new one, where they have beanbags and forts for quiet time, but you also have to pay for it. At least twice a week, Ricci complains of stomach trouble, or a headache, and either my mom or my dad, depending on who has us that week, has to stop everything and go get her. Each time, she miraculously improves the instant she gets home and my parents have an argument over the phone about what's wrong with her and whose fault it is and meanwhile I'm screaming inside my head *It's because our grandmother died and you got divorced and every day when she leaves the house she's afraid something else is going to change while she isn't looking and she is seven years old and can't take one more awful thing.*

Ricci hasn't told me this, of course. It's just a theory of mine.

"Okay," I say. "Wait here. I'll be right back."

"What are the topics tonight?" I ask my mother as I walk into the kitchen, pour Ricci some milk, gather Oreos in a napkin.

My mother's got deep shadows under her eyes and looks like she didn't get a chance to shower today. She shuffles work papers on the kitchen counter. "A woman in Arkansas saw Jesus in her grilled cheese sandwich and a man in Italy is marrying the Leaning Tower of Pisa."

"I hope they'll be very happy together."

"Unless Pisa turns out to be a nagging shrew."

I run my finger over the texture of the Oreos. That's something my dad said to my mom last year, before he moved out.

I don't know if he knew I could hear them fighting. They'd closed their bedroom door and lowered their voices to harsh whispers. *Look who you've become, Diana. A nagging shrew.*

"Go to work, Major Mom."

She gives me a grateful smile and moves to the kitchen island, sitting on the stool and popping open her laptop.

My sister is under the covers. I hand her the napkin with the Oreos and climb in, settling against her. I sniff her neck delicately. "You need to take a bath, Ricci."

"Water is itchy. Do the room!"

I sigh, getting back out of the bed, and Ricci finds the videos she wants to watch on her tablet. You might think being in front of a screen before bed would make her more antsy, but watching animal videos actually quiets her. She loves animals. If she had her way, our house would be a zoo.

Ricci needs everything a certain way before bedtime, so I walk around the room, carefully pushing her Minecraft figures back into place on her desk, arranging her coloring pencils by color (white, black, yellow, blue, green, pink), tapping the fish tank three times to say good night to the plump goldfish fluttering inside, checking the inside of the closet for monsters. The last thing is tucking her blanket around her tightly, under her legs and torso, but not over her arms. She needs those out. She calls it being "burritoed."

"Sergeant Sister, the quarters are clean. May I enter the bunk now?"

She nods happily. I lie down next to her.

"You need to let Mom work, you know," I tell her. "It's

her job. You have thirty minutes, then lights out, okay? I have things to do."

My voice might be a little sharper than I wanted, because Ricci's face squinches.

"Sorry," she whispers.

I make sure my voice is softer this time. "It's fine. But this is it, okay?"

She nods.

I set the timer on my phone.

Cue cat and hedgehog videos, the crunching of Oreos and slurping of milk, and soon my sister's eyelids are fluttering. I smooth her hair. Sometimes I forget that she's only seven and the world is hard for her. Seven seems so long ago, I can hardly remember it, just flashes of carefully reading aloud to my teacher and making sure my math sheet was neat and clean. I gently slip the tablet from her fingers and she snuggles into me.

I'm struggling to stay awake, but I don't want to fall asleep just yet, so I pinch my thigh through my jeans because I want to go to my bedroom after this, lie down on the floor and be alone and put on my headphones, finish my Sprodka while staring at the fairy lights strung along my walls and forget Dylan, and forget everything, alone and drifting and dulled in my very own private ocean.

SATURDAY

RICCI CRUNCHES HER GRANOLA steadily. "You look weird," she says. Pearly drops of milk slide down her chin.

I toss a napkin at her and pour cold brew coffee from the fridge into a big mug. I take a huge gulp. My head throbs and my eyes burn. "Shut up. I have a headache."

Ricci looks down at her bowl, stirring her granola. Her spoon clinks gently on the inside of the bowl.

I've hurt her feelings. "Sorry," I mumble.

"You're really mean sometimes lately," Ricci says softly.

"Well, sometimes you're really annoy—"

My mom wanders into the kitchen then, rubbing her face. "I'm so tired. I was up so late. Grilled Cheese Jesus is very complicated, let me tell you." She puts the kettle on for tea and looks at Ricci.

"Did you pack your backpack for Dad's?" she asks. "I'm taking you over in an hour or so."

My hands tighten around my coffee mug. I forgot we go to Dad's today.

Ricci sighs and blows a milk bubble. "Yeeeessss."

My mother looks at me. "How about you?"

"I have to work tonight. I'll go over after. I need to finish a group project for art class with some kids at the library first, because one of the guys was out sick and the teacher gave us an extension. It's due Monday."

"Are you going to get graded down because it's late? That doesn't seem like it should be your fault, if another student was sick. You don't look so great yourself."

She moves toward me like she's going to put her hand on my forehead. I back away.

She looks at me. "Geez, somebody's touchy."

"Just don't," I say. "I'm fine."

"Well, you should ask the teacher to extend—"

I cut her off. "Please don't start—"

But she's starting. I'm gripping the mug so hard I feel like it might break.

"Did you write your draft for the lit essay yet? You don't want to wait until the last minute. You always do. And then what happens? You start to panic. Your grades are shaky at the moment—"

I grit my teeth. My mother is obsessed with my grades. What makes it worse is that parents can look at this online school portal to keep tabs on what assignments are missing or late and see grades in real time, and honestly, I'm already anxious about school, I don't need my mother's anxiety on top of my own. I mean, what is so bad about getting a B in a class? Or a C? My mother didn't even *go* to an actual school for a long time. Laurel lived in an artists collective in the woods in Upstate New York for years before she moved them to the city. The parents took turns teaching the kids in a yurt. Sometimes a whole day of learning meant baking bread from scratch. Weeks might be devoted to putting on *Romeo and Juliet,* right down to sewing the costumes, painting the scenery, and building a stage and set out of cardboard, drywall, and scavenged wood. If you ask me, that sounds better than endless percentage points and advanced-this-and-that and everything pointing to this faraway, mythical dream of *college.*

"I have my book. I have notes. I'm set. I'll be fine. Don't worry about it."

"Is your dad picking you up after work? You know I don't like you taking the bus that late by yourself."

I swirl the cold coffee in my cup with my forefinger, trying not to smirk. My mother is worried about me riding the bus at night when I stand on the sidewalk outside sketchy liquor stores and ask literal strangers to buy us vodka.

"Yes, we texted about it." Actually, I think I forgot that, too.

I can feel things starting to pile up inside me: essay, art project, Dad, work.

My mother keeps pressing. "And did he respond to the text? You know, if he doesn't respond, it means he might not have read it, or—"

"He *responded.*" I make a mental note to see if he did, or if I even texted him.

"What did he say, exactly? You told him what time, right? That means he'll have to keep Ricci up later, and that's not good for her—"

"He said, 'Cool, ten o'clock, see you then, no problem.' Do you actually need to read the text? And it's Saturday. She can stay up and watch a movie. She's not a baby."

I have to lie to get her to stop, but my voice is too loud. It makes my head hurt even worse.

"Bella, your tone—" my mom starts.

"My tone is fine. I mean, my god, climb off my back, Mom. You're making me late and I need to shower," I say, getting up. "I'll check Ricci's bag before I leave and make sure she has her stuff."

And I'm out of the kitchen before my mother can say any more.

My hair wet and flapping in my face, I frantically search for my work shirt in my room. My headache hasn't gone away and my mouth is really dry. I find a bottle of water on the desk and take a long guzzle. I finally locate my shirt under a pile of clothes on my desk chair and give it a sniff. Not too bad, but there's a stain in the middle, which will irritate Patty. Maybe I can wear my apron higher tonight to cover it. I have two shirts, but one is at Dad's, and I don't want to go there before I have to, and who knows if he did the laundry anyway. There are so many things involved in living at two places. Like what clothes are where, whether you forgot your charger at this house or the other, remembering to pack school folders, who's picking you up and when. It's exhausting. Not to mention that Dad's way of parenting seems specifically designed to flip the bird at my mother: Ricci stays up too late, even on school nights, because he doesn't want to be the "mean" one; he doesn't give me a curfew, because he feels that "restricts a normal level of adolescent exploration"; there's no place to do homework except at the tiny table in the kitchen, which barely fits the three of us; dinners are mostly takeout or frozen pizza. And then there's Vanessa, which is a whole other thing entirely.

My head hurts so bad I can hardly think as I shove my school stuff in my backpack, make sure I have a couple of my favorite shirts and pairs of jeans, my makeup, and some tampons, because I'm trying to stockpile some at Dad's. He's not very good at remembering that sort of stuff.

I check Ricci's backpack, too. Like I thought, she lied to my mom, probably hoping that if she forgot something, my mom would bring it over, and then Ricci would have a meltdown and want to go back with Mom and not stay with Dad, which happens more often than not. She does it to both of them, in fact.

I shove in her green homework folder, her tablet and headphones, and a couple of shirts, socks, pants, and clean underwear. Done.

My mom and Ricci are in the living room, searching for Ricci's sneakers. They have the couch cushions pulled out and everything.

I hand my mom Ricci's backpack.

"You were very rude to me, Bella," she says, her eyes pinned to my face.

I sigh. "Fine. I'm sorry. Okay? Her sneakers are in the bathroom cabinet. She likes to hide them there, remember?"

My mom is flustered. "Ricci! You did that again?"

Ricci covers her mouth with her hands so we can't see her devious smile.

"I'm off. See you in a week, I guess," I say. Then I wait.

My mom doesn't notice. She's heading to the bathroom, muttering to herself.

"Okay then," I say softly.

There was a time after the divorce when my mom made a point of hugging me when she knew I'd be at my dad's for the week. "Let me get my love in. I'm gonna miss you," she'd say. She'd even do it before we got in the car to go to school on days Dad was scheduled to pick us up, because she knew I'd be embarrassed if kids saw my mom giving me a giant hug by the curb in the drop-off line. I love her, but I don't need to display that to my classmates.

She's been forgetting the hug a lot lately.

I look at my sister.

"See you later, Ricci. Be good."

But she's not paying attention to me now, either. She's making a fort with the couch cushions.

I stop by Grandma's house and fill up the Sprodka bottle and dump out a water bottle and fill that up, too. I'm going to need sustenance at Dad's. His is a beer-only house, and the few times I've tried to sneak one, he's figured it out. He might be lackadaisical about some things, but he's quite particular about his beer. I wash down a couple of ibuprofen with a can of Coke.

Outside, I slide my headphones on. It's a good fifteen-minute walk to the library. Hopefully, my headache will ease up by then.

I will not stop and sip from the bottle. I will not stop and sip from the bottle. I will not stop and sip from the bottle. I have to do this project. I have to go to work. I will not miss Dylan. I will not stop and sip from this bottle. I will not. I will not. I will not.

I find my group in the back of the library at one of the teen study tables. Like I thought, my group doesn't have any books out or laptops opened. I swear to god I've managed most of this project so far and it's been a lot of hassle, even though this is my favorite class, except that Ms. Green is making us do a presentation. Speaking in public makes me nervous—like, gargantuan levels of distress—but I'm going to try not to think about that. Maybe it will be better since we have to present as a group and I won't be alone.

The group is me, Cherie, Dawn, and Lemon, whose first name is Rudy, but no one ever uses that. He moved here in sixth grade and we already had a Rudy in our class, so Lemon became Lemon.

Cherie's head is on the table. I thunk my backpack down on the floor and she looks up blearily.

"You look horrible," I say. "Must have been some party."

"It was so much fun. The parts I remember, anyway. You look like shit, too, by the way." She sighs. "Party of one?"

I ignore her. Her eyes are bloodshot. I'm glad I remembered to use eye drops after my shower.

Lemon looks up from his phone. "You shoulda been there, Bella. Oh, wait, you're on parental probation after *the incident*."

"Ha ha," I say, sitting down.

"What incident?" Dawn says.

Dawn magically appeared at our school this year. I've never seen her at a party or the coffee shop or the mall or even hanging out with anyone, really. She keeps to herself, which must be kind of lonely. I mean, I have Amber, Cherie, and Kristen, and I'm lonely, too, but at least I'm not lonely *by myself.* I think there's a difference.

Dawn is wearing her usual outfit of overalls, Doc Martens, and a black long-sleeved shirt. She's in three of my classes, so I see this outfit a few times a week. As someone who basically has a uniform as well (T-shirt, flannel, hoodie, jeans, Chucks), I admire her consistency.

"Don't worry about it," I say, trying to be all business, getting out my school laptop and firing up our PowerPoint. "Did you finish typing the paper?"

Dawn nods.

Lemon stretches out in his chair, knotting his hands behind his long hair. He smells distinctly of weed. "Bella got hella wasted at Luis's party three weeks ago and totally *lost it,*" he explains to Dawn.

Dawn frowns slightly, which kind of ticks me off. I don't want her feeling sorry for me. No one needs to feel sorry for me.

Cherie says, "Knock it off, Lemon. Like you've never had a broken heart." She puts her hand on mine.

I can feel my face getting red.

"Lost what how?" Dawn says.

Lemon looks at Dawn. "You know, breakup bullshit. Booze plus breakup equals emotional implosion." He makes a sound like a bomb going off. The old people sitting a few tables over give us a couple of *Shh*s.

He makes a face at them and then leans close to me. "You know, Hella Bella, I'm available. I can pick up those painful pieces and glue you back together. Don't underestimate the healing power of the Lemon."

"You wish, Lemon. I think I'll stay smashed up if you're my alternative."

Dawn and Cherie giggle.

"Speaking of smashed," Lemon says, "you mind if I go outside and chill for a few minutes before we start this bullshit? I need to take the edge off."

We watch him get up and amble to the front door.

"He's just going to light up? Right outside the public *library*?" Dawn says.

Cherie shrugs. "That's his thing. Everybody has a thing, I guess. Don't you have a thing you do to like, de-stress?"

Dawn looks uncomfortable for a minute, that look somebody gets when they're thinking about saying something and they aren't sure whether to say it. Mouth pursed, eyebrows close together. That look.

Finally, she just says, "I needlepoint. Geeky, I know, but it makes me feel better."

"That's cool," I say, because she looks weirdly nervous, like Cherie and I are going to laugh at her, which, judging from the look on Cherie's face, might actually happen, so I distract Cherie by angling the laptop in her direction and pointing to a slide of *Aphrodite of Knidos.* "Let me guess. The ones that are misspelled are from Lemon?"

The text for the slide says *statutory* instead of *statuary.*

Cherie makes a face. "Actually, I think that was me. Sorry. I'll fix it." She starts typing.

Aphrodite is naked, or *nude,* as our art teacher, Ms. Green, prefers we say, holding some kind of draping and covering her *pubis,* another word that makes our class laugh. Aphrodite has just taken a shower, I think, and I remember that her pose is contrapposto, which sounds like a dish you'd get at Olive Garden. I tell Cherie to add that in and spell it out loud for her. I love this part of our class because the statues remind me of my grandma's photographs, not just the ones of my mom when she was younger but the ones she did much later, after her years of photographing musicians and artists and being a famous person herself. Older women, posed against the sky in the desert outside Tucson, their bodies seemingly fixed in time, beautiful and strong, like they know they matter. These statues have been through wars and plunder and maybe have lost noses or arms and legs, but still, they remain. They can't be erased or replaced.

They aren't *too much.*

Dawn says, "Hey, what's wrong?"

Cherie stops typing. "Oh, Bella, oh, no, are you okay?"

I wipe the tears from my face quickly with the hem of my flannel shirt. "Don't worry about it."

"Breakups are hard," Dawn says slowly. "Once, I—"

"Her grandma died, too," Cherie whispers to Dawn. "It happened right—"

"Oh my god," I say loudly. "Can we just *stop*?"

The old people at the next table say "Shush!" in their own loud way.

"Shush *yourself,*" Lemon says as he moseys by them. He drops so hard into his chair that he knocks our table. His eyes are pink and he reeks. "What did I miss?" He checks his own laptop, scrolling through the slides of classical Greek statuary on our project page.

"Ohh, baby. So many nips in this class. I love it." He makes a smacking sound with his lips.

"You know, Lemon," I say, glad that we've moved on from discussing my brief breakdown. I can feel Dawn watching me curiously, so I avoid looking at her. "The female body is a beautiful thing. It's not there for your gratification. It's *art.* It's made to be appreciated, not slobbered over."

Lemon shrugs. "Still makes me all jiggly, if you know what I mean. What's so wrong with that? Wait, were you crying?"

"Just shut up," I say. "Just shut *up,* and make sure you have your sources cited correctly for your slides, okay?"

"Yeah," Cherie says. "Step up, Lemon. I need a decent grade in this class."

"Me too," Dawn says. "My parents are super strict about grades."

"Okay, okay, Miss All-A Hella Bella and her minions. *Excuuuussse meee.*" He shakes his head. "Damn, somebody needs a *drank.*"

The bus is crowded and smells like sweat. I have to squeeze in the back right next to the window, hugging my backpack on my lap. My head is still rocking and there's a knot in my stomach. I haven't eaten anything yet; I just had that Coke and ibuprofen at my grandmother's. I clutch my backpack tighter and my fingers land on the shape of the Sprodka bottle inside.

Hair of the dog.

That's what my dad says sometimes after a long night out with his friend Hoyt, when I find him on the couch with puffy eyes, a beer in his hand, and it's ten o'clock on a Sunday morning. "A little hair of the dog always takes the pain away," he'll say with a wink.

No one would know. They'll just think I'm having some soda, right? It smells like soda. Maybe flat soda. Who would know? Who would even care? My heart starts to pick up a little. It might smooth out my head and my nerves. I have so much work to do before Thanksgiving break. That stupid art presentation. My actual piece of art for class, which looks awful. I never should have started drawing that damn tree, but I didn't know what to do and I had to do *something.* I don't even know what's going on in algebra. It's all just letters and numbers and lines swirling around. Lemon probably thinks I have all As right now, but I don't. My grades have dropped and I have a bunch of missing assignments I need to get in. I'm just lucky my mother's been so distracted she hasn't checked the grades portal in a while.

I sigh. I have five hours at work ahead of me. Helping ungrateful people and cleaning their dirty tables and picking up soggy napkins. My chest tightens.

Who would know? I can maintain. I think I can maintain. I know kids at school who guzzle NyQuil between classes like it's soda. And do other things. But that stuff seems dangerous and kind of scary.

This isn't scary. Literally everyone in the world drinks. I'm having a hard time lately. I just need to get through break and then I'll cut way back.

There's a squeezing inside my chest that feels hot and prickly. The lady next to me is twitching in a weird way and keeps mumbling "Sorry." The guy next to her is doing that sleep thing where his head falls forward and he jerks awake and sits up and then falls asleep again. The bus always makes me feel even lonelier. Like everyone on it is being held hostage by something inside them.

I guess I am, too.

The squeezing inside me gets worse.

My hand is around the bottle inside the fabric like I'm holding a precious gem.

The bus lurches and I pitch forward, almost hitting my head on the back of the seat in front of me. I haul myself back into my seat, take a few big gulps of air. *Jesus, get it together, Bella.*

I will not drink on this bus. I can't. I won't. I have to go to work. I have to be nice and put on my apron and haul plates of greasy burgers and salty fries and quesadillas, and wipe down tables, and fish tips from the bottoms of soda cups because some people think it's funny to cram money between ice cubes. Some people think it's funny to eat almost an entire triple-decker grilled cheese with avocado and then claim the bread was overtoasted and they want a refund. Some people think it's funny teenagers have to work, and keep them at the table asking questions like *Well now, girl, what are you going to do with your earnings? Buy more makeup?* Or they think it's okay to put their meaty hands on your arm like they know you, all *Aren't you just the prettiest thing I've seen all day?* or compliment the food while insulting their wives, all *If I didn't eat here, I'd die of starvation, heh heh.* Some people think it's funny to say *Now, where's my smile, give me a smile,* and it's all I can do to not say *I've got your smile right here* and dump that glass of iced tea on their head. The world sucks, but I will not drink on this bus. I will not drink on this bus.

It doesn't work trying to hide the stain on my red Patty's Place shirt. It's too high up, and if I tie my apron that high, it'll probably look like I'm trying to hide an impending pregnancy, so I just try to keep my order pad in front of the stain at all times, at least until I can legitimately claim that the stain happened today.

I'm working the five-to-ten shift, which means we're already busy by the time I get there, because people are having dinner before going to movies or whatever they're doing on a Saturday night. We'll have a lull around seven and then things will pick up again at nine and go until close, which is eleven p.m., but since I'm fifteen, Patty won't let me close, since closers don't get out until after midnight.

Patty's Place isn't big and it's kind of run-down, but it's been around for more than thirty years and has a pretty devoted old-school clientele and a lot of younger people who, I guess, consider it cool in an ironic way? Those types are always snickering over Patty's décor, which is pretty much whatever strikes her fancy at the thrift store, like purple-painted wooden fish, paintings of birds and seascapes, crocheted cacti, and old postcards that she frames. Not always with the picture facing out, but sometimes like, the actual written side, so you can read about what a great vacation someone was having in 1962 in the Catskills, or how much Edgar missed and loved Beatrice while he was in Paris in 1977. I like that one a lot. Edgar wrote, *The city without you seems a selfish place, or perhaps I am selfish to be away from you.* Pretty much whatever Patty likes, she nails or glues to the walls of the diner. I'm especially fond of her penchant for gold-framed mirrors of various shapes and sizes.

As usual, Patty is sporting a glittery scrunchie that can barely contain her out-of-control hair. If I were to describe Patty's hair using one of the paintings from Ms. Green's art class, it would be Klimt's *Nuda Veritas,* where the woman's red hair is like a cloud around her head, expanding almost beyond her shoulders, with some pretty flowers pinned in here and there. Patty's hair is red, too, but with a lot of gray, giving her a kind of wild, witchy look.

She's sitting at her desk in the cramped office off the kitchen, scribbling furiously on a schedule sheet. I try to sneak past her so she won't notice my stained shirt, but her head whips up just as I'm slinking by.

"Bella," she says. "Can you do a double tomorrow? Jess is out sick and I need someone to cover her dinner shift. I can have her sub for you next Saturday."

I hold my order pad over the stain. "Yeah, sure."

She squints at me. "You okay? You getting sick? You look a little . . . peaked."

"What? No, I'm fine. Just . . . tired. You know, school and stuff."

"I don't want you getting customers sick."

"No, I'm good."

"Why are you holding your stomach, then?"

Dammit. I slowly ease the pad away from the green chile stain.

Patty shakes her head. "You need to *wash* your shirt after *every* shift, Bella. How many times have I told you?"

"A million?"

She sighs. "If it happens again, I'm going to give you another shirt and take the twenty-five dollars out of your paycheck."

I nod, thinking of the money I had to spend for that replacement laptop. I can't afford to lose twenty-five dollars right now.

"Go on. Maura needs tables cleared. You can take some tables around seven, okay? Until then, bus and run the register." She turns back to the schedule sheet.

I walk by the kitchen, where Lonnie and Deb are working the grill and José is sitting on a milk crate by the dishwasher, reading a book of poetry. Sometimes when it's not busy he'll read everyone a poem out loud, which is kind of nice. José is even older than Patty, and I think he's been washing dishes here since she opened the place. He looks up and smiles at me as I pass, and I smile back.

Maura's tables are filthy and there's already a line of people at the door waiting for clean tables so they can sit. I start clearing plates and cups and dumping them in the bus tub and wiping down tables right away. It stays pretty busy, me bussing and doing the register until seven, when it slows down and Maura goes out back for a cigarette and her dinner and Patty tells me I can take any tables that come in.

I'm at the register, sorting order slips and receipts, when the little bell above the front door tinkles.

"Welcome to Patty's," I call out, not looking up. "Sit where you like and I'll be right with you." I try to keep my voice neutral but friendly, because Patty once told me I sounded "huffy," whatever that means.

I stack the sheets and file them neatly in the folder Patty keeps on the shelf under the register, slide my order pad out of my apron and make sure I have a pen.

And then I look up.

Dylan and Willow are sitting at B3, by the window. Tucked together on one side of the booth, holding the plastic menu between them.

Oh god no.

I panic. Turn around to face the kitchen, where Lonnie and Deb are fussing with onions and green chiles and cleaning the grill during the lull. Deb glances at me. "What's up?"

"Is Maura still on break?"

"Yeah, she's got fifteen left. She's gonna eat. Why? You okay?"

I look down at the counter, at my hands, which are shaking uncontrollably. My skin feels like it's on fire. Why would he come here? Why would he bring *her* here? Isn't this, like, in violation of the many millions of rules of breaking up, one of which is *avoid each other at all costs, except when you can't, like school, and in that case, change your daily class-to-class walking route and never make eye contact*?

In the summer, he would come in after the dinner rush and order some fries and wait for me, and then we'd walk to the park and kiss. Or take a bus to a movie, and kiss in the back row. Or take the bus downtown to 191 Toole if the show was all-ages, and kiss, the music fusing us together. My parents didn't know. I'd say I was staying with Amber and then she'd leave her back patio door open for me. Amber didn't like it, but she went along with it.

It felt thrilling, doing that with him, in secret. Something small and glowing and shiny that belonged only to me.

I have no choice but to take their order.

I walk to their booth slowly, gripping the pen and order pad tightly in my hands. It takes them what seems like an eternity to even notice me.

I'm not going to cry. I'm not going to cry. I'm not going to cry.

"Hey," Dylan says. "Hey, Bella."

His voice is neutral. Smooth. Like nothing is wrong. Like it isn't even wrong for him to be here with another girl. I can't look him in the eye. I look everywhere but at his face. At the menu lying flat on the table. At the table itself. At my order pad.

Willow says, "Are there red onions in the side salad? If there are, can you not put them in?"

Her voice isn't mean. Or knowing. Just normal, ordering food.

"No onions," I say in a low voice. "Got it."

"Cool. Can I have that with the cheese crisp and a Diet Coke?"

It would be so much easier if she was mean. I try not to see her face, her eyes. Her mouth. The mouth that he kisses now.

"Sure." *Scratch, scratch,* my pen on the order pad digging deep into the green paper.

Silence.

On my order pad, so hard I almost rip it, I write in very, very small letters, *I hate you so much right now.*

Dylan says, "You know what I like."

The green chile cheeseburger no tomato with a side of fries and ranch dressing and an orange soda.

I finally look at him. I can't help it.

Brown hair falling in his eyes. Blue flannel shirt. The freckle above his left eyebrow.

What I want to say is *I guess I do know what you like and it isn't me. It isn't me.*

My body was on fire, but now it's cold as ice, like when I have to get pickles and cheese from the walk-in cooler and it takes too long and by the time I have everything, my body is stiff.

What comes out of my mouth is "Yes."

"Cool. Thanks."

And then he turns back to Willow, who's scrolling on her phone and laughing. He bends closer to look.

Dylan brought Willow here and didn't think it mattered because . . . I don't matter anymore. I'm no big deal. I'm nothing. I'm erased.

I walk slowly to the kitchen, rip the green sheet from my order pad, pin it to the carousel, and press the bell. I open my mouth, but I can't even say *Order up.*

Deb turns around from the grill.

"What the hell is this?" she says, looking at the order sheet. "Something you want to tell me, Bella?"

Oh god, Deb read what I wrote about Dylan and thinks I meant *her.*

"Oh god," I say. My voice is so small. "That's not for you. I . . ."

I just want to die.

"Oh, shit," she says. "Are you okay?"

My whole face is wet.

I'm digging the pen into the order pad, deeper and deeper, until I'm just ripping the sheets.

"Lonnie," Deb says. "Go get Patty, quick."

Patty appears in an instant. "You are sick, I knew it." She puts a hand to my forehead.

But then she sees my face, and feels my tears, and turns around to see Dylan in the booth.

She sucks in her breath. "Oh, hell."

She likes him. She used to sit with him while he ate his fries and waited for me to get off shift. They talked about movies and music.

"Go out back. Take out the trash or something. Pull yourself together. Take a break. I've got this." She pushes me gently.

I walk quickly past Deb and Lonnie all the way to the back door and out into the parking lot behind the restaurant.

It isn't until I hear a soft voice say "Sit down, girl, take a load off" that I realize José is perched on an overturned pickle bucket, smoking a cigarette, listening to me hiccup as I try not to sob. It doesn't work. My eyes fill and my chest heaves. He stands, gesturing to the bucket.

I sit down. I hold myself as tightly as possible, as though I can stuff my sobs inside, but it doesn't work.

Dylan was the *one thing* that made me feel better after Laurel died. He was the *one thing* that came along and made me feel wanted and important, like she had. I told him things I'd never told anyone else. And he listened, like the things I said were important. Until they weren't.

"You want a cigarette?" José asks.

I shake my head.

"You want a drink?"

I sniffle, looking up at him.

My brain says: *Challenge him first, to be careful.*

My heart says: *Just take it.*

"What? I'm a *kid.*"

"Kids drink. Don't if you don't want to." He shrugs. "Under the pickle bucket. Maybe a little to calm you down. You might be a kid, but it seems like you're having a grown-up kind of feeling right now."

I stand up, lift the bucket. A pint of Smirnoff is sitting there.

"Sometimes you just need something to get to the next thing, you know what I mean? You just need to keep going and hope the *next* next is better," José says.

I hesitate at first, because, well, I have to go back in and work, and what if Patty notices? And also, what if José turns out to be one of those closet creeps and tries to touch me or something?

José chuckles, like he knows what I'm thinking. "Suit yourself," he murmurs.

I can have this. I know I can maintain if I have this. Just a little *this.*

I lift the bottle, unscrew the cap, and take two swallows before José shakes his head. "Not too much."

I take one last giant gulp, replace the cap, put the bottle back under the pickle bucket. The vodka burned my throat but replaced what was hurting inside me with a numbing warmth.

And kind of took my headache away. Hair of the dog, just like my dad says.

José holds out his palm. "Mint," he says.

I pop it in my mouth.

" 'As for me, I am a watercolor. I wash off,' " José says, looking at the sky.

"What?" I'm patting my face with my apron, hoping my eyeliner didn't smear too much.

"It's from a poem we're reading in my class at Pima," José says. "She's talking to her boyfriend, who leaves her and goes back to his wife. Those are the last lines. I think about them all the time."

He takes a drag from his cigarette.

"I'm not sure what the words mean, exactly," he says, staring at the stars just beginning to pop in the sky. "But I find them kind of comforting, you know? Sad things can be really comforting in a weird way."

I nod, because I'm not sure what to say.

"You should go back in. Patty will be wondering where you are."

I stand up, retie my apron, pat down my hair.

José smiles and points to the pickle bucket and puts a finger to his lips. *Shhhh.*

Patty and Deb are waiting for me by the dishwasher. I keep sucking on the mint José gave me. The drinks I took are making a warm cloud inside my body. I feel calmer now.

"You want me to tell him never to come back? I will," Patty says.

I shake my head. I'm buzzed, to be honest. That last big gulp helped, but it's also hitting me a little hard.

"He shouldn't have come in here. That's cold. There's, like, *rules.*" Deb shakes her head. She's got two new streaks of color since last week: pink and green.

"It's fine," I say softly, even though it isn't. I try to speak really clearly because I'm afraid I might slur a little. The warm cloud inside me is getting hotter.

"Whatever. Sorry I flipped out." I bite my lip. *Focus,* I tell myself.

Patty gives me a smile. "Go fix your face. Deb'll make you some eggs and toast. You eat, then you go back out and he'll probably be gone. You've gotta be tough with this, you hear? Don't let him get to you."

Deb nods. "Yeah. You have to just carry that shit until one day, you wake up, and it doesn't hurt so bad."

Lonnie appears, drying his hands on his apron. "On behalf of all men and boys, I'd like to apologize for our insensitivity. We really *are* that stupid."

"True that," says Deb.

In the tiny bathroom, I look at my smudged eyeliner, the tear tracks through my face powder.

The poem José quoted to me drifts through my head as I look at the mess I am reflected back at me.

As for me, I am a watercolor. I wash off.

It's ten-fifteen and my dad isn't here to pick me up yet. I'm about to text him when I see Vanessa's white Volkswagen Beetle pull into the lot. Ricci waves at me from the back seat.

My heart sinks. Perfect. Just perfect. Now I'm going to be subjected to my dad's girlfriend's relentless positivity for the night. The shots I took with José helped me power through the last of my shift. I'm still a little buzzed, so they'll get me through at least this car ride.

I climb into the front seat.

"Sorry," Vanessa says. "Your dad went out for a bit to hear some music. Looks like it's a girls' night. Are you okay? Your face is really pink. You getting sick?"

"I'm *fine,*" I mutter.

From the back seat, Ricci chants, "Girls' night, girls' night!"

"All right, then. I've got cheese popcorn and hot chocolate," Vanessa says. "Maybe a movie on Netflix?"

"I have homework," I say. "And I'm pretty tired."

"It's Saturday! No one should have to do homework on a Saturday," Vanessa answers. "You can take a break, for once."

"Saturday!" Ricci shouts.

I know it kills my mom that Ricci likes Vanessa so much. I mean, Ricci's just a little kid, so things like *new girlfriend* and *betrayal* don't mean anything to her. But at this moment, after having lost it at my job when my old boyfriend, my *first* boyfriend, brought in his *new girlfriend,* I'm not feeling too much like pretending to be nice to my *dad's* new girlfriend. Who, for all I know, was his girlfriend *while* he was with my mom. Parents lie to you all the time.

"Just drop it," I say sharply.

Vanessa stops smiling. From the corner of my eye, I can see her jaw tighten. I've hurt her feelings.

Good. Because who is she to just suddenly be in our lives, pretending to be important, making us dinner, watching movies, making hot chocolate, acting like . . . she's *family*? I didn't ask for a new family, or even an adjacent one. I don't know how to deal with the one I *have.*

I'm glad she's hurt.

I take out my phone, pretend to look at messages, like I don't know I've spoiled her nice plans for the evening.

Because I'm a watercolor. I wash off.

In the room I share with Ricci at Dad's, I throw my backpack onto the top bunk and climb up in the dark and click on the fairy lights I've strung around the railings and lie down.

I can hear the opening of *Frozen* out in the living room and Vanessa moving around in Dad's tiny kitchen. I know it's all he can afford right now, and it's actually kind of nice—the complex is pretty big and there's even a pool—but sometimes his apartment feels so tight and small, like I can't breathe. And there's only one bathroom, which is a pain when you really have to go and, say, Ricci is in there taking her sweet time. There's nowhere to *go* here, like there is at Mom's, where I have my own room and two bathrooms, plus Laurel's house when I need to disappear.

I unzip my backpack and pull out the Sprodka bottle and take a sip.

I'm kind of sorry that I know José keeps alcohol at work. Now I might be thinking about that all the time while I'm there. I sometimes have it in my backpack, but that's always for later, and it's not all the time, anyway. It's just lately. I just feel like if I can get through Thanksgiving and have a break, things will be better. I'll make them better.

I should change out of my work clothes. I'm still wearing my apron. I need to make sure I have a clean work shirt and apron for tomorrow. This means finding some quarters for the laundry machine in the next building over. I feel in my apron for my tips and I'm relieved to find some quarters in there. My dad isn't great about saving up quarters for emergency laundry. He likes to just dump everything off at the cleaners once a week.

My phone buzzes. Amber.

Hey

Hey, I type back.

You okay? How was work?

I hesitate. If I tell her about Dylan in the wrong way, she'll call, and I don't want to talk to anyone right now.

Dylan came in. With Willow.

OMG Are you all right? What a jerk!

It's fine. They just ate.

I pause.

It was all cool. No worries.

You sure?

Yeah. Gotta go. I need to do laundry. I'm at my dad's.

K. Call me if you want to talk.

I arch my back and untie my apron, counting my tips. After tipping out Deb, Lonnie, and José, I have thirty dollars. Not great, but not bad. It's something. I fold the paper money carefully and tuck it in my backpack, then count out six dollars in quarters.

I look at my phone.

I check Dylan's Stories.

I have a fake account, so he won't know it's me. I know that's all sorts of wrong, but I couldn't help myself after we broke up.

There they are, back row of the movie theater, nestled together.

I start crying again.

They're kissing.

Did he play air hockey with her in the theater arcade before the movie, like he did with me, our laughter mixing with the clack and slide of the puck across the table? Does she like to breathe in his smell, just like I did? She doesn't look any different from me, really, just a girl with messy hair and better eyeliner and jeans and sneakers, so why am I *too much* and she is not?

I slide down the ladder of the bunk and rip off my jeans and work shirt and jam on pajama pants and an oversize T-shirt and hoodie and grab the laundry basket from the corner. I throw my work clothes in there, along with some dirty clothes lying on the floor, and my headphones and phone, and tuck the Sprodka bottle under the clothes.

In the front room, Ricci and Vanessa are on the couch eating popcorn and watching *Frozen.* Ricci has a hot chocolate mustache.

Vanessa looks up at me. "A little late for laundry, don't you think?"

"I'm working a double tomorrow and I need clean work clothes. Dad's not a great laundry person, if you haven't noticed."

She gives me a look like she's considering very carefully what to say.

"Okay then," she says. "Maybe when you're done, you'll be ready to hang out?"

"No. Homework, remember?"

She tucks a strand of blond hair behind one ear and crunches a piece of popcorn. "Right. Homework."

She's wearing pink pajama pants and a tank top, which means she's staying over.

After the divorce, Ricci and I had barely just started getting used to Dad's apartment and, well, Dad, *alone,* without the presence of my mom, before Vanessa appeared. She was just there one night, like it wasn't a big deal, or anything my dad had to prepare us for, or even, I don't know, *ask* us about. He just slotted her into our lives, like our mom didn't matter, like maybe I wasn't kind of looking forward to just being with my dad by himself, away from all the fighting and tension with my mom, maybe figuring out who he was when he wasn't angry and sad all the time. No one ever asked me what I wanted.

And looking at Vanessa on this couch right now, even though she's being sweet and cool and nice with my little sister, I kind of hate her.

The laundry room is dead, so I have the machines to myself. I'm grateful that nobody left any wet clothes in the washer, because that's awkward, wondering if you should just pull out a stranger's clothes and dump them on the table. Who wants a stranger touching their clothes? Also, I do not want to touch anyone else's wet underwear.

I stuff my clothes in the washer, add detergent and quarters, and start the machine. Then I plug my headphones into my phone and go sit in the corner with my backpack and Sprodka bottle. If anyone comes in, I'm just some loser girl, doing her laundry on a Saturday night, listening to music and drinking her soda, occasional bursts of heat from the dryers keeping me warm.

I almost trip on the stairs going back up to the apartment and I have to stop and take a couple of breaths to steady myself. I'm not sure how long I was in the laundry room; I stayed long after the clothes in the dryer stopped tumbling, just looking at pictures on my phone and listening to music.

I'm unsteady. I was down there too long. I take a deep breath, standing outside the door to the apartment, listening. It's quiet inside. Ricci always goes to sleep for Vanessa, no problem, which I've never understood. I hope Vanessa is asleep, too.

I just have to get through the living room and to our bedroom. That's it. I try to imagine the path I have to take: being careful not to walk into the couch, which juts in front of the door; angle around the easy chair and then take a sharp right down the short hall to our room, open the door, set down the laundry basket with my clothes, manage the three steps on the bunk ladder—

No. I'm going to have to pee. No, I *do* have to pee. I start giggling at the absurdity of it, having to plan out my path like a master spy, but I'm also a little panicked. Please do not let Vanessa be up, please, please, please. I don't want to have to talk to her. My mouth is as thick as mud; I'll definitely slur.

No one is in the front room when I step inside. I breathe a sigh of relief. They're in bed. I'm almost around the sharp corner, one eye squinting because things are a little fuzzy, when Vanessa calls out from the room down the opposite hall, "Bella? That you?"

I freeze, then turn slightly. The door to the bedroom is half open. She's in bed with the light on.

"Yes." My lips are rubbery as I speak. Am I slurring? I cough to cover the possibility. Lick my lips.

"Okay. Did you lock the door? Your dad won't be home until later."

"Yes." Did I? I can't remember. Should I go back and check? No. Screw it.

"Don't stay up too late studying, okay?" She sounds sleepy. The light clicks off. "Good night."

"Night." I cough again.

There's a silence and then, "You sound a little off. I think you *are* getting sick."

"I'm just fine, thank you very much." I head as quickly and carefully as possible to our bedroom. I close the door behind me, my heart thudding with relief. It takes a minute for my eyes to adjust.

Ricci is splayed out on the bottom bunk, her thumb jammed in her mouth. I put the laundry basket on the floor and open the door again, pausing to listen. I don't hear anything, so I creep out as quietly as possible to the bathroom, waiting to flick the light on until I have the door closed. The suddenness of the light stings my eyes because my dad likes superbright bulbs. I sit down and pee what feels like a gallon of liquid and then stand up and wash my hands.

I look at myself in the mirror. Tired face. Sad face. Round and childish-looking, except for my smudged makeup. I trace the outline of my face in the mirror, leaving a fingerprint trail.

"That was stupid," I whisper to the girl in the mirror. "You could have got caught. Don't do that again."

I stifle a giggle.

Back in our bedroom, I fold my clothes in the dim glow of the fairy lights, set the alarm on my phone for tomorrow morning for work, squinting to make sure I have the time correct, because everything's getting blurry again, and start climbing up into my bunk with my backpack on.

But my foot misses one of the steps and I slip, jamming my chin on one of the rungs.

I freeze, pain slicing through me, and it's all I can do to hold back a scream. I take several deep breaths, try to refocus, my heart thudding in my chest. *Jesus.*

I grip the rungs again and slowly climb all the way up to my mattress, throw off my backpack, and turn on the small light clamped to my headboard. I feel under my chin, but no blood comes away on my fingers. That was close.

I check my phone. Put it down. Pull my school laptop from my backpack, lie down, rest it on my stomach, reach up behind me and click on the tiny lamp on my headboard. Maybe I should do some reading for English lit. We've got that paper due on Wednesday for the nonfiction module and I chose *Wild,* but I haven't finished it yet or even taken notes, even though I told my mother I did. I'm just filled with lies these days.

I slide the book from my backpack, but the words swim in front of my eyes. This book makes me sad, because the writer lost her mother, which makes me think of Laurel. I don't know if I would have what it takes to walk that far and for that long by myself, but maybe it wouldn't be too bad. No one to bother me. Just some trees and dirt and birds and a tent.

I start reading, forcing myself to concentrate on the words, as if I can stop their fluttery movement in front of my eyes. I shouldn't have stayed in the laundry room so long. I didn't pay attention. Bad Bella. I sigh; I can't concentrate. My chin aches.

The bottle is peeking from the top of my backpack. I look at it, then look away, then look back at it.

I mean, what does it even matter now?

I wake up with the book on my chest and the Sprodka bottle on its side, liquid pooling on the sheet under me and my bladder so full it's burning the inside of my body. Dammit.

I almost fall climbing down the ladder and catch myself just in time. I hold on to a rung, try to calm down. Am I seeing double? The room is spinning.

I blink a couple of times. The doubles go away.

From the living room comes the sound of soft strumming and low voices.

Dad.

The front room is separated from the kitchen by a breakfast bar, and after that, if you go left, you go to Dad's room. If you go right, it's me and Ricci's room. Right in the middle of our rooms, next to the kitchen, is the bathroom, so I'm going to have to see Dad in this state whether I like it or not.

Like I said, act like nothing is amiss and nothing will be amiss.

I open my bedroom door and stand in the doorway of the front room, trying not to sway. I don't think my dad would be mad if he thought I'd been drinking, since he's lazy in the parental enforcement area, but he would think it was weird that I did it by myself, on a night I was working, and not with friends or something. My mother told him about what happened with Dylan, and about Luis's party, but he didn't tell me to not drink or anything. It was mostly an awkward conversation about "taking it easy on the hard stuff" and "sometimes a broken heart makes us do some pretty crazy things" and my favorite, "what a little prick that kid is."

"Hey, Bella," my dad says. He's sitting on the couch, a guitar on his knees. "Did we wake you up?"

His voice is a little thick and his face is soft.

Oh. Right. Vanessa said he went out to listen to a band. So he's tipsy, too.

"Belly!" It's my dad's friend Hoyt. He's stretched out on the floor between the couch and the television, a couple of beer cans by his head.

I flinch. I don't like it when he calls me that. I feel like grown men should not be referring to girls by their body parts, even *if* it's because when I was really little, Hoyt could get me to lift my shirt by asking me, "Where's your belly button?" Which is also kind of gross, when you think about it.

"I don't like it when you call me that, Hoyt," I say. "Can you . . . not?"

He chuckles. "Aww, come on. It's your nickname. It's cute."

I look at my dad, like *can you make him stop?* But my dad is looking at his guitar.

Hoyt and my dad were in a band together a long time ago. Once, Hoyt said, "We traded guitar licks and groupies for Garanimals and goldfish and here we are, for better or for worse." I couldn't tell if he meant it in a happy or sad way.

"You didn't wake me," I say to my dad, making sure to speak slowly so I don't slur. "I just had to pee."

My dad pats the couch next to him. "You want to join us? I missed you. I could show you a couple of chords."

My dad is always trying to teach me how to play the guitar, but I'm not very good. I feel like my fingers are clumsy and huge when I try to play, but he says I just need practice.

I shake my head. "No, that's okay. I have to get up early. I'm doing a double tomorrow."

"Come here. Give me a hug, babe. I missed you."

Can he see me hesitate? The side of my shirt is wet from the spilled bottle.

"Come here," he says again.

I take the couple of steps toward him and bend down, kind of awkwardly, over the back of the couch, so he can't notice or feel the wet mark on my shirt. I keep my mouth shut, too, because of my breath. He kisses me on top of my head and ruffles my hair.

Then he sniffs the air.

I stop breathing.

He sniffs again. "You smell like . . . ," he says. "What is that smell?" He frowns.

Hoyt laughs. "She smells like a giant Patty's Place burger, bro, green chile and onions. It's killing me. You got anything to eat here?" He gets up, groaning a little, and staggers toward the kitchen. On his way, he peers at me.

"Damn, girl, you look like a soggy raccoon. What happened to you?"

I touch my face. Oh god. I fell asleep with all my makeup on.

My dad frowns. "Jeez, Bella, you really piled it on today."

He's not a fan of my makeup.

"It's my face," I say, my voice prickly. "I can do what I want with it."

"Ooooh, kitten's got her claws out," Hoyt calls from the kitchen. He's rummaging around in the fridge.

My dad's mouth flattens a little. "Well, wash it off and go to bed, all right? Good night, Bella."

He starts strumming his guitar again.

"Good night," I murmur, turning and walking to the bathroom.

I let the water run in the bathroom while I pee, just so Hoyt can't hear it in the kitchen, and then I wipe off my makeup and wash my face.

In the mirror, my bare face stares back at me, shiny and pink and puffy and tired and naked. I lift my chin. There's a red splotch there that will probably be swollen and purple by morning. That's just *perfect.*

I meet my eyes in the mirror for only a second before something flares up inside me, hot and sudden. Tears pool in my eyes. I shove the heels of my palms against them.

I don't like seeing that girl. That girl looks ugly and heartbroken and alone.

I turn away from the mirror and grab a towel to put over the wet spot on my sheet and go back to bed. I just want to disappear.

IT'S LIKE THIS AND *this is the only time I can say this, here in the dark, by myself: everyone is gone and no one understands what that feels like. It feels like a giant hole inside me sucking me in and churning me around as I break into bits until eventually I'll just be nothing. Speck on the sole of your shoe. A fluttery mote you swat out of your face. They have been fighting forever and I have been listening for years and she was my good place. And then he was. I know you don't like him because of what he did but really that was me. It was all me. My fault, always, just like with her. Please believe me. Please listen. I'm like a giant wrong thing. I'm all-capitals BELLA. I don't fit anywhere. I should stop. I know. I can't stop. If I stop, I'll start to crack and I can't crack because if that happens, I don't know if I'll find all of me. There will be too many pieces, too sharp, too tiny, and blood everywhere leaving stains that won't disappear. Please don't go. I didn't mean to frighten you. I'm sorry. I'm sorry. I'm sorry. I'm sorry. See. There is me again. All-capitals BELLA. Too much.*

SUNDAY

WHEN MY PHONE ALARM goes off, my mouth feels thick and dry, my head is spinning, and my stomach feels messy. I lean over the edge of my bunk. Ricci's not there. I climb down and grab the ever-present water bottle she keeps on the floor and drink it all in one gulp. That eases the pin-pricks in front of my eyes a little.

I check my phone for the time and see a message from Amber.

Call me. We need to talk.

I stare at the words, a vague feeling of unease creeping over my body. That . . . doesn't sound like Amber usually sounds. She sounds . . . terse.

My finger hesitates over my phone; then I shake my head. I don't have time to call her or I'll be late, and if she's mad at me for some reason, well, I don't want to hear about that until later. I toss my phone in my backpack and grab my work clothes, throw a blanket over my still-damp sheet and towel, and head to the bathroom for a shower. I feel dizzy and heavy-headed under the hot spray, so I hold on to the tiled walls until it passes. I'm a little afraid I might throw up, which is a thing that's happened a few times, and even though you think running water would make everything easier, it is not, in fact, easy to get puke down a drain.

In the mirror, my eyes are like red marshmallows and just like I thought, there's a swollen purple mound under my chin. *Fuck.* I do my face and eyes really quick, making sure my eyeliner is heavy to distract from my gross face. I swab some concealer over the wound on my chin, but it still puffs out. I swallow some ibuprofen and wash it down with water cupped in my hand from the faucet.

My stomach rolls. I lean over the toilet, panicked. I've only thrown up a few times after drinking, and it wasn't pleasant, and I had to spend the rest of the day in bed after telling my mom I had the stomach flu.

When I come out, Vanessa and Ricci are in the kitchen at the tiny table. Vanessa holds out a plate to me. "I made you a bagel. Your dad's still asleep. You need a ride to work? Wait, how late did you stay up? You look wrecked. What happened to your *chin*?"

I bristle, turning away from her so she can't have a better look at my face. "Wow, what a super nice thing to say to me first thing in the morning. And I slipped down the bunk ladder last night and hit my chin. That's what happens when I have to share a room with my sister and I have to climb up in the dark so I don't wake her up, okay? And *no,* I'm just gonna take the bus."

With her mouth full, Ricci says, "Bella had a nightmare last night." Bits of bagel flutter from her lips. Jelly's smeared on her cheek.

I frown. "What are you talking about? I don't remember that."

Ricci swallows some bagel. "You were weird. You were, like, crying about Dylan. And letters. Like the big kind. Are you in trouble at school?" She wrinkles her nose at me.

"I wasn't crying. Shut *up,* don't lie." What is she talking about? I don't remember anything like that. Why does she make stuff up all the time? Big letters?

But still.

Something is poking at my brain. I try to concentrate. I did my laundry, I fell asleep, I woke up, I saw Dad and Hoyt, I went back up in my bunk and . . . why did Amber text me that weird message . . .

"It isn't a *lie.* You were crying. *You're* the liar!" Ricci shouts.

Vanessa says, "Ricci. Honey, that's not nice."

Then Vanessa turns to me. "You okay? You want to talk?"

"It's *fine* and I was not crying. Ricci makes shit up all the time."

"I didn't!" Ricci yells.

"Girls," Vanessa says.

"Just forget it," I say. "I have to go. Don't forget Ricci needs to do two pages of her homework packet, if you're sticking around tonight, Vanessa."

Ricci's whining follows me out the door.

The bus is late, so by the time I get off at the stop closest to Patty's I have to run really fast so I'm not even later for my shift. I'm sweating inside my hoodie by the time I get there. My stomach hurts, too. I should have taken that bagel Vanessa offered. Maybe I can get Deb to fix me some toast before things get busy.

I'm hanging my backpack on the rack by the flour shelves when I feel my phone buzz again.

Amber. *I really need you to call me.*

Can't. At work. Double shift. Talk later.

I check my call history on my phone. It looks like I called her last night? But I don't . . . remember it? I must have rolled over on my phone or something in bed. Three missed calls from her last night after that.

I squint at the phone and then shove it in my back pocket. That's *weird.* My stomach flips nervously as I tie my apron around my waist.

What is *up* with Amber?

I'm on dinner break in the back when Patty pokes her head in from the kitchen and says, "Your friend is here. The nice one." She doesn't like Kristen, either, so I'm guessing she's talking about Amber or Cherie.

I take my plate of cheese fries out front, where Amber is sitting at the last window on the right, tucked away in the corner. She's rubbing her hands together and looks upset.

"Hey," I say, sliding into the booth across from her. "I'm sorry I didn't catch you earlier. Everything okay?"

She's quiet.

"Amber? What's wrong?"

"You look like shit, you know that?" There's an unfamiliar edge to her voice.

"I'm sorry, *what?*"

"Do you not even remember?" She looks up. Her eyes are glossy, like she's trying not to cry, but they're also . . . kind of mad.

"What? What are you talking about?" The cheese fries feel very heavy in my mouth all of a sudden. I swallow them in one lump.

"I'm so sick of this, Bella. I'm just so tired of it." She picks some green polish from her nails.

"Amber, whatever it is I did, I'm *sorry.* Just tell me what I did."

What could I have done? I didn't even *see* her yesterday. I'm struggling to think of why she's so upset and why she had to call me three times in the middle of the night. I mean, I couldn't answer. I was sleeping, for god's sake.

"Did I say something to you?" I start scrolling through our texts, looking for any place I might have offended her. "Whatever it was, I'm sorry, Amber."

The words of our texts whiz by my eyes, but there's something else, something eating away at a far corner of my brain. What Ricci said. About me having a nightmare. Dylan. Letters. I don't remember that. That didn't happen.

Did it? I was just reading *Wild* and I fell asleep and—

Amber pushes my phone down.

"You called me last night, like, at three-thirty in the morning. I could barely understand you, you were mumbling and crying about Dylan." She pauses. "You were drunk, Bella. *Again.*"

My stomach drops. I wipe my mouth with a napkin and then fold it carefully into a tiny square, hold it in one fist. I have to think fast, defuse this situation.

"I was really tired. I don't . . . honestly, I don't remember, and I'm sorry. I just . . . I don't know. Ricci said I had a nightmare or something. Maybe I called you in my sleep. I was sleeptalking! Get it? Like sleepwalking?"

I laugh, like it's a joke, but I feel kind of sick.

Amber's eyes are on the table. "You said you were cracking. That there would be blood. Do you understand how freaked out that made me? I almost called your dad."

I can feel my face drain and my blood run cold. I don't . . . I don't think I remember that. Do I? I felt unsettled when I woke up, my stomach messy. I had too much. A little too much, but I made it into bed, except for that thing with my chin, and I tried to read, and then I just fell asleep. Or I thought I did.

It's like it was at Luis's party, when I flipped out over seeing Dylan with Willow. Where one minute I was doing things and being *there* and then . . . nothing. And other people had to tell me later about what I was doing during that nothing.

Amber is staring at me.

"I mean, you were at your dad's, so, like, where did you even get something to drink? Do you go and shoulder-tap when you aren't with the rest of us? Do you think it's funny for me to hear you like that? And you're like that a *lot* lately."

"Listen," I say, carefully, trying to squash the panic down inside me. I can feel Patty watching us from the register. I keep my voice low. "I've been really stressed and I'm really torn up about Dylan. I'm *sorry.* I know . . . it seems bad, but . . . I just need this semester to end and then, I swear, things will be different. I need a break. I'm sorry. I guess I just . . . I don't know. I didn't mean to upset you. I mean, technically, I don't even *remember,* so I don't know why I'm saying sorry, ha ha."

"I can't believe you got that drunk by yourself." Her voice is flat and sad.

"I'm *tired,* Amber," I say defensively, my voice rising slightly.

"And I said I was *sorry.* I can't control something I can't even remember."

Her nails are almost completely free of polish now and she's pushing the green chips into a small pile on the white table.

"When did everything become about getting wasted?" She says this really softly, almost like she's not even talking to me, just talking to herself. She pushes a lock of her deep brown hair behind her ear. "Like, I feel like that's all we do now. I mean, that's what you guys do, I just drive." She flattens the pile of green chips onto the table. "And I don't think I want to do that anymore. I'm not even supposed to have that many kids in the car with me, you know."

"Amber, that's *not* all we do." My voice cracks a little.

She looks at me.

We're so different now, me and Amber. She's got a clean, washed face and I layer on a mask of makeup every day. She's on yearbook and does Science Olympiad and I keep to myself. She's got plans for this big car trip of ours, hope literally pinned on a map on her bedroom wall, and I feel like I'm just . . . just hanging on for the ride.

"It's not funny or cool, Bella. That one time a couple of months ago when I had to cover for you at your mom's, after we went to that stupid thing in Carter's garage? When I told her you must have gotten food poisoning from the drive-through burger. Do you think that was fun for me?"

She rips up a napkin, the little pieces sitting in their own pile next to the fragments of her nail polish.

"Do you even *remember* that night?"

My face heats up. I remember the garage was damp and smelly. The beer pong. And then being in Amber's car, a plastic bag on my lap while she mumbled "Oh shit oh shit oh shit" in the front seat. Then nothing until I woke up in my bed with her next to me the morning after, a worried look on her face.

But I thought we laughed it off.

Or maybe that was only me.

Tears slip down her face, splash on the chipped polish and napkin shreds.

"I think I can't hang out with—" she starts to say, but panic rises inside me and I cut her off.

I can't lose her, too. I'll have nothing, nobody. I grab her hands.

"I'll be better, Amber. I promise. Please," I say, leaning toward her, trying not to cry. "Please. I'll stop. *I promise.*"

"It's not good for me, Bella. I love you so much, but you're killing me."

"I promise, Amber."

I stand up and slide next to her, wrap my arms around her. Solid, beautiful, kind, and funny Amber. "Please believe me."

"You girls all right?"

It's Patty. She's looking down at us, concern on her face, holding two glasses of Coke. She puts them on the table.

"It's okay," I tell her, wiping my face. "Just friend stuff."

Patty nods and walks away.

Amber sniffles and takes a sip of her Coke. She still won't look me in the eye.

"Please, Amber."

"Okay," she says finally, finishing her drink. She hiccups. "I'll believe you. I have to go now. I have to get back home."

I slide out of the booth so we can both stand up. "I love you, Amber. I'm sorry."

"Stop *saying* that. If you were so sorry, you'd *stop* with all this," she says. Her voice is sharp.

I flinch.

"I mean, do you not even think this is a *problem*? You're calling me in the middle of the night and like, blanking out, and you can't remember things? That seems like a problem to me."

Little bricks of shame are stacking in me, one by one, weighing me down. I was *too much.* And now I'm a *problem.*

Blanking out, Amber said.

A little bit of last night flashes across my brain. Me saying I was all capitals. Too much. That's it. Like Ricci said.

And I am, I am, I am.

"I . . ." I swallow, trying to force out more words, something, but there aren't any. I feel hot and cold all at once. I bite my bottom lip, hard, to keep the swell of tears from erupting behind my eyes.

"Sorry," Amber says. "I'm tired. I should just go."

She scoops up her pile of green nail polish shavings and napkin pieces and slides them in her pocket. That's Amber: clean and neat, never leaving a mess for someone else to clean up. She pulls her hoodie over her head and looks at her sneakers.

"Amber." My voice is small. "Can't you just be nice to me? I'm just . . . Stuff is really hard right now."

"Oh, so it's my fault? *Nice.*" Her voice cracks. It's just as tiny as mine. She shakes her head. "See you, Bella."

I watch her walk out the door, the bell jingling as she leaves.

Problemtoomuchproblemtoomuchproblemtoomuch. So many letters jumbled together in my brain it's hard to focus, until I feel a hard elbow against my arm. A customer, squeezing by me to get to a booth.

Across the diner, Lonnie and Deb and Patty are standing by the grill, staring at me.

I put my head down and start moving, grab a bus tub, pick up dirty plates and stained glasses, vow to keep busy the rest of my shift so I don't disintegrate into a thousand pieces.

My dad is ten minutes late picking me up. He pushes the car door open for me from the inside. "Hey, kid. Long day in the trenches?"

I climb into the car. "Yeah. Pretty busy."

"You want me to spring for a late dinner? You hungry? I can swing by Sonic on the way home."

"Whatever."

"I just need to make a quick stop first, okay?"

He pulls into the bright orange Quik-Mart around the corner. "Be right back," he says, hopping out of the car.

I watch him through the glass windows of the store. He goes to the beer cooler.

When he gets back into the car, he dumps a twelve-pack in the back seat. "Gonna drop you off and head over to Hoyt's after. My turn for the libations." He winks and starts the car.

I hug my backpack to my chest. I can feel the extra bottle of Sprodka inside.

My dad and I are in a car and we both have alcohol, only one of us doesn't know about the other's.

He makes a left, honks at someone taking too long in the crosswalk.

Amber said I looked like shit this morning. I knew I looked like shit. I tried to fix myself up. It didn't work, I guess. I chew my fingernail. My head still hurts, even though I took more ibuprofen at work after the dinner rush. As my dad drives, I try to get a fix on all the things running through my head.

Memories. Or . . . the *not* memories. The things that got away from me, like Carter's party and that blank space between Amber's car and holding the plastic bag and then waking up the next morning with my head feeling like someone had stomped on it. Luis's party . . . That was . . . Seeing Dylan and Willow and the room shifting, spinning, and my cup always full and then . . . a bathroom? Crying in Luis's bathroom in the bathtub is how Cherie and Kristen found me. That's what they told me later. I had my knees up to my chest, people pounding on the door, and then

And then

And then

I don't remember what then.

Just that somehow I was in the tub and they were pulling at me and then suddenly I was in my room. Somewhere in the middle I lost an hour, two, maybe three. Poof. Down the drain. Gone forever.

I remember the laptop on my lap as I lay in bed in my room and seeing something Dylan posted in his Stories and then her, lanky Willow with her pretty hair, in a photo and the laptop . . .

There's another black space.

And then . . .

That's when my mother came in and then more black space, but it feels heavy in my mind, like there's something attached to it, but I just can't *see* it.

All day those bricks of shame and worry have been building inside me, getting heavier each time, and now they just keep going in this car with my dad and I can't stop them and do I have a problem am I the problem why doesn't anyone understand why can't *I* understand and don't I have the answer in my backpack? Don't I have the answer to make all this shit inside my head just stop for one second?

But I made a promise to Amber and I have to keep it.

Ricci is in bed when I let myself into the apartment after Dad drops me off. Vanessa is on the couch, the television on and a book in her lap. She smiles at me. "Hey. How was work?"

I drop the sack of Sonic chili dogs and fries on the breakfast bar. "Fine. Dad got food if you want some."

She wrinkles her nose. "I think I had my fill of macaroni and cheese with your sister, but thanks. You want to watch TV? You can pick. I just have it on for noise, really." She pats the cushion next to her on the couch.

I hesitate. I do kind of want to sit down and rest, because Patty's Place was really busy and I'm so tired and worried about what Amber said and still feeling a little sick.

"Okay," I finally say. I get a plate from the kitchen and slide a chili dog and fries on it and sit next to Vanessa, but not too close.

I tell myself if I'm sitting with Vanessa then that's just more minutes and seconds and maybe an hour that I'm not in my room not keeping my promise to Amber, so it's a good thing.

Vanessa is watching *Forensic Files.*

"You can switch if this is too scary for you," she says, tossing the remote next to me.

"It's okay. I used to watch it with my grandmother."

She nods. "I bet you're excited about a short school week. I was always dying for school breaks."

I almost choke on my chili dog. "Wait, what?"

"It's Thanksgiving! You don't have school Thursday or Friday. That's why I'm reading this." She holds up a cookbook. "You and Ricci will be here, so I thought I'd try something more than macaroni and cheese."

I chew my chili dog more slowly, my stomach sinking. Right.

Right.

This will be our first Thanksgiving without Laurel and we won't be with Mom.

The chili dog, which was delicious, doesn't taste so good anymore.

"Oh" is all I can say.

Vanessa closes the cookbook. "Bella, you okay? You know you can talk to me, if you want. About anything. I know it's been a hard year and this thing with that guy . . . Danny?"

"Dylan," I say sharply.

"Dylan. Right . . . well, I get it. I'm not trying to horn in or anything, but I'm here."

I crumple up the rest of my chili dog wrapper and wipe my mouth. "Doesn't it bother you that Dad goes out a lot? I mean, it can't be that much fun hanging out with me and my nutty sister."

She shrugs. "I don't mind. You guys are cool."

She pauses.

"Does it bother *you*?" she asks.

I pretend to be engrossed in *Forensic Files.* If I tell her it does, she'll probably tell Dad and then it will be a *thing.* But if I pretend it doesn't bother me, she might press me further, so I decide to just say, "Sometimes," and then I get up and take my plate to the kitchen, throw out the wrapper, put my plate in the dishwasher, and tell her I'm heading to bed.

In our bedroom, I pull the blanket over Ricci, take off my work clothes, slide on my pajamas, and climb up to my bunk with my backpack.

Lie down, stare at the ceiling.

Think about everything Amber said. The stuff I can't remember. The blank spaces. The way everyone at school kind of looked at me funny after Luis's party and made jokes about me being in the bathtub. I tried to shrug it off but it stung, and . . .

Everything was easier when Laurel was around. Just that tiny bit with her every once in a while. Well, maybe more than that, once everything got a little bad. Well, more than a little bad. The world was dying and we were suddenly locked inside. One day in March we went to school like it was a regular stupid day of sixth grade and we didn't go back for a year and half and going to Laurel's was two masks and feeling like the five-house walk to her house was *germs everywhere don't touch that,* sanitize yourself, don't breathe. All my friends were just screens, tiny heads on screens, and suddenly one day everyone went back to whatever it was we were supposed to do and no one talked about any of it and I was walking to Laurel's house and—

My body is so heavy with those bricks I can barely move.

Vanessa is still out there watching television and looking at that cookbook. My dad is gone.

I feel around my backpack for the Sprodka bottle, grasp it in my hands. I could just have one or two sips, that wouldn't be bad, would it? Just to soften these bricks, ease my tension. Help me sleep. Maybe tomorrow will be better. Amber will have calmed down by then. And really, she was kind of out of line, wasn't she? Maybe trying to make me feel guilty or something. I wonder if she's maybe jealous of me and Kristen and Cherie. Like I prefer them over her, which I don't, but honestly, it's not like we're the only ones who ever drink. Everybody drinks. Parents drink. There are commercials for it. Some parents *buy* it for you. It's a plot line in every movie about high school. There are those two YouTube ladies who make videos about wining it up while their preschoolers play on the carpet in front of them.

My phone buzzes.

It's a group text. Cherie, Lemon, Dawn.

CHERIE

hey we didn't say who was going to submit the project on the portal 2-night

LEMON

what

DAWN

I think Bella has the finished version

CHERIE

Bella u there will u do it

fine Dawn don't forget to bring the actual paper and our notes to turn in tomorrow

DAWN

ok

I dig out my school laptop, find the project presentation, do a quick once-over to make sure everything is in order and spelled correctly, log onto our account for art class, and submit it to Ms. Green. I watch the little circle go around and around as it loads to send. The Wi-Fi at my dad's is sometimes hideously slow, which is frustrating.

Pull the bottle from my backpack.

Hold it in my lap.

Look at the little circles going around and around on the class submission site.

Who would know? It would only be like the smallest bit. Not like last night. Just enough to chill.

I could have this and then quit for a while. I've done it before, a few times when I was with Dylan, but it was hard, because then I was just really nervous around him, and quieter, and it was easier to get a small buzz before I saw him so I could be happy and talkative, more relaxed. More normal. But I guess he didn't like that. "You seem a little ditzy," he'd say.

But then I think of Amber and how upset she was and how can I not remember calling her last night? How can that just be something that's . . . gone from my memory? What else did I say to her? My stomach feels like it's in knots.

I get up and shove the plastic bottle in the waistband of my pajama pants and creep out the bedroom door, peek around to see if Vanessa is still on the couch, and then go into the bathroom, locking the door behind me. I turn on the light.

My makeup is fuzzy and smeared and I have circles under my eyes. I put the bottle on the sink counter and slowly wipe off my makeup. There are deep blue shadows under my eyes. The purple mound under my chin is turning blueish. I wash my face, brush my teeth. My heart is beating really fast. Who would know? I could just finish this. There isn't even that much left, anyway, and then I'd be done. This week shouldn't be so stressful, because I have two days off from school, which makes four days total, counting the weekend, and maybe I can just sleep in every day. I touch the blue shadows under my eyes. I really need to sleep. I need a break. I feel like I could sleep for days. I wish I could sleep for days.

I unscrew the cap and place it on the sink top. Trace the bottle's lip with my pinky finger.

A knock at the door startles me and I yelp, turning toward the door so awkwardly that I knock the bottle into the sink with my elbow. All of the Sprodka bubbles down the drain.

"Fuck," I say, watching it go.

"Bella? Everything okay? You've been in there a long time."

Why does she have to be so *nice* all the time?

"Jesus," I hiss. "Can I have some privacy. Is that a crime?"

Silence.

Then Vanessa's soft footsteps on the carpet going into my dad's bedroom. The door closes.

The bottle is on its side in the sink, empty. I turn on the water, erasing the tiny remaining bubbles.

I guess that takes care of that.

It only takes a split second for me to reach into the cabinet below the sink, grab the NyQuil, and take a few giant slugs. When I look back at myself in the mirror, there's a small red drop at the corner of my mouth. It looks like blood.

I lick it off and turn out the light.

MONDAY

IN ART, I FIND my drawing in the file drawer and grab some supplies and set up at my easel. My drawing is a tree, which Cherie says is boring, and I agree, but I sort of like it, or the act of *doing* it, anyway, because I get lost adding branches and leaves and it calms me down.

From the front of the room, Ms. Green calls to me, Cherie, Lemon, and Dawn. Cherie looks at me and I shrug, like *I don't know.*

Ms. Green is wearing some fabulous, swingy silver earrings today that reach almost down to her shoulders. She's checking her laptop.

"Guys, I don't have your project for your presentation yet. You were supposed to submit it to me yesterday, since you're presenting tomorrow. I have the written paper, and thank you for turning that in, Dawn, but not the PowerPoint. What gives?"

My face immediately flames up. "No," I say. "That can't be. I submitted it last night."

Cherie says, *"Bella."*

"Bella was doing it," Lemon says. "Aw, man. Bella, dude."

I run to my backpack and dig out my laptop and run back to Ms. Green. I slide it on her desk, tapping away to get to our class submission site. "No," I say. "Look, right here."

But on my screen, the page from last night just says, *Your session has been timed out due to inactivity.*

Oh god. I forgot to check it before I went to bed. I never turned off my laptop. I forgot. And it didn't load.

I lick my lips, avoiding everyone's eyes. I had that NyQuil, but just enough to make me drowsy. That wasn't the reason. It wasn't. "My dad's Wi-Fi is really bad," I start, but Ms. Green cuts me off with a stern look.

"I've already given you an extension. It doesn't seem fair to allow you more time," she says. "You can resubmit today, but I'm knocking a full grade off."

"No," I say, my voice desperate. "No, that's not fair. Sometimes my dad's Wi-Fi is wonky and it takes forever to send. And I had to work a double. Please."

"Wow, this is just perfect. Thanks a lot, Bella," Cherie says, her voice hard. "I really needed a good grade."

Dawn is quiet.

Lemon shrugs. "Not much we can do now, you guys. Even a B or a C works for me." He goes back to his easel.

I start tapping furiously. The circle spins and then stops. *Submitted* appears on the screen. "There," I say. "You have it. You *have* it."

Ms. Green shakes her head. "Bella, I can't make exceptions at this point. Quarter grades are due Wednesday. I'm sorry about your circumstances, but as I said, I've already given your group an extension."

"But it's right *here,*" I say desperately. "It's not like you were going to check your submission box at midnight. I mean, come *on.*"

My heart says: *Just give up, you can't win this one.*

My brain says: *This isn't fair and she needs to know.*

I slap my hand on Ms. Green's desk, hard.

Cherie sucks in her breath and steps away. "I'm out," she says, walking back to her easel.

"Bella," Ms. Green says sharply. "I'm going to suggest you stop now and go back to your easel. Agreed?"

Dawn tugs my arm. "It's okay, Bella. It's not that big a deal."

I shake her off. "This is bullshit."

Behind me, the class gets really quiet.

"Bella," Ms. Green says. She stands up. She's so much taller than I am that I can see the tiny, pale hairs on the underside of her chin. "Go back to your easel. Now. Unless you want to take a walk to administration."

I slam my laptop shut and walk back to my easel, my head down so I don't have to see all the kids looking at me.

"Weirdo," someone murmurs.

Amber barely acknowledges me as I slide onto the bench next to her at lunch. Cherie slams her tray down, knocking her piece of pizza onto the table. "Way to go, Bella."

"Drop it," I say, unwrapping my peanut butter and jelly. It's pretty much all Dad ever has to make sandwiches for lunch. "I said I was sorry. I had to work. I was tired."

"It was one simple thing and you said you'd do it."

"I had to work a double. I was tired. Why didn't *you* do it, then? I practically did that whole project myself anyway."

"Uh, I don't think so." Cherie takes a bite of her pizza, cheese drooping down to her tray. Her mouth full, she says, "I helped with the slides, too, and the writing."

"You spelled everything wrong and Dawn wrote the paper."

"You guys," Amber says quietly.

Cherie wipes her mouth. "You think you're so smart, Bella, but obviously you aren't, because you couldn't even double-check that you submitted. Were you all fucked up again?"

"Cherie," Amber says.

My face burns. "Where did that even come from, Cherie? Like you're one to talk—"

But I stop talking because my heart suddenly drops.

Dylan and Willow are walking down the aisle, holding hands. He looks over at us and gives me a wave. My eyes fill up. I look down at my soggy sandwich.

"Jesus, Bella," Cherie says. "Get over it already. He's with *her* now. How long are you going to cry about this? *Enough.*"

I shove my uneaten sandwich back into my lunch bag and cram it into my backpack. Stand up and almost fall over the bench trying to get out just as Kristen is sliding in next to Cherie.

"Go to hell," I tell Cherie.

"Bella, stop," Amber says, trying to grab my arm, but I jerk away from her.

As I'm walking away, Kristen says, "What's with *her*?"

I sit in a bathroom stall, backpack at my feet, breathing hard. How could I have forgotten to check the project submission before bed? What's so bad about being a few hours late for an assignment? It was a mistake, that's all. I try to calm my breathing. I scan the walls of the stall to distract myself. It's like some sort of graffiti den in here. Stick figures fucking, phone numbers, swear words, song lyrics, stuff like *Help me* and *Make it stop* and *No it's not okay to be not okay because no one really cares life is not a slogan* scrawled in permanent marker. That stupid permanent sign on the stall door that reminds us SIT WASH SCRAM so we don't spend more than two minutes in the bathroom because god forbid we have a place to chill and get away from everyone. It's bad enough we only have four and a half minutes between each class; they can't even let us go to the *bathroom* without a stupid sign reminding us to hurry up? Why is Dylan waving at me like nothing is wrong? Why can't he just ignore me? Why can't he just *leave* me *alone*? Why can't everyone just leave me alone?

I can't calm down. I'm crying. I wish, wish, wish I hadn't knocked all my vodka down the drain.

Someone says my name.

I freeze.

"Bella, is that you?" Whispered.

I look around the stall, then bend down, peeking under the separator. Black Doc Martens, the frayed hems of blue overalls.

"Dawn?" I dab under my eyes with some toilet paper.

"Are you okay?"

"I'm fine. It's fine."

"It's okay about the project."

"Dawn, what the hell are you doing in here?"

Silence. Then, "Hiding, just like you. Usually I eat in the library, but I crunched an apple and got kicked out for being noisy."

That makes me laugh, but it sounds like a snort, because I'm still kind of crying.

"I know, it's funny," she says. "But I never know where to sit in the cafeteria. It's so crowded and just . . . overwhelming, sometimes. And I don't know where to sit in the courtyard, like who to sit by or *not* to sit by. This school is really big, not like my last one. I thought that would make it better somehow, but it didn't."

She's right. There are like three thousand kids here. Sometimes it's like trying to swim through thousands of mean hormonal fish.

That's true, too, about the cafeteria and courtyard. If you don't already have people to sit with, you're screwed. Everybody has their own group. Loners get weird looks and sometimes nasty comments if they sit at certain places. And we only get twenty-five minutes for lunch, so if you go through the line, you have maybe fifteen minutes left to find a seat and cram food into your mouth. A lot of kids just decide to eat outside in the yard, but even that's hard to find a spot. Kids get territorial over *trees.*

"I get it," I say quietly.

It's kind of comforting, talking to Dawn through the stall wall without having to look at her. It's just our voices echoing quietly in the bathroom.

"I wish I could have one whole day, one, where I didn't have to feel anxious and worried all the time," she says. "Do you ever feel like that?"

"Yes," I say, standing up. "But I'm afraid those days don't exist. At least, I've never had one."

I hoist my backpack onto my shoulders and squeeze out of the stall. I wash my hands and check my makeup. Slowly, the door to Dawn's stall opens. Her eyes meet mine in the scratched mirror over the sink.

She steps closer, turns on the water, and starts washing her hands. "I really like your eye makeup. It's so cool and smoky. Every time I try to do that, I mess up somehow."

"I could teach you sometime, if you want."

"Really?"

"Dawn," I say, turning to her. "Honestly, you don't want to spend the next two and a half years eating lunch on a toilet in a bathroom stall. You know? Just . . . sit with us tomorrow, okay?"

She doesn't smile, just regards me with a careful look.

"Are you sure?" she finally asks.

I dry my hands with a paper towel. "I'm sure."

"Deal."

"Deal."

TUESDAY

MY HEART IS POUNDING really fast. I try to take deep breaths to calm down, but it's not working. I brought the NyQuil with me to school today and swigged some in a bathroom stall between classes, but maybe I didn't have enough to ease my anxiousness. I've never done that before and I was nervous, like what if I spilled it down my shirt and someone was like, "What's that giant red stain on your chest?"

I hate this. My least favorite part of school is when you have to stand up in front of everyone and present something. I don't know why humiliation in the form of public speaking is required and then, to add insult to injury, *graded.* I don't like people looking at me. I don't like looking back at all of them, my fellow students, bored and playing with their hair, or scrolling on phones underneath the desk, or the ones who act like they're interested in what you're saying, but the way their mouths curl really means they are waiting for you to totally lose it.

The four of us are standing at the front of the room, our PowerPoint presentation on the pull-down screen. Cherie has the clicker. Lemon is supposed to do the first three slides, Dawn the next three, then me, then Cherie.

My palms are starting to sweat. I feel dizzy. Why isn't this cold medicine kicking in? Cherie is still not talking to me. I can feel her annoyance pouring off her like a kind of heat. That's freaking me out, too.

Lemon says *pubic* instead of *pubis* and everyone starts to laugh. "Chill out, people," Lemon says smoothly. "Be adults. This is *art.*"

"Fart," someone says from the back of the class. It's hard to see who, because of the easels.

Dawn starts talking. I can't really listen to what she's saying because I'm so nervous. Her words sound cloudy. This is not something I was built for. I wear baggy clothes. I like a lot of eyeliner and powder. I stay quiet, for the most part, out of the way of the usual high school bullshit. Those are supposed to be my protections. Staying at the margins, the edges of things. I'm thinking too much. Why can't I stop thinking? I need to calm down. Those sips of NyQuil are not doing the trick. Dawn's voice sounds warped, like she's talking inside a tube. I'm trembling. I lick my lips. Did I just get lipstick on my teeth? I think I'm going to pass out.

Cherie jabs me, hard, with her elbow. "Bella. *Go.*"

We're presenting on Greek statuary. Creamy nudes, ideal figures. The Greek goddess Nike. Hermes. The Venus de Milo with her missing arms. I have notecards in my hands, even though we have the slides. I just needed something to hold, but the cards are warm and damp and half crumpled now, the ink smeared from the moisture on my hands. I look at the first of my three slides, trying to extract the words somehow, make them leap from the slide to my brain, to my mouth, and out into the world.

The words blur. The words laugh and say *screw you.*

Just read the words, Bella. You love these statues. These statues are fixed and strong and you love them. They are like the women in Laurel's photographs, alive forever, and strong. You can do this, Bella.

My voice is shaking and my mouth is dry. Each individual letter in each word is slippery, sliding across the screen. I can't catch them, can't bring them to me.

"Um . . . ," I say. "So . . ."

"This is painful," someone whispers.

My face prickles with heat. My lips feel so dry I'm afraid they might spontaneously crack.

"When we consider . . . ," I try.

Thumpthumpthumpthumpthumpthump. I press a hand to my chest. It's like I can feel my heart trying to break out of my body. Now I've dropped my notecards. I bend down to pick them up, but my hands are shaking so badly I can't get a grip on them.

"Shoot me now," someone else says.

Next to me, Dawn leans over, picks up my cards, presses them into my hands. "It's okay," she whispers. We stand up.

Dizzy again.

"The."

The. That's all I have, all I can manage. I can't see anything anymore. Everything is out of focus. I can't breathe. Kids shift and sigh impatiently on their stools.

Thumpthumpthumpthumpthump goes my heart. I just want to disappear.

The familiar heat of warm tears whooshes up in my eyes. Oh no. No. No. *Do not cry.*

Dawn's voice takes over, ringing out, reading the rest of my slides. Then Cherie, smooth as silk, reading hers.

After the other group presentations, students clapped, but for us, there's just silence.

“Thank you,” Ms. Green says finally, clapping lightly. “Very thoughtful work.”

Her voice sounds very far away.

I’m frozen in place until I feel the tiniest movement against my elbow.

It’s Dawn. “We can sit now,” she whispers. “It’s over.”

I walk back to my easel, my legs rubbery, Cherie and Lemon staring at me, everyone staring at me. I hide behind my easel. The underarms of my flannel shirt are damp and sticky. I look at my stupid tree with its stupid charcoal branches and I no longer love it. It’s just a stupid sketch of a stupid thing that proves I can’t do anything right, no matter how hard I try.

I hate everything.

I have to take the bus after school to pick up Ricci, because my dad has a meeting and Vanessa is working. We stop at the 7-Eleven by the bus stop near her school to get her a snack before our bus to Dad’s comes. “I petted the goat today,” she says as she grabs a bar of chocolate. “Her name is Teddy.”

“Cool,” I say.

We’re across from the beer cooler. I always see those kids in movies who grab beer and stuff it in their coat or pants. Is that really a thing? I would so much like to just chill now, after the art presentation debacle. Just smooth everything over. Look at all those bottles. They aren’t that big. Who would notice? There’s a giant line at the register and just one cashier. I look up. Cameras in the ceiling corners and on the wall above the coolers. Maybe Ricci and I could take the bus to Laurel’s and I could make a bottle there. But how would I do it with Ricci there? She'd tell. And what if Mrs. Rabinowitz saw us and told my mother? Or if my mother was out at the mailbox and saw us walking down the sidewalk when we're supposed to be at Dad's?

"Bella," Ricci says. "Earth to Bella."

"What?" I say, looking down at her. Messy hair falling out of her scrunchie. A smudge of dirt on her cheek. She was happy today when I picked her up, shoving a bunch of drawings at me, showing me her special beanbag in the quiet room, where she goes when the classroom gets too noisy for her. "Sorry. I wasn't listening to you."

"Are you okay?"

No, says my brain.

Ricci's blue eyes are wide and worried. "Are you sick? Did I give you icky germs again?"

"I'm fine, Ricci. Let's go pay. We don't want to miss our bus. I'll let you listen to music on my phone. I added to your bus playlist the other day."

She gives me a big smile.

At home, I set her up with her YouTube cat videos and look in the refrigerator. It's practically bare, except for a six-pack of beer, peanut butter, jelly, bread, and some yogurt and milk. In the freezer, I find a frozen pizza and a bag of frozen peas, so I guess that's dinner. I put the pizza in the oven and the peas in water on the stove.

My phone jingles.

"Bella," my mom says. "I miss you."

Relief floods through me at the sound of her voice. "Hi, Mommy."

There's a pause. "What's wrong?"

"Nothing. Just . . ." *Everything,* I want to say, but I don't.

"Did something happen at school?"

"It's okay. I'm fine." Can she hear me sniffle? Water is bubbling furiously over the peas. I shake some salt on them.

"Your sister okay?"

"Yes." I pause. "Mom? I forgot about Thanksgiving. It's the first one . . . without Grandma, you know?"

My mom is quiet for a minute and I'm afraid maybe I upset her. I know she doesn't like to talk about her mom all that much because it makes her cry, and I think she doesn't want us to see that, like we all have to be strong or something, but I kind of wish she *would* cry sometimes.

"I know," she says finally. I think I hear a catch in her voice, but I can't be sure.

"Are you going out to Agnes's?" I ask.

"I am," my mother says slowly. "I thought about not going, but then I realized how so many of Grandma's friends will be there, and how much they miss her."

Laurel has this friend, Agnes, who lives outside Tucson in a place called Tubac on an old former cattle ranch with a bunch of other older women artists. Some of them are still making art, some don't anymore, but I guess when they were all younger they made a pact that when they got too old, or too lonely, they'd buy a place together and live out their days. It's a shabby rose-colored hacienda with a lot of bedrooms and bathrooms and tons of couches and hammocks and a hot tub outside and a chicken coop. They retrofitted the old barn as an art studio, and every Thanksgiving and Christmas, they invite loads of people and there are these funky old musicians with long gray hair and tie-dyed T-shirts who play all sorts of interesting instruments in the studio after the potluck meal. Zithers, bongos, guitars, bells, gongs, anything you can think of, really. That's where we always go for Thanksgiving. It feels warm and homey and nice. I love it out there. I think it's so nice these women decided to take care of each other.

"I wish I wasn't missing it," I say.

My mom is quiet for a second. Then she says, "It's important for your dad to make his own traditions with you."

"I guess," I say. I clear my throat, hoping she doesn't notice that my voice kind of broke.

"Does he have anything special in the works?"

I think of Vanessa on the couch with her cookbook, planning a meal, and I decide not to mention that. The fact that Vanessa is a thing upsets her. When my mom picked us up from Dad's a couple of months ago and asked how our week was, Ricci shouted, "Good! I made cookies with Vanessa and we played Go Fish," my mom's face fell, like all the blood had literally drained from it.

"Who?" she said to Ricci, glancing in the rearview mirror, her voice really faint.

I turned around in my seat to motion to Ricci to shut up, but she was busy with her tablet and not looking at me. "Dad's friend," she said. "Vanessa."

My mother stared straight ahead through the windshield, not speaking.

"Mom?" I said softly.

"A girlfriend," she murmured. It wasn't a question. It was a statement. Her hands dropped from the steering wheel to her lap. She'd been about to start the car.

"Mom."

She was kind of scaring me, the way her voice was so flat

and so . . . hurt. The way she was sitting so still, her hands placed flat on her jeaned thighs.

She wasn't even blinking, her body had gone so still.

"I'm right, aren't I." Her voice sounded ghostlike and eerie.

In that moment, I felt a thousand things: I hated my dad for not telling my mother. I hated my dad for finding a girlfriend, like my mother was easily replaceable. And I hated my dad because the realization was slowly coming to me, in that car, the sounds of the cows on Ricci's game moo-mooing in the back seat, that he never planned to tell her. He was going to leave it to us, like this. Like it was an accident. A blip.

Yet another example of *Bella, do it.*

"I'm sorry." That was all I could think to say.

I knitted my fingers together in my lap, hard enough to make my bones ache. I waited for my mom to erupt. She could yell loud when she was really angry. I know, because of her fights with Dad and sometimes when she reaches her limit with me.

But my mom didn't erupt. She didn't yell, or scream, or go up and pound on my dad's apartment door or grab her phone and start mad-texting.

She just sat in her seat, her hands white and flat in her lap, as big tears splashed down onto her cheeks, not making a sound, until finally Ricci looked up and said, "Why aren't we going?" and our mom didn't even wipe her face; she just put the key in the ignition and started driving, her wet face shining in the late-afternoon sun through the windshield.

"I don't know," I say now on the phone, finally. "I'm sure we'll think of something."

"You sure you're okay?"

"Yep," I say, trying to make my voice sound bright. I put the phone on speaker and lay it on the kitchen counter. The pizza is bubbling golden brown in the oven, so I turn off the heat and pull it out, setting it on the counter on the cutting board.

Mom sighs. "Okay, then. Want to put Ricci on?"

I call for Ricci, who runs in and grabs the phone.

I turn the peas off and find the pizza cutter. Get a cup for Ricci's milk.

That's when I see it, on the top shelf, third one up, tucked behind the wineglasses my dad insisted on taking in the divorce, even though he doesn't drink wine.

A bottle of rum, the kind with the sexy pirate on the label.

I freeze, Ricci's chatter behind me splintering into bits.

My brain says: *Take it. You can pour it over ice, it'll look like soda. Add some water.*

My heart says: *No, if it's soda, Ricci will want some and pitch a fit.*

I could do it during her bath. It's bath night. She's fine in the bath by herself. She just plays with toys and dunks herself over and over and generally makes a big mess. Dad won't be home until later.

It's so high up, I'd have to climb on the counter, or use one of the kitchen chairs.

I'd feel so much better. Amber would never know. I could just have *some,* and then nothing tomorrow. I haven't had any in like two days. Just that NyQuil, and that shouldn't count. That's a long time. And I had a shitty day. That's what adults do: they drink after a shitty day. Why can't I?

Sweat is prickling at my hairline. My mouth is watering a little just thinking about how that first swallow will feel when it hits my stomach and the warmth starts spreading. My breath catches in my throat.

My brain says: *Bella, do it.*

The front door opens.

I whirl around, almost knocking the pea pot off the stove.

My dad throws his bag on the couch. "Hey-oh," he calls, coming into the kitchen. "Oh, peas, my favorite. Peas and pizza."

He grabs a beer from the refrigerator and pops the cap off. "Oof, I had a rough day," he says to me, taking a drink from the bottle.

I shut the cabinet door. Ricci shoves the phone back in my hand and grabs Dad in a hug.

"I petted a goat!" she yells. "Can we get one?"

Ricci's bath, then Ricci's two pages of homework, which entails twelve Skittles, one for each math problem, a lot of whining, four giant teardrops, a glass of milk, and six frog stickers on her homework folder. My dad is asleep on the couch. I spend an hour getting Ricci to sleep and then go back out into the front room.

I put the dishes in the dishwasher. Make lunches for me and Ricci tomorrow.

Turn around, look over the breakfast bar.

Dad's still asleep, dressed in his cubicle-job outfit of button-up shirt, chinos, brown shoes, hair in a ponytail. He works for a retailer helpline and takes phone calls all day from people complaining about faulty recliners and refrigerators, uncooperative ovens and misbehaving rice cookers.

Open the kitchen cabinet, look at the bottle, so high up.

You can make it another day, I tell myself.

My brain says: *Why do you have to? You had a bad day. A total suck day. You just need a little help.*

I can feel it then, the anticipation of maybe having a drink. The little pops of excitement pinging around my stomach, sort of like when Dylan and I first started kissing, how everything slowed down as our mouths crept closer and my body would flood with warmth, knowing that soon everything would fall away and it would just be that, our bodies pressed together, time disappearing.

Bella, you shouldn't drink so much. It's kind of not cool.

I shake my head like someone's slapped me. Why is Dylan's voice in my head?

Dylan, staring at me at 191 Toole, the music pounding around us, his face disappointed. *Bella, I can taste it. You don't need to do that so much, okay?*

Me pulling him back, wanting to kiss more.

Nah, let's go home.

Silent bus ride home, him letting me get off the bus by myself at Amber's corner, no kiss or hug goodbye.

"Baby?"

I slam the cabinet door shut and whirl around. My dad is rubbing his eyes. "It's almost ten-thirty. Did you finish your homework? Vanessa said something about a paper?"

"Oh my god," I say, the dish towel falling from my hands. "My paper. My *paper.*"

I rush out of the kitchen and into our bedroom. Rip my folder out of my backpack and grab the syllabus for lit. Tomorrow. Ten typed pages by *tomorrow.* I grab my copy of *Wild.*

I still have like a hundred pages to read, but I can't quite remember what or how far I read on Sunday, when I fell asleep in bed. *Shitshitshit.*

I feel like crying, but I can't. I look at my phone. Ten-forty. I can do this. I can do this. I only have one more day of school and then a break and I can rest. I can do this. I can do this. I can do this.

WEDNESDAY

I'M SO TIRED I can barely keep my eyes open in algebra. We're just doing problem-solving games in an app on our laptops, since we're off the next two days for Thanksgiving, but the equations swim around on the screen.

In English lit, I have to clear my throat twice before Mr. Deavers turns to me. He's writing poetry quotes on the whiteboard. I shift uncomfortably from foot to foot, wondering if everyone is staring at my back.

"Yes?" he says. He never smiles. It's always like he looks right through us, especially the girls.

As for me, I am a watercolor. I wash off.

That's how Mr. Deavers makes me feel. Like I'm something small and insignificant.

"Hello? Can I help you, Miss Leahey?" He sounds annoyed.

"I . . . ," I say. "I need a library pass."

"And, pray tell, what *for*?" He draws it out, like he's some fancy Shakespearean actor or something.

"Our paper, for today. My dad didn't have any printer paper, so I couldn't print it out last night and I need a library pass so I can go right now and print my paper in the library and bring it to you. Since you don't take stuff on the portal."

"Yeah, man, save the trees, for god's sake, let us turn stuff in online," someone says.

Mr. Deavers looks around. "Who said that?"

Silence.

He puts one hand on his hip and tilts his head at me. "Miss Leahey."

I wait.

"You've had your syllabus since day one of this class. You've had plenty of time to prepare and print out your paper so that you can hand it in *today* in this class."

"I just need a pass so I can go print it out right now and come back and give it to you."

"No, you can't, because we have a quiz, or did you forget that, too? Honestly, why do I even make a syllabus if you aren't going to *read it*?"

My brain says: *To be a giant asshole?*

My heart says: *Well, I have to agree on that one.*

He lets out a giant sigh and shakes his head. Puts the whiteboard marker on his desk and pulls out the drawer. Hauls out a pen like it's the most inconvenient thing ever and starts filling in the library pass.

"Very well, Miss Leahey. You'll have to do this over your lunch hour and then bring it right to me. Here's the pass in case you're late for your class after lunch. Points off the paper for lateness. Take your seat."

There are fifty questions on the quiz and I can't focus on any of them. I can't remember what Juliet's characterization in act 4, scene 2 is. All I know is Romeo and Juliet wanted to be together, the nurse was helpful, and they died in the end and were probably better off for it.

I've got nothing left.

* * *

In art, I'm smudging some tree branches on my drawing as Ms. Green wanders among our easels, checking work and making comments. She's wearing a floaty green floor-length skirt and a cool pink velvet blazer. I start to tense up as she gets closer to me. I feel bad about slapping the desk yesterday, but I also feel like she could have cut us some slack. It doesn't seem fair that we have to use laptops to submit work at home, but if something goes wrong, it's all our fault. I mean, my dad's Wi-Fi is crappy, though it usually works, but what about those kids who maybe don't even have *any* Wi-Fi? Like when we all had to stay at home for a year and a half and Cherie had to walk down the street with her mask on and sit in the Burger King parking lot for six hours to use their Wi-Fi just to log on for class?

Ms. Green pauses by my easel, watching as I move the charcoal around. I feel my fingers shake a little, knowing she's watching me. But they were also shaking when I woke up.

"Are we good, Bella?"

My hand freezes over a branch. "I'm sorry, what?"

"The issue with submitting your presentation. I just want to make sure we're back on even footing, you and me."

"Um, sure. Okay."

She studies my tree. "You had some trouble during the group talk yesterday."

I swallow hard, not looking at her, trying to concentrate on my branches. "I guess."

She speaks really slowly, which is something adults do when they know what they're about to say is going to freak you out, or make you mad, or sad. It's like by talking slowly, they think it will soften the blow. It never does, and my heart goes *thumpthumpthumpthumpthump.*

"I have to take some points off your individual participation grade because you didn't contribute to the verbal requirement for the assignment. It wouldn't be fair, otherwise, don't you agree?"

What am I supposed to say? I can't argue with her. I said two words, tops. Am I supposed to ask her to spare me because I freak when I have to stand up in front of people? I'm already standing on the thinnest patch of ice in this class, what with the slapping-the-desk thing.

"Dude, just let her do extra credit," Lemon says, putting down his paintbrush. "She had a meltdown. That seems mental and not, like, lazy or something. I mean, you gave us an extension because I was sick, right?"

I give him a grateful smile, but not so big that Ms. Green can see, because that might piss her off.

"There's no extra credit in my class, Rudy, and you had a doctor's note."

She looks back at me.

"I'm not trying to be mean, Bella. Just fair."

My shoulders sag. My mother is going to kill me when she sees my quarter grades.

"It's fine. Okay? It's just fine."

"Good. Let's move on." She steps closer to my easel. "I'm liking what you've done here with texture and the use of space. But I'm wondering, where are you?"

"What? I'm right here," I say.

"No, I mean here," she says, tapping my canvas. "Part of the assignment was to examine the process of self-portraiture. I'm not sure I'm seeing you here, unless you are the tree. Are you the tree?"

My face flushes with embarrassment. Beside me, Lemon giggles. "Be the tree, Bella."

I look at Lemon's painting and do a double take. What I thought for three weeks was just a mass of chaos is *actually* a painting that appears to *be* Lemon: his smiling, dope-happy face made up of many colors. A mosaic of Lemon.

"I'm in the tree," I say. "Just up high, where you can't see it. I'm going to put that in, I swear. I just wanted to get the branches down, since they're more elaborate."

"There are a lot of branches."

"Yeah."

"I wonder how you'll fit yourself in. You'll be all tangled up."

"Well, see, that's what I'm working on, but you're talking to me, so . . ." Honestly, real artists would never have gotten anything done if people were in their studio all the time, hovering around their marble and chisels and canvases and paints.

Ms. Green nods slowly. "Okay, Bella. I can't wait to see it. We'll have one more week after Thanksgiving break before projects are due."

She moves on to Dawn, who's doing collage for her self-portrait, cool stuff like yarn and paper and leather and buttons and seeds. Dawn's looks really good, fun and interesting. Patty would probably love that on the wall at the diner.

Lemon says, "You totally weren't going to put yourself in that tree, dude."

But I was. I just didn't know *how* yet.

I spend most of lunch hour in the library, waiting for someone to get off one of the computers so I can print out my *Wild* paper. The printer jams and the librarian takes a long time to fix it, fussing over the tray and roller. I make it to Deavers's classroom just as the bell ending lunch rings.

He's sitting at his desk, drinking a paper cup of coffee and eating a creamy-looking Danish, which makes my stomach growl. You aren't allowed to eat in the library near the computers, so my lunch is still in my bag. I slide the paper onto his desk.

"Happy holiday, Miss Leahey," he murmurs as I rush out the door to history.

Kristen catches up with me as I'm waiting for my dad to pick me up.

She's out of breath. "Hey," she says. "What's up with you and Cherie? You weren't at lunch. And that weird girl, what's her name? It looked like she was going to sit with us, but then she just kept walking."

Oh, *Dawn.* I forgot. Doomed to the toilet stall again.

"I had to print out a paper for Deavers in the library."

"The nonfiction paper? I barely finished my book. I had to copy stuff from the web."

"One of these days you're going to get caught, you know."

"Who cares. I just scramble the words in a different order. No one can tell, trust me. Anyway, what are you doing tomorrow? Some people are gonna hang out at Killian's. Want to go?"

"Kristen, it's *Thanksgiving.*"

She shrugs. "Eh. Everyone at my house is gonna be passed out by three, you know that. All that turkey. My mom won't care. Come with? Cherie's going out of town."

"I'm not supposed to go to parties right now, remember? You all put me on probation."

She shrugs. "Aren't you with your dad this week? I feel like Amber said that at lunch or something. He'll let you. Also, are you and Amber mad at each other or something? I'm getting a vibe."

"Maybe. She's being weird." I hike my backpack higher on my shoulders. "My dad's girlfriend is making dinner. I don't know if he'll let me."

Kristen rolls her eyes. "Oh, right, the *girlfriend* situation. I know it well, only with my mother's boyfriends. They'll want you to stay and be nice and pretend to be all family-ish and shit."

I nod. Funny how parents break up and then one day it's just like, *Here is a new person, please automatically like and accept them just because I said so.*

She reties her ponytail. Her cheeks are flushed from the chilly weather. "Well, if you can get away, let me know. I think Lemon said his friend is going to drive. No big deal. But if you don't wanna go, don't go. I'm not gonna beg you or anything."

She hops off the curb as her mom's red car pulls up. "Text me," she calls, stepping inside.

THURSDAY

I WAKE UP EARLY TO the sound of pots and pans banging around in the kitchen. Ricci's still asleep, so I tiptoe past her. I make a quick stop in the bathroom to pee and to check the NyQuil supply under the counter. It's low, but enough to tide me over, I think. I rub the edge of the sink. Possibly, since it's a holiday, I can convince my dad to let me have some wine or a beer. I'm betting Vanessa brought some wine. Or if I can get them out of the kitchen somehow, I can snag that bottle of rum. If he notices, I'll just say I was looking for something and it broke.

I brush my teeth, head into the kitchen.

Vanessa and Dad are in their pajamas, surrounded by boxes and cans and bunches of broccoli and carrots and a giant hunk of meat in a pan. Vanessa has the cookbook propped open on the counter. They look flustered. Sometimes it still throws me when I see them together, doing things, like a couple. Dad always seems happier with Vanessa than he did with Mom. He touches her more. He and Mom just seemed like the walking dead at the end, lurching around the house in slow motion, silent and disheveled.

"You know, this really isn't a great day, historically speaking," I tell them. "I mean, I don't know if you have to go to huge trouble to make a giant meal that basically celebrates genocide."

"This is true," Vanessa says, holding up a finger. "Mostly, I'm thinking of this day as a day off from work in which I can expand my culinary skills beyond macaroni and cheese and toast."

My dad rubs his face sleepily. "What she said," he says. "You want to help?"

I hesitate. If I help, is that betraying my mom in some way? Pretending to be family without her? But if I don't help, am I hurting my dad's feelings by not stepping into this new life he seems to have suddenly created? This is so incredibly tiring, learning new routines all the time because of the divorce. One week here, one week there, better remember all the clothes you want to take, and oh, by the way, one year it's Christmas here and the next it's there, and oh, right, did I mention I'm bringing my girlfriend to our family holiday? Like, you know, occupying the space your mother used to take up?

I think of my mom in our house, alone. Probably finishing a show script before going to Agnes's house. Watching television, maybe. I wonder if she's thinking of us over here, together without her. I mean, what *does* she do when we aren't there?

"You don't have to," Vanessa says cheerily. "Me, I always slept in when I was your age. I won't be offended if you go back to bed."

My dad catches my eye. He ducks his head a little. This means he wants me to help. To spend time with him and Vanessa. Be *nice.*

"I guess I could chop something," I say finally. "I'm pretty good at chopping."

"Great!" my dad says, clapping his hands together. He gathers some broccoli, carrots, and onions and puts them on the breakfast bar, then hands me a knife and the cutting board.

I start chopping everything into tiny pieces and scooping the bits into bowls.

Dad's staring at me.

"What?" I say.

"Nothing," he says. "I just realized. You're not wearing any makeup. I hardly ever see you without all the . . . goop." He makes this wavy gesture across his face.

A flush creeps over my cheeks. "So?" My voice is kind of sharp.

"It's nice," my dad says.

"Are you saying my makeup is ugly?" I ask.

"No," my dad says slowly. "My daughter is beautiful with or without makeup. It's just, maybe you don't need so *much*. It's a little dramatic."

"It's *my* face," I say. "I can do what I want with it."

From behind him, Vanessa says, "Dan, how about getting the roast in? Kind of busy with these potatoes at the moment."

The air feels tense. My dad hesitates, then turns around and starts prepping the meat. I put down my knife. "I'm going to take a shower."

I make sure to put on extra eyeliner after my shower, just because. And to take a few gulps of the cough medicine under the counter.

This is going to be a long day.

I'm getting dressed in our bedroom, pleasantly numbed by the NyQuil, when Ricci wakes up. She looks at me blearily and sits up. “Are we late?” she asks sleepily. There’s some dried drool on her cheek.

“No,” I say. “Food won’t be ready for a bit. You want some cereal?”

She gets out of her bunk.

“No,” she says. “I mean for Agnes.” She starts putting things in her backpack, stuff she likes to take on car rides, like her tablet and earbuds and markers and drawing book.

“Ricci,” I say, the realization dawning on me that no one told her we aren’t going to Agnes’s this year, “we’re . . . we’re staying here.”

She shakes her head. “We always go to Agnes’s house. The Fabulous Band is there. Mommy’s there.”

Oh, no. No.

Ricci stares at me, then dashes from the room. I follow her.

She runs right in the kitchen, plants her hands on her hips. “Daddy, it’s time to go to Agnes’s house. I want to go to Agnes’s house.”

My dad’s put a flowered apron on over his pajamas. He’s holding a bowl of mashed potatoes in one hand and a beer in the other. He looks at Ricci, then me, panic slowly creasing his face. Vanessa turns from the stove.

“You didn’t tell her?” he says to me.

“Me? Dad, *you* should have told her.”

“Daddy!” Ricci shouts. She stomps her bare feet on the kitchen floor. “We always go to Agnes’s. Let’s go, Daddy, *now*.”

Vanessa kneels down in front of Ricci. “Oh, honey, we have a nice meal here, see? It’ll be ready in a few hours. Then maybe we can go to the park. Or to a movie. I used to love to see movies on the holidays when I was little.”

Ricci starts sobbing. *The Fabulous Band. My chickens. I want to see Agnes and my chickens.*

"Oh, honey," Vanessa says helplessly.

Ricci suddenly reaches out and pinches Vanessa, hard, on the arm.

Vanessa yelps, standing up and holding her arm.

The bowl of mashed potatoes drops from Dad's hands and shatters on the floor. He slams his beer on the counter.

"It's you," Ricci chokes out. "It's your fault I can't go see my chickens."

"Goddammit, Ricci, what is wrong with you?" our dad shouts, grabbing her thin shoulders with both hands.

"Dan," Vanessa says sharply. She's rubbing her arm where Ricci pinched her.

"Dad," I say, trying to wrestle Ricci out of his grip. "Stop. Just *stop.* She didn't mean it."

He holds on and Ricci wiggles. My dad says, "Jesus Christ, Bella. You and your *mother.* You couldn't have *told* her?"

"It's not my freaking job, Dad, it's *yours.* Let *go* of her."

Ricci is like a tug-of-war rope between us and then she suddenly squeals and goes limp.

There's blood on the floor. My dad releases her and Ricci sinks to the floor, wailing, holding her foot.

I bend down, take her foot in my hand, pick out a piece of broken bowl. "I hope you're happy now, *Dad.* Oh, wait, let me fix this for you, like I do everything." I'm so mad I can barely feel it as I pick Ricci up and carry her to the bathroom, her arms wrapped around my neck. I kick the toilet seat down with my foot and set her on it gently. Then I slam the bathroom door shut as hard as I can and lock it.

Ricci is hiccup-sobbing. I dampen a washcloth and dab her foot with it.

"It's okay," I tell her. "Look, it's not deep. Just a little cut. You can pick the Band-Aid, okay?"

I rummage inside the cabinet, hoping there's a stray Band-Aid in there somewhere.

Outside the door, I can hear the scraping of the broom and dustpan across the kitchen floor, my dad and Vanessa talking in low tones.

"Did you hear her? Do you see the way she speaks to me?" he says. "I don't understand her."

"Well, you could have told Ricci, Dan. I would have been okay with them going to that farm, or whatever it is."

"I deserve to have a life, too, Vanessa. They have to understand that."

Great. Maybe now Vanessa and Dad are going to go at it like Mom and Dad used to. I thought we were done with all that, but I guess not.

I grit my teeth as I hand Ricci a Band-Aid and watch her peel off the protective layer and gently lay the bandage across the cut on her foot.

I get a fresh washcloth and wipe her damp face.

"I'm sorry we aren't going to Agnes's this time," I tell her, stroking her hair. "Next year we will. That's how it happens, remember? Now we trade holidays every year. One year we have Thanksgiving with Dad, the next year with Mom. Same for Christmas. Our birthdays. This year we'll be with Mom for Christmas, next year Dad."

"I don't like it," she whispers, rubbing her pajama bottoms. "It's too much to remember."

"I know."

Her face crinkles. "I hurt Vanessa." She bites her lip.

"You did. But you were mad and didn't know what to do, so you did that."

She nods.

"She will hate me now."

"No," I say firmly, rubbing her hands. "No, she won't. You can say you're sorry and I know one hundred percent she'll forgive you."

"I don't like our life," she says in a small voice.

A little bit of me breaks inside, hearing that.

I look at her tiny face, her messy hair, and give her a big hug, rubbing her back. "I know," I say. "I know. I don't, either."

I bring her back out, holding her hand. The kitchen floor is clean now and the roast smells nice, salted and garlicked and in the oven. My dad has a scowl on his face and won't look at me.

"Hey, girl. You okay?" Vanessa says.

Ricci looks at the ground. "I'm sorry."

Vanessa kneels down. "I accept your apology. Maybe no more pinching when we're upset, okay? Use our words?"

My sister nods.

"I bet you're pretty hungry, huh?"

She hands Ricci a bear-claw pastry. "Eat this. We have a few hours to go yet."

Ricci smiles, but kind of sadly, like she's worn out. She takes the bear claw and nibbles. Usually, she would wolf that thing down.

My dad says, "I don't want to see that again, okay, Ricci?" He's wiping his hands with a dish towel.

"Dad," I say. "Just drop it. She said she was sorry."

He looks at me long and hard. "This is my house," he says. "We live here now. Things are different. I need everyone to get that. Can you get that?"

"It's an apartment, not a house," Ricci whispers.

My dad stares at her. "It's just an expression. You don't have to be rude. I work very hard for what I have."

Vanessa is twisting the dish towel in her hands. I can feel my body tensing.

My brain says: *Your dad's getting ramped up. You know how he gets.*

My heart says: *Be careful.*

My dad looks tired. When did he start getting angry? Was it when Ricci was born? Before that, he always seemed happy, or maybe it was just me thinking that, because I was a kid and didn't know any better. But he played games with me and sang songs on his guitar and then it was like, one day, with diapers and bottles everywhere and my mom so tired with Ricci's crying, he just . . . changed. Got mad if I didn't clean up my toys quick enough. Got annoyed with me when I couldn't figure out a math problem, my mom in the next room, fussing with Ricci. So I started cleaning. All the time. Everything nice and neat. Toys away. Practiced my math even when I didn't need to so I would be better at it. Wouldn't need to bother him. *I can do it,* I'd tell him. *I'm good at it now.*

I feel like half my life has been spent smoothing things over.

"Is there something you want to say, Bella? You look like you have something to say."

I think I forgot about a lot of that. Dad's anger, way back then.

Ricci backs into me, pressing her spine against my legs, the nibbled bear claw snug in her fist. I stroke her hair.

And something in me breaks again as I think how Ricci said she doesn't like our life. She's too little to not like her life.

I don't like our life. *My* life.

All of a sudden, I just feel . . . lost. Defeated. Like all the blood has leaked from me. Like my bones have fluttered into dust. I tried so hard, all week, for everything, and got nothing. Just fucked up over and over and over again. And now this.

Vanessa clears her throat. "Let's all take a breath," she says.

"Bella." My dad's voice is loud. "Are you listening to me? Answer me."

"No," I say. "I don't have anything to say."

"Perfect," he says. "That sounds like heaven."

He turns away from me.

I stay in our bedroom with Ricci while she looks at cat videos.

I have to get out of here.

Dad and Vanessa have pulled the small round table into the middle of the kitchen. There are three regular chairs and one stool from the breakfast bar. Ricci sits on that. The roast and vegetables are on the counter. Vanessa makes the plates and sets them down. The edges of our plates touch since the table is so tiny. Vanessa ended up making macaroni and cheese for Ricci. We eat quietly. I make sure to tell Vanessa that everything is great, and it is, but it barely registers for me. I'm just mouthing the words. No one mentions the missing mashed potatoes or the broken bowl or the Band-Aid on Ricci's swinging foot. Dad drinks three beers and has two plates of food. Vanessa and Ricci make funny faces at each other. Dad finishes and goes to the front room, turning on football on the television. Stretches out on the couch, calls to me, "Bella, clean up. Vanessa did all the cooking. You can do something, too."

I do the dishes, waving Vanessa off. Put away the food. Wipe the table, push it back. Put the chairs back in place. Put the stool back by the breakfast bar. Make everything just so, like there was never a fight here, or an incident with a shattered bowl and a bloody foot. Vanessa gets dressed and takes Ricci to the park, lets her stay in her pajamas.

In my room, I climb onto my bunk and stare at the ceiling. I feel inside myself and outside myself all at once. I am not in a good place. I should stop my thoughts but I can't, my brain and my heart are fighting, like they always do, and one by one, all my failures flood back to me, like text floating by on PowerPoint slides and notecards, just like my stupid presentation for art:

Had a boyfriend.

He left because I was *too much.*

Got drunk and had a meltdown and cried in a bathtub at a party.

My grandmother died.

Amber hates me.

My mom is lonely and sad.

My dad is mad and sad.

My little sister is seven and already says she hates her life.

Cherie hates me.

I messed up the art project.

I didn't put myself in the tree.

I messed up my lit project.

Points off
Points off
Points off
Bella, do it
Bella, do it
Bella, do it

I pull out my phone.
Text Kristen. *What r u doing*

Hey!!!!!

Hey

I had a feeling you might ping me

. . .

You wanna go out

Okay. My dad's mad, tho, I don't know if he'll let me go

Ugh. Just tell him I broke up with my boyfriend or something

. . .

And that I'm crying

. . .

And you need to help me for a little while. Dads can't handle crying girls.

. . .

Okay

My dad is snoring softly on the couch. I push his shoulder a little. "Dad," I say. Then, louder, *"Dad."*

His eyes shoot open. "What? How long have I been sleeping?" He looks at the television. "Who's winning?"

"Dad, can I go to Kristen's? Her boyfriend broke up with her. She's really upset."

He blinks at me. He's confused.

"Kristen?" He asks. "Red-bow girl?" Unlike my mom, my dad likes Kristen. Says she has a "passion for life."

"Yeah. She's really upset. And crying."

"Oh, that's too bad," he says, rearranging the couch pillow under his head. "Okay. Sure. Wait, how are you getting there and back? I don't . . . I'm pretty tired. Where's Vanessa?"

He's buzzed from the beers.

"Vanessa is still at the park with Ricci. Kristen's coming to get me," I tell him. "I'll text you later."

He mumbles and closes his eyes.

I wait until his breathing gets heavy, then go into the kitchen, push a chair close to the counter, take the bottle of rum from the cabinet, and put it in my backpack.

I text Kristen.

Come get me

So Gucci

. . .

B there in 10

* * *

Kristen is with Lemon and Lemon's friend, who doesn't go to our school. He's got scraggly hair and black-rimmed glasses and seems older and doesn't say much, just looks at me in the rearview mirror as I slide into the back seat. He gives me that chin raise certain guys like to do, that one that means *Yo.* Why do they do that and not just say hello? I will never figure that out.

Lemon turns around. "Belllllaaaaaaa. You broke your party probation."

Holds up his palm. I high-five him. His palm is sticky with something and I wipe my hand on my jeans.

"You got anything?" Kristen asks. "Man, my house was crazy. My mom has, like, twenty people there plus my relatives. They've been hitting it since they woke up."

I pull the bottle of rum out of my backpack and hand it to her. "Sweet," she crows, unscrewing the cap and taking a drink. She hands it to Lemon, who holds it out to his friend, who waves it off. He's got a joint in his hand, though. I don't know whether to be relieved about that or not. Maybe if things get too weird later Kristen and I can Uber home.

Lemon hands the bottle back to me and I take a drink.

I decide not to think about anything. About my promise to Amber. My parents. My grades. Any of it. I'm going to make it all go away. Dull it down. Chop it up. Erase it. For a little while.

Bella, I tell myself. *Bella, do it.*

And I do.

* * *

Lemon's friend's car is dirty. Polar Pup cups rolling around in the back seat, moldy fast-food wrappers stuck to the floor. Lemon lights up a joint and passes it to his friend. The stereo is too loud, so I put on my headphones and listen to my own music. We drive around. The thing at Killian's isn't until later, I think. Kristen was vague when I asked her earlier and said we were just going to chill for a while.

I don't know where we're going. We're just driving around aimlessly. Sound of the engine. Music. Nothing hurting. I slide down in my seat, my body a pool of relaxation.

I take the joint when Lemon's friend holds it toward the back seat, because why not? What does it matter? It doesn't matter that I'm breaking the rules, because I don't care anymore. I've never actually smoked pot before and it tastes weird and I cough but all I want to do is feel numb.

I imagine everything I am inside now as a weird sandwich: the NyQuil on the bottom, the rum in the middle, and the weed on top, an odd green top to the sandwich. I giggle. Then Kristen giggles at my giggle and then we're full-on laughing.

My phone buzzes. Amber.

Hey you, she's typed. *What are you doing?*

My brain says: *Lie to her.*

My heart says: *Oh, Bella. Not again.*

Happy turkey day, I type.

I start giggling and I can't stop.

Type: *gobble gobble*

Funny, she types back.

...

I miss u. Hope u r ok, she types.

I'm good, I type. *Fine*

Talk 2 u later

I send her an emoji of a turkey and Kristen looks and laughs so hard tears come out of her eyes.

Lemon's friend drives us to eegee's. He and Lemon scrounge around for money in the console. Kristen gives them some crumpled bills. They get Skinny Berries and grinders and we park in the lot and they pour the rum in the slushies and I listen to them all eat and slurp and giggle and I'm high and drunk at the same time, I think. Everything is simultaneously amplified and dulled. My phone buzzes and it's my mom *Hi Agnes says hello* and I type *tell her hello back* and my mother types *Are you having a nice day* and I type *yes very good I miss you* because I do miss her and she types *Can I talk to Ricci* and I don't even feel nervous or anything I just text back *She fell asleep early from all that food and we took her to the park* because my mom will never call my dad to ask to talk to Ricci, he hates it when she does that, so she goes through me and just like I thought, my mom is all *Oh that's good she probably needs sleep* and I type *Yeah* and she types *What are you up to* and I text back *Oh just watching a movie* and she types *Okay sounds good* and I type *how is the farm* and I see the little dots appear and disappear and then she's all *Hard. Lonely* and I know she's talking about my grandmother and a sudden wave of longing and missing swells up inside me and I press the letters on my phone but I can't find the right combination of words to type *I'm sorry I couldn't save her* because that's not something we ever talked about, how I found her on the brick walkway on the set of particular bricks that I do not walk on anymore, and my heart hurts so much right now and my eyes are getting full. Kristen says *Girl, what's going on* and I manage to type *Okay bye* before Lemon's friend suddenly throws his grinder wrapper out his window and starts the car and presses the gas so quickly I lurch forward and my phone slips from my hands and smacks the back of Lemon's seat in front of me and we're off again.

Driving, driving. Up over Pantano Wash. Farther than I've been in a long time. Windows down. Cold air. Hard and angry music. How can Lemon and his friend even hear each other talk? But they do. They're talking about something. Lemon's friend keeps looking back at me in the rearview mirror. The streets are quiet, barely any cars, because everyone is inside somewhere, eating or watching football or arguing or drinking like we are and the only other people out are the ones who have nowhere to go, trudging along with their tarped-up shopping carts or sleeping in doorways, mounds of blankets piled on, panting dogs by their sides. Everyone is so lonely.

"True that," Lemon's friend says, meeting my eyes in the rearview.

Did I say that out loud? I guess I said that out loud. I feel like a roller coaster inside. Up and down. Up and down. Twist and turn.

"It's a dog-eat-dog world out there," Lemon shouts.

Kristen says, "Woof," and laughs and laughs.

My inside roller coaster takes a sharp turn and things get dim, like when clouds suddenly block the sun.

* * *

Kristen is pushing me and says, "Killian's. Wake up," and I didn't realize I fell asleep. It's dark now. We crunch across a gravel driveway to a brick house pulsing with music. Older kids, maybe college? Some kids from school. Kristen takes my hand and hers is very warm. She seems nervous. Should I be nervous, too? There are a lot of bodies here. Everyone bumping into each other. Keg in the corner. Red cups. The overhead kitchen light is very bright. Feel dizzy from that sleep. Need to wake up. Cold beer. That will wake me up. Nice in my throat. Kristen lets go of my hand and she bounces up and down, up and down, red matte lipstick glowing, red-bowed ponytails flying up, down, up, down. She's not nervous anymore, her red cup in her hand. She has a passion for life.

Lemon's friend has a gray tooth. How do you get a gray tooth? I wish he'd stop smiling at me, because all I can focus on is that gray tooth. I think he is much older than us, now that I'm so close to him. Like, not in high school at all. He's sweaty. Hot in here. He grabs my cup, pours something brown in it. It tastes sweet and sickly at the same time, like over-sugared Coke, but down, down, down it goes because you can't drown unless you let go. Lemon's friend's hand creeps around the small of my back. He smiles at me, that gray tooth like a stone in his mouth.

I angle away from him.

Drinking is good because you can be someone else. Not lonely. Not quiet. Not on the edges of things. Someone says *I love your eyes* and I say *Thank you* and they keep talking and I keep answering and see I can be normal. Just a girl at a party. Normal. Drinking gives you a voice and a person to be. Adds color to what was just plain and ugly.

Whose house is this and where are we? Why are there so many kids here on Thanksgiving? Maybe their parents don't love them, either. Maybe their parents are too busy all the time. Maybe their parents are drunk, too, right now. All those talks they give you in school. In one ear and out the other. *You matter. You belong.* It's a lie. If we mattered or belonged we would not be here right now, smoking and drinking and getting high. Right?

I try to find the bathroom, but I open the wrong door and there are just kids on a floor in a room in the dark, sitting against the wall, staring at the ceiling. I'm not sure what's so interesting up there but they seem fixated. I ease around them and open another door in the room and flick on the light, hurting my eyes. The door doesn't lock and there's toilet paper stuck to the seat and something pulpy and greenish in the sink. I almost fall trying to sit on the toilet and catch myself against the tank at the last minute. I take deep breaths. It smells in here. I'm having problems with the zipper on my jeans and when I finally sit down I've forgotten about the toilet paper stuck to the seat but all I can think about is peeing. There's no more toilet paper when I reach for some and I sigh. I stand up, peeling the paper from my ass and flicking it into the toilet. I get my jeans done and wash my hands, the greenish sink stinking. Is it vomit? I gag a little. I wipe my hands on my jeans. I feel very heavy. I think I should go home.

*   *   *

I'm getting hot, face red from jumping up and down with all the other kids jumping up and down to the music. What time is it? It must be late now. I wanted to go home but I can't find Kristen and someone gave me another red cup full of something. I'm starting to see double, maybe. I stop jumping and squint a bit. Something is tickling my leg. I swat. Oh. My phone. I squeeze my eyes together. Dad.

I'm sorry, he typed.

I can't really see. Must be careful. Not too many words. No misspelling.

Me 2

Your friend feeling better?

Gng 2 stay over, I type. I add a crying emoji.

Okay. Call me tomorrow.

K

Phone back in jean pocket. Room spinning.

Lemon is talking, but I can't hear him. Are there two Lemons or four? I can't tell.

I might be a little sick after the sickly sweet drink and the pot and I should go. I tell him that but I don't think he hears me.

Or maybe he doesn't care. Maybe all four Lemons don't care.

I should go lie down somewhere No, wait, that's not safe. I don't know many people here. Where is my phone so I can call someone.

Not Amber. She's so mad.

You have a problem, Bella but

I AM the problem.

It's me. I'm the problem no one wants to solve or love.

I made so many tree branches in my sketch because I don't want anyone to see me.

I am a watercolor, I wash off.

Feel in my pocket for my phone. Not there.

Jumpupjumpdownjumpupjumpdown.

Lemon's friend has his hands on my shoulders.

I don't like the way that feels.

It makes me feel trapped.

I bounce away. I don't like him very much.

I need to find my backpack. Wait, I didn't bring my backpack. Did I?

My phone. Call someone so I can go home.

Why can't I find Kristen?

My face is hot. Falling. Floor slick with spilled drink. Someone pulls me back up.

An ocean rises in my stomach.

Eyes blur, like someone stretched gauze across them.

Sick. Cover mouth. I don't know this house. Going to be sick. Need the bathroom.

Push, push, push, through bodies to a door.

Backyard. Oh, cold air, so good on my face. Then

Sick, sick, sick.

Everything comes up, up, up, and there is Lemon's friend with the gray tooth. *Gross.*

That's what he says. *Gross.*

He calls me gross and he does not help me.

I have to get away from him.

Back in house, stomach hurts.

Where is Kristen? Is that her? Gauze still over my eyes.

Oh, there is Lemon. Across the room.

He has his phone out—maybe he can drive me.

Wait, no. Can he? Is he fifteen and six months like you have to be to drive here?

Wait, no, it was Lemon's friend who drove us here.

I don't like him.

Maybe Kristen can Uber us to her house.

I can't find her.

Push, push, push, through bodies to get to Lemon.

Bodies push back. Stomach twirls.

And

No

There they are

Corner. Kissing. DylanWillowDylanWillow.

Her hands in his hair. His hands on her jeaned hips.

And I am a thousand things all at once none of them good.

I am a million things bursting into flame.

You're too much.

Why are they here Why can't they leave me alone

Why is he staring at me now when he was kissing her just then

Why is he talking to me What is he saying

Hey Bella you
But his words go in my ears and die inside me
You okay Bella
With that mouth that mouth that once was mine
Get away from me
I push
Just get away from me
Oh there is Lemon in the middle of the room
Shouting and laughing
Hey Bella show me your nips

Holding up his phone
Bella be like the statues, he shouts.
We did this art project, he tells the people around him.
The human body is a beautiful thing, he says.
Gray tooth's eyes are glistening he is watching me closely
Chanting all the kids chanting
Nip slip nip slip and
Dylan get your hands off me
don't touch me
your skin hurts me
all of you hurts me
and I'm flying apart and moving toward Lemon
chants in my ears
and I will be the statue
This is like a movie of me
That I'm watching
Like it's not happening to me
Dylan holding my arm
He took my heart and ate it up and swallowed it

And still looking at him
I'm all open yearning and *love me*
How pathetic is that
I'll show him
Everyone
If I am too much I will be all the way too much
I will break the world
Bella don't what are you doing Bella
Dylan is concerned, Dylan is in my way
Everyone chanting
Bella do it Bella do it
all I ever hear
Bella do it Bella will do it
Dylan's face is one face two face three faces four
Saying *Bella don't*
what are you doing Bella
I'll take you home Bella
but I'm moving toward Lemon like in a dream
On a cloud through rain
Everything hazy
Unbuttoning my flannel shirt
Because what does it matter
I am a watercolor, I wash off

My mother is screaming but I cannot move
The porch light hurts my eyes
Why am I outside my house
Why am I on the stoop
My mother is screaming and I close my eyes
I do not like this dream

TWO

I tried to scream
But my head was underwater

—Billie Eilish, "everything i wanted"

STOP.

I am underwater and I am drowning and it hurts.

My whole body hurts. The waves hurt.

Stop. Stop that now.

I'm pulling and pulling. Tangled in the seaweed. Have to get out. Need air. Getting strangled.

You'll hurt yourself, Isabella. Isabella, can you look at me? Isabella, can you hear me?

No one calls me Isabella anymore. Little, when I was little, my dad called me Izzy. I wish he still did that, but he doesn't anymore. I cleaned up the toys. Did my math. But he never called me that again. Better when Grandma moved out to us. I had somewhere to go.

"Sweet girl," she would say to me.

Some voice, some lady's face, blurry above the water. Blurred by the water? I don't know what's happening and why doesn't she help.

Isabella, you need to keep that in. That's an IV. Stop pulling.

IV. Ivy. That's it. Like seaweed. That's what's tangling me, drowning me. She should untangle me, pull me out. Adults are supposed to help you, but they don't. They tell you to suck it up. They take points off. They say things will get better and they don't. I'm so cold in this water. I don't like cold water. I like warm water. This is too cold.

The water is inside me, angry and bubbling, hot and sick. Have to get this water out of me. Once I am empty, I'll float to the surface. There's too much water inside me.

Hold on, Isabella. Let me get a tub. Can you hold on?

Another voice. New blurry face. *Can you roll on your side, Isabella?*

Roll her. Watch for choking.

I've swallowed too much water and it's coming up up up up up up up up up up.

Vomit. There is vomit everywhere. On me. Everywhere. Burning my throat. My body hurtles and heaves, a dying bird in the rushes. Feel like I read that line in a poem somewhere but I can't remember.

Isabella, we need to get you into a gown, okay? Isabella, we need to take your clothes off. Can you sit up? Can you help?

Please don't touch me.

I'm dirty.

Please don't look at me.

Mom, can you help Isabella, please? Isabella, your mom is here and she's going to help you out of your clothes, but you need to sit up. We'll have to cut them off if you don't sit up.

MomMomMom. Why is she here? What is happening. The lights are too bright and even though she is making me sit up, I still feel like I am underwater, my body is so, so heavy. And why is she crying? My face feels wrong, somehow. Is something wrong with my face? I reach to touch it; someone pushes my hand away.

I don't want her to see my body. I've fucked everything up again and again and I've made my mother cry.

In the nurse's hand I see a silver flash of scissors.

Oh, let me die.

"Bella." My mother's voice is silky with sadness.

I don't want to open my eyes and look at her. I just want to keep my eyes closed forever.

Her voice floats to me, sinks down deep inside me. Makes a nest there.

"Bella," she says again. "Bella, I love you and I'm going to take care of you."

Lemon's friend's dirty car. The rotting fast-food wrappers. Lemon's friend yelling. Don't let her throw up in my car. A girl's voice: You are messed up, Bella. Kristen? Red bows on brown ponytails, always. You guys I don't think she's breathing. Shit shit shit shit. Take her to the hospital. Shit no, we'll get arrested. Where does she live? There. Take a left. That's her mom's. It's closer. I'm sorry, Bella. I'm so sorry, Bella, but we can't get in trouble.

That is what I dream, and when I wake up I am alone and there is just light from machines and a tube in my arm and something plastic in my nose and very heavy very warm scratchy blankets and my mother is gone and the weight of me is so much I sink back to the bottom of the water.

"Bella," my mother says. "Can you hear me?"

I open my eyes.

Sunlight through the window sends thousands of sparks

through my head. My mother is holding my hand. My body is so cold. How can it be so cold under this blanket. This blanket is as thick as bricks but I am still so cold. Shivering so hard my bones are clacking. Her hand is hot on my cold hand and shouldn't I melt from that heat?

"They left me on the doorstep to die," I say.

I remember this.

"Yes," my mother says, touching my face. I flinch, because it hurts. Why does my face hurt so much?

"Yes," she says again. "They did."

My mother is gone again and now I am alone. I feel jittery and freezing and sick and hurt all at once. Hard to move under this blanket of bricks. The tube in my arm itches but the nurse says don't pull, so I don't. She says I need it to not get sick again, to rehydrate.

"You poisoned yourself by drinking too much," she says, checking a bag of yellowy liquid that hangs above me. But she doesn't sound angry or like she's giving me a lecture.

"What your friends did was pretty crappy," she tells me, feeling my face gently with her hand. Something must have happened to my face because it hurts so much, but I don't want to know what. She sighs. "But I tell you what, you aren't dead, and in my book, that's a win. I've seen too many dead kids in my job."

She sets the television remote on the tray in front of me. I look down at my hands. They feel separate from me. Too heavy to lift.

My fingernails are cracked. Blood in the tips.

Something happened to me. My brain is struggling, folding in on itself.

I was at Dad's. Then with Kristen. Driving. Lemon's friend. Party. Sick. Then nothing.

Until the stoop at my mother's house.

Until my mother screaming.

My brain says: *Not true.*

I close my eyes. *Think,* I tell my brain. *Think. Remember. Something happened in that darkness.*

My brain says: *No.*

My heart says: *It's for the best, Bella.*

Don't ring the doorbell. I'm not getting in trouble, man. She drank all on her own. Just leave her here. You can't just leave her. Prop her up. Look, she can stand. Bella, after we leave, ring the bell, okay, Bella? No, Kristen, you ring the bell and let's run. Let's just get out of here. She's fine, she's leaning against the door. Run. Bella, I'm sorry. I'm so sorry, Bella. Run.

That's it. Lemon and his gray-toothed friend and Kristen. The door to my house. Darkness sinking over me and washing away. I could see and not see. Held the doorknob to stay up, but too heavy. The doorbell went: *bing-bong.* They started the car and drove away. Too heavy. Have to sleep. Must sleep. Falling, falling. Then breaking into a million pieces.

They left me leaning on the door and I fell and I smashed my face on our concrete stoop and then there was nothing.

That is why my face hurts. Oh.

Gingerly, I reach my hand to my face. Touch it with my bloody fingernails.

Sparks of fire tear through my cheekbone. I jerk my hand away.

I don't want to see my broken face.

But there's a blank space in my brain. Something vapory. Something else happened.

My brain won't give it to me.

My parents are arguing.

How could you let this happen.

Me? I thought she was with her friend! She lied. That's not my fault. Kids lie.

I told you she wasn't to go out. Do you remember? I told you about the last party.

Kids make mistakes all the time. She'll learn from this. It happens.

It doesn't just happen. Look at her face. She could have died.

It doesn't even matter what I say, Diana. You'll blame me no matter what.

I open my eyes.

They look at me. Mom's worried, pale face. Dad's pinkish, frustrated one. Then he looks relieved.

"Bella," he says. "Baby. Thank god."

"Can you please both just. Shut. The. Fuck. Up," I say to them quietly.

I roll away from them.

A nurse turns on the television. "Do you want anything in particular?"

On the screen, M&M's are tied to some sort of pole. Bombs strapped around their chests. Another M&M is yelling at them. Why are pieces of candy wearing bombs funny? What is this world? We had three shooting threats at school last year. Someone left a fake grenade in a urinal in the Tech building and they filed us out across the long lawn and then we went back to school the next day like nothing had ever happened.

"No," I say. "I don't care."

A few hours later, another nurse arrives. She says, "I need you to sit up now and drink this. Take it slow."

She presses a button, raising the top half of the hospital bed. Thick liquid in a tumbler. Chalky. It tastes chalky and I gag.

"Careful," she says.

"My skin," I say. "I'm so cold. And my stomach feels like someone punched me."

She takes the tumbler from me, wipes my mouth gently, avoiding the bad part of my face.

"Well," she says. "You still have a lot of alcohol in your system. You depressed your nervous system. Think of it as your body trying to get rid of the bad stuff."

My brain says: *Like that will ever happen.*

I finish the chalky drink.

I'm rolled over in bed, staring out the window, when I hear the door open. Maybe the nurse is here to give me more chalky drink or to empty the bag on my leg. A tube is going up inside of me. That's how I pee, though I don't think there's very much. I don't remember them putting it inside me. They took the plastic thing out of my nose, but it's still hard to breathe. Slow.

I turn over. It's not a nurse.

Blond ponytail. Jeans. Clipboard. Green T-shirt.

"Hey, Isabella." She drags a chair from the corner of the room closer to my bed and sits down. "I'm Tracy."

"Are you another nurse?" I ask. "And it's Bella."

"I'm not a nurse, Bella." She smiles. "I'm a counselor. I'm here to check on you. Ask you some questions. I met your parents. They're really nice."

"I don't think that was my parents, then."

She laughs. "Pretty sure it was. They're really worried about you."

I don't say anything.

"So, I'm going to just talk to you, and have you fill out a questionnaire. Okay?"

"Why?"

She tilts her head. "Just to evaluate where you're at. Like, emotionally."

"Why?" I stare at her suspiciously. Evaluate me emotionally? There are kids at school who get sent off for "emotional issues." Like cutting, or hitting, or just blanking the world the hell out, I guess. Grippy socks. That's what they call the places they go.

"I'm fine," I say. "I had a bad night. I don't need to go to grippy socks. Or to do your stupid test."

"Grippy socks," she murmurs. "Hah. Interesting. That's not quite where I'm from, but close. I work at a place here in Tucson. Well, on the outskirts. Your parents wanted me to come in and talk to you."

"I don't feel like talking. I don't care about whatever place you're from. Things just went a little haywire for me, but it's over. It's fine. It was just a bad night. You can go now."

She leans forward. "Bella, you came here with acute alcohol poisoning, which is a lot more than just a 'bad night,' and you could have died, so my job is to kind of figure out what's going on. Can you at least let me do that?"

"What happens if I don't?" In my mind, *acute alcohol poisoning* is rolling around, along with *you could have died.* I shiver at the thought, but I mean, obviously I did *not* die, so whoever this person is, she is unnecessary.

Tracy looks at me steadily. "I would ask you, instead, what are you so afraid of that you can't answer a few questions?"

"This just seems like a stupid test. I'm not in school right now. I don't have to take a test and I'm not afraid of anything."

She takes a pen out of her bag. "Okay. Prove it." She balances her clipboard on her lap. "Do you remember what happened the other night?"

I roll my eyes. "I was drinking. I drank too much. Happy now?"

"Right, but do you remember what happened the whole night? Some of it? Pieces of it?"

The broken plate. My dad getting mad. Silent dinner. Texting Kristen. Lemon's friend's car. Party. Getting sick outside. Lemon's friend saying *Gross.* Dylan kissing Willow. And then so much chanting and shouting . . .

My heart squeezes. "Some. Not all of it. I made a mistake. I drank too much. Smoked some pot. Big deal."

Tracy's writing on her clipboard. "It's called a blackout. That's what we call it when we can't remember something that happened while we were drinking. Sometimes we even do things while we're blacked out. It's not like you go to sleep, you know? Your body is still functioning as best it can, but you . . . It's like your lights went out. But your body keeps moving. Until it doesn't."

I feel for the IV tube in my arm. Stroke it.

Did I . . . did I do anything else after the parts I can vaguely remember?

"Does that kind of sound like what maybe happened to you?"

"Maybe. I guess. But it's fine. Here I am. I learned my lesson, okay? Can you go now? I'm tired."

Her voice is matter-of-fact. "I'm sorry you had to learn some sort of lesson that involved your friends dumping you on your porch at three o'clock in the morning, Bella. And that that lesson involved fracturing your cheekbone and your mother opening the front door to find you unconscious."

The memory of my mother screaming flashes across my brain.

I start to cry, and then I stop, because pain is shooting across my face. I feel it, gingerly. It's lumpy and swollen. Fractured.

"What does my face look like?" Panicky.

"It looks bad. I'm not going to lie to you. But, Bella, you didn't do anything *wrong*. I just want to say that. You made a bad decision to drink so much, but you didn't do anything wrong, do you understand?"

I shake my head. *No.*

"Tell me what happened to my face."

Tracy says, "You passed out on your front steps after your friends left you. You fractured your cheekbone, but apparently the fracture is relatively stable, so no surgery, but unfortunately, your face absorbed most of your fall. You're a mess, I'm sorry to say."

She stands up. Touches my arm. I shift it away from her. She takes some papers from her clipboard and slides them onto the tray in front of me, along with a pen.

"I think you've been drinking for a long time before this, Bella. I don't think this is just a one-night bad decision. I need you to answer these questions for me as honestly as you can so I can help you. Can you do that for me?"

I slide down in the bed, roll over and face the window.

"I don't need your help," I say. "I just need to go home."

"I'll be back tomorrow, Bella. We'll talk then."

I listen as she walks away.

This time, the drink the nurse gives me isn't chalky. It's fruity, like a smoothie. Goes down better. My mouth is thick. Hard to swallow, but I do.

There are a lot of sounds in hospitals. Beeps. Intercoms. Hushed voices. Loud voices. Crying. The squeaky wheels of rolling trays. Sometimes the nurses laugh at the station outside my room.

I miss my little sister. I wonder what my mom has told her about me, about what happened. Ricci smells like milk and Oreos and Magic Marker and I miss that.

I try to go back to sleep, but I can't. I wonder when my parents are coming back. I want to go home. I don't even care to which one.

Maybe if I fill out the forms that Tracy person gave me, I can go home.

She said it wasn't grippy socks, so maybe it's just for therapy when this is over. That wouldn't be so bad, I guess. I could ride my way through that for a few sessions to make my parents feel better.

I press the button, raising my bed so I'm sitting up. My head spins a little with the movement.

Pick up the sheaf of papers.

Hard to focus. The words swim. I squint and try to concentrate.

How many alcoholic drinks do you consume on a daily basis?

Answers: ❑ 1–2 ❑ 2–3 ❑ 3–4 ❑ I don't know

Have you ever done anything you regret while under the influence of alcohol?

Answers: ❑ Yes ❑ No ❑ Maybe ❑ I don't know

How often do you have negative thoughts?

Answers: ❑ Every day ❑ Sometimes ❑ Never ❑ A few times a week

Have you ever thought about suicide?

Answers: ❑ Every day ❑ Sometimes ❑ Never ❑ A few times a week

Have you ever attempted suicide?

Answers: ❑ Yes ❑ No ❑ Never

Do you ever wish you weren't alive?

Answers: ❑ Yes ❑ No ❑ Never ❑ Sometimes

Do you ever feel hopeless?

Answers: ❑ Yes ❑ No ❑ Never ❑ Sometimes

How often do you feel anxious?

Answers: ❑ Every day ❑ Never ❑ Sometimes

Have you done drugs, like marijuana or prescriptions, in the past week?

Answers: ❑ Yes ❑ No ❑ A little

How often would you say you feel sad?

Answers: ❑ Every day ❑ Never

❑ A few times a week

Do you feel safe at home?

Answers: ❑ Yes ❑ No ❑ Sometimes

Do you feel safe at school?

Answers: ❑ Yes ❑ No ❑ Sometimes

Have you ever lied about consuming drugs or alcohol?

Answers: ❑ Yes ❑ No ❑ Sometimes

Has your employment or schoolwork suffered because of drugs and alcohol?

Answers: ❑ Yes ❑ No ❑ Sometimes

Have you ever “lost time” when drinking?

Answers: ❑ Yes ❑ No ❑ Sometimes

Have you ever suffered an injury as a direct result of ingesting alcohol or drugs?

Answers: ❑ Yes ❑ No ❑ I don’t remember

Have you ever sought treatment for drug or alcohol abuse?

Answers: ❑ Yes ❑ No

On and on and on and on and on and on and on and on.

I have a funny feeling that filling out this form is not going to get me out of here right away. But I can't not fill it out, can I? That lady, Tracy, might tell my parents and they'll get mad and tell me to fill it out. But I can't answer truthfully, either, because that might get me in trouble, too, because obviously, I'm *here,* in this hospital bed, with a broken face and tubes in me. There's no downplaying that.

But I'm not going to drink anymore after this. I'm not. I'm done. I won't. I'll be good. I will. This was pretty bad. I mean, I'm *broken,* literally. I just want to go home.

I mark "Sometimes" for most of the questions, "No" for a few, "Yes" for the ones that are obvious, like that second-to-last one. This really isn't a good questionnaire because there are so many extenuating circumstances. Like, I'm fifteen and life sucks, so *Yes,* I probably feel hopeless, at some point, every day. What teenager doesn't? And sure, I probably tell myself I wish I was dead sometimes, when things are really sucky, like with Dylan, and Laurel dying, but I don't want to *die* die.

Do I?

This is a stupid questionnaire and that woman is a stupid person and I don't have to fill this out. She can't *make* me.

None of this would have happened if Lemon and Kristen and Lemon's gray-toothed friend hadn't dumped me on my mother's stoop. They could have just let me sleep it off in the car. This is *their* fault.

I rip up the papers and dump the pieces on the floor and bury my face in the pillow, good side down, and will myself to sleep.

* * *

But when I wake up later, there's a fresh questionnaire on my tray table, along with a pen.

I take the pen and scrawl *LEAVE ME ALONE* across every single sheet and slam them back on the tray table.

I haven't seen my parents in a while. The hospital is strangely quiet. Are they going to bring Ricci to see me, ever? Maybe she shouldn't see me like this, actually. It looks dark outside the window. My face really hurts. They come in sometimes and give me a little pill but I don't think it's doing anything. I need something stronger. Why hasn't Amber come to see me? Or Cherie? I don't expect Lemon or Kristen to, after what they did. I can't believe they would do that to me, just leave me there. I'm not going to be friends with Kristen anymore. Lemon can go to hell. So can his creepy friend with the tooth. Who cares if I can't remember everything from that night? That probably happens to a lot of people. *Blackout.* Fine, so I blacked out. But I'm not dead. I'm not dead. I'm sorry my mother had to find me, but also, I'm glad, in a weird way, because now she knows maybe what it was like for me to find her mother on the brick path. We have never talked about that. That it was me. It was me. It was me. It was me. It was me.

A giant rush of something crests inside me, taking my breath away. I haven't thought of this in forever, so plainly. We don't talk about it.

That I found her.

(me)

* * *

I have the nurse's sleeve gripped in my hand and I won't let go and it's possible I'm sobbing or maybe I'm not because all I hear is the sound of myself imploding.

(My grandmother's body was limp)

I pressed that button over and over and finally someone came and they won't give me any more painkillers because it isn't time and they can only give me a certain dose because my liver is messed up and when did that happen and how but the nurse doesn't have any answer I can accept.

(I think she went out to get the newspaper. I asked them to put it on her step and they never did. They always dropped it at the start of the path.)

I am begging the nurse for something to stop what I'm feeling and telling her that I can't catch my breath and she says I'm sorry you're going to have to live through this pain, sister

(It was my fault. When I was at my mom's I usually got her paper first thing and put it on the front step before school. But I was late this time)

and I just need to feel better and the nurse won't listen won't listen and she is looking at me and saying you'll have to ride this one out, honey, and I call her a bitch and she just laughs and tells me that isn't the worst thing a patient has said to her today

When I wake up, I'm confused. Another nurse is puttering around my bed. I wonder how long I've been here. Three days? Four? Did I scream at the nurse last night or this morning or a day ago? I held her sleeve for a long time and she told me a story about her horse named Clarissa and it was a very long story. Then it was time for my pill and she gave it to me and I fell asleep, hard.

I look at the tray table.

The replacement papers the lady named Tracy gave me are gone.

The nurse is holding out a clear plastic bag of clothes for me. Not the ones I came in with. I remember vomiting, and my mother taking my clothes off, and me not wanting her to see me naked. Those clothes are probably gone and that's too bad because I really liked those jeans.

"Isabella," the nurse says gently. "We're going to take your IV and catheter out now and give you a smoothie. Then you'll need to change. Maybe shower. Your mom brought some clothes for you."

"My name is Bella," I tell her.

"Okay, Bella," she says smoothly. "Whatever you want."

She sets the bag on the bed and carefully pulls the thick tube from my arm. There is a bruise around the puncture hole. She presses a bandage over it.

"Sorry," she says, reaching under the blanket, startling me. "Can you spread your legs just a bit for me?"

I close my eyes and feel a little prick inside me, then a tube being slid out.

"Good girl," she says.

She points to a large pink tumbler on the tray in front of me. There's a pill next to it.

"Drink up, but slow," she warns. "Your body is very tender right now, okay? Then take your pill. It will help with your facial discomfort."

"I know that," I say. "I've been here awhile. Am I going home? I want to go home."

I want to disappear in my room. I just want to disappear. I want to be surrounded by my stuff and my fairy lights and my own blankets and my books and put my headphones on and zone out.

The nurse hesitates. "Not just yet," she says. "There's a toothbrush and toothpaste in the bathroom. It's probably going to hurt when you brush your teeth, so be careful and slow. You can take a shower if you feel up to it. I'll be here if you need help."

I drink the smoothie. It tastes nice, fruity and thick and cold. I feel like my teeth are covered in wool.

I swing my legs over the side of the bed and weave a little. I'm dizzy after lying down for so long.

"Careful," the nurse says, holding my arm.

She helps me to the door of the bathroom. My legs feel twisty and rubbery.

She opens the door, puts the bag of fresh clothes inside on the floor.

"Bella," she says as I'm about to shut the bathroom door.

"What?" I ask.

I'm cold, shivering really hard, air drifting up through my hospital gown. I just want to get in warm water, wash myself off.

"Your face might startle you, okay? It isn't good. I just wanted to warn you."

But I'm already staring at myself in the mirror above the tiny white sink in the beige-tiled bathroom.

The whole left side of my face is swollen, quilted with blue and purple. My left eye is an egg-shaped purple pouch. I look like a prizefighter. I start to cry because I don't know this person. This can't be me. I always try to keep all my hurt on the inside and now it's spread to my outside, where everyone can see.

My brain says: *Monster. You're a fucked-up monster. You really fucked up this time.*

My heart says: *I'm sorry, but I have to agree on that one, yes. You are a right mess.*

"Do you want me to turn the shower on for you?" the nurse asks gently.

I don't want to see myself. I can't look at myself.

I shake my head. I don't want her help. "I can do it."

I close the door. I turn the water on, hotter than I should, and peel off my gown. There are bruises on my knees, too, from when I fell. My elbows. I'm a punching bag, and the funny thing is *I'm* the one who punched me.

I step into the shower. There's no curtain.

I just stand there in the hot water, shaking and silently crying, trying to wash the monster off me, until my skin is bright red.

I'm afraid it's not going to work.

The nurse knocks on the door. "Bella? It's time to see your parents."

"Just a minute," I say softly.

I turn off the shower and dry myself gingerly, because everything I am aches. I pull the clothes from the clear plastic bag: bra, underwear, socks, and things . . . I do not normally wear. My mother has brought a plain white T-shirt, black sweatpants, and an oversize red hoodie that says University of Arizona Wildcats on it. A pair of slides I forgot I even bought.

It's all I have. Slowly, I put everything on.

We shuffle down the hall, the nurse holding my arm. My body feels very, very heavy, and I'm still shivering, even though I'm wearing the hoodie.

I keep my head down, watching the tiles on the floor, so no one can see my monster face.

I tug the hood up and pull the drawstring tighter, just to make sure.

We come to a room and the nurse knocks. The woman with the blond ponytail, Tracy, opens the door and smiles. She's wearing a T-shirt that says HEALING HEARTS AND MINDS ONE DAY AT A TIME.

Jesus Christ, I *am* going to grippy socks.

I step back a little, but the nurse has my arm and urges me forward.

"Easy," she says. "Take it easy. Don't make this hard."

I notice she's a lot bigger than the other nurses have been and I feel a little prick of fear.

"Hi, Bella. Have a seat," Tracy says.

It isn't just my parents in the room. Amber's here, too, but I don't understand why. It looks like she's been crying. Her eyes are puffy and pink. She shakes her head when she sees my face and covers her mouth with her hand, looks down at her lap.

Tracy points to a couch against the wall. "You can sit there, by your friend, okay?"

I walk over and sit down slowly. "I don't understand what this is. Mom, am I going home? What is happening?"

My mom is holding her hands tightly in her lap. "Bella," she sighs, starting to say something else, but then she stops.

My dad is next to her. He's pissed, I can tell, jiggling his jeaned legs, rubbing the arms of his chair. But he doesn't say anything.

Tracy sits down and pulls a clipboard from a backpack next to her. "Let me start. This is going to be hard for everyone, but especially for Bella, so I'm going to ask you all to refrain from interruptions or shouting, okay? This is a listening and learning time."

I look around the room. Dad. Mom. Amber. This person Tracy.

Oh my god. This is an *intervention.* Like those shows on television. Haggard, strung-out people slumped in chairs while their friends and family tell them what disappointments they are and how they're going to die and . . . Oh my god. I cannot believe this is happening to me.

And it wouldn't be happening if Kristen and Lemon and Gray-Tooth hadn't dumped me at my house. This is *their* fault.

Tracy looks at the clipboard on her lap.

"Bella, you came here five days ago because you drank so much alcohol you poisoned yourself. Blood tests show you were at nearly twice the legal limit. Other tests indicate that this isn't an isolated incident. Your liver is already showing signs of damage, which is definitely concerning in someone your age. I think you've been drinking a lot, and I think you've been drinking for a long time. I think you've been hiding it for a long time. Based on the questionnaire you filled out and then ripped up, which I pieced together, it's obvious to me that you have a problem with alcohol. You're an alcoholic."

I freeze, feeling my face start to burn red at all she's said, like she found my diary and is reading it aloud.

On the plus side, maybe no one can see how red my face is because half of it is like a crushed eggplant.

"I am absolutely fucking not," I tell Tracy, gritting my teeth, even though that hurts.

Beside me, Amber sniffles. She won't look at me.

My mother is gazing intently at her lap. My dad is clenching his jaw.

"Okay, Bella," Tracy says. "Tell me how many drinks you have on any given day. Were you truthful on the form?"

I shake my head. "I don't . . . What is this? This is bullshit. Who even are you?"

"Bella!" my mother says sharply.

"Like I said before," Tracy says, "I'm a counselor at a program for teens with substance-abuse and behavioral issues. I'm here to assess your problem with alcohol. How many drinks do you have in a day, Bella?"

"I'm not an *alcoholic,*" I say, my voice rising. "This is insane. You saw my form. I just . . . like if there's a party or something. It's all normal. I didn't have much to eat at Thanksgiving and I just had too much—"

Next to me, Amber shifts. "She drinks a lot," she says softly. "She's lying. She's been drinking a lot."

I stare at her, the blood draining from my face. "Thanks a lot, Amber."

"Sometimes she calls me and the next day she can't even remember," she continues.

"That was *once,*" I counter.

She shakes her head. "No. Several times. Sorry. That was just the first time I called you out on it."

My mother shifts in her seat. "I went to Grandma's, Bella. Have you been drinking there? I talked to Mrs. Rabinowitz. She said she came over once and thought she smelled alcohol but was afraid to say anything, in case she was wrong. Was she right?"

My mother's eyes are so, so sad.

The way she's looking at me is ripping me up inside.

"I think we're blowing this out of proportion," my dad says suddenly. "I mean, she's been going through a lot. A divorce, her grandmother died . . . it's been a real shitshow this year. And granted, maybe we haven't been the greatest, most attentive parents—"

My mom's voice turns steely. "Oh, really? 'We'? *'We'?*"

My dad throws up his hands. "And so it begins. The blame game."

Tracy holds up a finger. "Deep breath, everyone."

There is silence.

Tracy looks at me.

I'm not going to get out of this, so maybe if I just admit to some stuff, I can go home, do some therapy, and be done with it.

"Like my dad said," I admit, "it's been really hard this year. And I've been drinking some. My boyfriend broke up with me, and I've just . . ."

"He broke up with you because you drink too much, Bella," Amber says flatly.

She's looking at me head-on, and she's mad and sad all at once, her face crinkling, tears pouring down her cheeks.

"You lie to everybody. All I've done is try to help you. I told you you had a problem and you, like, just blew it off. Just lied to me. Do you have any idea what it's like to be your friend? To see you hungover all the time and be afraid to call you out because I'm afraid you won't talk to me anymore? Do you have any idea what that's like?"

"Amb—"

But she cuts me off. She can't stop. "Do you even know what happened at that party? Do have *any* freaking idea?" She's fumbling in her bag. She pulls out her phone.

"Here. You want to see what happened when you were *that drunk*?"

"Oh god," my mother says. She covers her mouth with her hands.

The phone is shaking in Amber's fingers. She's shoving it at me.

I can't breathe.

There's me. Staggering, my face pale and sweaty and puffy. The sound on the video is a mix of music and chanting. *Nip slip nip slip.*

Snatches of memory come back to me. But are they real, or just because I'm watching this now?

Lemon's phone. His voice cackling off-screen. *Oh my god, she's really going to do it.*

Whistles.

Me, awkwardly unbuttoning my flannel, fumbling with the buttons, weaving toward him, raising the T-shirt underneath, pulling down one of my black bra cups. The crowd around me howling. My eyes look like they're falling down my face. And suddenly there's Dylan, swearing, trying to get the phone away from Lemon, his angry eyes right against the screen, and the phone flips and there's Kristen, flashes of the red bows on her pigtails, trying to pull my shirt back together.

I can't breathe.

I don't remember any of that.

Oh my god everyone saw my body.

I remember the car ride, the too-sweet drink. Lemon's

friend touching me. Dylan and Willow. That horrible sad feeling getting hot inside me, and then . . . nothing.

Nothing until the car. Voices. Holding the doorknob.

Falling.

My brain says: *I'm sorry. I tried to hide this from you.*

My dad grabs the phone from Amber. "Jesus Christ, how do we get this off here? My god. I'm pressing charges. Against those kids who dropped you off, the parents . . . Who leaves a house full of alcohol for teenagers?"

"You know what, Mr. Leahey?" Amber says angrily. "It's that, sure, but they were shoulder-tapping outside stores, too. And that's partly on me because I drove them. Because I didn't want to lose my friends."

Her voice breaks.

"And now you've almost died," she says to me.

"I *didn't* die," I say defensively. "I'm still alive. I'm right here, and everyone hates me. I'll stop, okay? I can go to therapy or whatever. Happy, everyone?"

My mother snatches the phone from my father and gives it back to Amber. "Put it away," she says softly. "I've seen it. I don't need to see that ever again."

I cross my arms over my chest, my face blazing. Oh my god, how many people have seen that?

I don't remember it, I don't remember it, I don't remember it.

"I'm going to sue," my dad mutters.

Tracy says, "Legal issues are another matter and up to the parents to pursue. I want to concentrate on Bella right now."

"I'm going to kill that kid," my dad says under his breath.

"Bella," Tracy says, ignoring him. "Let's try again. Would you say you drink alcohol every day?"

The room is silent, waiting for me. I feel sick.

"No," I say slowly.

"Liar," Amber says.

"I *don't,*" I say testily. "You don't *live* with me, you don't know."

"You guzzle cold medicine," she says.

"What are you talking about?" I try to keep my voice neutral.

"You stayed over at my house a couple weeks ago. I know you didn't really want to, but you felt like you had to so I'd shut up or something. And you said you were sick. You had a cough. You weren't coughing, but my mom gave you some cold medicine and we decided to go to bed early. In the morning, it was all gone and I couldn't wake you up. Do you think I'm stupid, Bella?"

My mother puts a hand over her mouth.

"I *was* sick," I say. "But I don't know what happened to the rest. Maybe *your mom* is the addict, Amber. Maybe it was *you.* Maybe you aren't so perfect after all."

Panic is coursing through me.

"Oh my god," Amber says, slapping her thigh. "I can't believe you."

I can feel a sheen of sweat on my upper lip and prickles in my armpits.

This is getting insane.

"Would you say you have a couple of drinks every day a few times a week?" Tracy's pen is poised over her paper.

"Maybe," I say. "I mean, who cares? Everybody does it. *Dad* does it—"

My dad says, "Hey now, I'm an adult, there's a difference."

I ignore him. "I have to work and go to school. Like, I have all As . . . well, I mean, I did. Anyway. It's not like I can be wasted *all the time.* This is absolutely stupid, you know?"

Tracy's pen moves on her clipboard.

"Have you ever blacked out, not been able to remember what happened the night before?"

"Well," I say sarcastically, "obviously, yes. The other night."

"Do you remember when you took your first drink of alcohol?"

I look down at my lap. I can't answer that. I can't. It will kill my mom.

"A little something sweet for my best girl," that's what Laurel said.

I don't say anything.

"Come on, kiddo," my dad says. "Let's just answer the questions so we can get out of here and then we'll move on, okay?"

"There is no getting out of here," my mother says, her voice suddenly firm. She looks at my dad. "Don't tell her there is. We discussed this."

I frown. What are they talking about?

"I don't know that we agreed on that, Diana. I'm thinking now that that solution is a little extreme. She's scared, she knows she messed up, she's going to be better now. Aren't you, Bella?" My dad looks at me. Reaches over and pats my knee.

I look at my dad, then my mom. "Wait. What 'solution'?"

Tracy holds the clipboard against her chest and tilts her head at me. "Your parents think the rehabilitation program I work for might be beneficial for you, and I have to say I agree."

"Rehab?" I say, my voice cracking. I stand up, but waver a little because dizziness rushes through me. I try to steady myself. Everyone's staring at me.

"You want to send me to *rehab*? No, no. No way. I'm not

going to some place for losers and freaks who can't keep it together. I'm not an *addict.* I'm not on the street shaking and sweating. I get good grades."

I look at my mom desperately.

"Actually," she says, "I checked the portal. I talked to your teachers. Your grades are way down. You're missing assignments. You seem foggy in class. You argued with your art teacher. You hit her desk. You fought with the librarian over a printer—"

"I do *everything* for you," I tell her, my voice rising. "I take care of Ricci. I make dinner so you can work, and now you want to send me *away*?"

"Maybe you can stay with me for a while, Bella. How about that, everybody?" My dad looks around the room. "I'm not sure I'm on board with . . . putting her somewhere. That feels more like a punishment than a solution."

"Stay with you for a while?" My mom lets out a barky laugh. "Right. You can barely take care of yourself."

My dad opens his mouth, but Tracy stops him, holding a finger to her lips. "Amber has something she wants to say."

Amber turns to me. Her face is swollen from crying.

"You're my best friend, Bella, but I can't watch you do this anymore. I can't watch you hurt yourself anymore. If you don't get some help, I can't . . . I can't be with you anymore. That's all. I can't be your friend. Do you understand? If you don't go, I can't be your friend."

"Amber," I say, reaching out for her.

She pushes my hands away.

She's my only real friend. Cherie and Kristen are friends, but Amber is my *one.*

"Amber, no, please."

She looks at Tracy. “Can I go? My mom’s waiting downstairs.”

Tracy nods.

Amber holds her purse close to her chest and walks quickly out of the room.

“I’ve packed a suitcase for you, Bella,” my mom says, and takes a deep breath. “I think this is the best thing. I don’t want you to hurt yourself anymore. I can’t . . . I don’t want to lose you, too. I cannot lose my daughter.”

She starts crying.

“Diana, just let her stay with me, will you? I can handle this.” My dad is pleading.

“Mommy,” I say. “*Mom.* Just let me go with Dad, then. I’ll be good, I swear.”

I get up and kneel in front of her, even though my body screams in pain, and touch her hands. She looks so tired, like she hasn’t taken a shower in days. In five days, apparently, because that’s how long I’ve been here. That means . . . school has already started up again after break. Everyone is back. Probably talking about me. Talking about what I did. Oh *god.*

My mom avoids my eyes.

“They said you might beg,” she says in a low voice. “This hurts me so much.”

This can’t be happening. I don’t want to go away. I don’t want to be away from my room or my friends—what’s left of them, anyway. Laurel’s. Ricci. To go where? Some stupid place with people who can’t get their shit together? I can get my shit together. I *will.*

I switch position, look my dad in the eyes. “Daddy, please. Don’t let them take me. Please.”

My dad’s mouth twitches, and he pats my shoulder tenderly.

"Sure, kiddo. We can do this together." Then he starts yelling. "You don't get to make all the decisions here, Diana. I have a say, too."

"They only need one signature," my mom says. "And she's on my insurance. And I don't think I can ever trust you to take care of her again."

And then they are off.

Screaming about everything.

Ricci, Grandma's house, Grandma, me, Vanessa, everything, everything, everything, shutting me out again. I shrink back against the couch, sitting on the floor, covering my ears under my hood, closing my eyes, and it's just like it used to be when we all lived together. Them angry and shouting or them quiet and furious; silent dinners, Ricci overacting to get someone to react, them yelling at each other to calm her down and me just invisible, spaghetti noodles curled on my tongue, going nowhere, sinking inside myself from all the noise and unhappiness.

And then, sitting there on the floor of the room, feeling Tracy's eyes on me while my parents fight, all I can see in my mind's eye is me in that video, moving toward Lemon's camera at the party, my fingers pulling my bra down.

If I had a million sweaters and ten thousand blankets, I would bury myself in them right now because I don't think I will ever feel not naked again. I start rocking back and forth, hitting my back against the couch. I can't take this. I cannot take this. I can't breathe.

Tracy has to raise her voice and clap her hands to get my parents to stop, and the instant the room falls silent, I uncover my ears and meet her eyes.

"Fine," I say. "I'll go. Just get me the hell away from them."

* * *

They don't let you say goodbye.

One minute I'm on the floor of the intervention room and the next I'm in a wheelchair being pushed down to the lobby of the hospital by the strong nurse, with Tracy holding the suitcase. The nurse helps me out of the chair and says a matter-of-fact "Good luck to you" before taking the chair and walking away. Like she does this every day. I guess maybe she does. I'm just another dumb kid to her.

I just stand there as Tracy walks toward the lobby doors. She looks back.

"Come on," she says. "It's time to go."

I look around. "But my parents. Where are they? Don't I get to say goodbye?"

"No." She shakes her head. "That causes an extra level of tension that we don't advocate."

She waits.

I stare back at her, my stomach curdling a little.

She motions to two guys I didn't notice before, sitting on chairs in the lobby. They get up and head toward us.

Toward me.

"Are we going to have a problem?" Tracy asks.

A nervous laugh trickles out of my throat. It's like I'm being kidnapped or something. Pinpricks of fear race through me. Who is this person, and what have my parents signed me up for, exactly, that would require two burly guys, one of whom has a disturbingly precise crew cut, to be staring down at me like this?

"Are you like literally going to use force if I don't go?" My voice is shaky.

The crew cut guy shrugs. "Maybe. If that's what it takes."

There's an awkward silence. I feel like I can't breathe.

"Bella," Tracy says finally, gently. "It's time to go."

One after the other, slowly, I lift my feet and walk toward her.

Because what choice do I have?

THREE

Someday, you will ache like I ache

—Hole, "Doll Parts"

DAY ONE

"BUCKLE UP."

That's what Tracy says to me in the van in the hospital parking lot.

Phil, one of the guys from the hospital lobby, turns around and hands me a Pedialyte. I don't know what happened to the crew cut guy.

"Stay hydrated," he says. "And if you're thinking of running, my advice is . . . don't."

Phil is bearded and ponytailed and rumpled and weathered in that way that so many older men are in Tucson. Tie-dyed shirt. Cutoff chinos. Birkenstocks with socks.

He goes back to scrolling on his phone.

My stomach feels tight and hot. I feel trapped.

I can't crack the plastic seal on the Pedialyte bottle. I gnaw it off with my teeth.

Familiar places drift by my window: the abandoned movie theater on Campbell and Grant with the whale mural on the side; Raging Sage Coffee; India Oven, with its creamy tikka masala and garlic naan. Laurel liked to go there on her birthday.

Tracy turns down a residential street. A neighborhood of adobe houses and ocotillo fences. She stops at a pink adobe and honks the horn.

"Billy Lewis," Tracy says to Phil. He jots something down on a clipboard.

The front door opens. A lanky kid steps out, yells something back into the house. Slams the door so hard the chile pepper ristra that hung there shatters on the ground, spraying red bits everywhere.

The boy hurls himself over my lap and jams himself against the window.

"Buckle up," Tracy murmurs.

"This is some bullshit, right here," the kid says angrily. "Major child abandonment, possible kidnapping. I should sue."

"Feel free to hop out and go back," Phil says, not looking up from his phone. "Find a lawyer. Make a lengthy TikTok with a sprightly background sound. Be my guest."

The kid doesn't answer, just clenches his jaw and stares out his window.

Then I can feel him looking at me intently. Heat spreads across my face.

"The hell happened to *you*?" There's a sneer in his voice, mixed with curiosity.

"Shut up," I say. I turn away to my own window.

"No, like, seriously, because you had to do something extremely bad to make someone do *that* to you. I don't know whether to be impressed by you or scared of you," he says.

"Billy." A warning from Tracy.

From the corner of my eye, I see the boy named Billy tuck his longish brown hair behind his ears and roll his head.

"How long are we going to be in this car?" he asks. "And why does she get something to drink and I don't?"

Without missing a beat, Phil backhands a water bottle to

Billy, who misses the catch. It bangs off his knee and onto the floor of the van.

"The abuse begins already," Billy murmurs.

There are dogs in the front yard of the next house, straining at their chains.

"Holly Shields," Tracy says to Phil. She doesn't honk the horn this time. They both stare at the dogs.

Phil sighs. He and Tracy do rock paper scissors. Tracy loses, and groans as she gets out of the van. She makes a wide path around the dogs. They don't bark, just hurl themselves in her direction. A thin girl dressed all in black emerges from the house, clutching a black backpack tightly to her chest. Her face is pale as she walks behind Tracy to the van.

I have to scoot closer to Billy so she can climb in.

"Wow, you look like crap," she says to me. Her voice shakes.

"Yeah?" I retort. "Well, it's crap you treat your dogs that way. How about that?"

"Why do you even have dogs if you're going to do that to them?" Billy chimes in.

Her face crumples.

"They aren't mine," she whispers. "It's not my fault."

As we drive away, the dogs whimper and whine.

We are in the foothills now, not far from where Amber and I dropped off Kristen and Cherie for the party. I wonder what they're doing. Are they wondering what *I'm* doing? Do they even care? I take another slug of the orange Pedialyte.

This house is enormous. Huge windows, two floors, expertly landscaped front yard, tucked up a hill at the end of a long dirt drive. Teal-colored iron sculptures of saguaros bracketing the immense front doors.

"Brandy Sheff," Phil says, looking at his clipboard.

Tracy honks the horn.

A girl so contoured and perfect she could be a Kardashian steps out, phone in her hand, awkwardly pulling a giant suitcase. A woman appears behind her. She sets down three other bags and then goes back into the house and closes the door.

"Princess," Billy snickers.

Tracy gets out of the van and grabs two of the girl's bags, throwing them in the back. She and the girl struggle with the giant suitcase. The van shakes as it plops in the back.

The girl, Brandy, climbs in and wedges herself into the seat behind us. A cloud of vanilla body spray fills the van. Next to me, Holly coughs quietly.

"Do you think this is going to be a vacation, sis?" Billy says. "Did you remember your bikini?"

Smoothly, as she snaps her seat belt, Brandy says, "You can fuck right off."

In the front seat, Phil chuckles. "Ah, the dulcet sounds of discontent. My favorite part of the journey," he says.

Tracy laughs. "About an hour to go, my friends. Try not to kill each other before we officially begin the rest of your lives."

She turns on the radio. Classic rock, wailing and mournful.

On cue, the three other kids in the van shove in their earbuds and listen to their phones. I don't have a phone, so I can't block anything out.

IhatethisIhatethisIhatethisIhatethisIhatethis.

* * *

The drive down Gate's Pass through the Tucson Mountains is slow, slow, slow, curves that make me feel sick as we descend into the valley and everything is disappearing, all the buildings and people going, going, gone.

The van is very quiet, until Brandy, the very beautiful one, says, "I'm Brandy, if anyone cares."

And then, "Billy."

"Holly," whispers the girl in black next to me.

It's like we're on a plane that's going down, we're going to die, and suddenly we have to make sure at least one person knows us before we, and everything we ever were, disappear forever.

"Bella."

Tracy drives down a long dirt road to a sprawling, ranchlike compound of brick and adobe buildings. It feels like the middle of nowhere, just desert with cacti spreading out in a repeating pattern of brown and green, brown and green.

She stops at a wide iron gate with SONORAN written in curly letters on one side and SUNRISE in the same lettering on the other side. She enters a code on a keypad and the gates open, severing SONORAN SUNRISE in half. She drives the white van inside and the gates whine shut behind us.

WELCOME TO THE BEGINNING OF YOUR LIFE, says the mat outside the adobe building. Tracy leads us inside. I hang back, behind Holly.

A woman with spiky gray hair and faded jeans stands up from a fraying couch in the lobby.

"Hey, everyone," she says. "I'm Fran. I'll be taking the four of you to Detox, where you'll stay for three days while we figure out what shit you put into yourselves and try to get it out."

She smiles, like this is funny. No one laughs.

"You'll need to leave your bags here," Fran says. "Just set them anywhere and say bye to your stuff."

"Excuse me," says Holly. "Why?"

Holly is so thin her black clothes hang from her shoulders. There's dog hair on the back of her hoodie.

"Bag search," Phil says amiably, taking a seat on the worn couch. "Have to make sure you aren't bringing in drugs, alcohol, weapons, stuff like that."

Holly hesitates, her dyed-black hair falling over her eyes. She steps back. I step out of the way so she doesn't bump into me.

"No," she says, holding her backpack tight in her arms. "No. Uh-uh. This is my personal stuff. I don't want your hands on it."

Tracy and Fran look at each other. Phil sighs, like he's used to this, and I guess he is.

"Okey-dokey," Fran says, shrugging. She checks her clipboard. "You're Holly, right? If you don't consent to search, you can't come in. You'll have to call your people to come get you."

"No." Holly's voice wavers. "They'll kill me."

All three of the adults are looking at her, faces impassive, waiting.

"Just give it *up* already," says the Kardashian girl, Brandy. "I have to *pee.*"

"Shit," Holly says, looking at her feet like she'll find an

answer there. Or a way out. I feel kind of sorry for her. She's obviously got something she doesn't want anyone to see or have.

Slowly, as though it's very painful, Holly lowers her backpack to the floor.

All of us line up our suitcases and bags in a row. I'm not afraid of what might be in mine. My mother packed it; I know there's nothing in there.

I wish there *was.*

Then Phil holds out a plastic tub. "Phones, too."

Brandy yells *no* so loudly my ears ring. Billy clutches his phone with both hands, and Holly trembles as she holds hers. I have no phone, so I have no dog in this fight, but I have to listen anyway as Tracy says "Phones are a distraction and not conducive to your recovery if you are in contact with people who may hinder that process" and "You may use the house phone after ten days, but we need to approve your call list" and "In time you'll earn the right to use your own phone for an hour a day, but not until you *earn it.*"

Honestly, I do not care. I don't have my phone, and I don't want to talk to my parents anyway. And I don't have any friends left, apparently, so there's that. As Billy and Brandy complain, I look around at the room.

Not fancy, kind of dumpy. A desk. Two old couches and some chairs, one of which has a duct-taped leg. Potted plant in the corner that looks rather thirsty. Posters taped to the walls chirping *You matter* and *The only way out is to lift yourself up.*

I shove my hands into the pockets of my sweatshirt. My face is starting to throb. If I was back in the hospital, it would be medication time. Are they even going to give me anything?

I look at the posters again.

I do not matter. I'm as insignificant as this flattened piece of gum on the floor that obviously needs mopping.

Phones thwack into the bottom of the tub.

"You've taken my whole existence now," Brandy says bitterly. "Happy?"

All the kids look at me. Brandy gestures to the bin. I shrug.

"No phone," I say.

Tracy motions for us to follow Fran. Brandy slinks up next to me as we walk.

"How," she says breathily, "are you even alive without a phone?"

I ignore her, because I'm too busy looking back at Tracy and Phil on their knees, unzipping and unlatching backpacks and suitcases, dumping out our clothes, toiletries, books, magazines, makeup. Everything is being piled on the dirty floor like our belongings don't matter. On my other side, Holly whimpers, tears silently running down her face.

Fran is a walker-talker.

She's hustling us down corridors and pointing things out, barely giving us time to ask questions or get our bearings. "Meal room," she says, pointing to a small room with round tables and plastic chairs. "Breakfast, lunch, dinner, snack. Detox kids eat here until you go to General Population. Detox is three days of rest, physical tests, and mental health evals." She points to a door to the left. "Activity room. Board games, cards, art supplies, movies, a sad selection of paperbacks donated from our finest local used-book stores." She grins. "In Gen, we've got a rock-climbing wall, pool, trails, a gym. Lots of good stuff."

This is sounding more like some sort of Olympics training

camp than rehab. But what do I know? I've only ever seen this stuff in the movies, and there, people mostly sit in chairs and cry and stare at koi ponds, and then they have an emotional breakthrough with the therapist of their dreams and end up perfect. Or at least slightly less damaged.

All this walking is exhausting. I don't think I'm ready for . . . rock-climbing. At. All.

Back down the corridor and then outside, to a smaller building, this one brick, painted teal. The sun is slipping down the sky. It's getting chilly. I look up and around. The drive was maybe an hour and a half, but we had to pick up those other kids, so I don't think we're that far out of Tucson. There are mountains in the distance, but which ones? The Rincons? The Catalinas? The Tucsons? Where *are* we?

Fran sidesteps into the teal building. Like me, Holly is lagging behind. Billy is next to me, studying his nails, which are colored black with marker. The tips are jagged from being chewed. Fran snaps her fingers at him.

"You're the only boy in Detox dorm right now, lucky you, which means you're bunking alone for right now." She opens a door to a room filled with two sets of bunk beds.

"Sweet," Billy says. "Like summer camp. Except without the kid who cries for his parents every night. Perfect."

Fran beckons to me, Holly, and Brandy.

"Bella, Holly, Brandy, this is your room. Pick a bunk, don't fight, respect each other's privacy."

She looks at all four of us.

"You can go in your rooms and rest before Search, and after that, we'll do dinner."

"Search?" Billy says, and for the first time, he sounds a little nervous.

"This is a drug and alcohol behavioral rehabilitation program, Billy. We have to do a body search before we can admit you. There will be two people in the room with you: a counselor, and a nurse who will do the search. If anyone has specific trauma issues that need to be addressed, please tell us and we'll do our best to make you comfortable. But we can't let you go any farther until we make sure you're not holding anything at this very moment."

"This is like a prison. And where would I even hide anything anyway?" Holly laughs nervously.

"No," Fran says. "Not a prison. And you'd be surprised what and where people hide things. But if you're here to get healthy, hiding something in your patootie isn't the way to start, wouldn't you agree?"

Brandy shrugs. "I don't have anything to hide."

Billy says, "I don't have a patootie."

"You have another hiding area," Brandy points out, and Billy frowns.

"Ouch," he says. "Yuck."

Brandy walks into our room and stretches out on a bottom bunk, arranges her voluminous hair behind her on the pillow, and begins to inspect her long pink nails. Billy goes to his room.

Holly looks at her sneakered feet and then at me, her sunken eyes like dark pools.

I stare into our room from the hallway. None of this seems like a good thing. Like Holly said, it seems prisonlike and kind of . . . dumpy? I thought rehabs were more hospital-y and clinical-looking. So far, everything seems kind of like a very low-rent apartment complex. Ratty furniture, spare walls.

I'm beginning to regret agreeing to come here, even though

I don't think I had much of a choice. Anger and fear flare inside me. They're going to search me? I've never even been to a gynecologist. I shudder. This can't be legal.

Amber and Kristen and Lemon. Amber snitching on me in the intervention room and Kristen and Lemon abandoning me.

If it wasn't for all of them, I wouldn't be here. I hope they go to hell. And when I get out of this place, if I ever get out, I'm never speaking to any of them again.

I look up and down the hallway for exits. Maybe I could sneak out. Run. Make it . . . somewhere? But where would I go? I'm not even sure exactly where this place is.

I can't even call my mother and beg, because I don't have a phone. And my body really hurts—

I give up and walk into the room. Holly is already on the bunk over Brandy, so I sit on the bottom of the second bunk bed set.

"I can tell what you're thinking," Holly says to me. "Because I thought about it, too. But it would be hard to leave. There's nothing around out here for miles. It's all desert. We're all alone."

"This is really the worst," I say. "I don't deserve to be here. I didn't do anything wrong. I just messed up."

Holly nods slowly. "Yeah. Right. Me too, I guess."

I could sleep for a thousand days, I think. That might be the only decent thing to come of this whole shitshow—not having to deal with my life for a little while.

"Girl," Brandy says, leaning out of her bunk and angling her face up to Holly, "whatever you got up your vajayjay, get it out now."

Holly rolls over toward the wall, her shoulders starting to shake.

Brandy turns her eyes to me. "You stashing?"

"Stashing?" I say. "What even is that?"

"You're a boozer, then," she says. "Stashing is hiding shit in your holes. Like Fran said. Little baggies of whatever. Or swallowing a baggie beforehand and shitting it out while you're here. Not that I've done it. I just know about it. That's a little too gross for my taste."

"That's absolutely disgusting," I say. "That's completely desperate."

"You do what you have to do, I guess," Brandy answers. She reaches up and pokes the underside of the bunk, where Holly is curled and silent.

"Isn't that right?" Brandy calls to her. Holly doesn't answer.

Brandy shrugs, lying back down and looking over at me. "But I can't wait to find out what happened to your damn face."

"It's not really that interesting of a story," I say.

From her top bunk, Holly whispers, "So if I did have, like, something . . . what am I supposed to do with it?"

"Well," Brandy sighs. "You have a couple of options. Not that I know personally. I've just heard things. One, you can go in that bathroom over there and take it out and flush it down the toilet. Two, you can take it out and swallow whatever you have and, like, OD, or whatever, since I don't know how much you're packing. But they're gonna take a blood test and make you pee, so they'll find it in your system and you'll spend longer in Detox. Three, you can take it out and hand it over when they come get you for Search. Option three shows you're being honest, which may score you some points."

"And you know all this how?" I ask Brandy.

"I did this once before, but at a different place," she says.

"Which, by the way, was *a lot* nicer than this one. I'm guessing Detox rules are the same at most places." She kicks off her pristine white sneakers and lets them fall to the tiled floor.

Holly shifts in my direction and blinks, like she's thinking very hard about something, then climbs down the ladder, walks into the bathroom, and shuts the door.

In a few minutes, we hear the toilet flush.

When Holly comes out, she looks triumphant. "I flushed some," she says. "But I took most of them. I needed them."

Brandy nods. "I get it."

"*What* did you take?" I ask Holly.

"Many, many good things," she says.

Her face seems bright with anticipation now, when just a minute ago she looked like a ghost.

Holly climbs back on her bunk. She closes her eyes.

I look around the small room. I'm going to be stuck with them, and then other kids, who knows how many other kids, for, what? Twenty-nine days? My stomach sinks. I'll never get to be alone. I'm losing my alone space. I won't have anywhere to go. I won't have anywhere to—

Drink.

I squeeze my hands together hard.

I suck in my breath.

There's no way out of this. And I won't have the *one* thing that gets me through.

There's a knock at the door; then Fran comes in again. She's carrying several bottles of lemonade.

"I heard the toilet flush," she says. "Who peed?"

Brandy points to the top bunk, and Holly sits up and looks down at Fran, her face panicked.

"I . . . really had to go," she says softly.

Fran looks up at her carefully. "Uh-huh," she says, and hands her one of the lemonade bottles. "Finish this by the time I get back. We'll need a urine sample."

Holly's hands tremble as she takes the bottle.

"Can I have an extra?" Brandy asks. "I don't need to flush anything. I'm just thirsty."

Fran gives it to her, then points to me. "You're up first. Drink fast as we walk."

She leads me down the hallway to a room that looks like a doctor's office: examining table, scale, sink, tray table full of stuff. I gulp the lemonade but gag a little. It's too sweet.

"I'm going to pat you down," she tells me, taking the empty bottle from me and placing it on the counter.

"Why?"

"Some kids trade pee before the urine test. Stuff ziplock bags in their pockets, pee in the bag, give it to a friend."

"That's disgusting. How can you pee in a bag?"

"When you have an addiction, you do a lot of things you never thought you'd do. But you know that already, right?"

I frown. "I'm not an addict."

"Then you should leave now, I guess."

We stare at each other for a moment. I'm the one to break eye contact.

I'm not an addict. I'm not an alcoholic. Are they even the same thing? I take a deep breath to calm myself.

Fran has me lift my arms and spread my legs. She pats me gently all over, slides her fingers in the pockets of my sweatpants and sweatshirt, and then grabs a plastic cup from the tray table. "Bathroom's in there. There's a gown hanging on the door, so put that on for Search. No bra, no underwear, no socks."

I go into the bathroom and do everything she says, avoiding my face in the mirror above the sink. I pee in the cup and screw the cap back on. The cup has my name and birthdate, *Leahey, Isabella, 5/30/2008,* and today's date. I do some quick math in my head.

December 1. If I have to be in here for thirty days, that means I'm here for Christmas (oh my god, Christmas in *here*? What can that possibly entail?) and then home through school break and then one week until back to school and all those kids and—

Don't think about that, my brain tells me. *They're probably all talking about you anyway, so really, be glad you aren't there. They've all seen that video by now. Heard about you.*

I don't know what to do with my clothes, so I just fold them very neatly and leave them on the sink. Then I open the door.

Fran and a woman in nurse's scrubs are standing there. The nurse has latex gloves on.

"Bella," Fran says, "if this is going to make you anxious or upset in any way, or if you have physical or emotional barriers to a physical search, like sexual trauma, please let me know now."

"I don't have anything to hide," I say. "I don't know why you have to do this. You're basically feeling up kids, you know."

"Honey," the nurse says, but not in a mean way. "I've had kids shove baggies of Oxy up their butt."

"Remember the kid who duct-taped a pint of schnapps to his stomach and thought he'd get away with it?" Fran says.

"Mm-hmm," the nurse says. "And the one who hid the pills in her dreads?"

They chuckle. I can't believe they find this funny.

"We've seen it all," Fran tells me.

"It'll be over in just a second," the nurse says. "And I have very gentle hands."

No one has ever touched me like she is about to touch me, not even Dylan.

I start to tremble.

Did my parents know this would be part of it, me getting my very private parts felt up? Did they sign off on this?

I think . . . I think I hate them both at this very moment for the humiliation I'm about to undergo.

"What if I refuse?" I say suddenly.

Fran shrugs. "Then you stay in Detox longer and you stay at Sonoran Sunrise longer, Your parents signed for you at the hospital. You initialed the form, too. This is what you signed up for. Or you can leave right now, remember? We won't stop you. But it's dark out and getting colder. If you have nothing to hide, this will go very quickly."

They're both watching me carefully.

I wish I was brave like that. To run. To push both of them against the wall and take off into the desert in my flapping gown.

But I'm not.

My face aches and my bones are tired and I just want to go to sleep.

I'm just a stupid and scared girl with nowhere to go.

"Can I close my eyes?" I ask finally.

"Yes," Fran says.

When the nurse is done, she takes off her gloves and drops them in the trash. "Clean," she tells Fran, who writes something in a folder. Then she starts asking me a bunch of questions.

Are you sexually active?

I tell her no. That I had a boyfriend, but we didn't do *that.*

Are you on birth control?

No.

Have you had any alcohol or drugs in the past forty-eight hours?

No. Well, the painkillers.

Are you suffering from depression, anxiety, or self-harm?

"I'm fifteen," I say. "I'm sad and anxious all the time, but I don't cut myself, no."

They keep asking questions and I'm getting more tired. My brain feels like mud.

They take a blood test.

The nurse examines my face. She gives me two ibuprofen and tells me to ask for more if I need it.

"I can't have what they gave me in the hospital?" I ask, looking at the ibuprofen in the palm of my hand. That stuff in the hospital was really good. If that's what people are stuffing up their butts, I can kind of see why.

She barks out a laugh. "Oh god, no, honey, this is rehab. We're trying to get you *off* stuff like that. What, you want a cocktail with dinner, too?"

Fran tells me I can get dressed.

Instead of taking me back to the room, she takes me to the vending machine. It's chained to the wall.

"Chips, chocolate, what would you like? It's going to be a bit before dinner. We need to finish the others."

"I'm not really hungry," I say.

"Something to drink?"

"I left my Pedialyte in the van."

"I can get you more of that." She makes a note on her phone. "Have this for now."

She presses some buttons on the machine and out pops a Gatorade. She hands it to me.

Back in the room, Fran points to Holly. "You're up."

I can tell by the way Fran looks at Holly that she absolutely knows she took something. I peer at Holly closely. Her eyes are glassy and she's not trembling anymore. Whatever it was must be kicking in.

Brandy is asleep, her hair a glossy fan on the mattress, so I lie down on my bunk. I open the Gatorade and sip it slowly, staring at the bottom of the empty top bunk.

The one thing I notice is how quiet it is here. Just faint traces of noise: maybe the nurse and Fran in the room with Holly, talking, but nothing else.

It's peaceful.

But not the kind of peace I like.

I'm so tired. It feels like my body has been beaten with rocks, turned inside out and back again.

Now there's a distinct sound of laughter far down the hallway. Thin, desperate.

Holly.

I cap my Gatorade and set it on the floor. I lie back, rest my head on the pillow.

I fall asleep.

I'm rolling on the surface of the sea on my back, the waves pushing me up and down, water filling my mouth, and I try to reach up, grab the stars, pull myself out of the water, but I can't get a grip on them. They're slippery.

"Isabella."

Where is that voice in the ocean? Help me.

"Isabella, wake up."

I blink.

Fran is standing above me.

"It's dinner. It's time for dinner, Isabella."

My mouth feels thick with sludge. My head is heavy.

"It's Bella. Not hungry," I mumble. "Just want to sleep."

"Okay," she says softly.

I pull the blanket up to my chin. The ibuprofen did nothing for my face. It throbs now, worse even than this morning. I hear the door close behind Fran.

I fall back into the ocean.

The nurse comes in later and nudges us until we wake up and takes our blood pressure and then we go back to sleep.

When I wake up again, the room is still dark. Slowly, I make out a lump on the bottom bunk across the room. It's Brandy, snoring gently, the blue wool blanket pulled all the way up to her nose. The top bunk is empty. Our bags and suitcases are here now, lined up against the wall.

Where is Holly?

I go to the bathroom. Don't look at my face in the mirror. There's a lever on the wall by the toilet. PULL FOR HELP says the square sign above it.

I stand by the window in our room. The sky is a shimmery purple-blue, studded with stars. You can see the stars in Tucson, too, but they always look better on the outskirts of the city, away from the streetlights and buildings. I remember that from Tubac, from Agnes's farm, sitting outside with Laurel by a crackling fire, a glass of something she called a Vesper in her hand.

I try it, just to see, but the window doesn't open. I guess so nobody tries to escape from the room.

I get up and go out into the hallway. It's quiet. There's a light at the end, so I walk toward that.

A woman is behind the desk, watching a show on a laptop. I hear the strains of the *Golden Girls* theme song before she notices me and pauses her show.

"Hello," she says. "Can't sleep? Are you Isabella or Brandy?"

"Bella. No one calls me Isabella."

She nods. "Cool. Tell me what you need, Bella."

"Where's . . . where's Holly? The other girl who was with us?"

"Holly's been segregated. We have to wait until whatever she took is out of her system."

"Oh."

The woman looks at some papers on the desk. "You were sleeping and missed dinner. Do you want something to eat?"

I hesitate. I can't tell if I'm hungry or not. My body just feels really . . . exhausted.

I tell her that.

"Alcohol poisoning really does a number on your nervous system," she says. "The effects can last for quite some time. Things inside you are trying to adjust. It's complicated."

I can't help it; I start crying. "My face really hurts and they won't give me anything but ibuprofen. I just miss my mom. Can I call my mom, please?"

I expect the woman to say *oh, don't cry,* but she doesn't. She just says, "No calls with parents right now, Bella, unless you want to leave. I know everything is hard at the moment, but we have rules, and they're meant to protect you." She hands me a tissue and I wipe my face. "Parents get to visit on the fifteenth day for two hours, if that makes you feel better."

I don't think it does. That seems really far away at the moment. Eons away.

"I'm Janet," she says. "I'm the night shift. I can play a board game with you, or you can watch a movie until you're ready to go back to sleep. Or we can just talk. It's up to you."

She waits for me to answer.

I want to be home. I don't even care which one. I just don't want to be here, in this dumpy place in the middle of the desert, in a too-bright hallway talking to a woman named Janet, *The Golden Girls* paused on her laptop.

I look down the hall desperately. I wonder if the doors have alarms. If I run, will they try to catch me? And if I run, where will I go?

My shoulders sag. I'm too tired and achy to run.

"Bella?" Janet asks.

I don't answer. I just walk back down the hall and into the bedroom, climb under my own blue wool blanket, and wait for the waves to come to me again.

DAY TWO

BRANDY IS ON THE floor, rooting through her suitcase. Dental floss, underwear, and very lacy bras fly through the air in clouds of pink, purple, mint green. She's pissed. Her voice tumbles out in a rush.

"They took everything. *Everything.* Makeup, toothbrush, toothpaste . . . Heathens."

I get up from the bed sleepily and walk over to my own suitcase, pushed against the wall under the window. Outside, I can see it's still early. There's a grayness to the sky; the sun is just beginning to rise.

I unlatch my suitcase. It's not really mine; it was Laurel's. It's old-fashioned and hard as bricks and she decorated it when she was a teenager, Mod Podging funny stickers, old post-cards, and photographs of bands cut out from magazines. "My parents were so mad," she told me. "It was quite expensive. But I had to make everything mine. Put my own stamp on things."

I don't care about makeup. I only have one good eye any-way.

T-shirts, jeans, a hoodie, underwear, my copy of *Wild,* like that's any use to me now.

The door opens.

It's Tracy, fresh-faced and smiling, blond hair pulled behind her ears.

"Breakfast," she announces.

On each bunk, she places a stack of brand-new toothbrush, toothpaste, shampoo, hairbrush.

"Why would you take my makeup?" Brandy asks angrily. "That's something that makes me feel better *naturally.*"

I study Brandy. She looks a lot different than she did yesterday. She must have taken off her makeup at some point last night while I was sleeping. She looks so much younger with a naked face.

Tracy shrugs. "You could hide drugs in it. But also, we don't want *you* to hide, if you know what I mean."

"I don't *hide* behind my makeup," Brandy mutters, sweeping her hair into a scrunchie. She stands up, grabs the things Tracy gave us, and stomps into the bathroom. She slams the door. Tracy smiles at me and leaves.

"I do," I say to the empty room. "I hide behind my makeup."

"Good for you!" Brandy yells from behind the bathroom door. "Good for effin' you."

Billy is already at the table, surrounded by bowls of scrambled eggs, plates of sausage, plates of toast and butter, boxes of cereal and cartons of milk. Brandy wrinkles her nose at one of the bowls. It's filled with scrambled tofu. Tracy points to another table with urns of coffee and juice.

"Not you," she says as I start to head over. "Pedialyte for you. No coffee just yet."

"That's not fair," I say.

"You wrecked your body," she says simply. "We're still rehydrating you. You can have that or water."

"One cup of coffee isn't going to kill me," I argue. This is ridiculous. It's coffee, and I'm not dead. I didn't die. I'm very much still alive, apparently, and in this awful place.

"Rules are rules," she says. "And speaking of . . ."

She places booklets in front of each of us.

Desert vista, a shining sky, *Sonoran Sunrise* in beautiful lettering on the cover, with *Welcome to your future* across the bottom.

"The handbook," Tracy tells us. "Read it, initial each page, give it back when you're done."

She sits down and starts making a plate of fruit and scrambled tofu.

"I'm not much of a reader," Billy says, flipping through the booklet. "Somebody just tell me the good parts." He shoves a sausage into his mouth with his fingers.

I use a fork to break the seal on my bottle of Pedialyte and dump some eggs onto my plate. The bad side of my face throbs. I take a small bite of egg and chew very, very slowly as I flip through the booklet.

> *Welcome to Sonoran Sunrise, a behavioral and rehabilitation program for adolescents in crisis.*
>
> *We are a healing, empathy-based recovery program that emphasizes personal responsibility and growth. Addiction recovery treatment is not one-size-fits-all because adolescents are not one size. We tailor our program to each individual in need, utilizing a variety of methods: self-awareness training, self-reliance, physical and adventure activity, emotional therapy.*

Images of kids hiking, with backpacks and trekking poles. Campfires. Swimming in the sparkling blue pool. Gathered in circles listening to some extremely healthy- and positive-looking person talk. It looks like a summer camp, for god's sake. It looks like all cheeriness and good health and good living and I am none of those things.

There's a list of rules.

At Sonoran Sunrise, I agree to:

Participate fully and openly in my recovery program.

Respect myself and the other residents.

Respect the counselors and other health staff.

Refrain from ingesting drugs and alcohol at any time, with the exception of medication approved by staff.

Refrain from violent or disruptive behavior toward myself, fellow residents, or staff.

Not abuse, harm, or put at risk any of the camp animals.

Respect the confidentiality of my fellow residents.

Refrain from sexual activity with my fellow residents or with staff.

Report any and all instances of inappropriate or violent behavior, sexual activity, drug use, or bullying to staff.

Follow all rules pertaining to mealtime, therapy, assigned physical activity, and any other activities.

By signing this document, I agree that I am ready to accept myself as a valued, spiritual, empathetic, and important person on this earth.

"Animals?" I say, breaking the silence that's settled over the meal room.

"Goats," Brandy says, rapidly turning the pages of her book. "They have goats and chickens here. That's what my mom said. She said it's a bunch of damn hippies. That doesn't seem so bad, though, honestly. My last place, everyone was like a prison guard, practically. The food was great and the sheets were luxurious, but the staff sucked. I might prefer the goat thing."

Oh my god, I'm like Ricci now. At a place with cute animals that are supposed to calm me down. I'd laugh, but it would hurt my face. Someday I'll have to tell Ricci about this. The place with animals and—

Ricci. What even have my parents told her? She's never been away from me for so long. She's going to freak out. *They're* going to freak out, trying to take care of her without me to run interference. It's going to be a nightmare.

My brain says: *Good. Make them suffer.*

My heart says: *Poor Ricci.*

There's a lot of other information in the book, about meal prep and phone calls and visitors, but I can't process all of it, so I just sign every page. This is my life for the next month. I can't believe it. My head starts to swim.

I grab a pen from a pile in the middle of the table and initial every page, throw the booklet next to the pens.

"What a good girl you are," Brandy says.

I ignore her, sipping my Pedialyte.

Brandy finishes signing her handbook with a flourish and then grabs Billy's, signs all his pages, too, as Tracy watches.

Billy looks at Tracy.

"Suit yourself," she says. "Don't say I didn't warn you."

* * *

No.

That's what I tell Tracy.

No.

We're in the activity room, which I didn't really get a good look at yesterday when Fran was marching us around. I'm feeling a little bleary after breakfast, and the two ibuprofen Tracy handed me haven't kicked in.

Tracy is standing in front of a wall of Polaroids. A veritable cornucopia of dysfunction, rage, and sadness. Kid after kid after kid after kid posing against the wall: disgruntled, beat-up, stitched-up, giving devil horns; red-faced, woozy-eyed, flipping off the camera; shit-eating grins, resolute fury, stone-faced; apple-cheeked and smiling like absolutely nothing is wrong or ever has been.

"There's no *no,*" Tracy tells me. She's holding the camera in her hand. "This is part of your process here. Every day, a photograph. Day Fifteen, which is halfway through, you look at all of them. You'll see a difference. You'll see yourself becoming a healthier person. You'll become more aware of yourself."

I notice that she does not say *happier.*

Also, this sounds suspiciously similar to the stupid art class self-portrait, and that just makes me angrier.

Brandy and Billy are inspecting the Polaroids and giggling at some of them. Brandy points to a photo of a pink-haired girl.

"Who's this here, flipping you off?"

Tracy gives a half smile. "That's Charlotte. You'll meet her later in Gen. She's a real charmer."

"Anyway," Brandy says, "this is weird. We didn't do this at

any of my other places, but what the hell. I'm gorgeous, snap away."

She finds a blank spot against the wall, releases her hair from her scrunchie and fluffs it around her shoulders, and pouts. Tracy takes the photograph. When it slides from the camera, she puts it on the chair to develop. Brandy skips over to watch.

"Wait a minute. How many places have you been in anyway?" I ask Brandy.

"Technically, only one rehab," Brandy says. "The other two were purely mental. And they were *nice.* One even had massages and a sauna."

"Damn, girl," Billy says, standing against the wall for Tracy. "And you're still not better?"

"It's not about being better, Billy. It's about managing your addictions and behavior," Tracy says. She holds the camera up to her eye.

"I'm not addicted," Billy says. "I manage my pharmaceutical behavior just fine, thanks. I'm only here to do the time for my crime, ma'am."

He sticks out his tongue. Tracy hands him his photograph, then motions to me.

"You signed the booklet," she says evenly. "This is a required part of the program."

"*Look* at me," I say. "I don't want to."

She gestures to the wall of kids. "Look at *them.* Everybody's face has a story here. These are all Detox photographs. You need to face yourself, Bella. If you can't face yourself, you won't do well here."

I think I hate her. Her blond hair, her perfect, unblemished face. She's like one of those smooth and beautiful rocks you find on a walk along the beach: glistening, unmarked, special. You slip it into your pocket and keep it forever.

That will never be me.

Tracy walks up to me very slowly.

"I know what you're thinking, Bella," she says quietly. "I know it. You think you know my story just by looking at me. You have a whole idea in your head. You've written a whole novel about me."

Brandy and Billy have gotten very quiet. My heart is knocking in my chest. Is Tracy going to hit me or something? Her face has changed, somehow. There's an edge to her voice.

She opens her mouth and gently, with one hand, pops out her entire top row of teeth, just for a second, revealing the emptiness there. Then, as quick as if it never happened, she pops it back in.

"Someday I'll tell you how that happened, Bella, and how I came to be at Sonoran, but for right now, don't judge people based on what you think you see. Your face is part of the story that's going to be written here over the next month."

Billy nudges me toward the wall.

I walk over, fit my back against it, look at the ground.

"Who's going to write that stupid story?" I mumble. "I wouldn't want to read it."

"Bella!" Tracy shouts.

Startled, I look up.

She presses the button, catches the photo as it slides out.

Smiling, she says, "You are. And you will."

DAY THREE

"YO, YO, YO, YO."

Clonk, clonk, clonk.

"Yo, yo, yo, ladies!"

I shoot out of my bed so fast I almost slip on the floor and crack my head open. I stand in the middle of our room, staring at Brandy, who's wiping her eyes.

It sounds like someone is trying to break our door down.

I drag myself over and yank it open.

A muscular college-aged guy with a crew cut grins and shakes his metal water bottle at us. He must have been using that to bang on our door.

A ping goes off in my brain. He's the crew cut guy that was with Phil in the hospital when I left.

"Move it up and out, ladies! Time for some sunshine. Sneakers, sweatpants, hoodie. Let's go, go, go!"

"I'm sorry, for what, now?" Brandy asks.

"Daily run. Move the body, free the mind. Five minutes until we leave. The name's Chuck. Pleased to meet you."

He shuts our door. In a minute, I hear that same metal water bottle being banged on Billy's door.

"I do not run," Brandy says. "I treadmill, slowly. But I do not run."

I look at myself. I'm already dressed in sweatpants and a sweatshirt, since I never took off my clothes from yesterday before going to bed. I haven't showered since I left the hospital. What does it matter, though? I pull my sneakers from under my bunk and drag them on.

"We used to do a twelve-minute mile in middle school in PE," I tell Brandy. "Sixth grade. PE was right after lunch, and it sucked. If you stopped, you had to start over. I am not looking forward to this."

"Well, I'm not doing it. The sun isn't even up yet. It's inhumane." Brandy shoves herself back under her blanket and turns to the wall. I go into the bathroom and pee and brush my teeth, moving the toothbrush carefully around the bad part.

Clonk, clonk, clonk. "Let's goooooooo!"

I yank open the bathroom door and walk to the bedroom door and open it. Billy is standing in the hallway with Chuck, his eyes half closed.

"Where's your friend?" Chuck asks. He's bouncing up and down.

I shrug.

Chuck leans his head into our room. "You don't want to come, that's all right with me. But it's a demerit."

"A what?" Billy asks.

"I don't care!" Brandy shouts, her voice scratchy.

Chuck turns to Billy. "It counts against you. You don't follow the program, you get a demerit. You get too many, you lose things."

"Like what?" Billy asks, alarmed. "How many demerits? What things? I'll get my phone back, right? Right?"

Chuck starts jogging down the hall. "Fuck around and find out!" he calls over his shoulder.

* * *

Outside, he leads us in stretches. When I reach for my toes, a wave of dizziness spreads over me and needles of pain spread up the backs of my legs. Billy can barely reach past his knees.

There's no track or anything, just desert. About fifty feet away, there are more adobe buildings and what looks like . . . a mini-farm? That must be the goats and the chickens. There is already a bunch of kids out there dressed in parkas and hoodies and jeans, raking the coop and throwing hay and grass from a bucket for the goats to eat.

"Don't worry," Chuck says. "You'll be one of them soon."

Billy shivers. "It's freaking cold out here."

Then Chuck takes off. Like, *fast.*

Billy and I stare at each other.

"You first," I say.

"You," he says, and scowls. "I'm not much of an athlete."

Far into the desert, Chuck yells, "Demerits!"

"Shit," Billy says. He starts running.

I watch him run awkwardly, his feet slipping on stones in the desert sand. His arms fly everywhere.

There's no *path.* I could run into a cactus, get needles in my sweatpants. Fall and crack my head open. Are there tarantulas out here?

I look back at the kids with the animals. They're kind of laughing. That guy Phil, the one from the first day, is with them. He puts his hands on his hips, watching me.

"Go, go, go!" the kids chant.

I don't like people looking at me, and I can't tell if the kids are being encouraging or mean. One of them has a shaved head and is covering her mouth, she's laughing so hard. I start running just to get away from them.

Billy is a black-hooded blip far ahead of me. I can't even

see Chuck anymore. What if I get lost? My lungs start burning right away. I land on a stone and almost twist my ankle. The bouncing of my body makes my face shake, and it pulsates with pain.

I can feel rivulets of sweat running down my back. Up ahead, Billy seems to have gained his balance. He's figured out how to move his arms in time with his legs. I'm like a flailing baby bird.

I stop, put my hands on my knees. Drops of sweat sting my eyes. I feel like I'm going to die. Maybe I should just lie down and die in the desert. I cannot do this. I don't want to do this.

I hear footsteps and pull myself back to standing, turn around.

It's Brandy, hair flying in her face, in matching pink sweatshirt and sweatpants, winter hat, and sneakers, stumble-running, face splotchy red.

When she reaches me, she pants, "Never. Leave. A. Man. Behind."

She grabs the fabric of my sweatshirt and pulls me forward with her.

I don't know how long it takes us to finally catch up to Chuck, but when we do, he's casually perched on a boulder, drinking from his water bottle. Billy is flat on his back on the ground beside him, looking like he's going to throw up.

"Fancy meeting you here," Chuck says, grinning.

"Sadist," Brandy says. She collapses next to Billy. "Do you have water for us, at least?"

Chuck shakes his head. "Nope. You should have thought of that yourself."

"You should have told us," I say.

"I'm not here to hold your hand," Chuck says, pulling a cloth from his pocket and wiping his face. "Somehow all of you figured out how to lie and steal and cheat and keep secrets so you could keep getting high or drunk or whatever, but you can't remember a basic function like bringing water if you exercise? That's on you. You need to learn how to take care of yourself in a good way. You lost that somewhere. Maybe you'll get it back here."

"Unlikely," Brandy says. Her neck is shiny with sweat.

Chuck stands up. "Ready?"

"I can't," I say. "Running, it hurts my face. I don't think I should be doing this."

He guffaws. "You don't run with your face, girl. You run with your legs. Stay here if you want. I'm headed back."

"Wait," I say. "I need to rest longer."

"Time's up," Chuck says, checking his watch. "Like I said, stay here if you want, but I'm headed out. Isn't it a beautiful day for a run?"

"No," Billy moans from the ground. "It is not."

"But how will I get back?" I say, looking around. "I don't know where we are." We're pretty far out. I can't see the buildings of Sonoran Sunrise anymore. There's no path; Chuck just ran wherever he wanted and we followed.

He takes off, calling over his shoulder, "Figure it out."

Billy quickly gets up and runs after Chuck.

Brandy wipes her face with a sleeve of her sweatshirt. "I'm not sticking around here. I don't want to get lost. I want to go home."

"That's *not* our home," I say.

I watch her run away, hair flopping against her pink back.

I sit on the boulder Chuck sat on. It's still warm from his body. My legs hurt.

It's really quiet out here.

I hate everything. I hate that stupid little bird peeking at me from a nest-hole in that saguaro. I hate that my face pulsates with pain. I hate that I'm coated in sweat. I hate that they left me here. Even Brandy left, despite that bullshit of "Never leave a man behind."

I don't think I've ever been in a place this still. Usually I'm surrounded by noise. School. My sister. My parents. My phone. Music through my headphones or my own thoughts careening inside my brain. Only drinking quiets everything down.

Now there's just . . . nothing.

And it's kind of scary. I don't know what to do in this quiet.

All of a sudden, my stomach rolls and I double over, coughing out leftover food from yesterday. I splutter out the last bits and wipe my chin with the hem of my sweatshirt.

The stupid little bird in the saguaro nest-hole cheeps at me.

"That's right," I say to it. "I'm disgusting. A disgusting, dirty thing."

I look down at my pile of vomit. Red ants are already crawling over it. I use my sneaker to push some sand and stones and twigs over it. Cover it up.

That was weird, what Chuck said. About us being good at keeping secrets and lying.

Covering things up.

Maybe I lied sometimes. But I had to maintain, didn't I? Everything has always been chaos around me. I just wanted to make it go away somehow. But I never cheated or stole.

Suddenly I remember what Amber said. How I lied at her mom's just to have an excuse to get the NyQuil. I did finish it off after Amber went to sleep. Sat in her green-tiled bathroom on the toilet and sucked the rest down, stuck the empty bottle way in the back of the bottom cabinet.

I guess that was stealing, in a way.

A swell of pain rises in me, but I push it down. I don't want to cry. I'm sick of crying. I'm sick of all of it. Everything.

I don't know how I'm going to get through this.

I slide off the boulder onto the ground and wedge my face between my knees. The darkness feels comforting.

"Jesus Christ, just get up."

I look up.

Strands of hair stick to Brandy's cheeks.

"I thought you were behind me," she pants. "I ran all this way back, so the least you can do is get off your ass and come with me. I need a ride-or-die in this place, and it looks like you're it, so get up and let's go."

She's waiting, hips cocked.

"If we die in the desert, at least we'll die together," she says. "Also, you have puke on your sweatshirt. Extremely gross."

She grimaces.

"Fine," I say, reaching down and grabbing some sand. I smear it over the vomit on my sweatshirt.

I stand up.

I'll need at least one friend here if I'm going to survive.

"Wait," Billy says suspiciously. "This looks like school. If I wanted to do school, I'd be *at* school. Not that I want to be *here,* but I did not think *here* meant school."

We're in the activity room after running with Chuck, eating, and taking showers. My body is sore from the run. Although

I'm glad I finally took a shower and changed out of my puke clothes, it was also weird to shower with Brandy right outside the door. I did it as quickly as possible.

We're sitting at round tables. There are easels and giant buckets full of art supplies and Legos against one wall, and things like a beanbag toss and plastic darts near another. There's a wonky mural of upraised hands reaching toward a starry night sky, which I didn't notice before.

Fran has given us stapled packets of paper. She takes a sip of her coffee.

"Not school, Billy," she says. "Not a test or a quiz. Just some looking inward."

I didn't sleep well last night. I kept tossing and turning, which hurt my face. I couldn't settle down. I kept doing the math in my head, like, *I have been here two days. But I have been away from home for a total of seven days. I haven't had a drink in seven days, but the first three days in the hospital might not count because I had so much alcohol in my system, right? So I was okay. And they gave me painkillers. I was tired the first two days here and mostly slept, so maybe that doesn't count. But now it's going on seven days without alcohol and I'm getting a little anxious about that.*

Those things just ran through my head. Over and over. Sometimes my brain won't stop.

I'm fidgety at this table, rolling a pencil between my palms.

The first sheet of paper is titled *Decision-Making Worksheet: Cost-Benefit Analysis.* Under that, it says *The substance or activity to consider is,* and then there's a blank line, where I guess we're supposed to write whatever it is that got us here. Over two blank squares, it says *USING* and *DOING.*

Above the left-hand column, it says *Advantages: Benefits and Rewards,* and above the right, *Disadvantages: Costs and Risks.* The bottom two squares are titled *NOT using* and *NOT doing,* and one square says *Advantages: Benefits and Rewards* and the other says *Disadvantages: Costs and Risks.*

Billy groans. "This *is* school." He drops his pencil on the table.

Brandy takes some colored pencils from a bucket and draws hearts in her grids.

Billy is right. Who knew there was going to be school in rehab? This assignment is as stupid as the forms Tracy tried to get me to fill out in the hospital.

"The point is to think about what, say, drinking does for you," Fran says. "Does it have positives? What are the negatives to your drinking? Or if you like your pills, why? How does getting high on Oxy help you? Are there ways it makes your life harder? Less manageable?"

"I don't know," Billy says. "I feel pretty good when I'm high. That's a plus right there."

"Sometimes we spend so much time trying to get high or drunk that we forget about the risks involved," Fran says. "Emotional risks. Financial risks. Familial risks. Friendship risks."

Friendship risks. Like me, with Amber. Maybe Dylan, too.

Kristen certainly doesn't count. She can be fun, but she doesn't really care about people; look what she did to *me.*

Cherie? She was pissed at me about the art project, but that wasn't really my fault, was it? It was the Wi-Fi's fault. Granted, I might have a been a little woozy, but that didn't stop me from trying to do the work. I mean, I guess I could have done it earlier. Remembered to do it earlier, anyway.

Dawn? She's an unknown. She's too new, though I feel pretty bad for forgetting about her during lunch when I had to print out that paper for Deavers.

I stop rolling the pencil. Look at those squares on the paper.

"What's this 'substance' line for?" Brandy asks.

"It's whatever you do. Your poison of choice." Fran smiles.

"Did *you* ever have a poison?" Billy asks Fran. "Me, I'm kinda a Mom's-painkiller type person. Valium. Stuff that evens you out. Stuff that has an end date, you know? Like, I know it'll last four to twelve hours, depending on how many I take. If I don't have a lot, I can supplement with my granddad's beer. He doesn't care. Then it's smoooooth sailing."

I perk up at the word *granddad.* I guess Billy and I have that in common. Drinking with our grandparents.

Billy looks almost dreamy, thinking about it.

Fran sets down her coffee cup. I think she's the oldest person I've met here so far. Gray hair spiking from her head. Hiking boots. Roses tattooed on her wrinkly forearms.

"Child," she says to Billy, "you name it, I did it. If it messed you up, I was all in. But then I watched my very best friend die, right in front of me. Under a tree in Anza Park on Stone. I've been in recovery now for seventeen years. And yes, some of what you'll do here will seem like school, because, like me, you need to *learn.* You will not live if you cannot learn how to live."

I sigh. This place is going to be an endless source of feel-good affirmations and slogans, just like those posters in the lobby when we arrived.

I look at my sheet and let out a long breath. I write *alcohol* in the *substance* line.

Under *advantages,* I write:

Feel more normal, like other people

Talk easier to people

Don't feel so anxious

Relieve stress

Don't feel

Be alone

Under disadvantages, I write:

Headaches

Making sure no one knows

I listen to everyone scratching away. Fran is on her phone. She looks briefly at my sheet.

"Those aren't headaches," she murmurs. "They're hangovers."

I ignore her. This is *tedious.*

I grit my teeth and tell myself to play nice and just get through it and move down the sheet to *NOT using* and *NOT doing.*

In the grid for *advantages,* I write:

My family wouldn't be mad at me anymore.

Amber would be my friend.

Maybe I wouldn't have lost Dylan.

I wouldn't feel so tired all the time.

I would remember more things, like homework (or Dawn).

I pause, thinking. Then, in very tiny letters, probably too small for anyone to read, I write, *the video wouldn't have happened.*

In the grid for *disadvantages,* I write:

I would feel anxious all the time again.

School would be harder.

I don't know how to feel.

I can't handle stress.

No one will be my friend/won't go to parties.

I don't know how to feel.

Lonely or lonelier

Then I write, *This is the most ridiculous test I have ever taken and whoever wrote it sucks completely and 4-ever.* I draw a smiley face with Xs for eyes and an arrow through its head.

Brandy slams down her pencil. "Done!" she announces. She shoves her paper across the table to Fran. "What grade did I get?"

"It's not a test like that, Brandy." Fran scans the sheet. "You don't have many disadvantages to drinking."

"Nope," Brandy says. "I like it. It makes me feel *better.* I have lots of friends. I go to parties. It helps me chill."

"Hmm." Fran puts Brandy's paper down. "But you're here."

Brandy scowls. "So?"

"Well, somewhere, somehow, something happened that brought you here. And while your *being* here is positive, the reason *behind* it is not. Get what I'm saying?"

Brandy twists a strand of her dark hair. It's still wet from her shower. She was irked that there wasn't a blow-dryer. "I'm just here because my mother hates me, to be frank. She'll do anything to get me out of the house so she can be alone with her boyfriend. So what?"

"What mom would want you out of the house so bad she'd pay all this money?" Billy asks.

I look over at him. "Wait, how much is this costing?"

Billy rubs his fingers together. "Probably mucho moolah."

"Well, it doesn't *look* like it," Brandy says, and sniffs.

How *are* my parents paying for this? My dad works in a cubicle and my mom has insurance through her radio job, but it can't be all that great. I think there was estate money from Laurel, but I don't know how much. My mom kept pretty quiet about that stuff. That was something else my parents fought about after she died. Selling off some of Laurel's photographs to museums. Auctioning them at special art houses. Some curator calls once every few months, but my mom gets really agitated and lets it go to voicemail.

Great. Now I'm costing my parents money they don't even have, so I'll feel guilty about *that* forever.

"Listen," Brandy says, raising her voice. "There is simply no limit to what my mother will spend to get me away from her, okay?"

Her face is flushed; her eyes have grown damp.

She stands up quickly, slamming her pencil back in the bucket. "I finished my homework. Can I go back to my room? This is lame."

"Sure," Fran says.

Brandy wraps her arms around herself and stomps out of the activity room.

"She just gets to leave?" Billy says. "That doesn't seem cool. I'm not even done with my sheets!"

"I can't force anyone to do anything they aren't ready for, Billy. If somebody chooses to be here and not put in the work, well, that's on them. You just need to worry about yourself. Do you want to put in the work? Do your advantages outweigh your disadvantages? Maybe by the time thirty days is up, you'll have an answer."

Billy sighs. "Thirty freakin' days."

He goes back to scribbling on his sheets.

Fran looks at me. "How are you doing with yours?"

I hand her my sheets.

"Interesting," she says. She peers over her glasses at me. They're pink with fake stones at the corners. Like something my boss, Patty, would wear.

"What do you mean, 'the video'?" she asks.

"Video?" Billy says. "Do tell. Sounds saucy." He leans forward, very interested.

"Shut up," I tell him. "I don't want to talk about it. It's none of your business."

"That's all right," Fran says gently. She makes a note on her clipboard.

She inspects my packet again. "I see a lot of anxiety. Loneliness. You must be carrying a lot. Would you say that's accurate?"

Don't cry. I grind my teeth, but that hurts my face, so I stop. I pinch my thigh under the table and shrug.

"Bella, tell me what kind of kid you are. Do you need me to say you did very well on this worksheet, do you need me to ask you to work harder, or do you need me to just accept it?"

"That's a weird question," I say slowly.

"I'm just trying to get a sense of you," she says.

"Well, I like good grades," I say. "I try to get them."

"Why?"

Billy is drawing ghosts with devil horns on one of his worksheets. I watch his fingers working carefully, gracefully. The ghosts are actually pretty good, with nice shading.

I think of my art project, that tree. I guess I'm going to fail that now. Along with every other class. By the time I'm out of here, school will be over for the fall. It will be after Christmas. I'll be so far behind everyone else.

"Because it makes people happy," I finally say.

"Who?"

"My parents. Teachers."

"Does it make you happy?"

"Well, if they're happy, I'm happy."

"But, see, I don't think you *are* happy. I don't see that on this sheet. If you get all As and your parents are happy, why are you still not happy? Has it ever made *you* happy to get good grades?"

"I don't know? I mean, it's stressful. All that work. Most of it I don't even care about."

I'm getting confused. Because now I'm thinking my grades don't actually make my parents happy. They're always angry/mad/sad no matter what.

Don't cry.

I grip the pencil between my fingers. I'd like to snap it in half.

"I'm the kind of girl who just wants you to say I did a good job on this stupid packet and let me go be by myself. That's the kind of girl I am," I say.

"Then you did a good job on this sheet, Bella. You can go."

I stand up.

"Dammit," Billy says. "I'm always the last one to finish a test."

Fran laughs. "Again, not a test, Billy. Not a test."

We spend the afternoon napping. Or rather, Brandy naps. I just stay in my bunk staring at the bottom of the mattress above me and feeling the soreness of the run with Chuck in my legs. Holly still isn't back. I'm very jittery. I can't tell if I'm bored or if I'm anxious. I get up and look through Laurel's suitcase. I didn't bother to put my clothes in the dresser by my bunk since we're supposed to go to Gen tomorrow anyway.

I flip through the things my mother packed again. My favorite gray wool cardigan from Tucson Thrift. A swimsuit. Flip-flops. Mittens. A wool hat.

I take off my hoodie and put the cardigan on.

I paw through the rest of my things. A Cormac McCarthy paperback. That one I asked her to buy me after watching this guy talk about it for four hours on YouTube but I've never been able to finish it. It's complicated and I kept getting distracted. The copy of *Wild.* My fuzzy slippers. And an embroidered black velvet pouch.

I unzip the pouch, curious.

Inside are photographs.

Ricci, her face pink with sunburn, smiling madly in the hot tub at Agnes's farm.

And Laurel and me, playing Scrabble at her kitchen table, our faces creased in concentration, her hair a long black and white braid down her back, her fingers heavy with the silver rings she liked to wear. She was wearing a tie-dyed T-shirt that Kurt Cobain made for her after she photographed him for *Rolling Stone.*

There I am across from her, squinting at the board, dressed in my flannel and jeans. Was this last year? The year before? I can't remember. My mother took the picture, one of the few times she came to Laurel's when I was there.

I press the photo to my good cheek.

Then I slide the photograph back into the velvet pouch, my body swelling with grief. I relatch Laurel's suitcase, walk out of our room, and keep walking until I reach the end of the hall, and then I turn around and go all the way down to the other end.

And then I do it again, and again, each time passing the person who sits at the desk, watching me curiously as I walk faster and faster. Eventually, she just puts some music on her laptop, something that sounds Broadway show tune–ish, and honestly I don't care. I just want to walk and walk until I can't feel anything anymore, and the sound of someone singing about seventy-six trombones is just fine with me. I'm a walking cartoon, a bobblehead doll, a mess of bruises and sore legs and failure.

After dinner, they let us watch television. Billy chooses some crime show. Brandy picks at the polish on her toes, complaining that she's bored. I try to focus on the show, but all I can think about is that worksheet and Fran's question about if good grades make me happy. Well, it's stressful to work for them and to worry about deadlines and doing things right and presentations and all that, but I wouldn't say I ever feel particularly accomplished when I'm done. I liked my tree, because that wasn't like checking off a box or filling in a blank or remembering a specific historical term or something, but then that got ruined because Ms. Green said I wasn't in it.

Billy changes the channel to a house show. People are complaining about countertops and kitchen cabinets and how they want two sinks and not just one in the bathroom.

Brandy perks up. "Oh, I love these shows. It's like the pinnacle of selfishness. Have you ever noticed how if they have kids, they're extremely concerned with making sure there are rooms *only* for the kids? And their toys? 'We need this third floor so Timmy can keep his toys here because I'm sick of stepping on them.' These people should not have children. They do not understand childhood at all."

"Shit, I would have died to have my own toy room," Billy says. "My dad was always kicking all my toys around when he got mad."

"Why didn't you just keep them in your room?" Brandy asks.

"I didn't have a room," Billy says. "My brother and I slept on the pullout in the front room. My dad had the bedroom."

His voice is tight.

He switches the channel.

"Gumball," he says, relieved. "This is better. Much better."

"Is that a talking cigarette in an elementary school?" Brandy asks. "What in the fresh hell?"

I can't believe I'm going to spend thirty days with these people, and with a bunch of other kids soon. I wonder what Ricci's doing. What my mom told her. How much she told her.

What is Amber thinking right now? Did Kristen and Lemon get in trouble? That video. I hug myself tightly, leaning away from Brandy on the couch, close to the armrest.

How many people have seen it? It's probably everywhere by now. School. I won't be there. I'm going to miss so much work. Am I going to have to repeat fall semester? What's going to happen to my grades? What are people saying about me? I was supposed to work at Patty's this past weekend. I'm going to have so much homework to make up when I get back. Am I going to have to go to summer school? When I go back to school, who will even talk to me? Amber cut me off. I'm not talking to Kristen and Lemon ever again, and Cherie was mad at me. I'll have no one. Why am I having these thoughts again, I've already had them, why won't they just get out my head—

My mind is spinning. I'll probably lose my job at Patty's and then I can't go on the trip with Amber but Amber won't want to go now anyway—

I can't breathe and I am breathing too fast, all at once.

I'm not going to have anything or anyone when I get out of here.

Jesus, I just want a drink. Something, anything, to make this go away.

My heart: *thumpthumpthumpthumpthump.*

"Hey, dude, what's going on?" Billy says. "You okay?"

I'm pounding on my chest, trying to keep my *thumpthump-thumpthump* heart inside my body.

"Shit," Brandy says. She jumps off the couch and runs out of the room.

I miss Ricci. What if Ricci had been the one to find me? That would have killed her, seeing me bloody on the front stoop. Like, she'd remember that forever. *Once, my sister got so drunk she broke her cheek open on the front stoop of my house.* Who's taking care of her? My mom has no idea which cat videos work the best for calming her down (it's the YouTube account with the tuxedo cat named, inexplicably, Justin Bieber); she doesn't know it has to be three Oreos, not two, not one, not four, and how to say good night to the tree frog and mist the tree frog and arrange the Minecraft figurines just so and tap the goldfish tank—

How many people have seen my boob? How far did that go? I'll have to see all of them again someday at school and somebody will probably write something about me on that one particular stall in that one particular bathroom and then what about the complete strangers, seeing me, drunk and pulling down my bra, laughing at me, reposting, reposting, endless, endless, endless, my tit forever out there, my eyes falling down my face, and I just wanted to feel better, you know, and my dad was so mad at Thanksgiving but who asked them to even get married in the *first* place and school was shit, and I just wanted to feel better and did Tracy say I had liver damage what does the liver *do* anyway what is its *function* can I fix that somehow is that how I'm going to die—

I need, right now, to not feel, but my way of not feeling has been taken away from me, which seems like the cruelest thing in the world.

Janet, the night person, is kneeling in front me. She takes my balled fists in her hands.

"Easy," she says. "Easy. Slow. Look at me."

Can't focus. Brain on fire.

She's massaging my hands. Kneading the bones.

"I want you to lie on the floor, okay, Bella? I think you're having a panic attack. Can you do what I do?"

She leads me off the couch and down to the concrete floor,

arranging my legs. "Get me that cushion," she says to Billy. I stick my hands inside my cardigan, twisting the fabric.

He hands her a couch cushion. She puts it under my feet so they're elevated. She lies down next to me, stretches her arms up behind her head, flat on the floor. "Mimic me," she says.

I untangle my hands from my cardigan and stretch them above my head.

Thumpthumpthumpthumpthump

"My heart's falling out," I gasp.

"No, it is absolutely not, and I tell you that as a medical professional," Janet says.

"Just give me something. Anything," I plead.

"I can't," she says softly.

"I'm going to die. I can't breathe."

"If you're talking, you're breathing, dude," Billy says. Above me, his face is worried.

"Billy, Brandy," Janet says. "We're all in this together. Get down."

They both lie on the floor.

"Breathe. In, out, in, out. Slow. You can do it, Bella."

I stare at the ceiling.

There are painted birds and coyotes and moons and stars up there. How do you do that, paint on a ceiling? Oh, yes, I remember from art class. A scaffold, like Michelangelo at the Sistine Chapel.

"Damn, that's a cool ceiling," Billy breathes.

"I didn't even notice that," Brandy says. "That's nice. What kinds of birds are those?'

"Wren, sparrow, roadrunner, quail," Janet says. "Say that for me, Bella."

Thumpthumpthump. I can't focus on what she's saying.

"Bella," Janet says. "Try."

My lips are dry, my voice hoarse. "Wren, sparrow, roadrunner, quail."

Thumpthump.

Wren, sparrow, roadrunner, quail.

Looking at the sparrow on the ceiling. Little thing. That's what I saw in the desert in the saguaro after the run with Chuck. A little sparrow cheeping at me. I think of its tiny sound. It wasn't lonely in the desert, like me. It had made a home in a sharp and pulpy place.

Thump.

Slower now, heart tired. Heart sleeping. Brain off.

Wren, sparrow, roadrunner, quail.

I don't know how long we stay on the floor, all of us, saying the names of those birds, maybe it's a few minutes, maybe an hour, but in time, I get so invested in the words, and in the ceiling story, that my body softens, and I can breathe, and then I am just tired, tired, tired.

DAY FOUR

WE ARE MOVING TO General.

Holly reappeared early this morning, after our Chuck run (and we remembered our water bottles this time), her eyes no longer glassy but with dark circles underneath. She clutched that black backpack to her chest. "They took my picture," she says. "That was weird. Is that going to happen every day?"

They took ours, too, right after the run. They didn't let us shower first. I leaned against the wall and didn't even bother pushing my hair away from my face. This was photo number three. I still haven't looked at them. I haven't looked at *myself.* Maybe if I never look at myself again, I'll just . . . disappear.

"It's a thing here," Billy says.

"Weird," she whispers. "Very weird."

"Why are you whispering?" Brandy snaps.

"I don't know," Holly says. She laughs nervously.

"Was it worth it?" I ask.

"Was what worth it?" Holly says.

"Swallowing . . . whatever it is you had," I say.

The smile she gives me is kind of scary, it's so calm and perfect.

"Yes," she says. "It was Oxy, and abso-fuckin'-lutely."

"Well, did you save some for me?" Billy asks.

Holly shakes her head. "No, sorry."

"Too bad," Billy says. "I'm starting to get really fucking bored here."

We're standing in the activity room, our suitcases and bags around us, waiting. Someone will come get us soon and move us in with all the other kids, and I'm starting to feel anxious. Not like last night, but anxious nonetheless.

"God, I'm starving," Billy says. "When are we going to eat?"

"In a little bit," Tracy says, coming up behind us, zipping her parka. "You ready? Big day."

"Whatever," Brandy says. "I'm ready to just *go.* Let's get this shitshow on the road."

Outside the Detox building, we walk along a dirt path by the goat and chicken pens. The goats bleat and nose around the fencing and the chickens scurry about. Other kids are in the pens in blue hoodies, tossing out hay with gloved hands, scattering feed from silver buckets.

"You'll be doing that soon," Tracy says. "We take care of each other here, including the animals."

"It smells like shit." Brandy slips a little on a muddy patch. Billy catches her arm.

"Because there *is* shit," Holly mutters behind me. "This is so weird."

Ricci would love this. Fresh air, animals. My heart aches a little, thinking about that. About her, and what she must be feeling right now.

For thirty days, she's an only child.

The General Population building is much bigger than the Detox building. Our room doesn't have bunk beds, like in Detox, but single beds. There are five and they're all neatly made, each one with a small bedside table and dresser. I notice that the bedside tables are fixed to the floor. Above the headboard of each bed, screwed to the wall, is a small light. On one side of the room, the cream-painted brick walls are bare, but on the other side, there are postcards and photos taped up. Someone has a lot of books under their bed; someone else has a fluffy black blanket, no blue wool like on the other beds.

"Just what I love," Brandy says sarcastically. "More communal living."

Tracy points to three beds on the left side of the room. "Those are yours. You can unpack later. Let's head to meal. Billy, you're across the hall. Find an open bed."

There's a meal room, like in the Detox building, but with really long tables with attached benches. It's like a small version of a school cafeteria. Brandy heads straight for a table and sits down.

"I'm famished," she says. "Where's the coffee?"

"In there," Tracy says, and motions to some double doors at the side of the room. I can hear movement and clanking behind the doors.

"Are you going to bring it out or what?" Brandy frowns.

"Nope," Tracy says.

"This is getting weird," Holly says.

"Can you please use another word besides *weird,*" Brandy says. "It's getting annoying."

"Sorry," Holly mumbles.

"If you want to eat here, or drink here, or have a clean plate and clean fork, or clean clothes, you do it yourself. We don't do it for you," Tracy tells us.

"The hell?" I say.

"Yup." Tracy starts toward the double doors. "Come on."

We follow her into a big kitchen. There are maybe fifteen kids inside cracking eggs, setting up yogurts on trays, standing at a grill flipping bacon.

A tall girl in an apron and latex gloves comes over to us. She's got tons of freckles on her face and red hair pulled back in a bun.

"Hey," she says. "I'm Lara. Kitchen manager. Newbies set the tables and do cleanup. When you've mastered that, you move to meal prep."

"Um, what?" Brandy says. "I did not sign up for this nonsense."

"The three rules of survival here: shelter, fire, and food." She sighs heavily. "Why doesn't anyone ever read the handbook?"

Shelter, fire, food. I don't remember that from the booklet, but then again, I skimmed it.

Also, *fire?*

Holly's the one who asks. "Uh, fire? What . . . does that mean, exactly?"

Lara grins. "You'll see. You'll learn to make one, kid. Fire happens later in the program. It's very exciting." She ticks the rules off on her fingers. "Keep yourself safe, keep yourself warm, keep yourself fed, and you'll live. We cook all our meals and we clean up after ourselves. If you don't help make the food, you don't get to eat the food. I would learn that right away. You can start by taking out the plates and utensils and then the drinks. Don't forget to count how many you need and give out, and how many come back. We need to make sure everything is accounted for."

"Wait," Holly says slowly. "So, like, we starve if we don't help?"

"Listen," Lara says. "Are you hungry?"

"Yes," Billy says.

"Well," Lara answers, "then you need to learn how to feed yourself. Because out there, in the world, maybe somebody will do it for you, but not forever. And what then?"

"I don't get it," Brandy says.

Lara smiles. "You will, trust me. You will. Wash your hands, grab some gloves, and get started."

We wash our hands in the sink and pull gloves from a box. I drag the gloves onto my hands. I'm not particularly happy about this, but I'm also hungry, so that's my priority. Brandy starts grabbing plates, swearing under her breath.

"Wait," I tell her.

"What?" She's impatient.

"Like, count everybody first, like Lara said, so you know how much stuff we need to take out."

She blows a strand of hair off her cheek and faces the kitchen, her lips moving slowly.

"Sixteen, plus us. Twenty, then. Wait, Tracy, too. Twenty-one."

"Holly," I say, because she's just standing there. "You do the silverware. Billy, you do the napkins. I'll do the cups and stuff."

I find a cart in a corner of the kitchen and start loading it with plastic coffee cups and plastic glasses. There are coffee urns and pitchers filled with orange juice, so I add those, too. They're heavy and I almost drop one.

We get everything set up on the tables in the other room, and gradually, kids from the kitchen start coming out with bowls of eggs and tofu and bacon, platters of sliced fruit, trays of yogurt and cereal and cartons of milk.

They arrange the food on the tables and begin sitting down.

It's like a Thanksgiving with total strangers. Only I guess all of us would rather be high or drunk or anywhere but here.

"Okay," Lara says, coming out of the kitchen. "Eat."

She waves me to a table and I scoot myself in. She slides next to me on the bench. Kids start passing trays and bowls from person to person. I scoop out eggs and fruit.

"Everyone, say hi to our newbies," Lara says. "I'll start. I'm Lara and I'm the queen, because I've been here the longest and I'm getting out the soonest. Well, second soonest. Sarah's tomorrow."

She points to the person on her right.

One by one, everyone says their names. Marshall, Gideon, Sarah, Nick, Josh, Charlotte, and they keep going. It's a blur. I don't think I'm going to be able to remember them all. I kind of wish they'd all say their name followed by what they're here for, because *that* would be interesting. Like, *I'm Larry, cokehead. I'm Molly, and I like molly.*

The girl named Gideon says, "Hey, roomies."

She winks.

Her head is shaved. She's the one who was laughing at me when I did that first run with Chuck. I look away from her.

There's a silence. Lara nudges me.

It's my turn. I say my name in a low voice.

"Don't be shy," she says. "Is it your face? No one cares. Shyness and shame will eat you alive. Nick!"

A kid with long braids looks up, mouth full. "What?"

"Do you think Bella's face is funny?"

"Aw, no." He smiles at me, breaking a piece of toast in half.

"Charlotte, what about you?"

The girl with pink hair nods. She's the one who was flipping off Tracy in the Polaroid in the activity room. "Yeah, I actually do. Sorry. I mean, the shit that happens to us, right? It looks painful, though. I hope she's okay." She pauses. "Once, I was so high I let a guy tattoo *booty* on my . . . actual booty. Wanna see?"

She stands up.

"Yes," Billy says immediately.

Charlotte puts a hand on the waistband of her leggings.

"Charlotte," Tracy warns.

"Fine." Charlotte holds up her hands and sits back down. "It is what it is. At least I didn't let him tattoo *face* on my face, you know?"

"I actually know someone who did that," Nick says.

Laughter.

"Everybody has a story, right?" Lara asks the table, and everyone nods.

Lara looks at me.

"Own it," she says softly. "And move on from there. There's really no other option at this point."

Brandy stares at the pile of dirty dishes. "I have never washed a dish in my life," she says, holding up her hands. "I'm not about to start now."

"How can you get through life without washing a dish?" I ask, filling the sink with water.

"Duh," she says. "We have a *maid.* Her name is Mary and it's her job and we pay her."

"I don't think there are any of those here," Holly says. "Maids. I think we're the maids."

She's dumping the coffee urns into an empty pickle bucket

that says *for the garden* in Sharpie on the side. She barely ate at breakfast, even though she said she was hungry. A slice of melon here, a bite of toast there.

Billy looks around the kitchen at all the pots and pans and the butcher table littered with eggshells and fruit rinds. "Do we have to clean all of this?"

Lara comes out of a back room holding a sack of flour.

"Yup," she says, hoisting it onto a metal rack. "Breakfast, lunch, and dinner. Next week you can move up to cooking. Then you learn the animals. But don't ever try to be the one who helps the feed dude with the animal food. That's Charlotte. She's very particular about it. Until then, chop-chop. You've got gym after this."

"Gym? I don't even want to know," Brandy mutters. "Just kill me now."

She drags on some rubber gloves and starts plunking silverware in the sink full of soapy water.

"Did you count the utensils and stuff to compare what we put out?" I ask.

"What?"

"Like Lara said," I tell her. "To make sure everything comes back."

"Why does it even matter?" Brandy asks.

From across the room, Lara calls out, "Because. Sometimes . . . people take them. And use them. Do you want me to elaborate?"

I shake my head no.

Because no, I do *not*.

* * *

We have to change for gym. Lara said our parents were told to pack certain stuff for us, like workout clothes, T-shirts, sneakers, swimsuits, hiking boots. I think my mother forgot my hiking boots. Maybe I don't even have hiking boots. I am not a hikey-type person. Maybe that's why I couldn't finish *Wild.*

"Oh, right," Lara says. "Tampons. Pads. Whatever you use. If you don't already know, you have to ask for them from Tracy or one of the shift desk people. If you had them with you when you came, they were confiscated during Search."

"Right," Brandy says. "Because I'm going to somehow put drugs in my tampons. Got it."

Lara laughs. "You know why they give you that awful hard hairbrush when you get here? Because some are super flexible, you know? Like, you can even peel out the part with the bristles really easily and there's space inside? That's where I used to hide my stash when I lived at home. *That's* why you can't bring hairbrushes in. You can put stuff in tampons, believe me, and seal that back up."

That seems like a lot of work to me, but then again, I had my Sprodka bottle to hide vodka in.

The five of us sharing a room are me, Brandy, Holly, Charlotte and Gideon. Everybody gets dressed pretty quietly, turning our backs to each other or changing in the dorm-style bathroom down the hall. There are toilet stalls and shower stalls in there and a long row of sinks. On each of our dressers is a little basket to carry our toiletries to and from the bathroom.

"It gets easier," Charlotte tells us, tying her pink hair into pigtails. "It's not so bad. I mean, it sucks, but it could be worse. At night, you're so tired you basically fall right to sleep."

"Whatever," Brandy says, pulling on some yoga pants. "I didn't come here to wash dishes and feed shitty goats."

Charlotte and Gideon look at each other, but I can't tell what they're thinking. That look Charlotte and Gideon gave each other . . . Are they the mean type?

On the way to gym, Holly whispers to me, "I don't feel so well."

"Are you sick?" I ask her.

"No, I just, like, I need to . . . you know."

Charlotte glances back at us. "Are you still in withdrawal? Sometimes that can last longer than just a few days. You shouldn't be out of Detox if you aren't ready."

"No," Holly says. "I just . . . I'm thinking about it all the time. Getting nervous, you know? Itchy."

She's rubbing her hands together in an anxious way.

Gideon falls back and walks with us. "I get it. I remember. Gym will help. Work some stuff out of you. They keep you pretty busy here, so it's kind of like, every task we do? Takes the place of using, you know? I think when we leave, we're supposed to do that."

"You want me to just go for a run if I want a drink?" Brandy says, pulling her long hair back. "Do some push-ups?"

"Yeah," Charlotte says, chuckling. "Exactly that. Get ripped while you get clean."

"Is that what *you're* going to do when you get out and you want to get wasted? Exercise?" Brandy asks her.

Charlotte laughs loudly. "Fuck no. I'm gonna get high as a kite and rob my biology teacher's house and then set fire to my rich-ass-bitch dad's Benz. That's the first thing I'm gonna do."

She gives us the thumbs-up and then saunters ahead of us.

Brandy looks at me. "Do you think she's joking?"

"That was kind of specific to be a joke," I say.

Charlotte stops in front of a brick building and looks back at us, waving. She pushes open the double doors.

We walk into a giant gym. Weight machines, rowing machines, mats, a thick rope that goes all the way to the ceiling, and a huge climbing wall. It looks like whatever they didn't spend money on in the other buildings, they spent here. Everything is gleaming and shiny.

Phil, the guy who was in the van with us and took our phones, comes over and checks us off on a clipboard. Charlotte and Gideon head over to the climbing wall. Chuck is standing there, watching some kids inch their way up the wall.

My stomach curdles. I am definitely not doing *that*.

"Newbies," Phil says, "welcome to workout. One thing that's going to help you in recovery is getting stronger not only inside but outside. Exercise is a way to create positive energy and release dopamine naturally. When we use, we release giant amounts of dopamine in our brains, giving us tremendous pleasure. That's one of the reasons we like being high and drunk. It makes us feel gooooood, right?"

"Hell yes," says Billy.

Phil gestures to the large and airy gym. "I want you to learn how to create that feeling of pleasure without damaging your baby brain and baby bodies. I want to retrain your brain. You're used to getting your pleasure artificially, so I'm going to teach you how to begin to rewire your impulses."

"I'm not good at PE," Holly whines.

"Um, my face," I say. "I'd really like to not mess it up any further."

"There is no good or bad here," Phil tells me and Holly.

"There is only trying. That's all I ask, is that you try. Can you do that?"

Holly shrugs.

"And you," he says, turning to me. "You've been medically cleared, or you wouldn't have been able to run with Chuck. But I got you. Don't worry."

He walks us over to a series of balls. They look like they're made out of thick leather. The biggest ones are about as tall as my knees.

"I want you to move those balls," he says. "Over there. Use your knees, you don't want to hurt your back."

He points to the end of the mat.

"Whatever, it's just a freaking ball," Brandy says, bending down. She tries to lift one, but groans and stands back up.

"This thing is like fifty freaking pounds!" she says, rubbing the small of her back.

"Pick a smaller one to start," Phil says.

Brandy reminds me of a very cranky old person on a TV sitcom. Complaining about everything. Worried about her nails. I kind of like it.

Phil sits cross-legged on the floor.

"Brandy, how heavy is your addiction?"

"What?" she says. She looks pissed.

"Everything that you carry around on a daily basis. You're a drinker, right? Thinking about how to get a drink, how many drinks to have, how many lies to tell so you can take that drink, how many lies to cover it up. That's a pretty heavy load to carry every day, but you've been doing it. If you can carry that, you can carry this ball."

"I'm not an alcoholic," Brandy says. "I'm not addicted. I can stop any time I want."

"Are you sure about that?" Phil asks.

"Yes," Brandy says. "Yes, I am positive."

Holly starts to fidget. She's tearing up. "I don't like this. I don't."

She's scratching her wrists.

"Me neither," Phil says. "But the fact that you're crying right now tells me you've got a big weight inside and you need to release it. I'm showing you a healthy way to do that."

He looks at me.

My brain says: *Move the ball. You'll get points.*

I look at the balls.

"What kind of kid are you?" Fran asked me, and I told her, "I'm the kind of kid who wants you to tell me I got a good grade so I can go."

If nobody else is going to start, I will. I bend my knees, put my hands on the sides of one of the midsize balls. Take a breath.

Jesusgodchristohmygodohnothisthingissofreakingheavybut Imnotgoingtoletthemseemefail.

I heave the ball up, stagger back, catch myself.

"Focus," Phil says softly. "You can do this."

I take a step, then another, grunting. Another step, another.

It is so, so heavy. Sweat is starting to drip down my temples. This might be worse than running with Chuck.

My stomach is starting to clench. My elbows are trembling.

One step, another.

I stop. My knees are starting to buckle.

Phil is next to me, now, talking low, near my ear.

"You were willing to lie, cheat, hide, and steal to drink," he says. His voice sounds far away.

"Well," I grunt. "You're wrong. I never cheated. I didn't steal, not really. I paid for my alcohol or I drank my grandmother's. So there."

"You've got to be pretty strong, somewhere deep down, to be willing to do all that just for a drink. If you can do that, you can carry this damn ball."

"I'm just carrying this ball because you told me to do it and I do what I'm told, *Phil,*" I say. The ball is getting heavier by the minute. I feel like my whole body is going to crack in half.

"That's so interesting, Bella. Was drinking the only thing you could do that wasn't preordained for you? Is that why you did it? Your little 'fuck you' to the world? You too afraid to tell anybody you're freaking out inside?"

My breath comes in waves. I think I would tell him to go to hell, but forming the words would make me pass out at this point.

One step, another. One step, another. One breath, another. My arms are burning.

I will not let my knees buckle. I will not fall down. I will not let go of the ball.

My mind loosens in a weird way. A litany of complaints bubbles up in my brain.

God, I hate Dylan. Why did he have to love me and then spit me out? Why does my dad have to be so angry all the time? Why did I lift up my shirt? Why can't I just be normal? Why can't I—

The ball slips out of my hands and almost drops on my sneakers, and I jump out of the way.

But I made it to the end of the mat. Almost.

My arms are going crazy, shaking like branches in the wind. My heart is thundering.

Phil claps me on the back. "How do you feel?"

"Like I'm going to die. Like I deserve a drink, to be honest. Like I hate it here, really."

He laughs. "Expected. But you have to learn to reward yourself for the difficult stuff without taking a drink, you know?"

"I think I'd prefer the drink."

"Gotcha."

"And I think I hate my ex-boyfriend."

"That works, too."

"Can I be done now?"

"Nope. Now you have to pick it up and take it back. And then you have to support your friends."

I turn around. Holly is bending down, her face red, trying to pick up a very small ball, her hands slipping off the leather. Brandy is pushing hers very slowly down the mat, like Sisyphus with a ponytail.

"Okay," I say. "Okay."

I take a deep breath, shake out my arms, bend down, and pick up the freaking ball, one more time.

I just want to go home.

Beanbags. Like at Ricci's school, in her time-out room.

They're brightly colored and scattered all around. Brandy sinks into one. "I'm not going to make it. Hauling balls, making food, cleaning. I'm not going to last. I'm literally going to die. This is the worst place I've ever rehabbed. The last place we got to keep our phones and I could make TikToks in the bathroom. They got a lot of views. I have no idea what's happening in the world without my phone."

Kids are filing into the room, plopping down onto bags. I find a yellow one by Charlotte and Holly. I like Holly. She's interesting and sad. She reminds me of Dawn.

Fran is in her own beanbag, hands folded in her lap. She waits until everyone is comfortable.

"Just to go over the format, for our newbies," she says. "What do we do in group?"

Charlotte raises her hand. "It's a safe space to talk and work out problems."

She kind of singsongs it.

"What *don't* we do?" Frans asks.

Lara says, "Talk over other people, invalidate their emotions and experiences."

I feel like I'm learning a whole new language in this place. *Invalidate. Safe space.*

"Do we *have* to share?" Fran asks.

Some kid, I can't remember his name from breakfast, says, "No, but if you keep stuff bottled up, it's not going to help with your recovery."

I wonder how many of these kids are just repeating what they know they should say, just to get on with this and get out of here, and how many really believe it. I'm pretty sure Charlotte is just playing a game. No one can be this perfect. But I guess I'll try to get out of here in one piece and get home, and once I do that, I know I can do better. I messed up, but I can make sure that doesn't happen again. I just have to be more careful.

I'm not sure I'm like everyone else here. Like Holly, shoving things up herself and then swallowing half of them in one go.

"Right," Fran says. "Because one thing I think we all had in common, out there in the so-called real world, is that sometimes we never told anyone how we were really feeling, if we were struggling. If we needed help. With even the little stuff, like schoolwork."

"Homework isn't little, it's enormous," Nick-with-the-braids says. "It's, like, everything to my parents."

"Being healthy is more important than a grade," Fran says. "Don't you think?"

"Try telling that to my dad," Lara says, shaking her head. "He never even finished high school. I'm his second chance."

Fran nods. "Sometimes the expectations of our parents are overwhelming, it's true. Trying to live up to what they want."

She looks around the room. "Who are our newcomers? Introduce yourselves, with as little or as much as you want."

Silence, then Billy, on a purple beanbag, sighs really loudly. "I'm Billy and I drink and take pills. Is that good?"

"Perfect," Fran says.

I fold my arms across my chest. I can feel my heart starting to *thumpthumpthumpthump* at having to speak in front of so many people.

Beside me, Holly clears her throat. "I'm Holly. I'm here because . . . I do a lot of stuff."

On cue, all the kids say, in unison, "Like what, Holly?"

Holly looks taken aback. "Um, you know. Oxy. Pain pills. Pot. You know, whatever is around. I don't really drink, though."

Silence.

"Fine," Brandy says. "I'm Brandy. I drink and I like it. I don't think it's a big deal. Everybody drinks. How can you not? It's everywhere. My mom has, like, a bottle of wine before dinner. You can't get away from it."

Gideon nods, shaved head gleaming under the ceiling light. "That's true. Parents will buy it for you, for a party."

"They will drink *with* you," Marshall says.

People are nodding.

Somebody else says, "There was a kid in my eighth grade who was taller than everybody else, wore glasses, and was already growing a beard and nobody ever carded him at the store. Bro was popular, I'll tell you that. He made mad bank on the side."

Laughter.

"When I was ten, at our family Christmas party, my dad let me drink beer," Nick says. "Everybody thought it was funny, this little kid staggering around." He pauses. "That wasn't right, what my dad did. I'm pretty mad about it now, when I think about it. I didn't even know what beer was, I thought maybe it was like soda, but it made me feel funny in a good way, like more relaxed, and I liked it. A lot. I mean, before I threw up all over the sofa."

I think about my grandmother. Our little drinks over Scrabble in the beginning.

Just a taste.

I was keeping her company. She would never *hurt* me. And sometimes if she had too much, or started seeming too tired, I put her to bed. We took care of each other. Is that so bad?

"And after that, I just wanted more," Nick says. "Isn't that weird? My family isn't the greatest, we have a lot of problems, so I started sneaking beer every now and then, just to, like, cut the edge. And when I got older, it was still there. Parties. Somebody's house. Asking someone to buy for you outside the store."

I look up from my lap. That was me. Shoulder-tapping with Amber and Cherie and Kristen.

"My mom used to put spoonfuls of Bacardi in my milk to make me go to sleep when I was little," Charlotte says, picking at the edge of her orange beanbag. She has thick eyebrows and dark roots that fan off into her pink hair. "She had to work night shifts and couldn't get babysitters for me, so she had to make sure I was out. The first time I had a glass of real milk, I spit it out. It didn't taste right!"

I think of my grandmother again and get kind of uncomfortable. I don't want to have to talk about her here. I feel like that would be a betrayal somehow.

"Bella?" Fran says.

Thumpthumpthumpthump

"Bella," says a kid on a white bag way off in the corner. "Hey, Bella, where's Edward?"

He's got brown hair down to his shoulders, like Dylan, and deep blue eyes.

Those eyes are fixed on me. I think I remember him from breakfast.

Josh.

Something in me shifts in a warm way.

My brain says: *Oh, for the love of god, really? Really?*

My heart says: *Sigh.*

My god, I'm going to have to look at alternate-Dylan for the next twenty-six days, and that thought makes me so mad I forget about my racing heart, and before I can stop myself, I blurt out, "Oh, that's so funny. Like I haven't heard that approximately six million times in my life. What an original thinker you are."

The kid just smirks at me.

"I was always Team Jacob myself, Josh," Charlotte says.

I make a mental note to make myself hate Josh for the next twenty-six days, even though his eyes are a perfect shade of blue. He's still looking at me.

I can feel a furious blush creeping over my face, but then I realize . . . oh, right. He's probably only looking at me that way because half of my face is purple and blue. Superb. Way to go, Bella. *Pathetic.*

I shift my eyes from his. That's the last thing I need right now. A stupid crush. Another person to eventually tell me I'm not good enough. Fuck that.

"Those movies were *good,*" Brandy says.

"*I* would like to sparkle," Billy says. "No lie. Chicks dig it."

"Okay, okay," Fran says. "Back to Bella. Do you have anything to add?"

People looking at me.

Thumpthumpthumpthumpthump.

People waiting for me to talk, to make a mistake.

And then I remember. The birds on the ceiling in the activity room.

Wren, sparrow, roadrunner, quail.

I say it three times in my head before I feel safe enough to speak.

"No, just . . . I'm Bella, and I'm here because of . . . drinking. Whatever. That's it. That's what you want to hear, so there you go. It's not a big deal."

"We want to hear whatever you want to tell us, Bella," Fran says slowly. "It's a safe space."

"I don't really like talking in front of big groups," I say tentatively.

"Then you came to the wrong rehab, girl, because this place is all about sharing." Charlotte laughs. "It's a veritable buffet of emotional vomit."

"It isn't about what we want to hear, Bella," Fran says. "It's about you learning to say things that maybe you've kept inside? Things that might be feeding your drinking problem."

"I don't have a problem," I say. "Things just got out of hand all of a sudden. That's all." My voice is prickly.

"I'd say that Bella isn't ready to talk yet," Gideon says quietly, her fingers thrumming the side of her pink beanbag. "Which is fine. And we should move on."

I look at her and smile gratefully. She shrugs.

"Okay," Fran says. "Well, Sarah is leaving us tomorrow and she's going to talk about how she's feeling about that. Are you ready, Sarah?"

A girl on a red beanbag nods and stands up. She pushes her blond hair away from her face; there are a lot of empty holes up and down her earlobes. She looks nervous, pawing at the hem of her faded Mac Miller T-shirt.

"Well," she says. "I'm worried. I'm scared. What's school going to be like? Do I have any friends left? Do I have any friends who *don't* use? How am I supposed to find new friends? Also, I kind of despise my parents, so . . . that's going to be an issue, for sure."

She talks, and everyone listens, or seems to, except me. I'm still keeping my face down because that kid Josh is still looking at me.

My brain says: *Do not.*

My heart says: *This is going to be tough.*

"Ages," Gideon says into the dark room. "Everybody say how old you are. And how many times you've done this."

We are in our beds. Holly is rustling around in hers, agitated. I brushed my teeth and peed and got ready for bed next to about a bajillion other girls in the long, brightly lit bathroom. Gideon smashed a roach with her slide. Brandy squealed.

"Seventeen, almost eighteen and freeee," Charlotte singsongs. "Three."

"Seventeen," Gideon says. "Two. The first time I was sixteen. I got better at it after that, but I slipped up this last time."

From beneath her blanket, Holly mumbles, "Sixteen and can you please all be quiet."

"No," Gideon says. "Put your pillow over your head. Don't be a drag."

"Fine," Holly says under the blanket. "First time. But I did grippy sock by accident. Does that count?"

"How on earth do you get sent to the nutbin on *accident*?" Gideon leans up on one elbow.

From her bed, Holly's voice is hoarse. "I went a little too far . . . with something."

There's a silence.

"You a cutter?" Charlotte says finally, her voice curious.

"Sometimes?"

"You either are or you aren't," Charlotte presses. "Let me see."

She gets out of bed and starts walking toward Holly's bed.

"No," Holly whimpers.

"Let her alone, Char, get back into bed. Jesus, you're so invasive." Gideon's voice is firm.

Charlotte turns around and pads back to her bed, stuffs herself under her blanket.

I'm processing them. Charlotte is the instigator; I'll have to be careful. Gideon seems like the leader. She's the one with all the books under her bed. Charlotte listened to her, so obviously she respects her.

A loud snore snakes up from Brandy's bed.

"Looks like it's your turn, then, Bella," Gideon says.

"Fifteen," I say, staring at the ceiling. Why aren't wren, sparrow, roadrunner, quail here, too? There should be paintings on all the ceilings. All the rooms should have bird Sistine Chapels in this place. "First time."

"Oh my god, you're a *baby,*" Charlotte exclaims. "Innocent, unsullied, and somewhat pure."

"She's not the youngest ever, though," Gideon says, lying back down and crossing her arms behind her head. "Phil told me they had a twelve-year-old once. But he got kicked out."

"What for?" I ask.

Gideon's voice is sleepy now. "He kicked a goat. They tell you you can't do a lot of stuff here to frighten you so you stay in line. I've seen some stuff. But the one thing you truly cannot do is hurt the animals."

Charlotte giggles. "Or fuck in the bathrooms."

Gideon snorts. "Right. Emmanuel and Shelly. That was a trip."

"They're still together, you know," Charlotte says. "She texted me. She goes to St. Gregory and he's at Marana, but they make it work. True love, born from addiction, pain, and fucking on a sink top."

"Well," I say. "I don't think I'll be doing *that.*"

Gideon and Charlotte snicker.

"You never know," Gideon says. "I met my first girlfriend at my last place."

Charlotte makes a sound like she's eating a piece of delicious candy.

Gideon shifts in her bed, her voice becoming muffled. "But

one thing you never do here is tell. If you see something, don't say something. Walk away. Vault it."

I roll over onto my side. Charlotte is on her side, too, facing me, her eyes bright. She's still in her pigtails from gym.

"That's right," she whispers. "Never snitch."

DAY FIVE

WHEN THE BANGING ON the door happens, it's still gray outside our dorm window. I blearily look around. Gideon is already up, lacing her sneakers. Charlotte rubs her eyes.

"God, I hate that guy," Charlotte says. "He's like a combination of every awful jock and PE teacher at my old school. All testosterone and slogans." She swings her legs over the side of her bed and reaches under it for her running clothes and water bottle. "Just give us a freaking minute, you monster!" she yells at the door. The banging stops, then starts up again somewhere down the hall.

I get up and shake Brandy awake.

"Oh, good lord, no, not again. I was hoping it was all a bad dream," she moans.

Gideon stands up, stretching, cracking her neck.

"Welcome," she says, "to your first real day of hell."

There are ten of us, running through the cold desert as the sun rises, panting and swearing. Holly stayed behind. We tried to get her up, but Gideon waved us off, saying she needs the rest, even if she gets a demerit. "Some things you can't push through," she said. "You just have to let them happen. I don't think she should have left Detox yet."

I'm at the end of the group with Brandy and Charlotte.

"This sucks so bad," Brandy pants.

"Indeed," Charlotte answers. "But this is how it is, every day. Run, eat, feed the animals, rest, eat, do all your therapy, go to gym, shower, eat, then fuck off the rest of the time. It's better when you get your phone back, at least. Something to do."

"How long have you been here?" I ask.

"Too many days to count," Charlotte answers lightly, twisting her head around to look at me. "I had a little snag and got some days added, but I'm pushing through."

" 'A little snag'?" Brandy says. "Like what?"

"Oh, you know. Some of this, some of that. But listen, if I can keep it together and not go psycho, I'm out, and I'm gonna wreck shit up, I tell you what."

" 'Go psycho'?" I say, coughing a little. My lungs are starting to hurt and there's sweat in my eyes. I stop, bend over, and clutch my knees.

Charlotte runs in place while Brandy lumbers ahead.

"It happens. I haven't seen it too bad yet, but someone told me Gideon did once. Flip out, I mean. Like, just snapped in half like a branch. Then you have to go to Seg until you can calm your shit down. She didn't really want to talk about it, but if it's bad enough, it adds to your days."

"Seg?" I ask.

Charlotte jumps up and down for minute. "Segregation. Like a time-out, only it can last a really long time and you're stuck in a room with nothing and no one."

She stops jumping and runs ahead of me.

I am dead last. I am so far behind that Chuck and the kids who were in the front are starting to pass me on their way back.

"Turn around at the red boulder," Chuck calls out, thundering by me.

I swear at him inside my head. All the kids behind him are splotchy-faced and intent, concentrating on not falling on stones or rocks, which is me right now, because the direction we're going in today has us going up a slight hill.

I'm chugging along, just fast enough that I can still see Brandy, Gideon, and Charlotte up ahead. I'm not completely alone yet.

I look up from watching the ground at the sound of my name.

"Hey, Bella, hey, Bella, hey."

Smooth and silky. Smiling. That guy, Josh.

He turns from the kids he was with and starts running by my side.

"You want company? I can do another round," he says. "Ah, nature. Don't you just love it?"

"No," I say. "No, I do not, and no, I don't need your company. You can go back. I'm fine."

My heart is beating a little too fast, and it's not just from this run.

"You still mad about the Edward comment?"

"I don't even remember it," I lie, picking up my speed a little, even though it hurts. "I don't even remember your name, frankly."

"Josh," he says. "It's Josh."

"Good for you, *Josh.*"

"I'll stay with you. It's cool. Isn't that what they want here? For us to stick together?"

"Whatever," I say. We're almost at the red boulder Chuck

mentioned. Gideon zips past us, Charlotte and Brandy behind her. Brandy looks at me and Josh and rolls her eyes.

I sit down on the boulder. "I have to rest for a second," I tell Josh.

"Cool." He sits on the ground a little away from me and brushes his damp hair out of his eyes.

We're quiet for a bit. Then he asks me what school I go to, and when I tell him, he says, "Damn, that's a big one."

"Three thousand kids," I say.

"I wish I had that," he says. "My school's pretty small. Hard to hide, you know?"

I'm staring at the ground, at a cluster of darkling beetles. I can feel his eyes on me. I drink a few sips from my water bottle.

"Can you not do that?" I ask finally. "Like, look at me for so long? I know it's funny, my face and all, but it hurts, and I'm kind of embarrassed about it, okay?"

"I wasn't . . ." He falters. "I wasn't looking at that. I mean, that *part* of your face. I wasn't . . . making fun of you."

I keep my eyes on the ground. If he wasn't looking at the bad part of my face, then he was looking at the okay part. The flutter that happens in my chest is swift and hot.

I glance up at him.

Our eyes meet.

"It's not even that bad," he says quietly. "I mean, I've seen a lot worse."

"Really?" I say. "Like how? How could you have seen worse?"

He looks away from me, into the distance. "I have some experience with it, is all. Busted faces." He abruptly stands. "We should go. I'm starving, aren't you?"

I get up and we start running together. We're quiet except for the sound of our breath. He keeps pace with me, which he doesn't have to do, and which is kind of nice.

I can't stop thinking, though, about what he meant by "busted faces."

Tracy's office is a lot nicer and cleaner than the rest of Sonoran Sunrise. She has tons of potted plants and tiny pincushion cacti in painted pots on her shelves, along with a lot of books: *The Language of Letting Go; Breaking the Chains of Addiction; Refuge Recovery; The Courage to Heal.* There aren't any beanbags in here, though, like the group room. Just some comfortable-looking easy chairs. There's a large window behind her desk, the desert stretching out beyond it.

"So," she says, settling into her chair. "Tell me how it's going. How do you feel?"

"It's okay," I mumble.

"Pretty good, pretty bad, horrible, awful, scary?"

"I guess all of that."

"These sessions," she says. "They're for you. Whatever you want to talk about. I'm a sounding board."

I nod. "Okay. Sure."

She's quiet for a minute; then she says, "I heard you had a moment the other day. You got very anxious. With Billy and Brandy. Janet helped you."

"Yeah."

"It sounds like you had an anxiety attack. Do you know what that is?"

"I think so. I guess so? I don't know." I start picking at my cuticles.

"Some people have a very physical response to certain stressors," she says. "Maybe we're worried about something, or many things, and it can build up before we know it. Shaking, crying, can't breathe, fast heartbeat. Has this happened to you before?"

"Yes," I say, thinking about what happened in art class. But I'm not going to tell her that. She knows about what happened in the class where I yelled at the teacher and hit the desk, but not about the presentation. I don't think, anyway.

I will give some information, but not everything. Just enough, like Charlotte said.

"A lot?"

I avoid her eyes. "Maybe. I guess."

"For how long?"

I shake my head. "I don't know. I really couldn't say."

I pick harder at my nails. Even though I didn't exactly answer her question, something's pushing at my brain, some memory, maybe more than one, of other times. I grit my teeth to make it stop. Bite my lip.

"Have your parents ever noticed your anxiety?" Tracy asks. She gets up and goes to a mini-fridge under the window and takes out a bottle of water. She sits back down and hands it to me. I don't open it, though. I just wrap my hands around it. The coolness feels soothing in my palms. I feel a little calmer.

"Bella?"

"What?"

"You didn't answer my question."

"I'm sorry, what did you ask, again?"

"Have your parents ever noticed your anxiety?"

"I don't know," I answer slowly. "Maybe? They don't exactly get along, if you hadn't noticed."

"I did notice," she says softly. "That's hard on you, I can tell."

I shrug. "It is what it is. They aren't bad people. They just have a lot going on."

"Have you ever told them how anxious you get sometimes? Some parents need to be told when their child needs help."

I start ripping the paper from the plastic water bottle, the pieces falling onto my jeans. "No, not really. Like I said, they have a lot going on. I don't want to bother them."

"Mmm," she says.

"I don't know what that sound means," I say tentatively. "Is that a good sound or a bad sound?"

She laughs lightly. "It's a sound that means I wonder what it's like for you at home that you feel like a *bother* to your own parents. How that's been for you, growing up like that?"

I drop my eyes to the strips of white paper in my lap.

It feels like shit, that's what it feels like.

It's hard to insert yourself into the lives of two people whose sole reason for being seems to make each other as miserable as possible. Even when I got my first period three years ago, it became a *thing.* Some kind of contest, with my mom saying I should use pads because I wasn't ready for tampons and my dad saying I should use period panties because he'd done research online and that seemed to be the new thing and wow did my mother lose it at that and it wasn't even because she didn't like the idea of period panties. I know for a fact she'd looked them up, too, and it was totally her jam—environmentally responsible, comfortable, all that stuff. But she wasn't expecting him to have done that work on his own, without her. Like he was encroaching on her motherly duties. So she fought him just on principle. *Like you're going to wash them out every night, Dan. You never even help with the laundry!* In the end, I just went down the street to Laurel's and she hauled out a box of Tampax and showed me what was what in her crazy bathroom with the framed and autographed album covers she'd shot for Iggy Pop and the Cramps and PJ Harvey.

"Bella?"

I snap my head up. "I don't remember the question?"

"That's all right. I think I have my answer." Her eyes drop to my lap. I've ripped the label into a pile of tiny, tiny white bits.

DAY SIX

Hello—

At the end of our session yesterday Tracy told me I should think about writing letters to myself. I'm not sure how to address myself. Is that weird? Right now I'm sitting in the Gen Pop activity room. Brandy is playing Uno with Billy, and Gideon and Nick are building Legos and arguing over something. I don't know where Charlotte is. She seems to disappear a lot. Gideon told me to be careful around Charlotte and that she lies. She says Charlotte's been here a lot longer than twenty days,

Anyway. Should I say "Dear me"? Or "Dear Bella"? Or maybe I should say "Dear Isabella," because it seems like no one here can remember I just want to be called Bella. I don't know. Anyway, I'm writing this letter to myself because Tracy said I have a lot of things inside (duh) and it might help me to get them out, rather than letting it all bottle up. Actually, I think she used the word "metastasize" (I don't think I spelled that right, but whatever—I'm the only one who is going to see this).

After I ripped up all the paper from the water bottle, she had me scoop it onto her desk and she was all "I asked you difficult things and I watched you begin to pick your cuticles and bite your lip and then decimate this label. This pile is your anxiety. It's what you're carrying around." Frankly, I think that's stupid. Not the anxiety part, but because what I feel is way heavier than a bunch of paper fluffs.

Try enough paper fluffs to equal ten thousand bricks and then maybe we can talk. She said it's possible I may have an anxiety disorder that contributes to my drinking. She said there are a lot of different types and people can sometimes go their entire lives without being diagnosed. She said she'll suggest outpatient therapy for me to my parents (good luck with that, Tracy!).

I have to be careful because I don't want to tell her too much. I know she's an adult and all and this is her job, but I will never be over Dylan telling me I was too much. Like, I thought when you were close to people, that's what you did, and I turned out to be wrong. Even Kristen and Cherie got sick of me talking about Dylan. So. Tracy can get dribs and drabs, just enough to satisfy her.

I did tell her, though (because it felt like not too much to say) that things are hard for me, in general, and that I kind of like to avoid people and certain situations because they get me all nervous and anxious.

And then she looked at me and said, "Unless you're drunk. Then you can manage." Like, point-blank just said that to my face, easy as pie. And so, I answered, "Yes." I know what she's going to try to get at. I've seen the movies. She'll peck and poke until I break down or something and say "I'm an alcoholic" and she'll swoop in and music will swell and she'll save me, but that isn't going to happen. Because I'm not going to say that because that is not what I am.

It isn't.

Gideon and Quinn have managed to build a pretty tall Lego house over there. I think I'd like a me-sized Lego house to hide in. Maybe I can get them to build me one. Tracy also said that when I write to myself, I should note some positive things about being here. Like things I feel physically and mentally. So here they are:

I think I have some friends (Brandy, Holly).

I think I might have some others (Gideon, I hope—she seems cool enough right now, and maybe I can get that story about her going psycho and what that's all about).

Josh is a positive (it was nice he came back for me on the run yesterday).

Josh is a negative (I do not need another Dylan).

I only had to stop once on the run this morning with Chuck and it was maybe a little nice to be outside and I did have more energy after that run than before. Josh ran with me for a little bit until Gideon doubled back and kind of gave him the side-eye and then he ran ahead. Maybe she thinks I'm headed for whatever those kids Emmanuel and Shelly did, but that's not going to happen.

So far I feel like I'm dragging myself around and can barely function, but I felt . . . I don't know . . . refreshed after that run.

Look at me, I sound like I'm in a feminine hygiene commercial.

Tracy mentioned that it sounds like I've been self-medicating. Soothing myself. I'm not opposed to that term. It actually sounds like I'm just trying to take care of myself in a weird way, doesn't it? Applying some sort of wonderful balm to my hurts.

Today was the fifth day of daily photos. I managed to not flinch when Tracy clicked the button (positive).

But I still didn't look at my photo. I'm an expert now at looking at myself in the mirror without actually looking at myself when I brush my teeth or wash my face. I kind of let my eyes go blurry so whoever that is in the mirror is cloudy, indistinct.

I don't want to see that person.

I'm not sure who she is.

Goodbye—

DAY SEVEN

I STILL CAN'T SLEEP VERY well at night; I just roll around in my bed. It seems like everyone else gets to sleep just fine, even after the night nurse comes in to do random urine or blood tests. You don't know when that's going to happen, I guess. I don't even know how you'd get something in here to take, anyway. They came in last night and took out Holly and Gideon. It was hard for me to relax after that. I don't know why I'm so jittery so late at night. I should be tired from that god-awful ball exercise Phil made us do again this morning and the running every day, but mostly it's just making my muscles ache.

So I get out of bed and walk up and down the hall. Sometimes Janet is on duty, sometimes it's someone different. I like Janet because she plays music. If I had my phone, I'd wear it. I'm jealous of the kids that do.

But I just walk. I'm up to forty laps now. I try not to think of anything as I walk. I'm focused on chipping away the time, because each second, minute, day that goes by is one more day and night down.

On one wall of the activity room in Gen it's like a chapel of Polaroids. Tracy takes extras so some kids can take them home when they leave, and the others stay on the wall if they give permission. If you stand far away, it kind of looks like one whole face, almost, made up of hundreds of people. It reminds me of the mosaic mural through the Fourth Avenue Underpass. I don't know who did it, but it's cool. It's like thousands of photographs of actual people on small panels all put together so when you walk through the Underpass, it's just faces, faces, faces.

Tracy was right. You can see a difference in some people's faces in these Polaroids. They start out angry or afraid, eyes pinched, mouth tight, and gradually there's a softening, a brightening of their skin. Sometimes a smile.

Sometimes there isn't, though. Sometimes it's just the same face all the way through: set and determined, a defiance in the way the kid looks at the camera. The same stance every time.

I know I'm there, too, but I know also where *not* to look for my pictures so I can avoid them: the far right-hand corner, where all the new kids are. It's kind of funny to occupy a body that you actively avoid looking at.

The wall reminds me of the Polaroids Laurel took of people, the ones they sent to her service after she died. People caught quickly in time and then that time disappears and that person they were in the moment is gone in real life but kept forever on film. The color of Polaroid film is pretty: the skin tones slightly off, too bright or too murky, just a slight blurriness to everything, like paint has been applied in a gentle brushstroke and then smeared the tiniest bit.

Laurel would really like this. She would like this wall of moments immensely; she'd probably have a lot to say about each portrait. I like that my grandmother was full of words.

Maybe I can be like that someday, if I can just figure out the right ones.

It's a little scary and breathtaking, too, that there are so many kids on this wall. This place isn't that big, and yet there are an awful lot of faces here.

And there will be more, and more, and more. How many of these faces are repeats? How many of these kids have come back here again and again?

I would like to not be one of them.

DAY EIGHT

"YOU HAVE A JOB, you had a boyfriend, you took care of your grandmother and then she died," Tracy says during our session.

I pick at my nails and then stop, because she notices if I do it, and that makes me nervous. It hasn't escaped me that for a person who doesn't really like to be noticed, I have landed in a place where it is all *about* being noticed and observed.

"Wow, you must have interviewed my parents for hours to have all this information on me."

"Something like that," she says. "I just needed to piece you together. Tell me about it."

I think quickly about what to parse out to her.

We're having this session on two boulders outside. In the distance, I can see the goat pen and hear them fussing around among the chickens. Tracy has brought two coffees, because I can finally have coffee now. It feels good and warm in my mouth. She brought creamer and I added a lot.

"I bus tables at a diner. Well, I should say I used to, because I'm pretty sure I lost that job after what happened. I was supposed to work and, well, I ended up in the hospital. And now here." I shrug, like *What are you gonna do? Oops.*

"Maybe you haven't lost it. Sometimes people can be pretty forgiving. You'd be surprised how many people are willing to give second and even third chances."

"Maybe. I really only had it because I was saving money to go on a trip after graduation with my friend."

"That's a good goal."

"Mmm," I say, rubbing the toes of my sneakers together. "I guess. It was really Amber's thing. She keeps maps of where we'll go and stuff. I mostly was going just to be with her and to get away and do something. It doesn't matter, though. We probably aren't friends anymore, after this."

It hurts to say that, so I take a big gulp of my coffee.

It feels really good to be able to drink coffee again. I can feel it perking me up for the first time in a long time.

"Were you worried about how you'd be able to drink on the trip?"

I practically spit out my latest sip of coffee. "Wow, you really just go for the jugular, don't you?"

"I like to get to the point," she says.

"I don't know," I answer. "I don't think I ever thought about it, really. I was more worried about saving my part of the money, which I lost some of because I had to buy a new laptop after breaking my old one."

Tracy is writing something down.

In the back of my mind, though, I realize I *did* think about that. Like, if it was just me and Amber, and we weren't with Kristen and Cherie, would she get pissed with me if I wanted to drink or something? And how would I do that anyway, on the road? Away from Laurel's house? What, was I going to shoulder-tap in some small town in the middle of nowhere while Amber watched television in a motel room?

Probably.

"Your mother said you were inebriated when you broke the laptop and that was the first time she realized things were going on with you, but she didn't realize the extent at the time."

Extent. What an odd word. *Ex*-tent.

I sigh, long and hard. "There was a dumb party and I saw my ex-boyfriend there with his new girlfriend and I went too far and I freaked out and when I went home, I broke my laptop for . . . reasons. It's kind of a long story, but yeah, she could obviously see I was wrecked."

"She says she didn't know about the boyfriend at the time. How long were you lying to her?"

"I'm sorry? I didn't lie. I just didn't tell her. She would not have been into me seeing someone. She says fifteen is too young."

"You lied by omission. You didn't tell her about the boyfriend, you didn't tell her about your drinking. You drank at your grandmother's house with your grandmother and then later, when she passed, correct—"

" 'Passed' makes it sound like she walked by me on the street and kept going. She *died.*"

There's a crack in my voice on *died.*

"If you prefer that term, that's what I can use." Tracy's voice is neutral.

The boulder I'm on is suddenly very uncomfortable. I stand up with my coffee cup, a little ways away from Tracy.

"I don't want to talk about my grandmother right now, okay? Is this over yet? I don't want to be late for whatever it is I'm supposed to be doing next. I'll get a demerit. I'll get in trouble."

"No, it's not over, and you won't get in trouble. I think you worry about getting in trouble, or troubling people, a lot."

I blink. "Of course. I'm a teenager. There are rules to follow.

Adults give them to you: Grow up. Take this test. Get a good grade. Brush your hair. Don't wear so much makeup. Be happy. Be grateful. You have your whole life ahead of you. On and on and on and on."

"Was your grandmother not like that?" Tracy asks. "You had a special relationship?"

"It wasn't *creepy,* if that's what you're getting at," I say, my voice edged. "She was my grandmother, but she was also my friend. I could talk to her. About things."

"Do you think it was wrong that she gave you alcohol, Bella? I'm curious."

I sigh. "Probably? I don't know. But parents give their kids alcohol all the time. Sips of wine and stuff. They buy it for you for parties. It's *everywhere.* You can't get away from it. It's *legal.* Amber is really the only person I know who doesn't drink. Or do *something.*"

But even as I say that, I'm not sure that's true. Amber, Cherie, and Kristen are just the only people I hang around, is all.

Tracy puts her notepad on the ground and picks up a dry leaf, crackles it into dust and watches the dust fall to the ground. She looks up at me.

"It is legal. But not for you. And many people can drink responsibly. Even teenagers. One or two drinks at a time and call it a night. I don't think you can."

I try to take another swig of coffee, but my cup is empty. "Well, maybe I can later in life. I'll just have to be very strict about it."

"I think the amount of work you put in to hide your drinking for so long points to high-functioning alcoholism. You were managing and maintaining several lies at once. Until you weren't."

I stomp my foot and immediately feel embarrassed. I'm not *five.* "I'm not an alcoholic. I thought we agreed on self-medicating? Now you're changing the rules, just like I said adults do! I drink a little too much, that's all."

Suddenly being outside, which had been nice, what with hummingbirds at the feeders in the mesquite tree above us and a good cup of coffee, is not so pleasant anymore. I can feel agitation burbling in me. I look around anxiously. I need . . . something to make this go away.

"You're upset. I can tell," Tracy says. "If you had something to drink right now, would you?"

"Yes," I spit. "I would. I would. To shut you off in my head."

"Well, you don't have a drink, so what are you going to do about it?"

My lips are shaking. I miss Laurel *so* much. Why did she have to bring her up, anyway? Bricks are piling up in me. One, two, three. I need to smash them. I need to calm down. There are no wrens or sparrows here. I need to not flip—

I turn and throw my coffee cup as hard as I can. It smashes into pieces against the side of a shed by the goat pen. The goats look at me, perturbed.

Gideon, Josh, and Nick run out of the shed, look at the broken pieces of mug, then at me.

Josh's eyes crinkle with concern.

"Damn," Nick says slowly. "You flipped *out.* I didn't think you had it in you."

There's a weird shine in Gideon's eyes, like she's almost . . . pleased?

Oh god. Was that a *psycho* thing to do, like Charlotte says Gideon did?

Maybe Gideon isn't really my friend after all, if this is funny to her.

"I'm sorry," I say quickly. "I didn't mean to do that. Please don't give me a demerit. Please."

I run over to the shed, the earthy smell of the goat pen enveloping me. The chickens are rooting around the legs of the goats. I drop to my knees and start gathering the pieces of the cup, my hands shaking.

Tracy kneels next to me. She puts her hand on my shoulder.

"Stop," she says gently. "Breathe. I don't want you to cut yourself."

I'm trying to breathe, but something is sitting in my throat, blocking it. I'm choking a little. The bricks inside me weren't smashed. They're rising up.

Wren, sparrow, roadrunner, quail.

Is that the right order? Does it matter?

I close my eyes, even as my shaking hands are pawing around, feeling for the sharp pieces of broken mug.

"Bella," Tracy says. "Let me help you clean this up. You don't have to do it alone."

What I do have to do, apparently, is go for another run with Chuck so that I don't get a demerit for behavior.

"Let's make this one count," he said when we started. "Let's rip it up."

Neither of those are things I particularly wanted to do, but I followed him anyway.

Now we're running up a hill, and even though it's cold

outside, we're sweating like dogs in the middle of the summer. Or, I am, anyway. Chuck seems unbothered.

At least he didn't totally leave me behind. He's only a little bit in front of me, occasionally tossing out things like "I don't know why people live in cities, all cooped up. You miss all this, the air and the majesty" and "How you doing, Bella?"

I can only grunt in response.

Because this hill is hard. I think it might actually be more of a mountain than a hill, and I'm tripping-running my way up it, hoping I don't slip and slide back down.

And suddenly, my chest aching and my throat dry, and whatever muscles are in my calves burning in pain, I get really mad at my mother and father.

Like, I am busting my ass on this hill, getting cactus spines in my hands, sweating through my sweatshirt, my stupid swollen face probably getting sunburned, because my mother and father were fuckups who fucked us up.

All I know is that things seemed okay until Ricci was born, and after that everything shifted. My mother was solely mine and then she wasn't, because she had this little thing in a Baby-Björn on her chest all the time. A thing that screamed and cried and did not like to sleep. And she was so tired. So I did bits and pieces to help her. Put the dishes in the dishwasher. Made sure all my Legos were put away. Kept the television down very low in the rare instances she could get Ricci to sleep and take a nap herself. Got myself dressed in the morning and fixed my own cereal.

Because my dad changed. Or had he always been that way, but it got worse? Because it became . . . something. It was like a *before* and an *after*. Before Ricci he worked, he came home, then he went out and my mother was always there to be with me.

Except sometimes, when she had her classes at night. Those nights, he'd read to me and then sing. After Ricci, he didn't do that so much, even though my mother had her hands full with a baby.

And there I was, suddenly. Something . . . he didn't want to take care of. Or didn't know how to. At least, that's how I felt.

"What's going on back there, Leahey?" Chuck calls over his shoulder. "We're almost up to the peak."

"I . . ." I grunt, slipping on a rock and nearly cracking my head on another one. I swear.

Chuck has reached the top. He's grinning down at me.

I'm still scrambling to reach him, my thoughts tumbling in my head. Only, instead of guilty or anxious about all of them rushing around at once, I feel . . . good. It feels good to think these things.

Nothing I did was right. I didn't clean up my toys quick enough. I wanted an extra story at night. I didn't like seeing my dad's face that way. Annoyed. I didn't like seeing my mother so tired and sad. So I stopped being a bother and became better. I built a better Me.

Or so I thought.

And oh, how they fought.

I'm really doing it now, scrabbling up this mountain. I think I can make it, even though there are pinpricks of blood on the palms of my hands because I have so much . . .

. . . anger right now.

And just as I think I'm getting there, I stop short, sliding a little ways back.

I'm not going to make it. I'm not going to make it because I'm not a whole person. I'm just random flaps of flesh stapled together to resemble a person on the outside.

Chuck is clapping his hands. "Do it, Leahey. Fight. You can make it. Don't give up now. You're almost here. Almost *here.*" He takes a deep breath and looks around. "And it's beautiful up here. You don't want to miss that, do you?"

I claw into the ground, get a good grip, dig the toes of my sneakers into the earth, and will myself to move up, move forward. Not backward.

When I'm close enough to touch the fabric of Chuck's sneaker, he reaches down and pulls me to my feet. I fall against him, then steady myself.

Chuck is right. It *is* beautiful up here. The vista is golden with tinges of green, cocoa, and burnt yellow, everything below us studded with stately saguaros and organ pipes and prickly pears. In the distance, I can see the adobe and brick buildings of Sonoran Sunrise, the faint shapes of kids moving around outside. The prettiness makes me ache a little inside.

And it also makes me sad, all of a sudden.

If I was at home and none of this had ever happened, I'd be figuring out ways to drink myself to sleep right now. I'd be checking the level in my Sprodka bottle. Looking to see if there was NyQuil under the bathroom sink. Wondering if I could have just a little more or if that would be too much because I'd have to get up for school in a few hours. Thinking about going to Laurel's to sit by myself and look at our last Scrabble game on the kitchen table and sip my lonely and my sad away. Checking my phone endlessly to see what great and enormous lives everyone else was living while I was making mine smaller, and fainter, by the day.

I would not know this existed.

"When I was coming up this hill, I hated my parents," I tell Chuck. "Now I hate myself."

"Yeah," he says, gazing at the vista. "But plenty of people hate their parents and themselves and don't try to drink themselves to death because of it. What's your excuse?"

"You're an asshole," I answer.

I turn away from him and begin to run back down the hill, slipping and sliding in the sand, pebbles, and rock, skirting lizards and grazing saguaros with my arms.

I run all the way back to our dorm, where I start stripping off my socks and shoes the instant I get into the bathroom. I shove myself into one of the shower stalls and yank the curtain closed, turn on the water as hot as I think I can stand it and strip off the rest of my clothes and sit inside on the hot tile, the water pouring over me, making sounds I didn't think could come out of me, biting my shoulder to make them not so loud.

I wonder what I might have been like if my parents could have gotten their shit together sooner and ditched each other.

I wonder what I'd be like if I'd never been a *sweet girl* and taken that first drink.

DAY NINE

Dear Mom,

I'm writing this letter to you to get some things off my chest. I'm sorry if that sounds aggressive or angry, but I just don't know any other way to say it. Tracy says it's sometimes easier to write things down in a letter than it is to say them out loud, especially for me, since I seem to have a problem getting my brain and heart to work together. I'm wondering if my anxiousness started after Ricci was born, when you and Dad started to get really snippy with each other. Remember that? I guess I was so scared of that that I tried to be good and make sure everything was neat and clean and that I wasn't being a bother to him and you, because you were really busy with Ricci and he was busy working. So I kind of learned to keep things inside. Did you even notice? Why didn't you notice me? I was so relieved when Laurel moved out here.

Anyway. Sometimes I wonder why you stayed with Dad so long, because things were really not good. I'm blaming you and I'm also not blaming you because of course I have no idea what it's like to be in a marriage, all the deals you maybe have to make with each other, but also, we were and are kids and it was obvious something was wrong and that you weren't happy and didn't you think that was going to affect us? Maybe someday we can talk about that, if you want. I do want to ask if you could not fight with Dad in front of me and Ricci, though. I feel like you have been fighting for a million years and I'm so tense inside waiting for it and then enduring it that I feel like I'm constantly on the verge of shattering, just like this mug I threw against a shed yesterday. I'm broken and I'm breaking things. That's my life now. I guess it actually has been for some time.

And if you and he could come to some sort of agreement not to use me as a conduit for communication because you don't want to deal with each other, that would be great. You know, like when you text me to tell him something because you don't want to text him yourself. That. That really stresses me out, because then you two just fight through me, if that makes sense, and that makes everything worse. I didn't think I should ask you to do this, but Fran said in group that we need to tell parents our limits, like what we can and can't handle, and that parents want us to tell them that so they know what's going on, and somebody in group said, "No, they don't want to know that, trust me, they'll just tell you to grow up and deal with it" and Fran said, "Then you have to tell them you're only a teenager and that you aren't supposed to be a grown-up yet and their job is to help you," and let me tell you, the room dissolved in laughter at that point.

I'm going to tell you something now that will probably upset you, and if I do decide to ever give you this letter, I reserve the right to cross this part out in permanent marker.

It was Grandma who gave me my first drink, when I was eleven. We were playing Scrabble in her kitchen, like we always did, and she had some in a cup, and I said it looked like melted candy, and she poured some in a cup for me and said, "Something sweet for my best girl." And man, did I like it. It was like the best, most wonderful thing after a few minutes. It was like I turned into candy and everything was suddenly more colorful and happier. I know it's a weird thing to say, but it felt like I had "arrived" somehow. Like I'd come home. Like I finally knew what normal felt like.

She didn't do it all the time. Not at all. Only every once in a while. But she did let me do it on my own later on, maybe when I was thirteen or so. And as you know, after she died, I would go drink there when I was checking on her house for you. I feel a lot of things about Laurel. I loved her so much, and I still do, and I will never not love her, but I do know that it was probably wrong for her to do that. But she was also a peaceful thing for me, since our house was so tense all the time. And she talked to me about a lot of things that you didn't want to talk about with me, like art and photography. She took me seriously. She taught me how to use a tampon. Did you know that? Maybe you thought it was Amber, but it was Grandma, because you and Dad had that awful fight about my period.

Maybe you didn't want to talk about art with me because you had grown up with that, with Grandma. You never want to talk about or see the photographs she took of you when you were young, and I think they are so beautiful. I don't know why you don't want to claim them and be proud of them or why you don't call that curator back about Laurel's archives. You must have your reasons. Maybe you didn't like that your childhood was on display. I get that. But they were beautiful, and you were beautiful, and I hope you aren't ashamed.

Anyway. I don't want you to hate Grandma for what she did, so I will probably cross this out. She might have started it, but it was me who kept drinking. And I'm going to be honest and tell you that I love it. I love drinking. I feel so much inside me right now that is cutting me to shreds and I'd like nothing more than to be sitting in her house by myself, drinking.

I know I'm seeing you in six days. I can't say I'm excited, even though that sounds mean. I do miss you and Dad, but I also don't. This is the longest I've ever been away from you. I'm not angry that I'm here anymore, at least I don't think so. It's actually kind of nice to be away from you and Dad. You know how sometimes you get very frustrated with me and Ricci and you say "I need a break"? That's how I feel. Sometimes kids need breaks from their parents, too.

I'm sorry it had to happen this way. Sometimes I'm bored here, and sometimes I'm scared, and they ask way too many questions and make us do an awful lot of exercise, but it's starting to feel okay. I work in the kitchen now, helping to actually cook the food. Everybody has to do their part. I burned some pancakes yesterday, but most of them turned out okay. That's all for now.

Love, bella

DAY TEN

IT'S PHONE DAY.

Fran finds us in the activity room and hands Holly, Brandy, and Billy their phones from the plastic tub. Brandy cradles hers like a baby, rubs it against her cheek.

Holly punches in some numbers and waits, her forehead creased in concentration. Then she puts her phone back down on the table. I guess whoever she tried to text didn't answer.

Billy's fingers are flying as he texts.

"I've missed you, my little friend," Brandy says. She pets her hot-pink phone tenderly.

"Congratulations," Fran says. "You've made it to Day Ten and you have your phones back. The rule is one hour a day, so use it wisely, then we'll collect them again. No filming of any kind, in any place in the compound, no photos of other residents without their consent. This is also your time to call your parents or caregivers if you'd like. But remember, *one* hour. Don't screw it up, or you lose phone privileges."

She tucks the plastic tub under her hip.

"Bella, since you don't have a phone, would you like to use this time on the house phone to call your parents? We've notified them that this is the hour you'll call if you feel up to it."

I nod. I follow her out of the activity room and down the hall. She opens a door. Inside there's a table with a phone and chair.

"I have to dial for you, okay?" Fran says. She takes a little slip of paper out of her jeans pocket and dials the number. She hands me the phone and then whispers, "I'll be back in fifteen minutes. This one is to your mom, then I'll come back in and dial your dad."

She leaves.

My mom picks right up.

"Bella," she says. I can tell she's been crying even before this call. Her voice is shaky and soft. "Oh, my baby, I miss you."

"I miss you too," I answer. It's true; I do. I can feel my lips shaking. I press the receiver closer against my face.

"How is it? Is it okay? I don't really know much about it, it was recommended by a friend of Mom's, you remember June at the farm? She has a friend who works there and—"

I cut her off. "It's fine, Mom. It's fine."

I sit down in the chair. On the wall, in very small writing, so small I have to lean closer to see it, someone has written *kill me now.* Soft, with a pencil.

There's a silence. "Are you mad at me? Bella, I did what I thought was best. You hurt yourself so badly. Can you understand why I had to do it?"

I think about that letter I wrote to her.

"I am," I say. "I am mad at you. Maybe not for sending me here, exactly, although I was when I first got here. But mad about other stuff. I don't . . . I don't know that I want say it right now. We only have a little more time and then I talk to Dad."

"Bella . . ." She hesitates.

Her voice sounds . . . scared, almost.

"What?" I say. "What is it? Is he okay?"

"He's not going to be able to talk to you today. He had a meeting come up, and—"

My stomach drops.

Of course.

"Oh," I answer.

"He's very sorry. He'll be at parents day on the fifteenth. That's all set. He promised. I don't know why he can't get out of this meeting, either. It's not like this call hasn't been scheduled since Day One, but you know your—"

I close my eyes, listening to her voice, which sounds far away to me now. He couldn't even reschedule a meeting for a, what, seven-minute phone call?

My mother is still complaining.

"Mom," I say sharply, opening my eyes. "Stop, please stop. Just stop. I can't . . . I can't take it. Please just stop."

"Bella? Bella, are you all right?"

kill me now, says the wall.

I get it. I do.

I miss her so much. I miss him. And I want nothing more than to ask her, in what little time I have left, how Ricci is, but I can't quell this burning inside me.

"Mom," I say, my voice shaking. "I don't want to see you on parents day. I don't want to see Dad. I don't want to listen to the both of you complain about each other any more in front of me. I don't want to sit at a table at parents day and not have him show up and if he does, to listen to you be mad at each other when I am literally in a drug rehab because I almost *died.* I am so sorry I was even born right now, you have no idea. So don't come. Please. I'm begging you."

"Bella, baby, n—"

I hang up the phone.

I open the desk drawers, looking for something, anything. I

feel around. My fingers close on a pencil shoved far at the back of one.

already dead, I write, even smaller, under *kill me now.*

The door pops open. I drop the pencil, kick it under the desk. Wipe my face.

Fran says, "You need a tissue?"

She holds out a box.

"No," I say. "I do not.

Bite my lip.

"You ready for Dad now?" she asks gently.

I stand up.

"He's in a meeting. Maybe you can call and leave a message and he'll get back to you. If he can fit you in."

"Oh, Bella," Fran says. She touches my shoulder. I brush her hand off, squeeze past her and her stupid tissue box and walk as quickly as I can down the hall, turn the corner, and run into our bathroom.

I lean against the wall, hot and cold at the same time. Bang the back of my head a little against the tiles to try and clear it.

The first time we talk, and all she did was complain about him. And ask if I was mad at *her.* And he could not even be bothered to make time for *me.*

God, there's nothing in here to break. Even the mirrors are a weird texture; not glass.

I take deep breaths. *Wren, sparrow, bullshit, bullshit.*

In between my breaths, I hear gulping sounds.

"Hello," I say. "Anybody here?"

I kick off the wall and walk down the stalls and shower cubes. In the last shower cube, I lean down, peeking under the curtain. A body, all in black, curled up, making sounds.

I yank the curtain open. Holly's head whips up toward me.

But her hand is moving, even as she's looking directly at my face, her eyes wide and frantic.

She's scrubbing the underside of her forearm with a toothbrush. Scrubbing it raw.

"Holly, stop." I try to grab the toothbrush, but she angles away.

Scrubbing, scrubbing, pinpricks of blood starting to appear. She always dresses and undresses and showers before or after us, in here, alone. Never with us. With her sleeve pushed up, I can see them.

Pinkish scars along the soft flesh of her arms. Some old, some that look almost new.

"Holly, no." I get on my knees. "Give it to me. Please. Let's talk. Don't."

She shakes her head. "Get out. No one was there. I called. I thought they'd be there. I know they were mad. Disappointed in me. But I thought—"

"The fuck are you two doing?"

Holly's eyes dart over my shoulder. I look back. It's Gideon.

Help, I mouth at her.

"Jesus H. Christ on a crutch," Gideon mutters. She reaches down and in one quick move rips the toothbrush from Holly's hand and throws it to the side. But Holly's fingers pick up the slack; she digs into her arms with her fingernails. I grab them, hold them tightly in my hands. I don't know what to do.

"I can't . . . There's so much inside me. I need relief. I was going to steal a fork from the dining hall, but they count those." Holly's eyes are filmy. Her teeth are chattering.

"Get someone," I say to Gideon. "We should get someone."

"No," she says. "No snitching. Remember? They'll send her to Seg." She narrows her eyes at Holly. "Or do you want to go to Seg?"

Holly shakes her head violently. "I can't be alone. I don't like to be alone. I can't . . . do that. I just . . . Let me do this. It'll go away. Then I'll feel better."

Gideon pushes me out of the way and hauls Holly up by her armpits, props her against the wall of the shower.

"We have to calm her down," she tells me.

"I'm going to help you," she tells Holly. "Just trust me."

"Go," she says to me. "Run and get her some clothes, a towel. And don't tell anyone what's happening."

Even though I'm afraid of what Gideon means by "helping" Holly, I do what she says, walking as quickly as I can out of the bathroom and to our room. I tear through Holly's stuff in her dresser, grab clothes and a towel, and speed-walk back, my heart racing.

Gideon has turned the shower on full blast. Sprays of ice-cold water hit my face.

But Holly is unfazed by the temperature. In fact, she looks calmer. Comforted, even as she's being soaked to the bone.

"Better," she says.

"Good," Gideon answers.

"I can't live inside myself," Holly whispers.

"I know," Gideon says.

"Things have happened to me. When I was little. They said it was my fault."

"I get it," Gideon says. "Someone mess with you?"

Holly nods.

I feel a little sick.

Holly's eyes swivel to me. "Those dogs. At my house. They aren't mine. It's not my fault, how the dogs are. He has stuff he needs to hide. People after him."

I wish she'd stop talking, even though that's a cruel thing to wish.

"He isn't even my stepdad," she goes on. "I just said that. I don't know where my parents are. I never have. This is a foster. This place, here, is court-ordered. I know they aren't going to take me back when my time is up. Everyone gets rid of me sooner or later."

"Some people should not be allowed around children," Gideon says grimly.

Holly's breath has slowed. Her black hair is a curtain over her eyes.

"I hit a teacher," she says. "I don't even remember it. But that's why I'm here."

I shudder, thinking of when I hit Ms. Green's desk.

"I think I'm done now," Holly says to Gideon.

"Okay," Gideon says. She reaches past Holly and turns off the shower. She takes the clothes and towel from my hands. "Turn around," she says to me. "Watch the door."

I do what she says, listening to the slide of the shower curtain, the wet smack of Holly's clothes dropping to the shower floor, Gideon murmuring to her through the curtain.

I'm still watching the door when I feel Gideon's breath on my neck, feel her words curl inside my ear.

"You did good, kid," she breathes. "But remember, *don't tell.*"

I nod.

DAY ELEVEN

BRANDY SIDLES UP TO me in the goat and chicken enclosure. It's our first time here. Gideon is naming all the chickens for us, and the goats, but she's going really fast and I can't catch them all. Holly is sitting in a corner on the ground, a chicken in her lap, rubbing its downy back.

"Hey," Brandy whispers. "What's up with her? With you guys. Did something happen yesterday? You've all been acting really weird. You disappeared and then you were all so quiet."

Gideon's eyes flit to me as she talks about how much feed to put in the buckets.

"No," I say evenly. "Nothing's up. Bad phone calls, I guess."

"You're lying," she says. "I can tell. You're sticking to that girl like glue. Why?"

"Just being nice, is all. She's sad. Not a big deal. We're supposed to watch out for each other, remember?"

"Right," Brandy says. But I can tell by her voice she doesn't believe me.

Gideon sighs, shaking an empty bucket. "Hold on," she says to us.

She goes to a door at the back of the coop and raps on it. Raps again.

"We need more," she says. "Come *on.*"

Charlotte comes out with a big bag in her arms, staggering a little under its weight.

“Right here,” she says. “Don’t have a cow.”

She giggles. Something’s weird about her face, somehow.

Gideon yanks the bag from Charlotte’s arms. Released from the weight, Charlotte falters backward.

“Cool it,” she tells Gideon, her voice sharp. “Just chill.”

Gideon stares at her in a hard way.

“No,” she says. “*You* chill.”

Beside me, Brandy sighs. “What is *up* with everyone today?”

I walk away from her, into a nest of goats, petting as many soft heads as I can.

Tracy walks up to the gate, two cups of coffee in her hand.

“Ready?” she calls to me. “It’s time.”

“It’s time,” Charlotte singsongs. “It’s time for emotional vomiting!”

I ignore her, opening the gate.

Tracy hands me one of the coffees. “Lots of creamer, just the way you like it.”

“Two peas in a pod,” Charlotte mutters under her breath as I walk away with Tracy.

We don’t sit on the boulder this time. She walks us farther, to a cluster of mesquite trees. There’s a cement bench beneath one. We sit down.

“Your mother called me,” she says. “And your father.”

“Great,” I say, taking a big swig of coffee, hoping it burns my mouth. It doesn’t. “Am I in trouble now?”

“No,” she says. “She said you don’t want them to come for parents day.”

“I don’t. but I’m guessing you’re going to make me. Whatever.”

"Actually, I'm not."

"What?" I turn to her.

She's gazing at a hummingbird twitching by a feeder.

"If you don't want them here, they don't come here. This place is for you, not them. I'm glad you spoke up. I'll bet it hurt, whatever you said to your mother, but that means it needed to be said."

I'm kind of stunned. I don't know what to say.

"If you change your mind, that's fine, too. And if you stick with it, I stand with you."

"Okay," I say slowly. "Thank you."

"It takes a lot of courage to tell people what we need, even when we know it might hurt their feelings."

I look over at the goat pen in the distance. Gideon is leading Holly around gently, helping her toss feed.

I hesitate. I should tell Tracy about Holly. I *should* tell her. Holly could really hurt herself.

Gideon glances in our direction. Ever so slightly, she shakes her head.

I look down at the coffee cup in my hand.

I can't tell. Holly doesn't want to go to Seg. That might be even worse for her. And didn't Phil say we have to help our friends? Gideon and I can take care of Holly. Ride or die, Brandy told me.

"Is there something on your mind, Bella?" Tracy asks.

"No," I say quickly. "What are we going to talk about today? Should we get started?"

"This is it," Tracy says. "We're done. Standing up to your parents was enough for a little bit, don't you think? We can just sit here and enjoy the morning. Oh, and I have this for you."

She takes a slip of paper from her jacket pocket and hands it to me. I unfold it.

In quotation marks, it says *"Hi, I just wanted to tell you I was thinking of you. We don't really know each other that well, but I've been places, too, and I just wanted you to know that.—Dawn."*

I blink at the paper. "What—"

"A friend of yours?" Tracy says. "They aren't on the call list, so we couldn't put you on. But we took the message. Is this a good thing? Or someone we should be aware of?"

I barely know her and she was nice enough to actually call me. Nicer than anyone else, even. My eyes get wet.

"Yes," I say. "It's cool. I know her."

I know her, and she's *been places, too.*

DAY TWELVE

I'M ALMOST ASLEEP AFTER my ritual forty laps up and down the hallway when I hear Charlotte shift in her bed and whisper my name.

"What?" I ask in a quiet voice. Moonlight is ribboning the floor through the window. Brandy, Gideon, and Holly are quiet in their beds. Gideon reads herself to sleep every night, thick fantasy paperbacks with intricately designed covers.

"That thing," Charlotte says in a low voice. "You with the cup the other day and breaking it. That was impressive, but you gotta watch out for Tracy. I saw you two yesterday. She's zeroing in. She's . . . she's an instigator."

I roll over to face her. I can make out her bright pink hair, the sharp bones of her shoulders poking through the thin fabric of her T-shirt. She's sitting up in bed looking in my direction.

"A . . . what, now?"

"She's an instigator. She picks at something you say and when you get real defensive or sad, she'll pretend to move on to something else, but then she'll zap right back to it when you least expect it and crush you until you snap."

I blink at her, my eyes still fuzzy from sleep. "But isn't that . . . kind of her job?"

"Partly, but—"

Gideon's voice, raspy with sleep, cuts her off. "Can you give it a rest, Char? What are you doing? Just because you and Tracy had your little skirmish doesn't mean—"

"Oh my god," a voice calls out faintly. "Why don't you all just shut up? My god, I'm so sick of being with all of you twenty-four-seven and I was just having the best dream about chocolate cake. You do not know how much I miss chocolate cake."

It's Brandy. She rolls over on her side toward us.

"And I miss the tamales Mary gets from La Estrella," she murmurs. "And the champurrado."

Her voice sounds wistful.

"Who's Mary?" Gideon asks. "That your mom?"

"No," Brandy says. "She's our maid. She's knows all the yummiest places."

"A *maid,*" Charlotte says. "No wonder you can't even cook an egg. You've never done anything for yourself in your life, have you?"

"I do plenty of things, thank you very much," Brandy shoots back.

"What skirmish?" I ask, pinning my eyes on Charlotte. "Did you go to Seg? What happened?"

She just smiles at me in the half moonlight. "I did what I had to do. She just would not stop talking."

"I miss getting high."

I don't think any of us even noticed Holly sit up in her bed. Her knees are tucked under her chin.

"I miss holding the foil in my hand and lighting the foil and watching everything get liquidy and snorting it up through a straw and dying a million warm deaths. I miss walking on First Avenue and waiting for the right person to come and not knowing what I'm going to get when I give them my money. Is it going to make me feel like cotton candy or am I going to die? I miss being on my bed or someone else's bed and not knowing how much time has passed, hours or days."

Her voice is filled with longing.

Charlotte sighs. "I miss counting out Valium and Xanax and planning what my day would be like with them in my body. Is it the mall? Is it TV? Is it actually making it to school, only now school is so much better because it's all rounded and not sharp edges anymore? Am I topping off my day with some cognac from my dad's extremely wonderful bar? Yes, yes, I am."

Gideon sucks in her breath and leans back on her pillow, thin arms behind her head. "I miss everything but I miss nothing. I'm here, but when I get out, I have nowhere to go. That was the deal. This was the last thing my parents said they'd do for me. The last time." She pauses. "I can't afford to get nostalgic. If I relapse on the outside, there's nothing to lift me back up. Not after what I did."

"What did you—" Brandy asks, but Charlotte lifts a finger to her lips and says, "Shh."

"What do you miss, Bella? Out with it," Gideon says. Her voice sounds sleepy.

"I—I . . . ," I stammer. "Mine is just . . . I mean, I liked vodka with Sprite. We—my friends and me—called it Sprodka."

Gideon bursts out laughing. "Oh god. The starter drink for babies."

"I'm not a baby," I say defensively. "I drank NyQuil, too. And the one night, I got really stoned and drank a lot of stuff I'd never had before, so—"

Charlotte pulls her blankets back up to her chest. "Oh,

Baby Bella. What I wouldn't do to be like you again, new and fresh and thinking booze was the best. Let's talk in a few years when you're back here and have a little more under your belt."

"I'm not *coming* back here," I say. "I'm never coming back here."

Charlotte and Gideon exchange looks. Brandy has fallen back asleep.

"Me neither, Bella," Holly says, giving me a small smile. "I'm never coming back here, either."

DAY THIRTEEN

Dear Me—

I would like not to be here.

I'm not sure I have anything positive to say today.

I'm up and down, like a plastic bag in an unpredictable wind. Empty, blowing no particular way.

I'm worried about Holly.

But I don't think it's right to just come out and ask someone, what was done to you?

Because I think I know.

And that's disgusting.

I don't understand the world. At all. How is she supposed to live like that?

If drugs are the only thing that make her feel better, why do people keep trying to take them away?

Why doesn't the world have anything else to offer her but to live with her pain and suffering?

I did laps in the pool today for the first time. It felt comforting to be in the water and just hear the sound of the water and not all the sadness here, including my own.

Maybe I shouldn't have said my parents can't come.

But if they can't make time for me, why should I make time for them?

It seemed like the days were going by really quickly, but now it seems like they've slowed.

Now it seems like I'll never get out.

And what even will happen when I do?

I don't think a goddamn thing will be different for me.

Wait, there are two things.

There was a new kid today. I don't even remember his name because he just appeared and didn't say anything at breakfast, even when Gideon, who is now the kitchen manager since Lara has left, asked him if he wanted to introduce himself. He didn't.

He had bushy black hair and a thin mustache and he didn't eat much.

But he ran.

Right after breakfast.

You'd think he would have done it on the Chuck run, but maybe he didn't because Chuck would have caught him. Probably.

We were in the goat and chicken pen and I was fussing over Binky (I've finally learned one goat's name) and this kid . . . just shot past us. Running like the wind.

Into nowhere. Into nothing.

And here's the second thing.

When someone runs, this extremely loud alarm goes off and everyone has to dive flat on the ground wherever they are and wait until staff come by to count you and escort you to your room and you have to wait in your room until they decide to let you out.

So today I learned that even if you're in an animal pen, which hasn't been properly cleaned yet because Billy is really a slacker, you have to lie flat in very close proximity to shit for an ungodly and unfair period of time.

Kind of like the real world.

—me

DAY FOURTEEN

EVERYONE IS A LITTLE on edge today.

Fran says in group that she understands, because tomorrow is parents day, and *do we want to talk about that*?

No one says anything.

"Anyone?" Fran asks. "It can be hard, I know. A lot of complicated emotions."

Charlotte says, "Frankly, Fran, I'm all talked out. I think we all are. Maybe you could talk about yourself for once."

Fran looks at her. "Well, what do you want to know?"

Nick pipes up. "Like, I know we've heard the story of you and your friend in Anza Park, am I right? We all hear that, like, the third day in Detox."

"Get new material, Fran," Josh says.

Everyone laughs.

"But what about after that?" Nick asks. "Like, what was it like for you after? When you tried to kick? What was the hardest part? You're always telling us we have to do our work, like on ourselves, inside and out, but you never actually tell us what that's like. After. Trying to live."

Fran thinks for a moment. "It's different for everyone," she says slowly. "But if you want to know the truth, the hardest part was quitting cigarettes."

"Fuck off," Charlotte says. "No way."

"Language," Fran says.

"Sorry," Charlotte mumbles.

"I had tried to kick drugs before. I tried cold turkey. You get pretty sick. It's one of the most awful things I've ever experienced, going cold turkey. You think you're going to die. But after a while, the sick goes away and the work begins. And sometimes it doesn't take. For whatever reason. It was hard for me, for a long time. Stop, start, stop, start. There were a lot of things working against me. Sometimes it felt like the easiest thing to do was to sink back into it. Who cared about me? A dirty woman living outdoors. Some people think you deserve that life."

She clasps her hands together in her lap.

"I found some people who didn't. And they believed in me. Little by little, I believed in myself. They don't make it easy for you out there. There's a lot of shame. But I saw my friend die, and yes, you've heard that before, and I think, in the end, I was ready. To put in the work. Because I didn't want to die in a park. I didn't deserve to die in a park. No one does."

"Cigarettes," Josh says. "Back to the smokes."

"Right," Fran says. "I needed those when I was withdrawing. I needed them through the first parts of my recovery. I needed to do something to myself. Cigarettes are insidious, but they're legal. Glamorous, to some. Isn't it funny how no one wants to give more money to get people into safe living spaces with good therapy and safe withdrawal, but hey, smoke up, pal, even though this thing will eat you alive from the inside, slowly and, finally, painfully. Nobody shames you for getting cancer from smoking the way they shame you for other addictions."

She gets up and moves around the room, her hands behind her back.

"I have never missed heroin as much as I miss cigarettes. I used them partly to get sober and then I used them because they were my new addiction. I had to stop the first cigarette in the morning at first. Do something else. The laundry. Go for a run. Write in my journal. Every day, I went a little bit longer without one until one day it was nine o'clock at night and I hadn't had a single one. I promptly put myself to bed and stayed there, afraid I'd run to the store for a pack."

Brandy laughs. "Those things are like twelve bucks a pack now."

"But," Fran says, "I still get cravings. I smell it when I walk outside in the city and something perks up inside me. Pokes me. Tries to rile me up. I pass by people in trouble all the time, high as kites, and you kids coming in here high to Detox, and I never feel that way about heroin. I see you, and I don't have that craving to get high. But smell cigarette smoke? It takes me hours to get that out of my system."

"Just hearing you talk about it makes me want a smoke," Nick says. "I haven't here, although I know some kids can if they want. I'm trying not to."

"Addiction of any kind sits in your brain like a cat with yarn, Nick," Fran says. "Batting around your synapses and impulses and logic for sport. And then it says to your body, hey you, want to play? Hence, the shakes, the DTs, withdrawal symptoms, the whole awful lot of it. Then you're in for it."

I pick at the hem of my T-shirt. Maybe I had hangovers, but I never had anything like what she's talking about. I don't even have that craving right now. I miss drinking, but thinking about it doesn't make me salivate or shake or anything.

"Some of you are thinking, *well, that's not me,* and maybe it isn't. Not yet, anyway. But it might be, someday. Because the weird thing is, you might work hard and get sober and stay sober, but it never leaves your brain. There's always a little scrap left, waiting to take you down. Once I had nineteen months and there I was walking down a street and I noticed some people getting high and something came over me and I turned down that alley and blew my nineteen months. I cannot explain it. And then I started over."

She goes back to her beanbag and sits down with a gruff sigh.

"There's a lot of starting over," she says. "But isn't it great if you get that chance? Some of you are on your third and fourth chances. Some are on their first. But you have this chance, no matter the distance you traveled to get here. No matter how many times you've started over, here you are."

"It's tiring," Nick says softly. "It's really exhausting."

"I believe if you can walk into the darkness," Fran says quietly, "then you have the strength to walk back out."

DAY FIFTEEN

GET UP. CRACK OF dawn. Chuck run. Shower. Change clothes. Brush teeth. Cook breakfast. Eat breakfast. Stand against the wall in the activity room. *Click. Click. Click.*

Tracy has pulled our Polaroids off the wall and arranged them on separate tables so we can look at them privately.

At first I just look at the floor. My sneakers. The hem of my pants. The lip of the table.

I gradually stop, right there, at the lip of the table.

How bad could it be? I ball my fists in the pockets of my hoodie. I saw myself in the hospital, but isn't that the worst it could have been? The very worst? Because that was right after. When everything was the most fresh on my face. Math-in-my-head time: fifteen days.

Fifteen days.

My eyes waver at the edge of the table. I raise them slowly. I try not to do that thing I do in the bathroom, where I kind of blur my eyes when I'm by the mirror. I keep them focused.

She arranged them chronologically.

My heart sinks at the first one.

I'm a piece of meat, pounded and pulped. One eye is looking down; the other is lost in a swirl of purple flesh that stretches down my left cheek.

There's a hot ball in my throat. I force myself to look at number two.

If there's a change, it's imperceptible.

I sweep my eyes across them one by one, left to right, slowly, an agonizing crawl.

Gradually, the purple gives way to something else: a dark blue, then a light blue, then various shades of pink and lilac, with yellow beginning to creep in toward day ten, like a flower you didn't know you planted that suddenly sprouts in a thicket of weeds.

But in there, too, in all that pulpy, changing misery of my face, is something else, and it's in my eyes. They start out dull and ashamed, looking everywhere but at Tracy's camera lens, and then they get more focused. They get clearer. As the swelling in my face goes down, my eyes get stronger, even as I'm having a hard time here. I stand up straighter in each photo.

Something is happening to me. But—

Holly is next to me.

"Oh," she says, laying a finger on Day One. "I remember that. The first day. I'm sorry I said you looked like crap. I think I was just scared."

"Me too," I say. "It's my face. Imagine how I felt."

"You haven't said," she says quietly. "Like, how that happened."

"Someday I will," I tell her. "I promise."

"You kind of look unreal," she says. "Not in a bad way. But all the color. Like a painting. These look like little paintings of you, almost, but you're the painted thing."

"When you say it like that, my self-destruction almost sounds cool."

"Do you want to see mine?" Holly says. She's got them pressed against her chest. "I'm like Wednesday Addams in each one."

She spreads them on the table above mine. It's gradual, like with me, but you can see the difference as the days go by.

"What time are your parents coming?" she asks. "Can I meet them? My fosters are coming. I called. They promised. I had to beg, but they promised."

Her eyes are gleaming.

"I told my parents not to come," I say.

Her smile dies. "Really?"

"Really," I say. "And it's okay. I'm going to pretend it's okay. They'd just make me miserable, and I'm miserable enough, you know?"

"I get it."

"I'm gonna take pictures of these, okay?" She holds up her phone. "I want to remember all of them."

I hesitate. "Are you . . . you aren't going to post them anywhere or anything, are you? Because I'm not cool—"

"No, no," she says. "I'd never do that. It's just for me. I like to draw. Maybe I'll draw from them sometime."

"That would be okay," I say. "I'd like to see that, actually."

"When we get out," she says. "We'll hang out. Pinky-swear."

We link pinkies.

Visiting is three hours, from eleven to two. They can eat lunch with kids in the meal room, take a tour of the buildings, see the animal pens, walk the paths, admire the gym, sit in the activity room and talk.

I keep myself busy in the kitchen. Most kids have people

coming, so the kitchen is a little understaffed. Fran and Chuck have stepped in to help make lunch.

"You okay, kid?" Fran asks.

"Fine," I say. "I am, really. It's better this way. The only person I want to see is my little sister anyway, but she's too young to come."

Fran nods.

"We better take these out," I tell her, pointing to trays of sandwiches and salads and fruits.

"Your wish is my command," Fran says, swooping up a tray of sandwiches and disappearing out the double doors. I follow her with the cart of drink coolers.

As I'm setting the coolers and cups on a table, I peek at everyone.

Brandy is sitting with an elderly woman with gray hair in a bun and a concerned look on her face. They aren't talking. Brandy isn't eating. I didn't picture her mom that way at all, the way Brandy's been describing her. That seems weird. At the end of another table, Josh looks miserable, sandwiched between a tall blond woman and a surly man. They're peering suspiciously at their sandwiches. I look around for Holly, but I don't see her. Maybe she's giving her fosters a tour. I don't see Gideon, either.

I busy myself setting out extra cups. If my parents had come, I can picture what would have happened, can hear what they would've said. My mother would be sad but hopeful, and my dad would probably be critical of the food, or the dumpy quality of the place, and then my mom would say, *Well, why didn't you look for the place, then? You made me do all the research,* and then he'd say, *Well, I didn't want her to be here in the first place and—*

I stop. Take a breath.

I didn't want them here and they aren't. So I'm not going to think about what might have been. I don't need them in my head right now.

After Chuck and I clean up from lunch, I walk back to our room. On the way, I look into the activity room. Josh is playing chess with his mom while his dad looks at his phone. Gideon is there with a bearded guy. Brother? Too young to be her dad. They're at the table closest to the door and they're both wearing the same kind of blue sneakers, which seems weird, but okay.

Holly is at a table in the far corner, drawing, alone.

I hope her people come soon.

In our room, Charlotte is asleep, curled into a ball.

I lie down on my bed and stare at the ceiling.

That's what I'm doing when Brandy comes in and hurls herself on her bed.

I look over at her. "You're back early. It was nice your mom—grandma?—came."

Her eyes burn. "That was *not* my grandmother. Or my mom. That was *Mary,* our maid. My mother went to Cabo. Like I told you, I'm nothing to her. I made Mary leave, even though we still have time."

Her voice wavers. She takes off her sneakers and throws them against the wall.

"I'm sorry," I say.

"Whatever," she says. Then she sighs. "Sometimes I get my hopes up that she's going to start to care. It's good to be reminded yet again that she never will."

She flops onto her side and closes her eyes, her mouth trembling.

Gideon walks into the room slowly and sits down on her bed. Folds her hands in her lap.

"Are you okay?" I ask. "You don't look well."

She raises her eyes to me, only I feel like she isn't looking at me but through me.

"Gideon?" I ask.

She snaps to. "Sorry. I'm just . . . tired. My cousin tires me out. But at least someone came, right?"

She slides off her blue sneakers. Holds them in her hands and looks at them for a long time.

"Gideon?" I ask again. "Are you *sure* you're okay?"

"Yeah," she says. "Totally fine. I was just thinking I need to get a new pair of sneakers when I get out of here. These are getting kind of ratty. Don't know where I'll get the money, though."

Carefully, she puts them on the floor and bends forward, sliding them far back under the bed. Then she lies down.

I'm getting drowsy. I close my eyes.

A siren blaring makes me bolt off the bed, confused, my ears hurting.

Gideon yells, "Down, get down! Runner!"

I slam myself onto the concrete floor, press my cheek to its coolness.

The four of us look at each other on the floor.

I look toward the open door. Josh is flat on the floor in the hallway, his face turned to me, his parents looking down at him in horror.

Holly, he mouths.

DAY SIXTEEN

IT'S 2:04 A.M. AND we are all still awake in our beds.

We haven't left since this afternoon. No one is allowed to leave their room unless a staff member accompanies them, even to go to the bathroom.

The police came and questioned us.

What was she wearing?

All black, like always.

How did she seem? Happy? Sad?

She's always sad. Look around at where we are. But she seemed hopeful. Her people were coming.

(They did not come.)

Did she ever mention any friends or places she liked to go?

She scored drugs on First Avenue and Fort Lowell.

Did she say she was planning to leave?

She said we'd be friends when she got out. She was going to draw us.

Can you describe her mental frame of mind in the past few days?

She's been upset. She's had a bad life. Read her file, man.

(Tell, but just enough to *not tell.*)

They took her suitcase, her bedsheets (I don't know why), her pillow, her blue wool blanket, her toiletry bag.

(She's coming back, don't take those.)

Miss, let us do our job.

Gideon finally speaks.

"It's really cold out there," she says. "The last I saw her in the activity room, she was just wearing her long jersey shirt."

It's cold out there.

My insides feel like they're caving in. She's so thin and frail.

"The police will find her," Brandy says. "She can't get far. She's not that sturdy."

I press myself against the wall.

"When are they going to tell us what's going on?" I ask Gideon. "When will they let us leave the room?"

Gideon is silent.

"They'll keep us cooped up until tomorrow," Charlotte says sleepily. "Probably. And restrict us to indoors for a day or two. Just to make sure nobody copycats."

"We should do something," I say. "We should go look for her."

"There are people doing that," Gideon says. "They'd never let us, anyway. They say if you run, good luck to you, but we're minors, so they sent people out. The police were here. They didn't come for that one guy because they caught him right away."

"Just everybody go to sleep," Brandy says. "Okay? That's the best thing to do right now, I think."

But I can't.

DAY SEVENTEEN

"CHECK-IN TIME," FRAN SAYS. "Talk to me."

We are gathered in the group room, splayed out on the beanbags.

No one says anything. There's still no word on Holly.

"I know we're all worried," Fran says gently. "They're still searching. When we know anything, we will tell you."

"This sucks," Billy says.

"It does," Fran agrees. "Sometimes people run. Sometimes running is the only thing that seems like an option."

I feel like my heart is going to burst. I keep thinking about Holly out there, In December. In the cold. It's not like it's below freezing or anything here, but it still gets pretty cold at night. And she had *nothing* with her. And in the shower, she told me and Gideon she didn't like being alone. That she couldn't be alone, and what if—

"It's just—"

I stop myself.

Everyone's looking at me.

"Yes, Bella?" Fran says.

"It's just . . . I mean, what if she . . . I don't know. Didn't you notice her? The things she did? That she was—"

Beside me, Gideon nudges my arm.

Don't tell. Right.

I swallow. "Nothing. Forget it. I just feel terrible. And I feel ashamed."

"Ashamed?" Charlotte guffaws. "Why? It's not your fault. Girl was mad-mad. She snapped."

"She had a hard life, okay?" I say. "I feel stupid thinking about all my problems when hers were so much bigger, all right?"

"It's not a competition," Nick says.

"Yes, it is." Charlotte giggles. "Please, tell us your issues, Bella. I'm all ears."

"Shut—"

Fran holds up her hand, stopping me.

"Whatever problems you have, they're yours. They belong to you. And they are just as big to you as someone else's problem is to them. You can't compare experiences," she says. She takes a deep breath. "The problems in your lives are not going to go away just because you came here. We can't erase them. We can only give you some tools to help you deal with them in responsible, healthy ways. You'll live with what you live with for the rest of your lives. We're only asking that you not try to drown your problems. Drown *yourselves.*"

"Wait," Charlotte says. "You're going to read the poem, aren't you?"

Fran stands up. "Yes. Yes, I am."

"Oh god," Charlotte murmurs, closing her eyes. "I've heard this poem three times already."

"Shush," Nick says. "Let her cook."

Fran closes her eyes and begins to speak.

Something happened to you
It was awful, it was traumatic
Or maybe nothing happened to you

Whatever it is, if it is nothing, or
If it is something, it's still inside you
It still feels the same, a heaviness, a pain, a feeling of emptiness
It all weighs the same
So you smoke it down, or you choke it down
With whatever liquid drowns it quicker
You squeeze it into your veins to set you on sweet fire, burn it all down, burn it all down
You crunch, crush, mix it up, one on top of the other,
Four to twelve hours of bliss being NOT YOU
You become NOT YOU
But that is still you
Warped
Like a fun house mirror
You are still in there
And whatever the thing is that happened to you
Or the nothing that happened to you
It is still there, too
Because you can crush it smoke it squeeze it swallow it choke it down
But you cannot kill it
You cannot kill it
I am asking you:
Whatever lives inside you that is so great you must destroy it
Have you destroyed it yet?
Did any of the crush smoke squeeze swallow
Kill it?
No.
It is always there
It will always be there
I am asking you to face it
I am asking you to take it

And love it
Water it
Tend it
Talk to it
And tell it
We must live together
You and me
This pain
This nothingness
Because when you wake up after crushing smoking squeezing choking
It will always be there
You will still be that fist in your face
That scream in your ear
That one bad night or twelve
You will still be all the people who have died and left you here
You will still be alone
You will still be
You.
You must live in spite of all this.
Smash the fun house mirror
Stop the crush smoke squeeze choke
Be you in all your terrible things
All your lonely things
All your silences and screams
Be a human on this earth,
Unafraid
Of your heart-shaped glory.

DAY EIGHTEEN

THEY STILL HAVEN'T LET us outside. Tracy and Phil and Fran take turns talking to all of us, one by one. We eat breakfast, we clean up, they say we can go into the activity room, the gym, or our rooms, but nowhere else. We can't even go to the animal pens, which seems to upset Charlotte.

Tracy is waiting for me in her office.

"Have you heard anything?" is the first thing I say as I flop into one of the easy chairs. "It's been a long time now."

She shakes her head. "Just what I know. They have a search team out, still looking. Holly didn't say anything to you?"

"No," I said. "She seemed to be doing all right. She said her fosters agreed to come."

A dark look passes across Tracy's face, but just as quickly as it appeared, she wipes it away.

"What?" I press her. "What was that look? You know something. Tell me."

"I shouldn't be telling you this," she says in a low voice, pushing a pen across her desk. "They weren't going to come. They might have told her that, but we spoke a few days ago and they were in the process of relinquishing her."

"Relinquishing her?" My voice is a squeak. "What does that mean?"

Tracy licks her lips. "Giving her back, essentially. She'd have to go back to the group home and wait for another family."

I stare at her, a pit opening up in my stomach. "Like she's some dog they can just send back to the pound? That's hideous. She's a *child.* Do you even know what she's been—"

Tracy holds up a hand. "I know what her background is, yes."

I stand up and pace around her office. "Well, we should call the police on them. We should do something. They can't just *do* that."

"I can't do anything, Bella. When you're here, I do my best. When you're beyond the compound, it's out of my hands."

"So when we get out, we're just nothing to you? We just, *floof,* disappear?"

I'm raising my voice.

"Bella, take a breath. Sit back down."

"No," I say.

"Bella." A warning tone to her voice. "You have Fire in two days. You don't want to lose that. You've earned that step in the program. Think very carefully about what you're doing right now."

"I'm standing up for someone. Is that wrong?"

"The world can be a very bad place, Bella. Sometimes we try to help people and they slip away anyway. And you have to let them go."

"That's some bullshit, right there," I say, and I'm so mad, I don't even care if she takes Fire, whatever exactly that is, away.

I stomp out of her office and slam the door behind me.

I'm on my bed, looking at the stars through the window high on the wall, when Brandy comes in. "Let's go," she says.

"Where?" I ask.

"The Star Pit."

"The what, now?" I vaguely recall something like that from our handbook. I squint up at her.

"The Star Pit. We get to go now that we're past our halfway point. I finally read the handbook, can you tell?" She giggles.

"I don't want to," I say. "Whatever it is."

"Listen, they're letting us outside for this one thing. We can't do anything for Holly right now, so let's do something for ourselves, at least? I want to see it. Gideon says it's cool. Please?"

"Is it some mystical land of understanding and enlightenment?" I ask, getting off my bed and sighing loudly.

"God, I hope so," she says. "I could really use some enlightenment right about now because I am getting *very* bored here."

She grabs our parkas.

The Star Pit is a series of rocks arranged in a huge circle along the edge of a dug-out pit. It's farther out than the goat and chicken pens, and as we walk to it, I can see the sky getting bluer and brighter and the stars sprinkling the sky like white crystals. There are already some kids sitting and lying down in the pit.

"What did the handbook say, exactly?" I whisper. I can see tendrils of my breath in the frigid air.

"You get to come here unsupervised if you reach the halfway mark with no more than one demerit. It's just . . . I don't know. You can look at the sky. Or talk. Or whatever. At least it's something different at night than sitting in our beds or watching stupid movies and thinking sad things or dreaming about how fucked up we'll get when we're out." She points off into the distance. "And we aren't entirely unsupervised right now, anyway."

I look where's she's pointing. Tracy, Phil, Fran, and Chuck are sitting on lawn chairs, bundled up in blankets, around a fire.

As we get closer, I can make out Josh's face, and Gideon's, and Billy's. And two other kids, Nick and one whose name I can't remember. They all look up as we climb down into the pit. Gideon hands us a blanket.

"Welcome," she says, "to the party for people who can't party anymore. It's like group with Fran, only no Fran and no absolutely traumatic poem, but we get the stars."

Brandy and I arrange the blanket over our knees. It's woolen and warm. I pull the hood of my parka over my head and stuff my hands in my pockets.

"We're trauma-dumping," Billy says. "Care to join?"

"What?" I say.

"Just listen," Gideon says. "It will become clear soon enough."

"At my last place," drawls one of the boys whose name I can't remember, "trauma-dumping was forbidden. Granted, it was a loony palace, and people were maybe a little more on edge there, but I've never understood how you can expect fucked-up kids to get together and *not* trauma-dump."

"How do you even forbid that?" Brandy asks. "You can't forbid people to talk to each other."

"Heh. Like, yeah, a counselor would literally come up and separate you, that's how," the kid says. "And you'd get written up. I mean, we were in group therapy once a day! How is group not one giant session of trauma-dumping for everyone involved?"

Josh scooches over a little, closer to me. He gestures to the blanket. "Kind of freezing here. Do you have a little piece to spare?"

Brandy nudges me slyly. I open the blanket a little and Josh slides in, pressing his side gently against mine. I can feel my face heat up.

"But as we were saying," Gideon tells us, "before you showed up . . . Billy's dad once actually tried to sell him for drugs."

"Oh my god," I say. "That's horrifying."

But it comes back to me then, that comment he made when we were watching the house renovation show the night I had my panic attack. That he and his brother had to sleep on a couch and his dad would kick his toys. The way he stopped talking and his face got tight and how relieved he was to switch to *Gumball* and think of something else.

My dad might not be Dad of the Year, but at least he's not . . . that.

"Is it terrible I want to know what drugs and what price and also . . . like, to who?" Brandy asks.

"Whom," Josh says.

"Whatever," Brandy says. "The trauma, dump it."

Billy leans back on his elbows, looking up at the stars. "I was eight. We were living in Orlando then. At a motel. He'd stolen me from my mother. And he was going to sell me for Oxy. The price was fifty bucks. And I didn't know exactly what that meant, because I was so young, but I can guess now, and before your minds start racing, the dude buying me was an undercover cop, so it was actually a good thing, because my dad went to jail and I went back to my mom and she ended up marrying a very nice, fairly well-off gentleman named Stuart."

"What a fantastic children's book that would make, Billy," Gideon says. "I'm picturing very pastel illustrations to illuminate the warm relationship between addict father and innocent young child being sold into sex slavery."

Beside me, Josh shivers. "That's dark, man."

Under the blanket, his hand gently searches for mine.

I kind of stop breathing a little. I let him take my hand. His is very warm.

"It turned out okay." Billy shrugs. "I mean, *I* didn't, but Stuart keeps paying for my rehabs, so it's all good. He cares. I just keep not caring, is all. Stuff I can't get rid of, you know?" He taps his head. "Up here." He taps his chest. "In here."

Gideon reaches across the pit and holds out her hand. "I get it."

Billy takes her hand. "Solidarity," he says.

"Right on," she answers.

Brandy chuckles. "At least he cares. My mother could care less. This time? I passed out and vomited up a bunch of blood and stuff on her brand-new rug and all she could say when they were loading me into the ambulance was 'That rug was from Morocco.' "

In the distance, far off, I can hear coyotes howling. It makes me a little lonely for Dad's apartment. There's an arroyo behind it, and a lot of coyotes and javelinas travel up it to move through the city. It's safe there, covered by trees on both sides. Sometimes people live there, because it's safe for them, too. Sometimes Ricci wants to go play in there, but my dad has to tell her, "That's some people's home. We don't just walk into people's houses, do we?"

I can hear the coyotes from the room I share with Ricci. I miss her so much.

I tighten my fingers in Josh's. He squeezes back.

It's very peaceful out here.

"How about you, Bella? Are you going to drop the fabulous story of your face?" Gideon teases. "I love a good fight story."

I hesitate. I can feel Josh's eyes on me.

"It's not very exciting," I tell them. "The only fight I had was with a front stoop. My friends dumped me there and I passed out and smashed my face on the cement."

"They dumped you?" That's from Nick. "That's cold. You don't dump people. I mean, at the very *least,* drop them at a hospital and take off, but not on a front porch."

"I read about a girl in Minnesota whose friends dumped her at her parents' house in like fifteen-degree weather and she lost her feet to frostbite," Gideon says. "I sincerely hope they are not your friends anymore, Bella. Fuck that."

"Wait," Billy says to me. "I seem to remember you, on Day Three, said something about a video. I bet *there's* a story." He chuckles in a lascivious way.

My face flushes again. "It wasn't like a sex tape, dumbass. And that, I don't want to talk about that, right now."

"Come on!" wheedles the guy whose name I don't know.

"Drop it," Gideon says. "If she doesn't want to, she doesn't have to."

Josh presses his shoulder tighter against mine.

"I feel like Billy is winning the trauma-dump contest at the moment, anyway," I say to change the subject from me. "Anyone else? Josh?"

Josh stirs beside me. "No. I've got nothing. My life is pretty much picture-perfect. Parents love each other. They love us. Two cats and a dog. A pool. Lot of food in the fridge. Fancy private school."

Wait, that can't be true. He said something about "busted faces" on the hike, and it seemed like it was a family thing. Why would he lie?

Maybe he's like me, and there's something he doesn't want to share.

"No," Billy says. "There has to be something. Something that made you fuck up so bad you somehow ended up here."

Josh shakes his head. In the moonlight, his face is pale and soft, smooth. His hair is perfectly cut to look that messy. I believe him about the fancy rich part.

For a minute, my brain says: *Why would someone like* him *like someone like* you*?*

My heart says: *Just shut up for once and enjoy this starry night and handholding, will you?*

He takes a deep breath, like he's remembering something glorious and beautiful, and he says, "No drama for me. I just really, really, really love getting high."

A hush falls over the group and we're quiet for several seconds until Gideon says softly, "Yeah. Absolutely yes to that. One. Hundred. Percent."

A peal of laughter comes from the group of staff members.

"What do you think they're talking about?" I ask.

"Us," Brandy says.

Gideon and Billy giggle.

"They're obsessed with us," Josh says. "Obsessed, I tell you. They can think of nothing else."

We all laugh. It feels good to laugh.

"Come on, Bella," Billy says, "give us something, anything, if you can't talk about that video."

Before I can stop myself, because I'm feeling such a rush of warmth inside from the laughter and being out here with everyone, like I have *friends* or something, I say, "I held my grandmother in my arms as she died."

There's a brief, stunned silence, until the guy whose name I can't remember suddenly howls with laughter, his whole body shaking, falling backward onto the cold ground.

Brandy is laughing so hard tears are running down her face.

"I mean, it's not really funny," I say, even as I kind of start laughing a little. "It wasn't at that time, anyway. Or now, to be honest. We used to drink together."

That just makes everyone scream harder.

"Oh, Jesus," Billy says, wiping tears from his eyes. "I hate this goddamned life so much."

While they're all still hysterical, and not paying attention to us at all, Josh buries his face in my neck, just for a second, long enough to let his mouth rest there, and then he just as quickly brings his head back up again.

I can still feel it, hours later, back in our room.

A mouth-shaped warmth on my skin.

DAY NINETEEN

Dear Amber,

I'm writing this letter to you to apologize to you. They have us write letters here to people we have wronged in the course of our addictions. I still don't think I am an addict, but yeah, there might be a problem.

I'm thinking of you because I treated you in a bad way, and also because I made a friend here, and she ran away. I miss her, and I miss you.

I was thinking today that there are only two reasons I agreed to come here. One was that after you left the hospital that day, I was really afraid I would never get to be your friend again. You said if I didn't do this, if I didn't try, that we would be over and done, because I had lied and betrayed you and hurt myself and in the process hurt you. And you were right. I was hurting the both of us. And I didn't want to lose you.

The second reason was that after you left, my parents did what they always do: they yelled and screamed at each other about whose fault I was, et cetera, et cetera, and if I'm being completely honest, I just wanted to get the hell away from the both of them. I think I actually said that to the counselor. I can't remember. It's all a little fuzzy now and I still had a lot of alcohol in my system.

Thank you for scaring the shit out of me by telling me you wouldn't be my friend. I know that's a weird way to put it, but it's true. And I'm sorry for the many ways I have hurt you. I have to accept that my actions might have ruined our friendship forever. That's on me.

It's all right if you don't write back. One of the counselors, Tracy, said that sometimes you care about people, but they slip away anyway, and you have to let them go. I don't feel that way about you, but I understand if you feel that way about me.

Love, bella

P.S. I met a boy. I know. I know. I'm the problem, it's me.

P.P.S. I'm going to make Fire tomorrow. I'm still not sure exactly what that means, but maybe someday I can tell you about it.

DAY TWENTY

THE FIRST THING THEY do after waking you up on Fire Day is make sure you're prepared for Fire Night. There is no Chuck on Fire morning. You do not have to run, because presumably, all the walking and hiking and trying to not kill yourself out in the wilderness will be enough activity for you.

Phil runs a backpack check. Everyone gets a very big pack to lug around on this adventure. He walks the room, checking our supplies.

Parkas, hats, two pairs of thick socks, jeans, hiking boots, winter hat, warm gloves. I don't have hiking boots, so he sends Gideon to the lost and found to find me some.

I slip them on. They're a little too big and feel heavy on my feet, but Phil says they'll do.

Rolls of toilet paper, hand sanitizer, and a small shovel that fits in your backpack.

"So you can dig a hole and do your business and then bury it," Phil explains helpfully.

"Lovely," I say. "This gets better by the minute."

Backpack, personal tent, first-aid kit, flashlight, wool blanket, sleeping bag, tarp, mat, knife, bottles of water, and packets of dried food for snacks.

Brandy looks at the knives.

"Are you going to make us, like, catch and kill and cook our food?"

"Maybe," Phil says. "Want to?"

He winks.

She pales.

"No," he says, patting her on the shoulder. "The food will be taken care of. No killing out there."

The second thing is eating. You don't have to cook that day. You do get breakfast, though, and Phil says to load up, so Brandy eats three helpings of everything. I try to eat, but I'm still thinking about Holly. She should be here with us, since she was part of our core group.

I hope she made it somewhere safe.

Gideon is strangely quiet as we eat. She liked her Fire experience, so I thought she'd be more excited for us, but all she says is "Good luck."

We meet outside. There are six of us: me, Billy, Brandy, Josh, Charlotte, and Nick. Phil and Tracy are our guides.

"Single file," Phil calls out. "Keep up. We have a long way to go until we can take a break."

I sigh. The pack is heavy and it's hard to keep good balance with it on. I'm behind Brandy and Charlotte, who seem to be having no problem.

I stop to readjust my straps. They're thick and difficult.

"Let me." It's Josh.

"I can do it," I say. I give one more good yank on both sides and almost pitch forward onto my face. He catches my shoulders.

"Thanks," I say.

"No problem. I did this before at another place. It gets easier. I don't think this is going to be that bad, though. The one I did was a whole week long."

We start walking together.

"That's long. A week," I say. My shoulders are already starting to pinch under the straps.

"Yeah," he answers. "Hey, you know I'm out soon. I think a day or so before you. I can't wait. I feel cooped up."

"Where . . . the other place?" I ask. "What was that like?"

"It was in Colorado," Josh says. "Three months, mandatory. I crashed my dad's car. Last year. I wasn't messed up or anything. It was more like a behavioral camp."

"Well," I say. "You seem pretty well-behaved to me, so I guess it worked."

He laughs.

"I'm not an outdoorsy person," I tell him. "I mean, I like nature and I'm glad it's here, but I don't really want to spend an excessive amount of time in it."

"Same," he says. "I mostly play games, watch movies, stuff like that. Chess."

"I get lost at chess. I like Scrabble, though. I'm excellent at Scrabble."

"Cool. I think there's a board in the activity room. Let's do it when we get back. If we survive."

"Right," I answer, watching something kind of furry and disturbing skitter across the dirt in front of us. "If we survive."

After a few hours, we stop for lunch, which is dried fruit, nuts, water, beef jerky, and tofu nuggets. Tracy takes Charlotte and Brandy a ways off to pee, but I'm going to wait until we get where we're going, when it's dark, even though I'm feeling a little uncomfortable.

Before we start moving again, Tracy whips out the Polaroid.

"Yep," she says. "Even out here, we commemorate the moment."

We walk and hike for six hours. I know this because Charlotte has a watch.

Everywhere we go, I look for signs, even though I know I shouldn't because it's probably useless, but still . . . signs of Holly. A footprint. Maybe she dropped something. I don't know.

Anything.

But it's been five days. Someone had to have come and gotten her. Maybe she had a plan. Maybe someone knew to meet her out here.

When we finally stop, you can tell this is where they always do this, because there are remnants of other fires, like dark pits and blackened branches.

Phil claps his hands. "This is where we make camp. The first thing is shelter. Does anyone know why?"

"So we can get out of this stupid place?" Nick asks. His cheeks are red from the cold.

"Ha ha," Phil says. "Yes and no. One, yes, you need this step to complete the program. But two . . . what do we do when we need to stay warm and safe from the environment?"

"Um, go into my bedroom?" Charlotte says. "I mean, come *on.*"

"What if you don't have that? Play along nicely, Charlotte."

She throws up her hands. "I don't know, man. You tell me."

"You need to protect yourself. You need to start before it gets dark so you have something in place for the night."

I raise my hand. "And we do this . . . how?"

Brandy raises *her* hand. "I have spent a considerable amount of time watching *Alone,* so I feel pretty confident in saying we need to start collecting branches and stuff to build a shelter."

"Excellent," Tracy says. "Though we do have tents, in case we need them."

"Ohh," Nick says. "Shelter building. I think this is where the knives come in."

He looks positively glowing at that thought.

Everyone collects their knife from their pack. Tracy directs us to mesquite trees, warning us about the sharp stickers, and tells us to look for other types of fallen branches, like cottonwood.

Josh and I try to saw at some mesquite branches, but it's not as easy as it sounds, because they are sharp, and it's painful if you hit the wrong spot. We finally get some together and collect branches from cottonwoods. Everyone is fanned out, arms full, looking and wandering. We are allowed to use branches that have been left behind from other Fire trips, too. They're scattered around the site in loose piles that Phil pointed out.

When it seems like we have enough, Tracy shows us how to make a kind of A-frame for our personal shelter by lashing branches together with long strands we shave off the mesquite branches. The strands act as a kind of long, thin rope. It's very hard to cut the branches into decent strips, though.

After that, we have to drape our tarps over the A and secure them with actual rope, which Phil has been keeping in his own backpack.

This takes an incredibly long time. My A-frame falls twice, but I'm determined to get it back up.

"You need help?" Tracy asks.

"No," I say sharply. I'm still testy at her about Holly.

She holds up her hands. "All right, then."

"Well," Billy calls out to her. "*I* need help."

He's gotten twisted inside his tarp. Tracy heads over to him.

"Voilà," Josh says.

I turn around.

His shelter is perfect.

"A week in the Colorado wilderness," he crows.

"A-plus, bravo, good for you, mountain man," Charlotte calls out. Her frame is crooked, but she's done. I look over at Brandy. She's almost done, too.

My heart sinks. I'm on my third try. Why didn't I let Tracy help me?

Finally, I think I get everything solid and throw the tarp over. I hold my breath.

It stays.

I loop the mesquite rope through the holes in the tarp, tying the ends.

It stays.

I feel a little bloom of accomplishment.

Suddenly Brandy calls out, "UNFAIR," pointing to two huge, real tents on the edge of our campsite.

Phil and Tracy look at us like *So what?*, smiling away.

"Well," Phil says, laughing. "I mean, if something does happen during the night to one of your fine homemade establishments, you can seek shelter with us. And you do have your own little tents, just in case."

"I'm sure Bella will bunk with Josh if things get rough," Charlotte chortles. "Or maybe even if they don't."

"Oh my god," I say. "Shut *up.*"

Charlotte sticks out her tongue at me.

I don't even want to look at Josh, because I'm a little ashamed that while we were hiking here, I did have some thoughts like *Oh look a starry night in the wilderness what if we kissed,* that sort of thing. Not gropey, just kind of soft and fantastic stuff.

"Sorry." I finally look at him. "I'm sorry she's a jerk sometimes."

But he doesn't look mad or embarrassed.

In fact, he has a weird expression on his face.

Like maybe he was thinking the same thing about me when we were walking.

I mean, it's not going to happen, because if we got caught, we'd get in trouble.

I turn back to threading my mesquite rope.

And also . . . I don't even know how to kiss anyone when I'm sober, because Dylan was my first kiss and I was buzzed when it happened then and most of the times after. What's it like to kiss someone when you're sober? How much did my buzz contribute to how great I thought our kisses were? Maybe they weren't great after all.

I would, though, kind of like to find out if they would be.

What it's like.

Without being drunk.

"Bella." Tracy's voice snaps me out of my reverie. I can feel a blush creeping across my face. Can she tell what I was thinking?

"Let's get started on your fire, okay?" She pauses. "Are you all right? You look a little flushed."

"I'm fine," I say. "Totally fine. Ready for fire."

* * *

Phil gathers us in a circle. He shows us how to use our knives to carve a V-shaped notch in the center of one branch and to cut a second small branch in a certain way to make something called a spindle. Then he says we need to find tinder, which is like tiny leaves, dried grass, and twigs, and shape it into something that looks like a small bird's nest or bundle. He moves quickly, and it's hard for me to follow. I wish I had something to take notes with, but I do the best I can.

It's pretty hard to cut that V-shaped notch, which is small, with gloves on, so I take mine off, even though the temperature is dropping at a pretty speedy rate. I'm much better at finding the little things for the bundle. I'm pretty proud of my bundle.

And then it gets hard.

I hate this spindle. I'm trying to stick it into the notch in my wood, which is not a very good V, and I can't get a good latch. It takes me several tries. I finally do, and then I start rubbing the spindle back and forth, over and over and over, between my hands.

Like, *over and over and over.*

Like, for years.

I cannot get a spark, and you need a spark to blow on so you can add a small dry piece of bark to catch fire and then transfer that shit to your little tinder bundle and hope like hell the flames catch and you have a tiny fire that you can make into a big fire with more branches and keep going for god knows how long.

That's the plan, as far as I can tell, but it is not working for me.

My wrists are starting to ache from twisting this spindle.

It's getting downright freezing, too. It's December in the

desert, which means it's friggin' cold, no matter how thick my jeans and socks are. I don't know why they didn't have us wear long underwear, too.

I'm getting really frustrated that my spindle work is going nowhere. I decide to redo my notch. But the sun's going down and I'm losing light, so I have to dig my flashlight from my pack and it's way at the bottom.

Brandy is starting to lose it over at her spot and she asks Tracy for help.

And you know what Tracy brings her? Some sort of actual fire-starting contraption that's not a lighter but something akin to a tiny cell phone and does what a lighter does, and suddenly, Brandy has a spark that she desperately, lovingly blows, practically crooning to it as she transfers it delicately to her bundle and *bam.*

A fire.

I look over at Josh. He's sitting in front of a small, tidy fire, warming his hands. The flames glow on his face.

He's not even paying attention to me, he's so pleased with his fire. I look around. Everyone has their own little fire but me. And Billy.

Then something happens in me.

Like, a crack that starts spreading wider and wider, revealing stuff. Because I hate my unfire. I despise my nonfire.

And inside that crack is a bunch of stuff I have hated over the years.

I start frantically rubbing the spindle again.

This fire is the second grade and Hayley Mitchell pouring a tub of glue over my head and me having to get all my hair cut off to get it out. I mean, that was a shitty thing to do, right? But she was eight and so that stuff happens, you move on, blah

blah. But I guess I haven't, because there's Hayley Mitchell and her mean self in my unfire.

This unfire is Hayley Mitchell all over again, taunting me. Telling me I'll never fit in, I'll have glue on my head forever. *Glue girl.*

This unfire is me getting my period in sixth grade, before everything went haywire and they sent us home and we didn't go back for an entire year, and not realizing what had happened until a teacher pulled me aside and said, "Dear," because I had a big red spot on the back of my jeans. I swear to god, for years after, when someone would call me "dear," I'd flinch, thinking I had blood on my pants.

This unfire is my first period and those bloody jeans.

This unfire is Dylan calling me *too much.* This unfire is another example of me not being normal, because across the camp from me, I can hear Billy yell, "I have a spark!" and Phil getting all excited and then Josh asking me if I need help and even *Charlotte* has a fire.

Tracy is in front of me now, taking out that infernal fire-making contraption again. And look, here comes Phil.

Great, now I have a crowd for my unfire.

I tell them to go away.

It's so cold. I'm losing control of my arms. They feel like warm rubber and I'm trying to rub that spindle so hard and so well and still it's refusing me.

This unfire is everything, all of it, the whole past year and what guy breaks up with his girlfriend in a parking lot? JFC, sit down with her and hold her hand and do it. This unfire is my parents not breaking up sooner and my dad not having the balls to tell us he had a girlfriend before just planting her in his apartment one night. This unfire is Laurel thinking it was okay to give me schnapps and *dying* on me and me afraid to tell my mother how that felt and this unfire is me for letting everything awful take root in me and grow there into something too tough and strong for me to fight.

I can hear them cooking tofu hot dogs and roasting marshmallows over their fires and I think I even smell hot chocolate and I can't stop the eternal waterfall of silent tears that's drowning my face.

Then I see a spark. Some shit-tiny little spark. A flick of orange, and I throw my spindle away and bend down and blow and it gets brighter and smoke comes up and a little flame appears, a beautiful tiny flame, and I hold my bark over it and soon enough the bark's on fire and I swear to the stars above and everything else that if that bark will just stay lit until I get it in my tinder bundle I will stay sober until the end of time and

I have a fire. I shout it out.

"I have a fire!"

Everyone cheers.

I grab some rocks and make a ring and place my branches and twigs in just the right way like Phil showed us and add more twigs and more dried grass and there it is. And I thought I would stop crying, but I haven't.

It's like I've opened something that can't be closed.

Tracy comes over and sits down and pats me on the back and says, "That's a swell fire."

"It is," I say.

"Then why are you crying?"

"I think I broke something in myself," I say quietly. "I don't know."

She doesn't look sad or mad or disappointed at that. She just says, "Bella, it's okay to ask for help. You don't have to kill yourself proving something before you ask for help. That's kind of the whole point of this. We teach you basic skills so you can have tools out there in the world and survive, but we also teach you that when those tools don't work, you ask for help. You recognize that you need help before you . . . break something in yourself."

"So I failed. I didn't pass," I say. "So I'm going to have to do this again. Because I refused help."

She kind of laughs. "You didn't fail anything. In fact, you showed a tremendous amount of tenacity, and I think that refusal to give up is going to serve you pretty well."

"But I need to ask for help," I say.

"Yeah," she says.

So I say, "I'm goddamn starving. Could you help me cook some tofu and make hot chocolate? Because I don't think I can use my arms anymore."

The hot chocolate is good. I sit on a rock around the main campfire, next to Josh, while Phil plays guitar, and I'm so exhausted I can barely hold my cup; my arms are still rubbery. Josh's parka'd arm is slightly touching mine, and that feels really good. I know he can't exactly leave another warm mouth print on me out here like he did at the Star Pit, but this counts.

Not first-kiss-under-a-starry-sky kind of good, but good nonetheless.

I made fire.

And I only have ten days left.

DAY TWENTY-ONE

TRACY TAKES OUR PICTURES in the desert. Photos of our campsite, our fire sites, our sad-sack A-frame shelters (though Josh's is perfect).

Josh grabs Tracy's camera when she isn't looking and holds it above us.

Click.

Before I can even look at it, he shoves the photo in the pocket of my parka and races to put Tracy's camera back by her tent.

Phil cooks everyone sausages and toast over his campfire and makes coffee.

After that, we make sure all the fires are out, dousing them with water, kicking dirt on them, inspecting for any still-warm coals. We take apart our A-frames, careful to leave the branches for the next group. Roll up our tarps, stuff them in our backpacks.

It's a long walk back, but I don't mind. It's slightly downhill, which is a relief. Josh stays with me. We don't talk very much, but it doesn't feel uncomfortable.

It feels comfortable.

When we stop for lunch, Tracy's cell beeps. She looks at it, then frowns. She takes her phone off into the distance, where we can't hear. When she comes back, she whispers in Phil's ear and his face gets funny, but not in a good way. In a grim way.

“Let’s pack up, everyone,” he says, standing. “We need to head back a little quicker than we hoped.”

“What’s up?” Billy asks. “You look weird.”

“Nothing,” Tracy says. “Just some bad weather we should try to head off.”

“She’s lying,” Brandy whispers to me.

“Yeah,” I say. I wonder about what.

When we get closer to Sonoran Sunrise, Tracy and Phil stop and turn around, facing us.

Phil’s eyes are wet. He clears his throat.

“Everyone,” he says, his voice faltering. “There’s been an incident.”

My stomach drops. Josh steps closer to me.

Tracy licks her lips. “Early this morning, Gideon was found unconscious in her room.”

“No,” I say. I step forward. Tracy holds up her hand.

Everything inside me drains away.

“What are you talking about?” Brandy says, her voice cracking. “Is she . . . d—”

She can’t even say the word.

“No,” Tracy says firmly. “She was unconscious, she’s been transported to the hospital, she’s being cared for.”

“But . . . how?” I ask. “Was she sick?”

“No, dummy,” Charlotte says, her voice thick with bitterness. “Grow up. She OD’d. Didn’t she, Phil? Tracy?”

Phil nods.

“But . . . like, how?” Brandy asks. “What was it?”

“Is she going to live?” I ask desperately.

Phil holds up his hands. “Too many voices all at once. We

know only a little at this moment, but we wanted to prepare you before we get there."

"This happens," Tracy says. "Things get in. We aren't perfect. People devise new ways all the time."

"You got that right," Charlotte mutters.

"But she was all alone in our room," I say. "Didn't they do a bed check or—"

"That's why she probably did it," Charlotte says. "Because we weren't there. No one to bother her when she offed herself."

I turn toward her, angry. "Are you saying she tried to kill herself?"

"Again, grow up," Charlotte says, snapping her fingers in my face. "She's not just going to take a tiny bit here and there in this place. She was supposed to get out in a few days, but she doesn't have anywhere to go, remember? Her parents wouldn't take her back." She turns to Phil and Tracy. "Right?"

They nod sadly.

First Holly, now Gideon. My heart is racing.

"Why can't you take care of people?" I spit at Tracy. "You say you do, but you don't. Don't you have something in place for people who have nowhere to go, after? That isn't fair. Even with Holly, you knew she had nowhere but that . . . place. You knew her foster parents weren't coming and you didn't prepare her. She seemed happy. She had plans. She took pictures of me—"

"Bella," Tracy says. "I know you're upset—"

Beside me, Charlotte's voice is cold. "Like this?" she asks, holding up her phone. "Pictures like this?"

My voice, slurred and feral, rings out in our small group, across the quiet desert.

Dyyyyyylaaannnn . . .

Look at me

Look at me

Everyboooooooddddy

As if in slow motion, I turn toward the vision of myself on Charlotte's phone, slopping around in front of Lemon's camera, my face slack, my makeup smeared. My breast hanging out, fleshy and pale.

Josh's face is unreadable. Brandy covers her mouth. Billy steps away from us.

"Charlotte," Phil says. "My god."

"The internet," Charlotte says, "is a glorious place where things live forever, unlike the real world. Which Gideon was trying to leave. Maybe now, O dear overlords, you should tell everyone, now that they're already upset, that Holly's dead."

Tracy opens her mouth, but nothing comes out. She looks helpless.

That's how I know it's true.

Phil drops his eyes. "They found her in a house a few days ago—"

"We all need to take a moment—" Tracy starts.

Brandy starts crying.

Charlotte is still holding up her phone. She muted it, but I'm replaying over and over on her screen.

"Holly was never going to make it anyway," she mutters.

I grab the phone and throw it as far as I can into the desert.

And then, even with my heavy backpack on, I deck her.

I hit her for Holly, and for Gideon, and for the video, and for everything, everything, everything, until someone pulls me off her.

DAY TWENTY-TWO

I'M TWO AND A half deaths down in my lifetime and locked in a room with a futon and a beanbag.

Holly and my grandmother are fulls. Gideon is the half.

I'm in Seg.

If I had a whole bottle of vodka right now, I would drink it down as fast as I could.

I wouldn't even need the Sprite.

Anything to obliterate myself.

They say that you'll get better here.

You don't.

I shut myself down.

DAY TWENTY-THREE

DAY TWENTY-FOUR

THERE'S A KNOCK AT the Seg door.

I don't get up as it opens. Janet walks across the room and stands over me, a phone in her hand.

"Bella," she says. "There's someone on the phone for you."

"I don't care. Isn't that against the rules? I'm supposed to be in isolation." My voice is flat.

Being alone can really do a number on you.

"Yes," she says. "But it's a little girl. She says you're her sister."

From the phone, I hear a tiny voice say, "Bella, where are you?"

I grab the phone. Janet steps away but doesn't leave.

"Ricci," I breathe. "Ricci, are you all right? Where are you?"

Small hiccupping. "I'm at Daddy's. I'm supposed to be with Mommy, but they trade me every three days now, since you went away. Where *are* you? It is Christmas Eve. Mommy said you're on a school trip, but school is out, Bella."

My heart sinks. She sounds so sad. And what an awful way to put it: being *traded.* Like a toy.

"Ricci . . . where is Daddy?"

"He's right here. On the couch. He's sleeping. Bella, I heard my friend's mom talking at school and she said you're in the hospital. Are you . . . going to die, like Grandma?"

A thousand knives pierce my body.

"No, Ricci, I'm not." I take a deep breath. "I'm . . . I wasn't doing too well, but I went away to get better. I'm not . . . I'm not going to die."

She whimpers. "I knew you weren't on a field trip. Field trips don't last that long, and they don't happen at Christmas. You would have sent me a postcard."

"I would have. Ricci, where's Vanessa? Is she there?"

A pause. "Vanessa hasn't been here in a long time. Daddy doesn't want to talk about it."

I close my eyes. *Daddy doesn't want to talk about it.*

"Are you coming home soon? Tomorrow is Christmas. Daddy didn't get a tree. Mommy's taking me to Agnes's."

"I—" I look up at Janet like she can help me, but she can't. I know she can hear everything. She averts her eyes. I bet she knows if I got added time for attacking Charlotte.

"I'll be home, but I don't know when. But I'm not going to die, okay, Ricci? And I miss you so much."

"I love you, Bella."

"I love you too. Can you wake Daddy up, please?"

"Okay."

I hear the phone thunking on something hard and then her whispering, "Daddy, wake up. Bella's on the phone. Wake up, Daddy."

"Bella? What's wrong?" His voice is hoarse. "Are you all right?"

I suck in a breath.

"No, Dad, I'm not all right. I'm in rehab and one of my friends here died and another one OD'd and my baby sister called me to ask if *I'm* going to die. I'm not all right. At all."

"Bella—"

I cut him off.

"Listen to me," I say, gritting my teeth. "You go out and get her a Christmas tree, *right now.* She is *seven* years old. Then you decorate that tree with her *tonight.* There's colored paper in the drawer in her dresser in our bedroom. Staple some rings, glue them, I don't care. But decorate that tree. And if you didn't get her any presents because you were too tired or you forgot or you thought Mom or Vanessa would take care of it, you take her to Walmart and buy her whatever the hell she wants."

"Bella, listen—"

"No, I'm not going to listen. After all that's done, you and Mom are going to sit down and figure out how to tell Ricci the truth, by yourselves, before I come home, whenever that is, because I'm currently in a locked room for god knows how long. Do your job, goddammit."

Before I hang up, I add, "Merry Christmas."

I hand the phone back to Janet. My hands are shaking.

"Well done," she murmurs. "I liked that sign-off."

"Well," I say, "he is my dad."

She smiles.

"I don't understand how she got that number," I say. "She's seven. How would she get the number if they told her I was on a school field trip?"

Janet hesitates. "Listen," she says.

"What?"

"It sounds like there are some issues with your dad, and we don't need to go into that? I kind of got the gist by your very one-sided conversation, but you should know . . . he calls here every day."

"What?"

"Pretty much every day. He doesn't ask to talk to you. He knows you probably won't talk to him, I guess. But he just wants to know how you are. Good day, bad day, okay day, eating all right, that sort of stuff."

My dad has been calling to check on me every day and I didn't even know. Frustrated tears spring to my eyes.

"That's probably how she got the number. She looked in his phone, and he saved it with your name. That's my guess. I'll bring you dinner in a little bit and take you to the restroom."

Janet leaves.

My dad couldn't reschedule a meeting to come see me, but he calls every day. My dad and mom lied to my little sister and she thought I was going to die. One friend did die, the other almost, and I think I punched Charlotte at least three times before Josh pulled me off her.

And I'm stuck in this room.

I pick up the beanbag and rip it to shreds.

DAY TWENTY-FIVE

TRACY IS NOT HAPPY about the decimated beanbag. When she steps into the Seg room, she takes one glance at it, tucks her folder under one arm, and pulls out her phone to tap out a text. She slips her phone into her back pocket and looks me over.

"At least you didn't hurt yourself. Did you?"

I'm sitting on the futon, wedged in the corner. I don't answer her. I feel electrical, like wires are strung tight inside me and they're malfunctioning, sending up random sparks every now and then.

She sits on the floor and pulls her knees up to her chest.

"Charlotte is fine," she says quietly. "A few bruises, nothing more. I'm sorry I didn't tell you about Holly."

I feel like I might answer her, if I had words, but I don't seem to have any left. Maybe I've said everything I had to say and I'll be silent forever. Maybe I can just stay in this room until my time is done here, with whatever days they'll add on for my outburst on Charlotte, and when I leave, it will be as an empty sort of human shell. Skin with nothing left inside. Maybe that would be better for everyone.

"It happens," she says. "What Gideon did. Even here. Things aren't linear in recovery. No straight lines. One day things are working out; the next day, a little fissure, a crack, and we go right back to where we started from. There isn't any shame in that. We get up, we bandage ourselves as best we can, and we start over."

She sighs.

"I don't really like the sound of just my voice. It makes me feel lonely," she says. She pulls some paper from her folder and rips off a piece, slides it across the floor and rolls a pen to me.

I wait a moment before grabbing it, then I do, and I scribble, *is she dead?*

I shove the paper across the floor at her.

"No," she says after reading it. "Gideon is not dead. She's getting care. She'll recover."

A little weight is lifted inside me. I didn't want anyone else to die. I cannot have one more person die.

"There's no way we could have known, Bella. Things creep in here sometimes. Addicts . . . and I am one, and always will be . . . the most interesting thing to me is how absolutely crafty we can be sometimes. Like, the things we'll think of to get wrecked, do you know what I mean? It takes so much work, you know? If we could just put that amount of work into trying to take care of ourselves."

She laughs. "I mean, honestly. We search people when they come in for visiting days. We do! But that was a new one for me, for sure. How long do you think they planned that? Her cousin buying the exact type of sneaker Gideon wears, ripping out the insole, slipping drugs in there, and then gluing it back down. And then the way they traded, just one shoe each, under the table? It's impressive, truth be told."

The sneakers. The matching sneakers. The way she held them so carefully in her hands that day in our room.

There's a knock on the door. Tracy gets up and opens it.

Fran hands her a dustpan, a broom, a bag, and a little box, and then closes the door.

Tracy leans the broom and dustpan against a wall and sets the bag on the ground. She holds the box out to me.

"For you," she says. "You've made a mess and you need to fix it. By yourself. When we make messes, we're responsible for cleaning up the damage."

I don't take the box.

She puts the box down by me and sits back on the floor, cross-legged this time. She pulls out her phone again and begins scrolling.

"I have all day," she says. "I get time and a half on holidays. We had a meeting and we won't add days to your time here. The only person you hurt was yourself. Charlotte was equally responsible for egging you on, but you've put in some work here, and whatever you needed to get out of yourself, well, it sure did come out."

I reach for the box and open it.

Inside are a needle, thread, and a small pair of scissors. I look over at the scattered white beans, the ripped fabric of the beanbag.

"Merry Christmas," Tracy says.

I'm sleeping when I hear a soft tap on the door. It took me a long time to gather all the beans and sew and stuff the fabric of the bag, to sweep up the bean dust and loose threads. There was nothing to do after that except go back to sleep. If I didn't, I'd just sit there and think about Gideon, and Holly, and Laurel, all lost to me now.

The door opens.

It's Janet.

"I shouldn't do this," she says. "But for some reason, I am. Come on out."

She motions to me. I wipe the sleep from my eyes and go to the door. Janet opens it a little wider.

Josh is standing in the hallway.

"Everybody made a Christmas party in the activity room," he says. "It isn't any fun without you."

Janet closes the door to the Seg room and looks at us sternly.

"Ten minutes," she says. "That's it. And you stay here, where I can see you. Understand?"

We nod. Janet walks back down the hall to the desk and sits. She turns on some Christmas music, very low, on her computer.

"Hi," I say.

"Hi," he says.

"Thanks," I say.

"You really did a number on Charlotte," he says.

"Tracy said she was fine."

I look away from his face. He's seen me, now. Naked. Drunk. *Too much.*

"Hey," he says. "That thing, what she showed? I don't care. I mean, I *do* care, because it was hurtful to you. But I don't think you should be embarrassed or ashamed."

I look at him.

He speaks more quickly. "I mean, I'm here, too, you know? I've . . . Things have happened to me, too, or I've done them. That maybe I don't feel so great about. I guess what I'm saying is, if you think that video is something that will make me not feel what I feel for you, you're wrong."

"I— That's good to know," I say.

"So. Also," he says, shifting from foot to foot. "I'm leaving."

My heart drops. "What? I thought that was the twenty-seventh? What happened?"

He shrugs. "My parents are pulling me. They've had tickets to Cancùn for a while, and I guess they figure a few days early isn't going to make much difference. They wanted to pull me after they saw what happened when Holly ran. I think that really freaked them out. But I wanted to stay."

"That sucks," I say.

"I know. I don't make the rules. I just try to stay out of their way, you know?"

"I know," I say. "I know."

"I just wanted to say goodbye and . . . you know, well, I hope you're okay. With everything. I was worried for you. And I hope we can talk. After all this. When you're out."

"Yes," I say. "Definitely."

He reaches into his back pocket and hands me his phone. I punch my number in.

"Cool," he says, taking the phone back. "Cool."

There's a very warm pocket of something between us. Something I want to lean into.

Josh steps closer to me.

"Four minutes," Janet calls from down the hall.

He steps away.

"Do you want to . . . They're dancing at the party," he says. "Do you want to dance? I mean, Janet has that music playing and all."

Janet has a slow Christmas song on, something I don't recognize, old-timey, maybe from the fifties. A singer with a mournful voice.

I nod.

Awkwardly we step toward each other. Josh puts his hands on my waist and I put mine on his shoulders. Slowly, we move in a circle.

I don't really know where to look. I can feel his breath on my cheek, and if I actually look *at* him, our mouths would be like an inch away and—

I look at him.

He swallows. "Your face looks a lot better. I'm glad I can see the other half now, because they're equally nice. I've been meaning to tell you that."

He moves his face closer to mine. Time . . . sort of slows.

The Christmas music abruptly stops.

"Oh, no, no, no, no," Janet calls out sharply. "Nope, nada, separate, that's it, time's up, merry Christmas. Time to go, young man. And time for you to go back in your carriage, Cinderella."

She's marching toward us. We drop our arms from each other and stand far apart.

"Off you go," she says to him. "You need to finish packing."

"Right," he says.

"Goodbye," I say. My hands are shaking a little. I turn toward the door of Seg.

"Wait," Josh says. "I have something for you."

I turn back to him. He's holding out a candy cane.

"I took it from the tree," he says.

Janet slips the candy cane from his fingers and hands it to me.

"Go," she tells him.

"Bye, Bella," he says softly. "See you on the outside."

I watch as he walks down the hall, looking back at me once,

giving me a small wave, and then rounds the corner to the activity room.

"Don't tell anyone," Janet says. "It would ruin my reputation as a hard-ass."

"'Your secret is safe with me," I say. I step inside and she closes the door, leaving me alone in the room again.

I stretch out on the futon, lay the candy cane next to me, turn on my side to stare at it.

I wasn't with Dylan at Christmastime, so I never got anything from him. This is the first Christmas present I've ever gotten from a boy.

A candy cane in rehab.

DAY TWENTY-SIX

Dear Ricci,

Impact letter time. You are probably the hardest one for me to write, because you are seven, and obviously, I can't give this to you. One, you wouldn't understand it, and it would probably confuse you even more. After all, you thought I was away on a school field trip. (For the life of me, I don't understand why they came up with that excuse. I mean, I know anything is better than "your sister OD'd on booze and almost died on the front porch," but I think they could have tried a little harder. I hope they tell you the truth, like I asked them to.) I think as you get older you'll realize that parents make things more complicated than they need to be a lot of the time.

Anyway, I'm here. I'm at rehab, which is a place they send you when you have some sort of problem and need time away. I'll write this as though I'm going to give it to you when you're much older, and maybe I will. Or maybe I won't. We'll see. We call these impact letters because we're supposed to recognize the impact our actions have had on other people, like you.

I drank a lot of alcohol, and yes, I almost died on Mom's front porch. We can talk about the particulars of that years from now, when you can comprehend it. It wasn't pleasant and it was my fault, because I drank too much, and then I drank some more, and then some more on top of that. And I'm here because everyone would like me to stop drinking. I think that I would like to stop it, too, and I think I can. I mean, I've been here twenty-six days without a drink. I haven't run away. I didn't accept someone's drugs taped to the inside of the bottom of their shoe and relapse while in an actual rehab. I've been doing a lot and following along but I had a little blip a few days ago, which is too bad, because I missed Christmas here and I have to stay in a room all by myself. That's a story for another time.

What I want to say is: you annoy me, you irritate me, you make me laugh, I miss snuggling with you and reading to you in bed and your whole nighttime routine, and I am really sorry that what happened happened and that you're alone now, without me. I'm sorry about whatever you're thinking right now and how lonely you might be feeling. I'm sorry that at some point you probably asked Mom when you get to go on a monthlong field trip for school in the middle of Thanksgiving and Christmas and that she probably started to cry.

This hurts:

I'm sorry that sometimes my need to drink could have hurt you. There were times that I thought about drinking while making you dinner at Dad's. I thought about it sometimes when I was giving you a bath at Mom's. Like, I could have snuck something and left you in the tub with your toys. And what then? What if I had passed out and you got hurt? I could never forgive myself. I never want to hurt you, but I'm pretty sure I have, just by being here, and you don't even know it. You don't know why I haven't sent a postcard. Or called. Or texted. I wonder what you think about that. There must be a million thoughts in your head.

Those million thoughts? They are my fault, and I'm sorry. And I hope you aren't stuffing them way down deep inside you so you don't upset anyone, like Mom or Dad, because while I do disagree with some things they tell us here, I can one hundred percent say that stuffing yourself with your feelings is not a good thing. Eventually, that will land you in a small room like it did me, and you'll miss Christmas, and your people, like I miss you right now.

I'm going to see you soon, and I can't wait. I love you.

—Bella

P.S. There are goats and chickens here and they all have names, but I can never remember who is who. I bet you could.

DAY TWENTY-SEVEN

I'M OUT OF SEG now, but I can't go back to Gen Pop until Charlotte and I talk things through. It's called conflict resolution.

That's what Tracy said, anyway. Charlotte and I are sitting in her office, along with Phil and Fran.

"Right here, right now, the both of you can talk it out," Tracy says. "Charlotte, you can begin."

Charlotte is slouched in her easy chair, her legs crossed at the ankles. She straightens herself up and looks me square in the face.

"I'm sorry that I showed everyone the video, Bella. I think . . . I don't know. I have a lot of feelings about Gideon and Holly, too. And being here. I just lashed out. I wanted to hurt somebody. That's what I do. I'm not proud of it."

She looks at Tracy. Tracy nods and looks at me.

"I felt violated that you showed that video. I don't understand why you'd do that. I mean—"

My voice might be a little harsher than it should be.

Phil cuts in. "She just told you, Bella. Sometimes we have mechanisms we use when we feel scared or grieved or threatened. Sometimes they aren't the appropriate ones. But she apologized. That's a start. Give her a chance."

I take a deep breath.

"I accept your apology, Charlotte. And I'm sorry for hitting you. That wasn't the right reaction to what you did."

(I don't think I entirely believe this, but I say it anyway.)

"I accept your apology," Charlotte says, blinking at me. "I am really sorry. That was a shitty thing to do."

"We don't have to talk about it anymore," I say.

"Can we go?" Charlotte asks.

Phil, Tracy, and Fran look at each other.

"That was possibly the easiest resolution meeting we've ever had," Fran says.

"You can go," Tracy says.

I stand up and follow Charlotte out the door.

"Are you still hurt?" I ask. "I really am sorry."

"Nah," she says. "I'm good."

She stops and grabs me in a hug, tight.

"We're all good," she says. "We need to stick together, right? Shit happens, but we need to stick together in this place."

"Yeah," I say gratefully into her pink hair. "We do."

DAY TWENTY-EIGHT

IN MY DREAM, I'M floating in someone's pool. The water is warm and nice, so it must be summer, maybe July, when it gets so hot pools heat up and even by nighttime they're still warm when you step in. Someone is whispering to me from across the pool, but I can't see who it is and I don't know why they don't just shout.

Then I'm not dreaming. I'm awake. The room is dark, filled with the sounds of my roommates breathing softly in their sleep, and Charlotte is peering down at me, a grin on her face.

"Come," she says. "Come with me. I want to show you something. You can't say no, okay? It's very special. But *be quiet.*"

"Where?" I ask.

"Just come *on,* silly girl. Change your clothes first, though. We're going outside."

Her teeth shine brightly in the dark room.

In the hall, she pauses, looking both ways. The night person is way down to the left, headphones on, staring at her laptop. Charlotte creeps to the right and pulls me with her, toward the exit at the other end of the hall. As we near it, she puts a finger to her lips.

"I don't want to get in trouble," I whisper as low as possible.

“Shut up,” she says. “It’s fine. I’ve done it before.”

At the end of the hall, she pushes gently on the door until it gives and only opens it the merest amount, just enough for us to slip through. When I’m out, she holds it carefully until it latches back into place with a soft click.

My heart kind of spikes when I hear that click. Can we even get back in? Don’t these doors lock behind you at night? There must be some sort of alarm—

Charlotte looks at me. “I know what you’re thinking. I’ll just say we couldn’t sleep and went to the Star Pit and forgot to tell whatever-her-name-is in there. The new one. Do you even remember her name?”

She giggles.

I think a minute. “Lisa. Her name is Lisa. But what about bed check? What if they do a bed check?”

She shrugs. “Same story. Plus, that’s not for a few hours yet. And that one, that Lisa. I’ve been watching her. She’s been forgetting bed checks lately. I think she forgot about Gideon. Just follow me.”

She skirts around the edge of the dorm building and heads toward the Star Pit, which relieves me, because if we do get in trouble, sure, we can say we went there. It shouldn’t be too bad. I mean, I only have two days left. They can’t kick me out for sitting outside and looking at the stars and talking. I made it through Fire. I’ve *made* it.

But Charlotte turns right, veering away from the path to the Star Pit, toward the goat and chicken pen.

My stomach is in knots. I stop walking.

“Charlotte,” I whisper. “I don’t like this.”

She ignores me.

It's really cold out here. I should have put on my mittens and hat.

I run after her.

She opens the latch to the goat pen and I follow her, stepping carefully so I don't walk in shit, though I realize that's probably impossible. Charlotte takes my hand, pulling me forward across their enclosure, into the area where the chickens are nestled in their boxes, plump and sleeping. Their heat lamps are on. It's warmer in here.

Charlotte leads me back to where the feed buckets and supplies are.

I rub my cold hands together.

Charlotte is fiddling with the padlock to the door where the Feed Dude stacks the bags of feed and bundles of hay and grass.

She looks back at me, her eyes shining. "Easy-peasy."

She's holding up a paper clip. She slips it into her pocket, pulls open the door, and disappears inside.

This is not good. I just got out of Seg.

"I'm going to go back," I whisper. "I'll just tell them the Star Pit thing and—"

Charlotte emerges from the darkness of the supply room, grinning. She opens her jacket.

In the inside pocket on the left side, the top of a bottle peeks out.

The goats stir in their beds, bleat softly.

"No," I say. "No, Charlotte."

I'm panicking. My voice is high-pitched. I start to sweat a little, even though I'm shivering.

"Don't be such a baby," she says. "You can just sit with me. For a little while. *Please.*"

I shake my head.

"Fine." Her voice has changed. It's harder. "Be that way. I thought you were my friend. I thought we made up. I thought you, of all people, would at least hang out with me."

"Charlotte, I don't want to get in trouble."

She waves a hand. "Oh, please. You're the baby of the group. You had some slips, but they aren't going to kick you out or anything. They didn't even kick you out after you attacked me! You did *nothing* compared to what people have done here to get kicked out. You have two days. Trust me. I'm lonely. I just want someone to talk to. I'm getting out tomorrow. I've put up with a lot of bullshit here and I deserve this."

She walks away from me and sits on the ground, puts the bottle in front of her.

"I don't care. Just go. It's not even my thing, you know. Drinking. So it's not a big deal. I haven't done any of the stuff I wasn't supposed to while I was here, so what rule am I really breaking anyway?"

She shoves her back against the wall of the pen, kicks a boot against the ground.

"I just want someone to talk to. You don't have to do it. I won't make you. What, you can't even, like, be around it?"

I'm looking at the bottle. It's not vodka. It's something else, something brown. She unscrews the cap and takes a long drink. She coughs a little.

Then she closes her eyes and leans against the wall again.

I can see what's happening inside her from the outside. The way her shoulders loosen inside her parka. The muscles of her round face getting softer. I can feel the warmth spreading inside her as whatever it is makes its way around. Probably a little sizzle in her mouth.

My face gets hot. I . . . think I can taste that sizzle, too.

"No one understands what it's like, you know? I mean, people who aren't *us,*" she says quietly.

I'm being pulled in a thousand different directions. Seg. Two days left here. Made it through Fire, the last thing. The very last thing. Didn't I do everything they wanted? I did make it. I did last. Doesn't that prove that nothing is really wrong with me, if I could make it through? And if I did make it through all these days, well, I can do it out there, too. I'll just have to be careful.

But right now, right here, it's right *here.*

My brain says: *Stop thinking, Bella.*

And that is the only thing I hear, because my heart is eerily silent.

I walk to Charlotte in a kind of vibrating fog, each part of me alert and focused. I'm me, but not me. I am just a thing who wants one thing.

I understand what Fran was talking about in group now, when she had all those months and one day she went down an alley like in a dream and ended it all.

I cough. Charlotte laughs. My mouth feels singed; a thousand sparks go off in my throat and everything lands inside me with a fiery explosion of pleasure and heat.

"What did I do," I say. "What have I done."

Charlotte laughs. "It'll go away after a few more. That's

the nice thing. It makes you feel bad at first, but then it takes it away. And isn't that the best thing, when all the bad goes away?"

Yes.

The goats eye us curiously. Charlotte pulls out her phone. Giggles over videos. Texts her friends. Shows me memes.

"We should go," I whisper. "That's enough."

I take a few more sips.

It's hitting me a little hard. I waver, even though I'm sitting down.

"Your tolerance is shot," Charlotte says, pulling on the sleeve of my parka back toward her. "You'll have to build that back up when you're on the outside."

Things are getting a little fuzzy. Her voice sounds like we're underwater.

"Where did you even get this?" I ask, my words blurry in my mouth.

She laughs.

Charlotte made friends with the Feed Dude. That's why she always wanted to be the one to help him unload. That's why it was always Charlotte's job. A little flirting here, an exchange of money there, why should he even care? It's just a job to him. He doesn't care about anyone here. People need money. What's it to him? He puts a little smiley face on the bag that has the bottle. She's been picking locks for years. Her parents locked things up to keep her safe and she figured out how to unlock them with a few videos on YouTube, to keep herself the way she needed to be. She's been doing this off and on for weeks now. She isn't stupid. She figured out the pattern of urine tests and blood tests. She took her chances. Rolled the dice, so to speak.

"I'm getting out," she says after a while. "I have to prep myself. This is just a little last celebration, and I'm spending it with you. Isn't that cool? When you get out, we'll hang out. I'll take you to the mall. We'll use my dad's credit card. He loves that. Let's go to Claire's!"

She fingers her naked earlobes wistfully.

"I can't wait to be me again," she murmurs.

"God, I hate this world," she says.

"Take it easy." She giggles. "Don't overdo it. I don't want you to break your face again."

The chickens look so pert and fluffy in their boxes. The pen smells musty. What time is it? That night person surely must be doing bed checks by now.

But all those worries are muted in me, now.

I have missed this.

I try to stand up, because I have to pee, but my body is jelly.

Charlotte is standing above me, looking at me intently.

She snaps her fingers.

"Hey," she says. "Bella. Hey."

I look at her. Both of her. The two Charlottes flitting in front of me. I blink.

"I'm going outside to pee. I'll be right back, okay?"

She picks up the bottle. I reach for it.

"Uh-uh," she says. "Don't worry. I'll be back. Sit tight."

"Charlotte," I call, my voice thin and soft. "Charlotte, are you really going to set fire to your dad's car when you get out? I don't think he'll let us use his credit card at Claire's if you do."

She turns back to me and winks.

"That's for me to know and you to find out."

She doesn't come back for a long time.

And then longer.

I can't get up. I am jelly, water, soft bone, squish, becoming small and invisible in this pen of animals. A goat wanders over and nestles my leg with its damp nose. Soft. Soft fur. Sleepy. Me and the goat are sleepy.

Please come back, Charlotte.

I.

DAY TWENTY-NINE

IT'S AS FAMILIAR AS an old sweater you thought you lost but find buried on the bottom of the closet under shoes and old comics. Or shoved inexplicably underneath the back seat of a car. It smells fusty from disuse but you put it on anyway and instantly its warmth, that feeling of comfort, rushes right back to you as you bury yourself in it. You feel like you're home.

Only, this home is not a comfortable sweater. It is sweat on my forehead and pinpricks of pain shooting sharply behind and in front of my eyes. It is everything inside my head and heart suddenly weighted down, again again again, after twenty-eight days of what I realize now, sitting in the stinking goat pen, curious noses pushing at my cheek, and staring at Tracy, who is watching me, who is sitting on the pen floor with me, who is waiting for me to say something, I realize now it was a gradual lightening I felt all this time, even though I didn't want to. Even though I fought it. Even though I didn't want to admit it felt good.

To not wake up this way. The way I am now. The way I was for so long.

I push myself up into a sitting position. Bits of hay and feed fall from my cheek. A few chickens skitter over with excitement.

Tracy takes a Polaroid of me and stands before me, flapping it slowly.

"I'm sorry," I say.

"The Feed Dude," Tracy says. She stretches her neck. I wonder how long she's been waiting for me to come to. "Was it the Feed Dude?"

I look over at the supply room door, the padlock hanging open. I know that inside, among the stacks of bags, is one with a tear and a small smiley face on the side.

I nod slowly. Which is a mistake, because I have a crick in my neck from being passed out on the ground. I don't know how long I've been in here. I only remember Charlotte, and the bottle, and *shhh shhh* and *doesn't this feel better now.*

"Where is Charlotte?" I ask. My mouth is dry. My tongue sticks to the roof of my mouth.

Tracy reaches into her jacket pocket. Her nose and cheeks are red from the cold morning. She throws a bottle of water at me. I catch it, drink, swirl the water in my mouth. I wonder why I don't have to pee and then I realize why. I peed myself. I'm sitting in wet, smelly jeans.

Tracy says, "She's gone. She was here for two and a half months. She turned eighteen yesterday."

"Oh," I say.

"I think," Tracy says slowly, "that the reason she acted out, didn't complete steps, maybe, was so she could stay here longer, until she turned eighteen."

"What do you mean?" I ask.

"I don't think she wanted to go home. And now she doesn't have to. Someone picked her up a few hours ago. It wasn't her family."

"Bella," Tracy says. "Charlotte didn't care about you. You were a sport to her. Today was your day twenty-nine and Charlotte did you dirty."

I burst into tears. Giant, slobbery, snot-from-the-nose tears. Giant, gut-wrenching, shame-filled sobs.

I had twenty-nine days. Charlotte didn't do me dirty. I did myself dirty.

"You'll meet more people in life like that, Bella," Tracy goes on. "They're all around us. Sometimes we don't see it right away, but we learn. You're fifteen. You're just beginning at life."

She stands up, brushing off her backside and knees.

"Come," she says.

I look up at her. "Where are we going? Are my parents here?" My stomach feels rotten; I'm filled with shame and sadness at the thought of having to face them.

"No," Tracy says. "They aren't."

"I don't understand."

There's no pity on her face. There's no sympathy or disappointment. There's only matter-of-factness. She must have been through this a million times before.

"We're going to Detox," she says. "You're back at Day One."

The thundering in my head gets louder and louder as my brain screams *Nonononononono want to go home, want my bed, my sister, my mother, my father, my fairy lights, my home my home my home, nonononononono.* The thundering mixes with my sobs as Tracy waits, patiently, hands in the pockets of her parka.

I worked hard and then I didn't and then I worked hard and then I broke but then I had hope and then I could just see the light at the end of the tunnel and all I had was one more day, twenty-four hours, and it was just going to be a little, just the smallest bit, and it felt so good in my mouth, my throat, and those first few sips hit hard, setting my blood on fire and it felt so good and I felt *me,* I felt *me* again, I felt—

I bury my head in my knees and smell the damp piss on my jeans as I choke and cry.

Tracy throws the Polaroid picture at my feet.

I lift my head and look at it in the dirt.

I look . . . unreal.

"Do you like sitting in your own waste, Bella? Is this how you want to remember yourself, years from now?"

That girl's face in the picture. Smudged with dirt and snot. Puffy and unkempt. Her body soaked in her own pee.

"No," I say.

"Do you need help, Bella?" Tracy asks.

Do I answer? Do I make a sound, other than my crying? I can't tell. I'm breaking into bit after tiny bit, watching myself float away.

"Do you need help, Bella?"

I wipe my face clean with my hands.

I had twenty-nine days and now I'm sitting in my own piss.

Wasted and hungover.

I can't do this anymore.

"Yes," I say. "I need help."

I look up. I take her hand.

DAY ONE

WE PASS A GROUP of kids running desperately after Chuck on our way back to the building. They seem angry, scared, tired, forlorn. All those things at once. They don't look at us. They don't want to lose sight of Chuck. They don't want to get lost. It's easy to get lost, even here.

Tracy sees me watching them.

"No one likes labels, Bella. But sometimes it helps to have a name for something. When we name things, we understand them. We know where we fit. It's not a cage. It's a field of possibilities," she says.

I know what she wants me to say.

"I'm an alcoholic."

The world does not break. The walls of Sonoran Sunrise don't crumble. Violins do not erupt from nowhere. Tracy doesn't clasp me in a bear hug as I weep on her shoulder.

But something, maybe the tiniest thing, loosens inside me. A relief.

In the activity room, Tracy gets the camera from the shelf.

I stand by the wall.

When she aims the camera at me, I look right into the lens and I do not blink.

FOUR

And oh, what do I do?
'Cause God how it hurts

—Julia Jacklin, "Pressure to Party"

I'M SITTING IN THE activity room with my suitcase and backpack by my feet, staring at my sneakers. Around me, kids are saying goodbye to each other. Long hugs. Tears. Phone numbers being traded. Adults waiting to take them away to whatever life will be like now.

I open the folder on my lap. A plethora of papers and brochures and a *You got this!* sticker. A plethora of information for me on how to live now.

"Bella?"

I look up. Tracy sits down in the chair next to me.

"Your mom is waiting in the lobby. Your dad and sister are outside in the car. How are you feeling?"

"I . . ."

"It's okay to be overwhelmed," she says gently.

I still can't get any words out of my mouth, but inside my brain, they're flashing, hot and confused: *worried hurt nervous scared sad help me.*

"Breathe," Tracy says, putting her hand on my shoulder. "It's supposed to be hard. It's not supposed to be easy, because living is never easy. Things are going to be hard. But you can do this."

"How do you know?" I ask. "Do you have a Magic 8 Ball? Gideon and Holly were too scared to live on the outside and look what happened. How do you know I'll be any different?"

She shakes her head. "I don't."

"Awesome," I say. "That's fantastic news."

"Life is hard, Bella," she says. "The world is uncontrollable, but you can claim your little spot if you want it, because everyone gets a little spot. It's up to you what to do with it."

She stands.

"And now," she says, grinning, "it's time to go home."

My mother hugs me so hard she squeezes all the air out of me. I'm buried in her shoulder, my eyes closed, breathing in the fact of her: comfort, home, the smell of cinnamon from the tea she probably had in the car, the vanilla scent she dabs on her neck in the mornings.

"I promised myself I wouldn't cry," she says into my hair. "Looks like I broke that promise."

"Mom," I say. "You can let go now, it's okay."

She doesn't.

"Mom," I mumble into the fabric of her sweater. *"Mom."*

"Bella," she breathes softly. "Bella, just stay here against me for a minute."

"Okay," I say.

"Listen to me," she says.

Her arms tighten even more around me.

"I sold Grandma's house," she whispers. "It was time. Emotionally and monetarily, it was time. It is not your fault, Bella. Not one bit."

I struggle against her, a thousand thoughts racing in my brain at once:

Nowhere to hide now.

My one quiet place.

Our last Scrabble game on the kitchen table—

Where is it now? Dumped into a box? Sold at a yard sale?

No more sitting at her kitchen table, shutting the world out—

The last little bit of her I had, gone—

I can feel my body tensing up like a fist.

"Bella?"

I push away from my mother at the sound of my sister's voice and turn around.

Ricci's standing in the lobby, just past the front door, twisting her fingers, her eyes clouded with worry.

My dad opens the door behind her.

"I'm sorry," he says. "She couldn't wait any longer."

I open my arms and Ricci crashes against me, clenching me tightly.

"You will not leave again," she says firmly. "Never, never."

I pet her hair. "Sure thing, Ricci."

I feel my dad's hand on my shoulder and look up.

"Hey, girl," he says. His eyes are watery and his hair is longer, sticking out past his ears. Grayer, too. "You look good. This is good."

Awkwardly, he hugs me over Ricci. "Missed you."

"Hey, Dad," I say.

My mother clears her throat. "I'm not pointing any fingers at anyone, but didn't you two forget about something?"

Ricci unclasps her arms from me and grabs my hand, pulling me to the door.

"Bella, come *on.* He's *waiting.*"

"Ricci, what—"

My dad sighs. "Don't question it, Bella. Just let it happen."

Ricci pushes open the door and drags me into the sunshine outside. I blink, trying to get my bearings. Ricci pulls me across the parking lot to Dad's car.

A scruffy brown-and-white one-eared dog is panting patiently in the back seat, staring balefully at us through the window.

"Bart Bingleheimer!" Ricci yells. "Mom got us a *dog*!"

In my dad's car, the dog wedges himself between me and Ricci, his warm dog breath on my cheek. He leans closer, sniffing me. I pat his head awkwardly.

"You got a *dog*?" I say to my mother. "We have a thousand pets already."

My mom turns around, shrugging helplessly.

"We have a yard," she says. "And he just—"

"Christmas," Ricci interjects. "He showed up at Christmas, at Agnes's. By the barn—"

"He wouldn't leave her side," my mother says.

My dad clears his throat. "Turns out buying whatever she wanted at Walmart didn't do the trick, because what she really wanted was a dog."

He glances at me in the rearview, but I drop my eyes.

Right. Our phone conversation when I was in Seg.

The air in the car is thick with dog breath and tension. I crack the window.

"Are you hungry? Do you need us to stop somewhere and get you something to eat?" my mom asks.

"We had a big breakfast," I mumble. I didn't eat much of it, though.

No one says anything.

My mom turns on the radio.

* * *

Outside the window, the greens and browns of the desert gradually give way to warehouses, motels, fast-food restaurants, strip malls. No more Chuck runs, no more meal prep, no more Fran group, no more Star Pit, no more asking for razors from the desk if you want to shave in the shower and having staff wait outside the closed curtain, no more goats, no more gym, no more friends disappearing in the desert, no more bed checks and surprise urine tests, wren sparrow roadrunner quail, daily Polaroids, my broken and aching face, no more, no more, no more.

Now it is:

School, people, do I have any friends left, one house one week, the other house the other week, no more house where I can find my peace, and a yellow folder with directions on how to live my life.

The closer we get to home, the more my stomach starts to roll and clench.

My dad drops us at my mom's. He drove the other way around the block so we wouldn't pass Laurel's, but it's only five houses away, so I can see the Sold sign from my mom's house when I get out of the car.

"I'll come get you in a week," he says. "Okay? Right back to where we left off. Easy-peasy. Back to the routine. Okay?"

He hugs me. It feels nice, being in his arms again. Maybe he isn't mad about that phone call after all. He did call every day. I should try to remember that.

"It will all be good," he says, his voice floating over my head.

"Yes," I say. "Yes. Absolutely."

* * *

Laurel's vintage velvet couch is in the living room. I stop short when I see it, a sharp pain of longing for her in my chest.

"You kept it," I say.

My mom bites her lip. "I did. I love that couch. I was thinking if you wanted it in your room, we can do that. It's a little crowded in here with two couches, but . . ."

The dog, Bart Bingleheimer, is springing from our old beige couch to Laurel's, testing for a comfortable spot. He finally finds one and settles down, burrowing his nose between the cushions on the velvet sofa.

"Well, you can see who really likes it." My mom laughs a little. "I did save some things, just so you know. Some we sold at the estate sale. But I have her archives and all the other photos. It's a lot. I put it in the shed. It will take a lot of time to go through, and I'm not sure, right now, that I'm ready—"

Her voice breaks and tears spring to her eyes.

"I'm sorry that I made you take on my grief, Bella. Having you care for Mom's house for me. All that. If I hadn't done that, maybe—"

I cut her off. Her tears are making me feel sad, and a little guilty.

"I would have found someplace else, Mom," I say. "To drink. And I was doing that before she died."

It feels weird to say that out loud.

"I started going to a grief group," she says. "It meets once a week, at night. It feels strange to me that I somehow feel comforted by a roomful of sad people, but I do."

"Life is strange," I say.

"A very true thing," she answers. "A very true thing."

Ricci appears in the living room, nearly crashing into the velvet sofa. She's holding a vase.

"Look, Bella," she says. "Look what Agnes made. It's Grandma."

I stare at the vase—urn—in her hands. It's heavy-looking and beautiful, winding lilac and aqua with spare shimmers, like someone added tiny, glistening jewels to the mix.

Ricci shoves it into my hands. Laurel. We never did anything with the white boxes that came home after she was cremated. They disappeared into my mother's closet.

Laurel. I'm holding my grandmother, just like I did on the bricks outside her house a long time ago.

I hug the urn tighter to my chest.

"Agnes gave it to me a few weeks ago. She'd been working on it for a while," my mom says. "I was thinking . . . maybe during spring break, you and me and Ricci can take a trip. Driving, to a couple of places. We could scatter Mom. It seems like she'd like that, bits of her everywhere.

"I'm sorry," my mom continues. "That my grief made you think you had to hide yours."

I don't know what to say to that, so I just look back down at the beautiful urn.

"Anyway," she says, "we have so much to do. Should we get you some school clothes? And we need to get you set with your new group. Tracy gave me a lot of paperwork. There's a therapist she recommended, but they aren't taking new clients right now, so I'm looking around for—"

Her words are tangling in my ears.

It's all a little too much for me. Being in the house is overwhelming after being at Sonoran Sunrise for two months. Seeing all our things, Ricci petting a strange dog, my grandmother in my arms, the thought of school and *everything everything everything.*

The real world is closing in on me.

I hand my mother the urn. My mind is racing. I try to breathe slowly, in and out, but I feel dizzy.

"I . . ." My voice falters. "I just . . . I think I need to go lie down."

I run to my room.

The bed is made, the room has been cleaned and straightened. There are boxes stacked neatly in one corner, which I guess are some of Laurel's things. I sink into my bed, drag the covers over my body, over my head. I breathe in the darkness under my blanket. I roll over and my cheek hits something flat and hard. I feel around, my fingers closing on a cord.

I peer at my phone, resting on the pillow beside me, charger plugged in. The phone I thought I lost at the party.

The party that changed my whole life.

Did someone bring it back to my mom? Was I just too drunk and thought I lost it but I didn't?

Maybe I don't need to know everything. Maybe it's better if I just let some things go.

Hesitantly, I type in my password.

There are sixty-seven text messages.

My finger shakes, hovering over the message box.

I press it.

My dad. *Bell, where are you? You okay?*

Right. They must have been texting me the night of the party. My stomach squeezes.

Mom. *Bella, please answer. I didn't like the tone of your last message. I'm worried. Please pick up.*

My dad. *Hey, Bella, let me know if you're good. You okay?*

Dawn. *Hi. I just want you to know I'm thinking of you.*

Josh. *Hey*

Cherie. *I'm really sorry. Call me when you get out. I hope you're okay.*

Dawn. *Hi. I was listening to this song today. Here it is. I think you'd like it.*

Lemon. *Hey Bella listen, it was messed up and I'm really sorry. You don't have to talk to me ever again I just wanted to say that.*

Dawn. *I hope you got my message. The one I left with the lady at that place. Anyway. I'm here. It was Cherie who told me where you are. I won't tell anyone. I just wanted you to know I get it and we can be friends if you want to when you get back.*

Josh. *Hey, what's up? Are you mad at me or something?*

Josh. *I'm not sure what's up. Text me.*

Josh. *I guess you don't want to hang out?*

Dawn. *It's me again. I guess you're going to be gone longer. I'm sorry about that. Here's another song.*

Dylan. *Hi Bella, it's me. I hope you r ok.*

I scroll through, the messages blurring. There aren't any from Amber or Kristen. There are, though, a lot from numbers I don't know.

Girl you famous lets hook up

Your video is my favorite send me more

Ur sexy

I feel sick.

I turn my phone off, my hands shaking, and shove it under my pillow.

But I feel like I can hear those messages from unknowns in my ears, so I get up, pull the phone out, walk over to my desk, and put the phone in my drawer.

Then I climb back under the covers and roll over, pressing myself against the wall and closing my eyes as tightly as I can.

* * *

I wake up in a haze, hot and sweaty. The room is dark except for the faint glow of my fairy lights. I don't know how long I've been asleep. I feel panicky. I look around.

Where are Brandy and Holly and Gideon and Charlotte? Why aren't they here?

Then I remember: I'm not *there* anymore, I'm *here.*

But that means . . . Where's Ricci? It's obviously late; I need her to get to bed so my mom can work, because I'm home now and that's how things are here.

I get up and stagger out of my room. The kitchen light is on, my mom's laptop and notepad are out on the kitchen island, but she's not sitting on her stool. I make my way down the hall to Ricci's room and hear faint voices coming from behind the half-opened door.

"Mom?" I say hoarsely, pushing it open farther. "What are you doing? I usually put Ricci to bed. You have to work."

Ricci and our mom are snuggled in Ricci's bed, reading a book.

Ricci says, "Mom learned how to put me to bed. It was hard, teaching her about the tree frogs and the fish, but she did a good job."

My mom smiles at me. "I really did, Bella. I even get stickers when I do a *really* good job."

Above her head on the wall are a bunch of cat stickers with googly eyes.

"But it's my job," I say softly. "I like putting her to bed. Mostly."

"Then get in and do your job!" Ricci shouts, scooching

closer to Mom, making a space for me on the inside, next to the wall, under her poster of Antarctica.

I clamber over her, wedge myself under the blanket. I have to lie on my side to make myself fit.

"My girls," my mom murmurs. "My beautiful girls."

"Mommy," Ricci says. "Shush now and keep reading."

I'm asleep again before I know it, in shelter and warmth.

I wake up with a start.

Out of habit, I shoot out of bed, kneel down, look for my running sneakers and folded sweatshirt and sweatpants under the bed, where I always put them before I go to sleep. I want to be dressed and ready before Chuck begins obnoxiously banging, because I hate the sound of his metal water bottle on the door. I like to be the first one ready now.

But nothing's under the bed except small pairs of underwear and a smattering of Woodzeez. I panic for a minute: *Where's my stuff? I don't want a demerit.*

Then I remember.

I'm not there anymore. I'm here. At home. In my sister's room.

There's no Chuck run.

I try to get my bearings. How long was I asleep? My mouth feels dry. I drag myself from the bed to the bathroom I share with Ricci, and pee. I flush the toilet, wash my hands, glance at myself in the mirror, still surprised at what I see these days.

It's been two months. I have the Polaroids to prove it, carefully slipped into a ziplock baggie in the suitcase in my room.

My face is my face again, whatever that means. No more

swelling. No more meaty bruising. I brush my teeth, watching myself, as though my face might suddenly change now that I'm back here in the real world. Might turn into something else.

It doesn't.

But I have circles under my eyes and I look tired. I *am* tired.

I spit the toothpaste into the sink. The tube is empty, so I throw it in the plastic bin next to the toilet and kneel down, open the cabinet under the sink to get another.

I search among boxes of Kleenex, rolls of toilet paper, a spray bottle of bleach. I don't see any toothpaste, so I stand up and check the medicine cabinet.

It's still filled with packets of dental floss, bottles of moisturizer, Band-Aids, nasal spray . . . but what strikes me is what *isn't* there.

Ibuprofen, Midol, the melatonin gummies Ricci sometimes needs, the NyQuil, even Ricci's children's Tylenol.

Oh. I guess we're going that route, although hiding the ibuprofen seems a little excessive.

I walk into the kitchen, where I find my mom sitting at the kitchen island with her laptop open, Bart Bingleheimer asleep at her feet. I smell coffee and eggs.

"Good morning," she says cheerfully. "I didn't want to wake you when I took Ricci to school. Thought you could use the sleep. There's coffee and eggs."

I walk to the cabinet where we keep our mugs and open it. Just to check, I glance up to the top shelf, where she keeps unopened wine. She doesn't drink a lot, but if she has it, it's on the second shelf, behind the cans of coffee and boxes of tea.

There's nothing.

I pour myself a cup of coffee and take a sip.

I turn around.

"So just so I know, for future reference, I need to ask you for ibuprofen if I have a headache and Midol if I have cramps and beg for a spoonful of cough syrup from the safe, or wherever you put it?"

My mother sets down her coffee mug. She gazes at me steadily.

"Yes," she says simply.

"You won't even trust me with an aspirin?" I say, exasperated. "That seems excessive, don't you think?"

"No, I don't," she says. "I read in an article that sometimes when kids come home from . . . rehab . . . they can suffer depressive episodes, and I'm just—"

"Jesus, Mom, I'm not going to *kill* myself," I say. "Thanks for the vote of confidence."

She blinks. "You did almost kill yourself. You did almost die. It's my job to prevent that from happening again."

I look into the deep brown well of my coffee mug.

"Actually, Mom, if I learned anything at that place, I learned that it's pretty much all up to me, when I die."

I raise my eyes to meet hers but look away when I see the tears brimming there.

"I'm sorry," I say. "I just . . . I'm still tired, I guess. This is hard."

"I know." She takes a sip of her coffee.

But she *doesn't* know. I'm going to have to do things she's never done. Our definition of *hard* will never be the same.

I turn around and put my mug on the counter, take the pan off the stove and shovel the cold eggs into my mouth with my fingers. Then I put the pan in the sink, turn on the water, soap the sponge, and start washing the dishes.

"Bella," my mother says. "What are you doing?"

"Washing the dishes," I say.

"We have a dishwasher," she reminds me.

I look down at the running water, soap on my knuckles, a plate in my hand.

I finish washing, rinse everything, and set it all in the dish rack to dry. "We did our own dishes at the place. And cooked our food. If you didn't make food and clean up, you didn't get to eat. I would wash, Holly would load—"

A sharp pain shoots through me. I blink back tears.

I turn around. My mom is looking at me curiously, and I can't tell if she's sad or worried.

"We all helped," I tell her. "I'm going to my room for a little bit, if that's okay."

"Of *course* that's okay," she says. "I'll come get you later when it's time to go out."

"Go out?"

She nods. "You need some . . . things."

Her eyes slide to the calendar on the wall.

It's Monday. There's a red circle around Thursday, and inside the circle it says *Bella back to school.*

I feel my bottom lip begin to tremble. I bite it to make it stop.

"A short first week back," my mom says. "I talked to your teachers and your school counselor. Everyone agreed that would be best. Just two days. Take it slow."

I look at the calendar again.

I look at Tuesday. *Bella, hair appointment, 11:00 a.m.*

Wednesday. *Bella, doctor, 9:30 a.m. Bella, group, 6:30 p.m.*

She has my whole week in red pen. A scheduled life.

"Right," I say.

I turn around and walk to my room. Behind me, Bart Bingleheimer shifts and sighs in his sleep.

I sit on the floor.

Bella, school things. Bella, doctor. Bella, hair. Bella, group.

Bella, breathe, I tell myself.

What did I think? That I'd just come home and sleep for days before life really began again? It bothers me that she set all that up without asking me. I mean, I dye my hair in the bathroom. And I don't mind how long it's gotten. When I get bothered by it, I can cut it myself, like I always have.

I look at the tiny pink clock on my desk.

11:03 a.m.

I would be in group with Fran right now, and then meal prep, and then lunch and cleaning. Then gym and the stupid medicine balls, which got easier. The climbing wall, which Phil finally got me on. I managed to get halfway up before I demanded to go back down. And then and then and then . . .

But right now . . . there's nothing. Just this eerily quiet house, my mother tapping away at her job in the kitchen, a strange dog asleep at her feet.

I feel itchy without something to do.

I grab my backpack from my desk chair and take out the folder Tracy gave me. *What Happens After,* it says on the front in lettering that seems entirely too optimistic.

Inside, there's a stapled packet of papers.

On the top of the first one, it says, *Congratulations, and welcome to the rest of your life.*

A sunset overlaid with a saguaro is beneath that.

I turn the page.

The first two weeks of aftercare are the hardest. There are adjustments to be made in the way you'll live your daily life. You should have some tools from your time at Sonoran Sunset to guide you. But remember: if you need help, ask someone.

Here are some tips for the next two weeks:

You are a fragile, valuable human.

You have undergone a tremendous life experience.

Your family or caregivers will want to help you and make things easier. Or they may not. Some families may impose rules and structure that you find suffocating. Some families may not have boundaries at all. It is up to you to find the balance that you need to thrive, and to make it happen.

Find a group right away. Meeting with others in similar situations will give you a space to talk, to feel seen and heard, and to receive validation for what you're feeling and going through.

Avoid situations that may trigger you or make you feel unsafe. This includes parties and family gatherings that may involve alcohol or other substances, and being with friends who may not respect your needs.

I close my eyes.

So I'm supposed to basically avoid everything, all the time, for the rest of my life.

Perfect.

I open my eyes and flip through the pages. Lists of resources in Tucson: sober book club meetups; sober teen meetups; sober horseback riding camp (this makes me wonder if a lot of people are riding horses drunk, who would have thought); yoga classes for teens; mindful retreats for teens.

Then, in the back, are fourteen blank pages. Well, not entirely blank.

On the top of the first one it says, *This is your journal for the next fourteen days. You can write whatever you want here. This is a space for you to think about your day. We've included some experiences you may encounter during the next two weeks on each page. These are not chronological or absolute but are common in the immediate days of recovery after returning home.*

Recovery. Like I've come back from a long illness or injury.

Perhaps I have.

I flip the pages. At the top of each one is a sentence. I flip back to Day One, which I guess is . . . today.

> You will feel scared, alone, hopeful, angry, unsettled,
> and unsure of what every day from now on will be like.
> Remember, you made it this far.

The little *You got this!* sticker that I saw when I was in the activity room before I left drifts out from the pages. I kick it under my desk, shove the papers into the folder, and cram the whole packet in my backpack.

Then I hide under my bedspread until my mother says it's time to go shopping.

The mall is filled with old people and tired parents pushing overloaded strollers. Of course: everyone my age is in school right now. At least I can be grateful for that.

"Where should we go first?" my mother asks brightly, hoisting her purse over her shoulder.

I shrug. "I don't care. I mean, I don't really shop here. I don't like new stuff."

"Well, where do you go when you come here with your friends?"

I look around, sighing.

"Well, Kristen likes Forever 21, mostly because she can steal something small, like a bracelet. Then we go to Claire's and mess around. Then we go to Spencer's and look at weird stuff and Cherie buys a T-shirt. Then we have Panda Express."

I don't tell her that sometimes Kristen brings something she stole from her mom's and we drink it in the photo booth and make funny faces.

"Well, then let's go to Forever 21, I guess," my mother says.

"I don't really like those clothes. I told you, I don't like new stuff. I usually go to Goodwill or Tucson Thrift."

"Try something new? Let me treat you. Aren't you tired of wearing the same old things?"

She gestures to my hoodie and jeans and then to Forever 21. In the display windows, the mannequins are wearing expertly torn and frayed jeans, rainbow beanies, crop tops and crop hoodies. There are bright gold balloons pinned behind them.

I look down at my ratty black low-top Chucks, comfortable and comforting.

"I'm still me," I say to the ground, not looking up at my mother. "A thirty-dollar crop hoodie isn't going to make it all better. Or make me what you wish I was."

"Bella, I didn't . . ." My mother lets out a long sigh. "I'm not trying to remake you."

"I feel like you might be. This, and the hair appointment tomorrow . . . I do my own hair, you know that."

"I was just trying to make you feel special," she says, a strain of desperation in her voice. "Tell me what you want."

"I don't know what I want!" I yell. "I've been back two days. How am I supposed to know what I want!"

A woman with curly gray hair in a pink sweatsuit huffs by us on her mall laps, giving us a concerned look.

My mother's face falls.

Great. Now I've hurt her feelings.

"I'm sorry," she says. "I should have asked you what you wanted to do today. Where you wanted to go. Let's reset. Let's go to Goodwill. How about that?"

"Fine," I say. "Let's do that."

Anything to get out of here.

But we have problems finding parking and my mother gets irritated. And I can tell she's disappointed that I pick out the same old things at Goodwill: baggy T-shirts, loose cardigans, jeans that are worn and comfortable-looking, flannel shirts. It's not great for me, either. I see some kids from school walking down Fourth as we leave. They must be ditching, because it's only two o'clock. I don't know them by name, but one of them looks at me and elbows her friend and then all three of them are staring at me.

My mother notices them. "Are those some friends? Would you like to say hi?"

I pull on her elbow. "No and *no.*"

I duck my head and look at the ground the whole way back to our car.

In the car, she says we need to pick up Ricci on the way home.

I shake my head. "Can you drop me at the house? I don't really feel like going all that way."

My mom pauses. "Just come with me. We'll stop on the way for eegee's."

"I want to go home. I'm really tired."

"I'd rather you come with me."

"Mom, what's the—"

She's not looking at me.

"Wait . . . ," I say slowly. It's dawning on me now. "You don't want me home alone. You don't trust me."

Her hands grip the steering wheel tighter. "It isn't that I don't trust you. I just—"

"Do you think if you leave me alone, I'm going to run right out and find some booze?"

"Can you blame me?" she says softly. "I mean, honestly, Bella, can you?"

She's staring hard at the road.

I turn my face away to look out my window, my cheeks burning.

"I just need to keep you close right now, Bella," she says finally. "Is that so wrong?"

I remember what the packet of aftercare instructions said: *Some families may impose rules and structure that you find suffocating.*

I pull on my headphones and slide down in the seat, staring straight ahead.

Wren, sparrow, roadrunner, quail . . .

HAVE YOU GONE TO YOUR FIRST GROUP MEETING YET?

MY MOM AND RICCI are down the street at a coffee shop. Mom said they'd be back in an hour. "A little early," she said. "Just so you don't have to stand outside alone."

But I am standing outside alone. I'm standing outside a church alone. I've never even been inside a church before. The meeting is in the basement.

It's cold. I clench my hands into fists inside my hoodie pockets. I look up one side of the street. Down the other. I don't have a viable escape plan. I'm not a brave person.

I do want to go in, but I don't want to go in.

My brain says: *Too many people you don't know, too scary.*

My heart says: *Do you want to die, Bella? Do you? Do you want to wake up in your own piss again?*

My heart can be very harsh.

But I remember, too, what my mom said about her grief group, that she was surprised to feel comforted in a roomful of sad people, but she did. And I remember how Tracy and Phil and Fran said we need to take care of ourselves and live day by day and keep up with our work on the outside.

I force myself to walk to the double doors and open them. In the hallway, a sign with an arrow pointing left says *Teen Group, Room 15, basement* in black marker. I turn left, go down the stairs, and find room 15.

Chairs set up in a circle. A table with cookies and soda and coffee and water. Kind of like the cafeteria at Sonoran Sunrise. For a minute, I wonder if anyone from there is here. Brandy or Billy or Nick. Even Josh, who I still haven't texted back.

All the faces are unfamiliar.

Kids just like me, milling around, taking seats.

A woman comes up to me. She's about my mom's age and wearing a shawl, her purple-streaked hair in braids.

"Hello," she says. "I'm Beth. Are you here for the meeting?"

"Yeah," I say.

"I'm glad." She studies me. "How many days do you have, if I may ask?"

"Thirty-four. Including rehab. I just got out a few days ago." I wonder if I should tell her that the part including rehab was actually a second round.

"Well," she says. "We're about to get started. Why don't you find a seat? We can talk after, if you like."

"Okay."

I find a seat between two girls. A sign on the wall says to turn off your phone, so I do.

My knees are jiggling and I press them to make them stop. These chairs are kind of uncomfortable. I miss the beanbags in group with Fran.

One of the girls says, "First meeting?"

I nod.

The other girl says, "You don't have to say anything right away. It helps, but you can take your time. Don't feel rushed."

"I didn't say anything for, like, ten meetings before I felt brave enough to really talk," Girl One says.

"Okay," I say.

"You do have to introduce yourself, though," Girl Two says. "That's kind of the rule. Just so you know."

"I remember that," I say. "From . . . rehab."

Girl One laughs. "You don't have to whisper it. Everyone here's in the same boat. Where were you? I was at Spirit Hills. That's in Phoenix."

"Sonoran Sunrise," I say.

Girl Two nods. She's wearing a huge puffy parka and has tattoos of tiny stars along one side of her neck.

"The goats," she says. "That place is all right. That's what I heard, anyway. I've been to some bad ones, believe me. Like prisons."

Beth is talking and suddenly stops. I realize everyone in the room is staring at me.

Girl Two nudges me gently. "It's okay," she whispers. "Just get it over with. Rip off the Band-Aid."

I look at my lap, at my fingers twisting together.

Wren, sparrow, roadrunner, quail.

"Hi. I'm Bella. And I drink a lot. I mean, I did."

Everyone says, "Hi, Bella," all at once.

And one by one, they say their names.

"Bella's been home, what did you say? A few days now?" Beth's eyes are kind. "Is there anything on your mind?"

I hesitate.

"It's all right," Beth says, sipping from her paper cup. "We're all friends."

"I start school again tomorrow," I say quietly. "I haven't been there in two months."

A boy—Ethan? Efrain? I can't remember, but it had an *E*—across the circle lets out a loud guffaw.

"Oh, man," he says, shaking his head. "School? Good luck. It was bad before, it'll be bad again. Just try to get through the day. And stay away from the bathrooms."

Girl One nods. "I got a UTI after my first week back at school because there wasn't a bathroom I could go in where people weren't doing *something.*"

"I just do online school now," a girl sitting next to Ethan-Efrain says. "It's so much less bullshit, really. And I can use the bathroom whenever I want. But that basically means I never leave my house, except for here." She laughs nervously. "My life now is like, *microscopic.* Get up, grab a Pop-Tart, sit at my desk, log in and sit there for six hours, then go back to bed."

"You can't escape the world, though," Beth says. "Not forever. At some point, you have to get back out there and figure out a way to exist."

"No thank you," says the girl primly. "The world is not a good place for me. It wasn't when I was using, and it isn't now that I'm not. I'm better off hiding."

"I'm with her," says another girl. She's knitting furiously, bright blue yarn in her lap. "Except I can't really even hide at home. My parents didn't stop drinking when I came home. I sit there all night waiting for them to pass out and then I pour out whatever's left over because smelling it literally makes me . . . makes me *ache* for it. You know?"

Everyone nods.

Next to me, Girl Two—Ashley, I think—says, "Just go to school. Keep your head down, do what you can, and protect yourself. I have fifty-two days now. That means something to me. Every night I text myself to congratulate myself, because the only person who truly cares about me is me. Everyone is all positive when you first get back, but that fades away. No one wants to deal with your shit long-term, you know? They just want you to get over it so they can go back to normal, whatever that means. And you know what? Sometimes you have to lie to save yourself. In a bad situation with unsupportive people? Lie. Get out. Tell them you've got to catch a bus. Or you have homework. Make something, anything, up. Just get out of there."

Beth looks at me.

"What are you hearing, Bella? What are your thoughts?"

I lick my lips. Having too many eyes on me is making me nervous, but I guess I have to say something. *This is me trying.*

"Well, to be honest," I say slowly, "it all sounds horrible. Going back to school. People . . . eventually not caring. If they ever did."

Ethan-Efrain shrugs.

"You can't always get a pretty rose garden, girl," he says. "Sometimes all that's left is thorns."

SCHOOL MAY BE STRESSFUL. EXPECT THE UNEXPECTED.

"BELLA," MY MOM SAYS.

We're sitting in the drop-off lane. Kids barrel out of cars and head through the school gates. I'm frozen, backpack on my thighs, seat belt pinching my shoulder.

"It's time," she says gently. "You can text me."

"We aren't allowed to use our phones during class."

"At lunch, then."

The car in front of us pulls away, leaving a gap. The car behind us honks.

Thumpthumpthumpthump, says my heart.

Wren, sparrow, roadrunner, quail.

"You can do this," my mom says. "I know you can. Remember, you meet with Ms. Ferris first, okay?"

Right. The counselor. To go over *the plan.*

"Who's going to sit with me at lunch?"

"Amber?" my mother answers. "Or you can go to the library."

"They don't let you eat in the library," I say, my voice tense. "And I haven't talked to Amber since before rehab."

I haven't talked to anyone. I haven't returned any texts. I just look at them every night and then put my phone away.

The car behind us pulls around.

Another car behind us honks.

"Bella."

"I'm going."

My brain says: *Run for your life, kid.*

My heart says: *Open the door, Bella. Put on your backpack, Bella. Walk straight ahead, Bella. Look at the ground. Look at a fixed point in front of you like you can see and not see. Make a protective shield around your body that no one can penetrate. You have your makeup. You have your baggy clothes. You are impenetrable.*

I get out of the car. My mother drives away.

I look everywhere and nowhere at once. I activate my protective force field and walk into school.

No one can touch me.

I pray that it lasts.

Ms. Ferris is sitting behind her desk, typing away at her laptop.

I just stand there, waiting. Finally, she looks up.

"Yes, yes, come in," she says in a rushed way. "Sorry, finishing up an email. Sit, sit."

I have to take some files off the chair across from her desk and I stand, holding them in my hands, until she notices and takes them, adding them to a towering pile of folders.

She peers at me over her glasses. "And you are . . . ?"

"Bella," I say. "We were supposed to talk about—"

"Yes," she says, snapping her fingers. "Bella. I have you right here. Sorry. Three thousand kids, I have a lot of appointments."

She slips a folder from the pile and skims it. Looks at me over her glasses again. Her eyes are rimmed with pink, and there's a coffee stain on the collar of her gray shirt.

"Okay. So it looks like you kept up with some work at Sierra, that's good, that's good, you're not too behind, but there might be some summer school, just prepare yourself.

And I have a note from your mom about gym and your scars, so I did send an email to Ms. Greer about not dressing out—"

"Excuse me," I interrupt.

"Yes, what is it? You do want to dress out or you don't?" Her voice is impatient.

"I don't . . . That's not me. I don't know what Sierra is, and I don't . . . have any scars."

She stares at me.

"I'm Bella Leahey?" I say tentatively. "I was at Sonoran Sunrise for two months."

A light goes on behind her eyes.

"Oh," she says quietly. "I'm sorry. Excuse me. I have the wrong file. I've got two Bellas who were . . . well, you're Bella *Leahey.* Yes. I know you now."

I wince.

I know you now. She means the video. I know it.

She pulls another file from her enormous tower and opens it. After reading for a second, she closes it and takes off her glasses, leans forward on her elbows.

She clears her throat.

"You," she says, "are definitely going to summer school."

Ms. Ferris escorts me to first period since I'm late and she's run out of tardy slips.

I hesitate at the door.

She opens it and pops her head in.

Mr. Lopez glances up from his desk in the corner.

"Bella Leahey," Ms. Ferris says.

I look at my feet. My face is blazing with heat.

"Come here," Mr. Lopez says.

I walk to his desk. Every single kid in the room is looking at me.

He hands me a folder with a packet of paper in it.

"You'll need to make up the final exam for the fall. Let's set up a time during one of your lunches next week. Each of your teachers will have work for you. Check in with them today at the beginning of each class."

He snaps back to the room.

"Eyes down, do your bell work, nothing to see here," he tells them.

Heads duck down.

I take the folder, which is stuffed with assignments, and start walking to my seat.

"Bella," Mr. Lopez calls.

I stop and turn around.

"Do the best you can," he says gently.

I slide into my seat, stare at the desk for a minute, trying not to crumble, and then open the folder he gave me to find the bell work.

Between classes I have *thumpthumpthumpthump* and I try to do *wren, sparrow, roadrunner, quail* inside my head as I look and not look at the other kids, wondering when I'll bump into Kristen or Lemon or Dylan or Amber or wondering how many kids know, how many kids saw the video, what they're thinking, do I hear whispers or is that just my brain making the whispers up and it hurts. I want to run out of the school as fast as I can, but I can't. It's like gym with Phil: I have to keep picking up the heavy medicine ball when it falls, even if I don't want to. I manage to make it to a restroom at some point, but there are a couple of kids in there acting funny in a stall and I can smell something familiar and I remember what that girl said in group, that the smell makes her ache. It made me ache, too, in the goat pen with Charlotte.

For a split second, standing outside the stall listening to them giggle, I want nothing more than to bang on the door and say, *hey, save some for me,* but instead I turn around, my bladder burning, and get the hell out of there.

Fran said, "Some days seem to last forever but there is always another one in your future. Move toward that."

Lunch.

There are thousands of kids here, millions of kids, there is no space for me.

My brain says: *Make one.*

My heart says: *It's too hard, too tired, text Mom, have her come get you. Thumpthumpthumpthump*

"Bella?" Soft voice, fingers on my shoulder.

Dawn.

"Sit together?" she says. "Over there."

I can't move.

"I'm here," she says. "Follow me."

Table at the end, underneath the high windows. She's nudging me along.

Just sit, Bella. Take out your lunch, eat it, no matter how much you can't taste it. You only have three more classes and then home, the safety of home.

Dawn is quiet, opening her Tupperware, setting her water bottle on the table.

"I'm glad you're back," she says. "I didn't know today was the day. It's okay that you haven't texted me."

A backpack *thunks* next to me. I look up, startled. Cherie.

"Hi," she says. "Can I sit here?"

Slowly, I nod. She slides in next to me.

I take out my sandwich. My hands are shaking. I'm not hungry anyway.

No one says anything for a long time.

"I'm sorry," Cherie says finally. "About everything."

"It's not your fault," I say.

"I mean, I *know* that," she says, waving her hand dismissively. "I just meant *in general* that I'm sorry."

I don't say anything.

"You look skinnier," she says, giving me the once-over.

"I did a lot of running," I say. "And there was a gym."

"Swanky," she murmurs.

She pops open a bag of Takis, delicately cracking one in half.

"You know Kristen's gone, right?" she says.

"I haven't really been keeping tabs on her," I answer mildly. "What happened?"

"Her parents pulled her out. After it happened. It got really hard for her here. Lemon, too."

"Why?" I ask.

Dawn takes a sip of her water. "Because. It was a crappy thing to do, leaving you that way. You could have . . ."

"Died," Cherie finishes. "And kids were pissed about that. You were a whole assembly talk, you know that? Principal Cummings did it. About taking care of each other, watching each other's backs. Blah blah. And some kids started freezing Kristen and Lemon out."

"Did you?" I ask. "Freeze Kristen out."

Cherie crumbles some Takis into her yogurt cup. "I still talk to her. She's at Palo Verde now. But it's not the same, when we talk. I just keep wondering if she'd do the same to me. I mean, she's sorry. She's really sorry. Your dad threatened to sue her parents, can you believe it? You should probably talk to her."

"She doesn't have to," Dawn says. "If she doesn't want to."

"I know that," Cherie says, irritated. "But we were *friends* for a long time. That should count for something."

Dawn shakes her head. "I don't think so. I don't think you should have to forgive someone for something like that."

"*Everyone's* hurting in this situation, Dawn," Cherie says, shoving some Taki yogurt in her mouth.

"Actually," Dawn says, staring hard at Cherie, "I think the person who's hurting the most is sitting right here, and that's the person we should be caring about."

"Stop it," I say, suddenly exhausted. "I don't want a fight. It's my first day back. My friend from there *died.* It wasn't some sort of spa where I lost weight. Shit *happened.* I just want to get through this freaking day."

"Sorry," they mumble in unison.

I feel very, very, very old all of a sudden. I'm a sophomore sitting in a crowded lunchroom and I feel as though I'm a thousand years old.

Cherie and Dawn are telling me about the new art module for spring as we weave through the hall on the way to Ms. Green's. Something about clay and being excited to use the wheel. I'm trying to concentrate on their voices instead of all the faces around me when I hear it, rising above the crowd of kids, hovering in the air.

"Belllllaaaaa."

Some guy, I don't know him, maybe a senior, is walking

toward us. Toward me. Saying my name over and over. Dark eyes, wide grin, a pack of guys behind him with the same grin. Snickering.

They stop in front of us. Blocking us.

Cold, cold. My body is becoming ice.

The hallway gets eerily silent and still.

"You're my favorite sophomore, Bella."

Slowly, he raises his T-shirt, exposing his stomach, then his chest. He touches a finger to his lips and presses it against his hairy nipple. His friends laugh.

I feel sick.

"Don't be a dick," Cherie says to him, pulling my arm and trying to push through the cluster of guys.

"Nip slip," he says. "Nip. Slip."

Laughter everyone laughing at me

"Give me a little kiss, Bella, come on."

Leaning closer to my face. Breath on me, dirtying me.

Suddenly, I'm shoved to the side, into Dawn, who knocks into some other kids.

The guy has fallen backward into his friends. They stagger under his weight. He tries to steady himself but falls back again.

It's Amber. Amber who shoved me out of the way and is now shoving him, over and over, screaming things I never thought would come from her.

I can only catch certain words. *How would you like it* and *asshole* and *think it's so funny* and *your dick everywhere for everyone to see I bet it's so small you coward how about we see that how would you like it.* His friends are pushing her back, yelling at her, calling her those names boys like to call girls, but there are other girls now, girls I don't even know, stepping in and pushing those boys and yelling *think we're just pieces of meat* and *get your hands off her leave her alone sick of all of you.*

My brain says: *Run.*

My heart says: *Ride-or-die.*

Just like Brandy said.

And I go in, to get my friend.

Amber's shirt is ripped at the shoulder. She's pressing an ice pack to her head. We're in the vice principal's office, waiting for her to come in. Cherie and Dawn are sitting on the floor, in the corner, because there aren't enough chairs.

Very quietly, Amber says, "I'm still mad at you, you know."

"I know," I say.

"I'm also mad at myself. I was a bad friend. Your mom gave me the number at that place and said I was on the list to call you, but I didn't."

"I didn't know that," I say. "But it's okay."

She's quiet.

"I sent you a letter," I say.

"I got it," she answers. She takes the ice pack off her head and places it in her lap. Her hair is much longer now and a different style, wavy and layered. It looks nice. "Are you okay? After that place?"

"No," I answer. "But I'm trying."

"Good," she says softly, looking at me. "Because I found something. For our trip."

"I didn't think . . ." My voice shakes. "I didn't think you'd still want me to go."

"Don't be stupid," she says. "Who would I rather go with? Anyway, it's a corn maze. In Iowa. We should look at our map soon."

"A corn maze," I say. "I wouldn't mind getting lost in some corn."

"Probably no better place," she says. "We can literally be *Children of the Corn.*"

We smile at each other, and then Amber sighs, pressing the ice pack against my knuckles.

"I have never been in trouble before in my life," she says. "And now I'm probably going to get kicked out of school."

"I know," I say. "And what a way to go, am I right? With a bang and a whimper."

She starts to laugh, but it's laugh-crying, so it's not really funny, but is, at the same time.

Cherie and Dawn start giggling.

And then we are all laughing together, stupidly, until Vice Principal Stickler comes in, and then we immediately stop.

She leans her hip against her desk and crosses her arms, that stance adults adopt when you're in trouble and they expect you to start talking first, not them.

"It's my fault," I say immediately. "It was because of me. If you kick anyone out, it should be me. They were just sticking up for me."

She sighs. "Let me see your hand."

I hold up my right hand, the knuckles red and skinned.

"Miss Leahey," Ms. Stickler says, "where on earth did you learn to throw a punch like that?"

"Rehab, Ms. Stickler. I learned to fight in rehab. On a girl named Charlotte."

My mom is waiting outside Ms. Stickler's office. I brace myself.

"Well," she says.

"Well," I say.

"That was not quite the first day back I was hoping for." She stands up.

"Me neither, to be honest." I swallow hard. "How mad are you?"

She cups my cheek with her hand. It feels nice.

"Bella," she says, "let's just get you home."

FAMILY CAN BE A CHALLENGE.

My DAD OPENS HIS front door and sweeps me into a big hug. Ricci wedges herself between us to get some, too.

"I missed you," he says, kissing the top of my head. "I hear you got into a little scrape at school yesterday."

He pulls away from me, making boxerlike jabs at my midsection. I duck out of the way.

"She can't go back for like a week," Ricci tells him. "She has to stay at home and do her homework, *and* she's going to summer school, which sounds unfair."

"Ah, you can make up that work, Bella," my dad says, walking into the kitchen. "I know you. You can put your mind to it, get it done, and then voilà, a summer of freedom."

"I don't really mind," I say. "I'd rather not stress out about it."

I go into the room I share with Ricci and put my backpack on the floor. The room is a mess, Ricci's clothes all over from the last time she was here. I guess Dad hasn't done laundry, but what else is new? Probably some things are never going to change. I gather Ricci's stuff into a pile in my arms and take it into the living room, looking for the laundry basket.

"Hey," my dad says. "What are you doing? Put that down. No work! It's Friday night. I've got a pizza on the way, soda's in the fridge. Who's up for a movie?"

"Me!" Ricci shouts.

“I should get these in the wash,” I say.

“Put them down, Bella,” my dad says. “I’ll do them tomorrow. I’ll get to it. Don’t be silly.”

There’s a little edge to his voice. I take the clothes back to our room and put them in a pile in the corner. I look around again.

Clothes on the floor and hanging off my desk chair. Ricci’s crayons everywhere. I don’t think he’s changed the sheets since I was here that last time.

My brain: *Well, you should clean everything up. Make it nice and neat. You’ll feel more comfortable.*

Me: *I kind of wished he’d cleaned up so I wouldn’t have to. I don’t mind cleaning, but not all the time. I shouldn’t have to do it all the time. Why can’t he clean when we aren’t here?*

I force myself not to pick anything up.

Breathe, Bella, breathe.

I come back out. He’s handing Ricci a Sprite. It’s then that I see it.

A beer bottle on the counter.

Actually, two. And a few in the sink.

I swallow.

“What?” my dad says. He glances back at the kitchen, at the bottles. “Oh, right. It’s Friday and I’m in for the night with my girls.”

“I just thought . . . that you wouldn’t have any here. Mom doesn’t have anything in her house.” My voice is quavery.

“Well, that’s your mom’s house and this is mine. Hey, you look a lot leaner. Have I told you that? It looks good on you. Now if we could just do something about that raccoon-eye thing you have going on.”

He spreads his fingers across his eyes, like he's making a mask.

"We exercised a lot at rehab. You know, where I was for a drinking problem."

I let my eyes slide to the beer bottles.

The smile dies on my dad's face. He winces.

"I really don't like that word," he says. "*Rehab.* Like you're a house that needs work. You're fifteen, not fifty, you know?"

There's a tentative knock on the door.

"Ah!" my dad says. He clears his throat. "That would be Vanessa."

I stare at the door as he brushes past me to open it. I thought Vanessa was gone. I thought Ricci said that on the phone when I was in Seg.

But there she is in the open doorway, a big smile on her face. Ricci runs over to hug her.

"You're back!" Ricci squeals.

"Oh, just here for a little visit," she says, looking at me over the top of Ricci's head as she rubs her back. "To say hi to Bella and pick up some things."

"Well," my dad says, sounding a little nervous. "Come on in. We've got pizza on the way. You want something to drink?"

He heads to the kitchen. Opens the refrigerator door. Pulls out a beer.

"I'm going to my room for a bit," I say, gritting my teeth. "Change the sheets and straighten up."

I grab some sheets out of the hall closet on my way, slam the door a little too hard.

In the bedroom, I yank Ricci's sheets off the bottom bunk.

"You want some help?"

I turn around.

Vanessa is in the doorway, nervously wringing her hands.

"Sure," I say. "Whatever."

She grabs a fitted sheet from the pile on the floor and holds it up.

"This is a double," she says.

"Dad made a mistake when he bought them," I say. "We just tuck them under."

"That sounds like your dad," she says lightly. "Here, let me help."

She starts sliding the sheet onto Ricci's bed. Together, we tuck it under on all sides and start on the pillows.

"I just wanted to say, Bella," Vanessa says, flicking out a pillowcase, "that I'm really sorry I missed all the signs. I should have been better. I should have been more cognizant. More present."

"Actually," I say, "you were pretty present. I mean, I didn't really give you a chance, but you tried. I just rejected it."

She kind of laughs. "You are fifteen. That's to be expected. I seem to recall rejecting my parents quite a bit. I mean, I'm not your parent, but . . . well, you know what I mean."

She's silent for a minute.

"You seem good," she says after a while, pulling the blanket off the top bunk and folding it. She places it on my desk chair, moving a pile of dirty clothes to the one in the corner.

"Yeah, I guess." I'm trying to concentrate on the sheet I'm unfolding and not the fact that there are beer bottles on the kitchen counter and my dad is out there drinking.

I feel jittery thinking about them.

We finish putting the sheets on the top bunk, me climbing up and stretching them around the corners. I'd like to just lie down and bury myself in this bed and not go out in the other room. Maybe I'll have to be like that girl in group who pours her parents' booze down the drain at night, though my dad never seemed that bad. He's not like *that.*

Still, couldn't he have not had any here? At least when I'm staying with him?

"Earth to Bella," Vanessa says. "That's the doorbell. I think the pizza's here."

But from the front room, I hear a familiar voice bellow, "Ricci! My girl!"

I freeze. Why is Hoyt here? It's my first night back with Dad. It should just be . . . family.

"Bella, come on out and say hello to Hoyt!" My dad's voice is positively merry.

When I walk out to the front room, Vanessa behind me, Hoyt yells, "Belly!"

He's holding a bottle of wine and a twelve-pack of beer.

My stomach drops.

I haven't been around alcohol in a month, except for the bathroom-stall thing at school. But I got myself out of there. I can't get myself out of here.

My dad gives Hoyt one of those guy backslaps and takes the twelve-pack into the kitchen.

"Belly," Hoyt says. "You look fantastic, kid. I'm so proud of you. You made it."

And then, really slowly, almost so slowly I think I might be imagining it, the big smile on Hoyt's face disappears as gears and pulleys do the magic in his brain.

"Hoyt," Vanessa says gently.

"I'm sorry, Bella," he whispers. "I don't know what I was thinking."

"Dan," Vanessa says, turning to the kitchen. "Maybe let's skip beer and the wine, tonight, okay?"

My dad is already opening a beer for Hoyt. He looks at Vanessa like *what?*

"Yeah, man. My mistake. Let me just take all that back to the car."

Hoyt heads into the kitchen and starts taking the beer case out of the fridge.

"Hey now," my dad says. "Hold up. What's going on? Buddy, stop."

Hoyt stands in the kitchen, awkwardly holding the beer.

"Dad," I say, trying to keep my voice neutral, "I can't be around alcohol. I'm not supposed to."

He frowns, taking a pull of his beer. "No biggie. You don't even like beer, am I right?"

He winks, like he's making a joke.

But no one laughs. Hoyt looks at the floor. Ricci is glued to the television.

"It's my house," my dad says firmly. "I had a long day. I just want a beer and to hang out with my kids, is that so wrong? I'm not the one with the problem, and I don't, technically speaking, think my kid has a problem. Her *mother* thinks she has a problem. But don't get me started on that."

He pulls a plate from the cabinet and sets it down, hard, on the countertop, dragging some pizza slices onto it. "Now let's eat. I'm starving."

My dad walks past me and settles on the couch. "Come on, Bella. Eat. You look too skinny."

Hoyt comes slowly out of the kitchen. He looks ashamed and unsure of what to do.

My heart: *You know what you need to do, even though it's going to suck, hard.*

My brain: *I support your heart, wholeheartedly. Get it?*

I have to keep myself safe.

Because I can feel my stomach getting hot, thinking of all this beer. Because my brain is racing through so many scenarios: *he'll fall asleep later and you can just come out and have one, or just a sip, and he'll never know, and then you'll be satisfied. He's probably got NyQuil in the bathroom, too.*

My body starts to tremble, thinking of the night in the pen with Charlotte.

I'm supposed to have six more days here with him.

He called and left messages for me every day in rehab, but he can't not drink while I stay with him.

"Bella?" Ricci says, turning to me from the couch. "Come sit, okay?"

There's a piece of pepperoni sticking to her bottom lip.

I walk over and very gently wipe it away.

"Sure, Ricci," I say. "I'm just going to grab something from my bedroom real quick."

"Bella?" Vanessa says. As I'm walking away, I can hear her speaking in low tones to my dad.

What was it the girl in the group meeting said?

Sometimes you have to lie to save yourself.

In our room, I grab my phone and my house keys. That's all I need for right now.

"Hey, Dad?" I say when I walk back into the front room. Vanessa's in the kitchen.

"Yeah?" He's changed the station to a police show. Ricci's fidgeting and bored. Good, that will help. Hoyt is perched on the edge of the couch, eating a piece of pizza.

"I'm feeling a little overwhelmed, so I'm going take a quick walk around the block to get some air, okay?"

From the corner of my eye, I can see Vanessa watching me. "Sure. We'll save you some pizza."

"Cool," I say. "Well, I'll see you in a few."

I'm just about to shut the door behind me when Hoyt gives me an apologetic wave. *Sorry,* he mouths.

"Hey, Hoyt?"

"Yeah?"

"Can you not call me Belly anymore? It makes me uncomfortable. Maybe it was funny when I was kid, but I don't find it funny anymore."

He pauses midchew. "Yeah, sure thing, Bella."

I close the door behind me.

The air is crisp outside. The sun's already gone down.

I have a couple of bucks in my pocket. I could get a soda somewhere and then wait for the bus. The ride will be nice. I know it's weird, but I've always liked the insides of busses at night. The yellowy interior lights, the way the neon signs of stores flash by through the window. Might be nice to get away from people I know for a while.

"Bella, wait!" Vanessa is jogging down the steps.

I turn around. She's got my backpack in her hand.

"I'm sorry, Vanessa," I tell her. "I can't stay."

"I know. Let me give you a ride."

In her car, Vanessa says, "That was not good. I'm sorry. I talked to him about it, before you came back, and I thought . . . I thought he was on board."

I pick at my fingernails. "I don't think I can stay there for a while."

She's quiet for a bit as she drives.

Then she says, "I came tonight because I missed you two. When I was younger, my mom had this boyfriend and I got really attached, you know? He'd watch *Gossip Girl* with me, can you even imagine? I thought he'd be there forever." She shakes her head. "He wasn't. One day, he was just gone. I didn't know what happened. My mom didn't want to talk about it. I thought it was my fault. I mean, I know now it wasn't, that it was just two people who dated for a few years who broke up and didn't really think about me and how *I'd* feel. But he could have at least said goodbye."

She glances at me. I'm trying very hard not to cry about my dad.

"Anyway, I know you aren't attached to me, but I am, kind of, to you. And to Ricci. This is all just to say, if you ever need anything, I am here."

I look over at her.

"Thanks," I say simply.

"I'll go back after I drop you at your mom's and hang out for a bit with Ricci. Maybe do some of that laundry."

"I think you should let Dad take care of the laundry," I say. "For once."

She laughs.

I unlock the door to the house, waving to Vanessa as I go in, and my mom looks up from the couch, surprised. I think she must have been asleep. Bart Bingleheimer barks at me and wags his tail from one end of Laurel's velvet couch.

"Bella? Where's Ricci? What's wrong? What happened?"

I sit next to her.

I have to think really carefully about what to say to my mom, because it's scary. I don't know how she's going to react, but I have to be honest.

"I can't go back to Dad's house, Mom." I rub the knees of my jeans. "He was drinking beer, and when I told him I couldn't be around that, he . . . well, he didn't care."

My eyes well up, realizing the full weight of what I just said. What my dad did. What it feels like he chose, instead of me.

"Oh my god," she says, She pats around the couch for her phone, shaking her head. "I just . . . I can't even . . ."

"Mom," I say sharply. "Please do not call him right this second and start a fight. Just listen to me."

She looks at me.

"Vanessa drove me home," I continue. "She's going to go back and hang out for a little bit with Ricci. She's nice, Mom."

My mom nods. "Okay. All right. That's . . . fine."

"And I need you to do something for me." My voice breaks a little bit. "I need you to tell him that I'm not coming back, not until I can be sure he won't have alcohol there and won't have been drinking somewhere else. I need you to do that for me because you're my mom, and you should stand up for me with him. Because I'm afraid to tell him. He thinks I'm on a walk right now. I just kind of left."

My mom's mouth trembles. "I will do that for you, Bella. My girl. I'm so sorry. I'll call him, right now."

She gets up. Bart Bingleheimer hops off Laurel's couch and jumps up next to me.

My mom turns around.

"Bella?"

"What?" I say, scrubbing Bart's one ear. The place where his other ear was is just a nub. I wonder how he lost it, who he was with before us.

"I'll let your dad know, but at some point, you need to learn to tell him these things yourself. When you feel ready."

I'm in bed. My mother is asleep in her room. Bart is snuffling at the end of my bed. It's comforting, his gentle snores.

I can't sleep. I tried doing push-ups and sit-ups to tire myself out, but it didn't work.

I need to talk to someone who will understand, but who? It's midnight now, and Amber's probably asleep. I know she'll answer and talk to me, but she won't *understand.*

I pick up my phone. Pull the covers over my head.

I never got Brandy's or Billy's number because I went into the pen with Charlotte. Billy and Brandy got out on time; I didn't see them again.

Scroll through my texts. Finally delete the bad ones. Delete the one from Lemon.

Then I see the texts from Josh.

Without thinking, I text him back.

Hey

I wait, staring at my lit-up phone in the dark under my covers.

In a few seconds I get, *Hey, you . . . wow, it's been a long time*

Yeah, I text back. *I kind of ran into some trouble and had to do another month.*

Oh wow. Wow. That sucks. But you're back in the world now.

Yeah.

How is it for you? It's a trip, isn't it?

That's one way to put it.

I pause.

Can I talk to you? Like really talk to you?

Of course. U okay?

I had to leave my dad's tonight. He was drinking. Not bad. I mean, he always has. But I didn't feel cool around it and he got kind of mad.

Shit. I'm sorry that happened to you. Sometimes people make it really hard. My parents have a lot of parties for my mom's work and I just have to deal. Where are you now? Do you need me to come get you or something? I probably could.

It's okay. I went back to my mom's. I switch houses. It's that kind of thing.

Oh right. It's good you had a place to go, though.

Thanks for offering to come get me.

Of course. So do you maybe want to hang out sometime?

I stare at the phone, my heart beating very slowly, not quickly, like I thought it would.

I think so. My mom is keeping me close, but I'll see.

I get it. That's cool.

Do you miss Sonoran?

. . . I miss you. Our runs together. Chuck trying to run us to death. Our dance.

That was a good dance.

I kind of have to go now, Bella, but text me tomorrow?

Okay.

Bye

Bye

I put my phone down.

I get up and walk to my suitcase, half open on the floor. I still haven't completely emptied it from when I came back from Sonoran. I dig through it until I get to one of my T-shirts.

Wrapped inside is the candy cane Josh gave me.

I cradle it in my hand and then get up and lean it against the lamp on my desk.

I sit back down, pulling clothes from the suitcase. It's probably time to empty it and wash these clothes. I'm rooting through the contents when I find an unfamiliar paper bag.

I unwrap it.

It's a Polaroid camera and a pack of film. There's a note taped to the box of film.

I unfold it.

Bella—

A little gift for you.

—Tracy

I pull the film cartridge from the box and snap it in the camera. Find the flash function.

Aim it toward myself and click.

Dear Dad,

I know Mom already talked to you. I hope you two didn't fight. I hate it when you two fight. I feel like you've been fighting for a really long time. I'd like you to leave me out of that sort of stuff.

I'm sorry that I just left the other night, but I'm also not sorry. I had to go because looking at those bottles of beer, I could kind of taste them, and that was scary to me. When I had that relapse in rehab, it felt like something was pushing me that I couldn't control. Something inside me took over. I'm trying hard not to let that happen again.

I can't come back unless you make some changes. I know it's your life, but you're supposed to take care of me. I don't want to wake up in the hospital again. I just got home and I'm confused about everything, too, and everything is not fine, but I'm trying to make it work. I don't really know what else to say, except that I hope I can come stay with you again someday.

—bella

WAS THERE A ROUTINE YOU LIKED AT SONORAN? TRY IT AT HOME.

I GET UP. THE SUN is just rising outside my window.

I look under my bed for my running sneakers, my sweatpants and hoodie, my dark knit cap to keep my head warm, my mittens.

I'm almost out the door when Bart appears in the living room, looking up at me hopefully, tail wagging. I sigh, find his leash, and snap it onto his collar.

He is not a good running partner. He stops at odd times to sniff patches of grass growing out of the sidewalk, jerking me backward. I jog in place as he lazily makes his way down the rows of weeds at the base of curbs. He barks lustily at a cat in someone's front yard, and I have to pull him away when the light snaps on in the house. Once, he even just . . . stops and lies down on the side of the street, rolling over and flashing his belly. I have to rub it five times before he's satisfied and gets back up. Finally, he gets into a groove and we're at a good clip. Sweat is prickling on my face and the back of my neck. My lungs hurt, but in a good way. I'm glad not to be running on Chuck's crazy made-up trails with him yelling at us for being addicts and drunks and losers and leaving us high and dry as he runs merrily away, but I'm also glad to just be running, because it's making my body feel good, and I'm out so early not many people are up, so I don't have to worry about anyone staring at me. I mean, I don't feel great emotionally, but at least I'm not sitting in goat shit.

I have not had a drink in thirty-nine days.

PEOPLE WILL DRIFT BACK TO YOU.

MY MOTHER IS PUTTING Ricci to bed. I'm cleaning up in the kitchen. I made us quesadillas and steamed carrots for dinner, on my own, because I kind of miss making food like we did at Sonoran Sunrise. I'm also bored. If things were the way they used to be, I'd be a little buzzed by now, probably, and doing things in anticipation of being able to get more drunk, quietly, in my room, or at Laurel's.

It's hard dealing with the boredom.

I'm sliding dishes into the dishwasher when my phone buzzes.

Dylan's face appears on the screen. My heart sinks.

It's one of my favorite pictures of him, at the arcade at the movies, leaning over air hockey.

I can't ignore him for the next two and a half years.

I can hear how soft his voice would be on the phone, sinking into my ear. Or if we did a video call, how he'd look lying back on his bed, his phone above him, his head resting on the pillow, his eyes half closed. We kissed on that rumpled bed, a lot, when his parents were out.

I can see all these things; they flood back to me in a breathtaking wave. If I answer the phone, I'm opening something back up. Something I think I need to keep locked tight. I didn't ask him to save me the night of the party. It was kind that he did, though. I don't ask him to seek me out in the hallways or wave to me in the cafeteria. But he does.

Maybe it's not me who needs to let go. It's him.

I wait until the phone stops ringing and then I text him.

Please stop. Please, leave me be.

Then I block his number from my phone and go into my room and pull on my headphones and listen to the saddest songs I know as loud as I can.

EVERYBODY IS TRYING IN THEIR OWN WAY.

Dear Bella,

Do you remember when you were very little, about three or four or so? Your mother had that night class she was taking. It met once a week, for three hours. That's a long time to talk about books, but I've never been a big reader, really. Anyway, you didn't like her being away. You two had a very specific bedtime routine, and me being around, and her not, kind of threw you off. You were very specific with me that I couldn't read to you in the bed, like she did. "It's her spot," you said, as nicely as possible. "Her place is saved. You will have to sit there." So I sat in that awful wicker wingback chair Hoyt and his wife had given us. Not the best for reading. But I did it. And I was happy about it because I felt close to you. Because I loved you. We worked out our own routine, if you recall. The wingback chair was rotting in the seat, and my back was rotting, too, so I bought one of those outdoor loungers and some cushions at Savers, and every Wednesday night, I pulled it close to the right side of the bed, where you were, and we read. Then I'd sing you to sleep. I'm much better at musical things anyway. Or I used to be. Sometimes I wonder if you remember those songs. I do. I had a couple on rotation, like "Cigarettes and Chocolate Milk" and "Alive" (you really liked that one because no one can do Eddie's baritone like me. I've made a lot of money off that song in bars, let me tell you. And of course, I sang it kind of quiet, because I'm not a monster, and also you needed to go to sleep and Pearl Jam tended to rile you up, AS THEY SHOULD*). But your favorite was "Time of Your Life," so I always closed with that.*

And I remember exactly the night that I thought you were finally asleep and I started to get up, like usual, but you opened your eyes and said, "No, Daddy, stay right here, with me. Don't go. I'm scared." And I didn't. I said, "Never. I'm right here." I stayed right there on my little makeshift pool-lounger bed. I stayed there every time after, too. I stayed the whole night, every time.

Somewhere, though, I left you. Of course, I couldn't stay in your room forever and always while you slept; you had to learn how to sleep alone, and grow up, and do things without me.

But I left you, somewhere in all that time. Your mother and I had our problems and I disappeared. I was there, but I wasn't. I have a lot of shame about that, but that's my burden to bear, not yours.

My point is, I've been thinking about your letter and that song, "Time of Your Life," and that time in our lives, and this time, and especially the lyrics "It's not a question / but a lesson learned in time."

Maybe this is all a very sharp and painful lesson for me, like the song. I have to do better. I have to be there for you. You aren't grown up and you shouldn't have to do things alone. You're a kid. You're my kid. And I hurt you. I didn't hear or notice that you were struggling. I haven't paid attention to my own struggles, either, or the ways they might have affected you.

It's hard for me to look at you and understand what's happened to you, because then I have to look at myself and see all the ways I've failed you. I don't expect you to understand that. I don't think you'll truly understand unless you become a parent someday. That sometimes we inadvertently break our kids' hearts. Then we have to live with that.

When you're ready, I'm here. I'll be here for you. I can't promise everything will be perfect; nothing can be. But it'll be better. I love you, Isabella.

—Dad

DO YOU FEEL SAFE TODAY?

I'M COLORING WITH RICCI when my phone buzzes.

Josh.

Thumpthumpthumpthump but not in a bad way, in a nice way.

Hey, he texts.

Hey

How are you?

Good. You?

It's going okay.

Good.

I was wondering if you wanted to maybe hang out tonight, see a movie. My mom said I can borrow her car.

I don't know.

It'd be nice to see you.

My brain: *Say yes.*

My heart: *Say yes.*

Hold on, I text. *Have to ask my mom.*

My mom's at the sink, rinsing plates. She peers over her glasses at me when I come into the kitchen.

"Mom?"

"Hmm?"

"My friend from rehab, Josh, texted. Can I go to a movie with him tonight?"

She takes her glasses off. "I don't know, Bella. Isn't it too soon?"

"He's sober now, Mom. I have to, like, go out sometime, I guess, right? We're just friends."

"I don't know how I feel about this."

"We're only friends, I told you."

She looks at me carefully.

"I have to go out sometime, Mom," I say, pleading. "At some point, you have to trust me."

"Do you think it's the right thing to do?"

"It's just a movie. He's nice, I swear. And I have to go back to school next week. I want to do something a little fun before then."

"All right," she says finally. "But I'm driving you there and picking you up. You can text me when the movie's done. And I want to meet him first, outside the theater."

I stare at her.

"Those are the conditions. You're fifteen. You lied about dating Dylan and you're just out of rehab. I feel like I'm being pretty nice, considering, don't you?"

I run to my bedroom and plop on my bed.

It's cool, I text. *But she's taking me to the theater and has to meet you first.*

Okay. Wow. But sure.

He sends me the time and place for the movie.

* * *

Ricci jumps up and down in front of the theater.

"Stop!" I hiss. "So embarrassing. *Mom.*"

He's walking toward us down the sidewalk of the El Con, his hands in his hoodie pockets, smiling. I can tell he's a little embarrassed, too.

"Ricci," my mother warns. Ricci sticks out her tongue.

"Hey," I say as he gets closer.

"Hey." He smiles.

Those blue eyes.

"I'm Diana," my mother says. "This is Ricci."

Ricci hides behind my leg.

He holds out his hand. "Josh." He looks down. "Hey, Ricci."

"There won't be any drinking tonight, correct? Or anything else?" my mom asks.

Josh shakes his head. "Uh, no. Just a movie."

"Mom," I say. "I mean, honestly, I'm near death from embarrassment, here."

"Fine. Text me when the movie's out," she says. "And here, Josh, put your number in my phone."

She holds it out to him and he punches in his number.

"All good?" he asks.

My mother looks at me and then back at him.

"All good," she says.

We watch as she and Ricci start walking toward the car, and then we head inside.

* * *

In the lobby, he stops and pulls out his phone. "We have a while yet. I got the start time wrong. Sorry."

"That's fine." I look around. "We could go to the arcade. I'm pretty good at air hockey."

"Eh," he answers. He ducks his head, then looks at me, his eyes crinkling. "You wanna go see my friend? He lives right by here. We could hang out, come back."

"Well," I say. "I don't know. I'm just supposed to do this."

I twist my hands, nervous.

"It's right across the parking lot. That one street where the houses start. We won't stay long. I don't really like arcades. Too noisy."

"I don't know. I don't want to get in trouble."

He leans closer to me. "No trouble, I promise. I'll take care of you."

As we walk across the lot he asks, "Your parents cool now that you're back home?"

I put my hands in my hoodie pockets. "Not really. My dad wrote me a letter after that stuff I told you about. Well, I wrote him first, and then he answered. It's complicated."

He nods. "That's very old-school, writing letters back and forth."

"Did you write letters at Sonoran?" I ask. "The impact letters?"

"Nah," he says. "I did that the first time around at another place. I feel like writing them again kind of takes the impact out of the impact, if you know what I mean? Like how many times can I say I'm sorry for impacting somebody's life?"

"Right."

His phone pings.

"Oh, hey, hold on, I have to get this." he says, and turns away from me.

I pretend to look at my own phone. He's murmuring. Takes a quick glance at me. Puts his phone back in his pocket.

"Onward," he says. "It's right over here."

We have to hop a short wall. I scrabble a little going over it; he helps me down. We're in someone's backyard, where pathway lights lead to patio doors. I can see a light inside and people standing around. Josh takes my hand. Leading me down the path.

"You look really cute," he says, smiling. "I don't think you had any makeup on at Sonoran, did you? I like it. And like, here you are, with your whole real face, finally."

I'm hoping he doesn't notice the blush creeping up my neck.

"It's a good face," he says softly. "I'm looking forward to getting to know that face."

He slides open the patio door.

There's a crowd of guys and a few girls sitting in the living room, passing a bong. The television is on. YouTube. Skateboarding videos. A couple of the girls look me over.

I just stand there, not sure what to do. There are soft bells going off in my brain.

I don't know anyone here. I should be at the movies, safe in the dark.

Josh goes into the kitchen and comes back with two beers. He hands me one.

"Just a pit stop before the movie." He winks. "I swear."

The beer. In my hand.

It was all so smooth and silky. In the house, then the kitchen, and now back to me, handing me a bottle like it's nothing.

"Wait here," he says. I watch him walk over to a guy in the corner, who glances at me and then at Josh. He slips his hand in his pocket and then passes something to Josh.

Josh turns to the wall and bends his head slightly so I can't see what he's doing.

His friend laughs.

The bottle is a thousand pounds but also light as a feather.

My brain says: *oh god this will feel good can you even imagine you will get so fucked up so quick you've been sober so long*

My heart says: *Get out*

He just walked from the kitchen to here and it landed in my hand, easy-peasy.

Like walking down a street and turning a corner, an invisible hand at your back. Like Fran said. Everything is fine and then suddenly you are not you.

I am not me.

My heart says: *this boy is cute you don't have to drink it just put it down.*

My brain says: *Bella do it your mom will never know pop a mint drink some coffee just have a little no one will know.*

It's like walking into the animal pen with a girl you punched in the face and you're so starved for friendship you follow her and then you see what she has and your mouth starts to water and haven't you worked so hard aren't you so tired of trying and didn't Tracy say the world was uncontrollable anyway and if you did all those days before you can always do them again—

My mouth is tingling. My whole body is tingling.

Josh comes back to me, his amazing blue eyes bright and a little wild.

"Bella? You cool?"

It's hard to push the words out of my throat with the bottle in my hand. I feel my body splitting into a million little pieces. I'm flying everywhere, out of myself, disappearing cell by cell.

"You lied to me," I whisper. "You said you weren't doing this stuff."

My voice seems very far away, even though it's coming from inside the me that's rapidly disintegrating.

He leans in close, his breath on my cheek. A shiver runs through my body. His mouth is so close to mine.

"I didn't lie to you, Bella, I lied to your *mom.* And parents lie to *us* all the time. They tell you they love you, then they mess with you, and then they say they're sorry, then they do it again and again."

His voice has hardened.

That's right. In rehab he said "busted faces" when we were on the run and he asked about my face.

He presses his mouth to my neck, just like he did in the Star Pit.

"I told you in rehab that there's not much to me, except I just really, really like getting high. And I really, really like you. It's a shitty world. Let's break it together."

It is a shitty world, isn't it?

A mountain of schoolwork and summer school. Awful kids at school. Getting suspended. My dad not caring enough to not drink in front of me. Laurel's house gone, her things just piles of boxes in the corner of my room.

Holly and Gideon.
God, I'm lonely.
I'm slipping away.

It's a thousand stars exploding in my mouth, slipping down my throat and carving a warm pool in my stomach, that first sip.

It's a million volts of shame shooting through my veins and then drowning them with the second.

And then
It is something else
Rising inside the me that used to be me
The me scattered in piles all over the floor
A boy's mouth inching closer to mine
Something mad
And angry

And the third sip
The one resting inside my mouth
Itchy to go down my throat and drop into the warm-
And-getting-warmer pool in my stomach
Is just swirling there, tipping over my tongue
Crashing against the sides of my mouth
The back of my teeth

* * *

It comes out with vengeance
Pushed by that anger
That somehow rose from the broken me
All over his shirt
All over the floor
And he jumps away, his shirt soaked
And they all look at me
I drop the bottle on the carpet
And pick up all the broken parts of me
(I can put them back together I know I can)
And run, run, run

ONE FRIEND IS ALL YOU NEED.

SEEK SHELTER. THAT'S WHAT they said at rehab. Make one if you don't have one.

I'm on the sidewalk outside the front of the house, breathing in the cold February air, then spitting frantically on the ground, trying to get the taste out of my mouth. I feel dizzy.

I look around. I sort of know where I am and I sort of do not. I just have to go around the block, right, to get back to El Con? My phone is in my pocket. I wrap my fingers around it. I stand there.

My mom was right. It was too soon. It will probably always be too soon.

"Bella?"

I look up.

Dawn is standing across the street, arms wrapped around herself.

We stare at each other.

I walk across the street.

"Bella, what are you doing here?"

"You live here?" I ask, wiping my mouth frantically. I spit again.

"Yeah," she says. "Over there. What is going on? Are you sick?"

"I . . ."

She sniffs the air around me.

"Oh," she says. "Oh."

"I didn't . . . I thought we were going to a movie. Me and Josh."

"Josh?" She wrinkles her forehead. "Does he go to school with us?"

"He's from rehab."

"Are you . . . How much did you have?"

She puts her arm through mine and starts walking me toward her house.

"I don't . . . I can't really think right now. Two sips of beer. I swallowed them. And then . . . there was a third, but . . ."

"But what?"

"I spit it out. On him."

She stops walking. "Wait, you spit your drink out on him?"

"I had to get it out."

She giggles.

"It's not funny, Dawn. I have to get it out. I have to get the rest out. It can't stay in me, don't you understand?"

I whip over, facing the ground and shove my fingers down my throat, over and over.

Up comes some frothy liquid and leftover dinner in chunks. I choke a little.

Then I start crying.

"I thought we were going to a movie," I say softly.

Dawn pats my back. I'm still bent over.

"Let's go inside," she says. "It's cold out here, and we should probably call your mom."

* * *

Two women are inside her house sitting on a couch and watching television. One of them is knitting something long and gray. They both look up.

"Oh, hello," one says. "And who are you?"

"Mom, this is my friend, Bella. The one I told you about."

The women look at each other. I can tell they've *heard* about me, but they don't look unkind.

"Bella, these are my moms, Sharon and Claire."

"Hi," I say.

"Hello," they both say.

"Bella threw up on the lawn," Dawn says casually. "I'm going to take her to my room and we're going to call her mom."

Dawn's room has art posters all over the walls and tons of books. She's got a needlepoint project on her bed. She sits down.

"I like your room," I say. "Do you think this counts?"

"Do you think what counts?"

"The beer I had. Does it ruin my days? It was only a little, and I threw it up, so it doesn't count, does it?"

Dawn gives me a half smile. "Listen, Bella, I have to tell you something."

"What?"

"I'm a cutter. I mean, I was. I'm trying hard not to be. It's why I wear long shirts all the time. I'm all messed up. But listen: if I decide to one day just make a little nick, even just the smallest thing, only a little bit of blood? I still cut myself. I lose what non-cutting days I had, so . . ."

She looks at me.

"I feel like it's the same with alcohol. You have to reset the clock. Start over."

I look at her, my heart sinking.

"Sorry," she says.

There's a knock at the door.

Sharon, one of Dawn's moms, peeks in.

"Do you need a bucket?" she asks me. "Kind of want to save the carpet after what happened on the lawn."

I feel my face flush. "No. Sorry. I'm better now."

"Right. Glad to hear it."

She closes the door.

"Do you have any marshmallows?" I ask Dawn.

"I'm sorry, what?" She giggles.

"Marshmallows. And a fire pit. They told us in rehab to feed ourselves when we're hungry, and to seek shelter, and to stay warm, and we'd survive. So do you want to make a fire in your backyard? And eat gooey marshmallows on sticks?"

"I *do* have a fire pit, and that sounds really nice, but I don't think right now is the time to be giggling and eating marshmallows. I think you need to call your mom and tell her what happened. And then, after she's done grounding you for a million years, you can come back and have marshmallows. Give me your phone."

I hand her my phone.

"What's your password?"

I tell her.

She scrolls on my phone. "What did you say his name was?"

"Josh."

She makes a few swipes on my phone.

"There," she says. "He's blocked."

Then she calls my mom.

It doesn't sound great.

When she gets off the phone, she hands it back to me.

"I'm sorry for what's about to happen to you," she says.

"Thanks," I say. "I knew someone like you. In the hospital. Holly. She died. But not from that."

"A cutter?"

I nod.

"Well," Dawn says, "there are a lot of girls like me. And like you. Just walking around the world not knowing about each other. A silent, sad army, I guess. Welcome."

The first thing my mom says when we get in the car is "I'm so angry at you right now."

The second thing she says is "I'm so angry at *myself.* What was I thinking, letting you go out like that?"

The third thing she says is "We're going to a meeting. I texted Tracy and that's what she said to do."

The only thing I say is "Okay."

And then, "I'm sorry."

It's ten o'clock at night and there are at least seventy people in this church, only not in the basement this time. Up top, in the main part, spread out among the pews. It isn't all kids, either. It's mostly adults.

Someone is talking at the front of the church. My mother and I slide into a pew in the back.

I do not feel good. I feel sick and stupid and afraid and ashamed. I'm sweating, but I feel cold inside. I lost all my days.

I lost all my days.

No.

I threw all my days away.

It was me.

Because I'm not normal. I can't do this like other people. I can't drink. And now I'm sitting here with all these other un-normals late at night talking about how un-normal we are.

That girl in group, she said her life was microscopic.

I can see that now.

How your life has to get very small, somehow, before it can get bigger, and I probably won't know when that time will be for a very, very long time.

I start to shudder with sobs, pressing a hand against my mouth.

My mother puts her arm around me and takes my hand with her other hand and squeezes hard.

Again and again and again and again and again and again and again how many times will I have to start over all my days?

TODAY YOU WILL REDISCOVER SOMETHING YOU USED TO LOVE.

I'M SIFTING THROUGH THE boxes of Laurel's things that my mother put in my room. There are beautiful velvet pouches filled with vintage jewelry. Books of poetry with her handwriting in the margins, which makes me think of José and Patty's Place and the snippet of poetry he recited to me. *I am a watercolor / I wash off.* He shouldn't have given me alcohol at Patty's, but I also shouldn't have taken it, and I did. I'm not going to tell Patty, because like Gideon and Charlotte said, don't be a snitch.

There are so many old photographs of Laurel, so many when she was young—my age, I think. In her school uniform on the Upper East Side, an A-line skirt with a crisp white shirt, a boxy-looking camera strapped around her chest.

In the last box, I find our Scrabble game, everything neatly put away, the letters mixed together and the last words we made gone forever. I run my hand over the worn cardboard box.

I get up and go to the living room. My mom is in the bathroom, her laptop open in the kitchen. Technically, I'm supposed to be doing schoolwork while I'm on suspension, but I'm so far behind and will have to do summer school anyway, I'm not trying to stress out about it.

I position myself at one end of the vintage blue velvet couch and begin pushing. It's heavier than I thought, and I'm grunting a little by the time my mother emerges from the bathroom. I've essentially blocked her in the hallway.

"What in the world are you doing?" she asks.

"I think I want this in my room," I say.

"All right," she says. "Let me help you, then, so you don't hurt your back."

It takes a lot of time and maneuvering for us to get it into the hallway, me pushing and her pulling, and then to figure out how to get the couch on its side and angle it through my doorway.

When we finally finish, it's sitting in the middle of my room. I tumble over the back of it and heave my desk under the window next to my bed, and my mother and I push the couch into place.

She flops down on it.

"You were supposed to be doing homework," she says. "You don't want to fall further behind."

"I know," I say. "But I was looking through her boxes and then I just wanted her couch in here."

My mother places her hands on her stomach.

"It still smells like her," she murmurs. She gets up abruptly. "Well, I should get back to work and so should you," she says.

"Maybe we could take a break," I suggest. "My brain feels a little mushy at the moment."

I lean down and pick up the cardboard Scrabble box.

"Do you want to play a game?"

She looks at the box for a long time.

"You know how old that is, don't you?" she asks. "It's from when I was little. I used to play by myself all the time, or with some of the other kids at the compound. She was always too busy, or off working."

The box feels suddenly heavy in my hands. My mother's voice sounds lonely.

"I was a little jealous, you know, that you two spent so much time together and got on so well. The only time she really noticed me when I was growing up was when she put me in front of her camera."

Her eyes look far away; then she snaps back, blinking at me.

"Let's do it," she says suddenly, her voice strong. "Let's clear off the kitchen table. I want to play some Scrabble with my daughter."

IF IT ISN'T WORKING, FIX IT.

MY MOTHER SETS THE piece of paper in front of me on the kitchen table.

"The rules," she says. "Tracy says we need clear rules."

I look down.

Wake up.

Go for a run. Take Bart.

Come home. Shower.

Take the Polaroid.

If it is a school day, get ready for school. Make your lunch. Eat breakfast.

Go to school for Power Hour before first period. Catch up on your work.

Go to class. Text your mother at lunch.

Go to class.

Your mother picks you up.

Come home. Clean your room.

Do homework. Make dinner. Clean up.

Go to group.

Come home.

Journal for twenty minutes.

Read, listen to music, watch TV.

Go to bed.

Repeat as needed.

Your friends can come over if your mother is home.

You can go out with your friends if a parent comes along.

If your mother wishes, at any time, she can give you an at-home test.

If you fail this test, you go back to rehab.

In time, certain parameters can be lifted after discussion with your group leader and your parents.

"That's a lot of rules," I say.

My mother shrugs.

"It's what we have to try. There are friends in there, and things to do. You have Dawn. And Amber. I don't understand the Polaroid thing, exactly, though."

"I'll tell you about it sometime," I say.

YOU CAN START OVER AS MANY TIMES AS IT TAKES.

THE SHED IN OUR backyard is cluttered, and the ceiling is quilted with webs. Old bicycles, gardening equipment, roller skates, boxes and boxes and boxes labeled *Mom,* as in Laurel. My mother's mother. I put my backpack on the ground.

I wedge myself between dusty suitcases to reach Grandma's dented green trunk.

I lift out cartons of unused film, albums of black-and-white images, notebooks in Laurel's messy handwriting. She told me once she always took notes about what she wanted to portray before she would do a shoot, like she was drafting a story before bringing it to life.

At the bottom of the trunk, I found it, wrapped in a thick blue wool blanket. Her large-format 8x10" camera. It's heavy in my hands, boxy and big. I'm going to learn to use it someday. I think Laurel would like that.

But for now, I put it away.

I reach into my backpack and take out the baggies of Polaroids from rehab and the ones I've been taking here with the camera Tracy gave me.

Carefully, I tack them to the walls in chronological order and then stand back and look at them.

There's the story of me.

Puffy and bruised and beaten down in the beginning, and

then, gradually, a lightening, shades of something else, or someone else, trying to break through.

I still haven't finished last semester's final project for Ms. Green. I think I'm going to use these instead of the tree, where I tried to hide myself behind branches.

I think I could make a whole diary of the last three months in these Polaroids. I'm sorry if Ms. Green won't like it. I don't mind whatever grade I get. But if she wants a self-portrait project, what better than these images of a certain girl who is me? Who started out one way and ended another? I understand now what Tracy meant when she said they were telling a story, one that I was writing about myself without fully realizing it.

The door to the shed opens suddenly, startling me. I jump.

There's a smartly dressed woman staring at me, an elegant black bag slung over one shoulder.

"You must be Bella," she says warmly. "Your mother said you were out here. I'm Clara Comstock. I'm an old friend of your grandmother's."

"Oh," I say. "Hello."

She steps carefully into the shed and looks around.

"Oh, dear," she says. "Are you really storing Laurel's work out here? I'm worried about the temperature."

Her eyes land on my Polaroids. She peers closer at them.

"Very interesting," she says. "Little bit of a rough start, I see."

She motions to the first set of pictures.

"I was in rehab," I say softly. "I got really hurt."

She looks over at me.

"I'm an alcoholic."

It sounds weird, saying that out loud, for the first time, really, to anyone.

She blinks.

"I'm not inexperienced with addiction myself," she murmurs. "Good for you. Very nice eye."

She's moving along the rows of my pictures, leaning close.

"You look like her," she says finally, turning back to me. "We met at Brearley. Pretending to be perfect little girls in our A-line skirts during the day and then coating our faces with powder and false eyelashes and ratting our hair and pulling on fishnets and boots at night to go to impossibly exciting and dangerous parties with impossibly exciting and dangerous people. And she recorded all of it. Like she did everything. She never wanted to forget a thing. And I want to make sure no one forgets her. There was a period in her twenties when she did some captivating self-portraits. Mostly nudes in abandoned buildings. I'm very interested in those. The exposed self."

"You're the curator," I say. "The one who's been calling for months."

"Yes," she says, smiling. "Your mother finally returned my calls."

"Okay, but can you come back?" I say. "I'm kind of thinking. I have some homework to finish. I missed a lot of school and I have an art project."

She holds up her hands. "I'll go inside. Your mother is making tea. Perhaps when I come out again you can show me Laurel's work?"

"I guess that would be all right."

She closes the shed door behind her.

I think about what she said, "the exposed self."

I look at my photos again, walk along them, touching each image, one by one, with a finger.

Each one contributes to the whole story of me as written so

far. I am too much, too little, too bruised, starry-eyed, scared, wren sparrow roadrunner quail, and one day I hope I look back at all these photographs and think I was beautiful in my brokenness, in all the pieces I keep gathering up and trying to suture back together.

One day.

But for now, I reach into my backpack and slip out my Polaroid, position it in front of me.

Because I don't want to be a watercolor. I don't want to wash off, or away.

Click.

AUTHOR'S NOTE

There's a photograph of me and my sister in front of a table crowded with bottles of wine and liquor. The photograph is worn and blurred with age, but there we are: my sister with her beautiful red hair, me with my tangled blond hair. We're fancied up; it looks like I'm in some sort of pretty, zippered velvet dress. Maybe it was Christmas and a family party, lots of cousins and aunts and uncles and tumult. I'm four or five in the photo. I know this because my kindergarten picture is the last one of me with long hair. After that, it was cut short, never to be long again.

I think about that photograph a lot. Was it some portent of what my life would someday be? Because a long time ago, I really, really, really, really liked drinking. And I was good at it, until I wasn't. Like it did for Bella in *The Glass Girl,* everything began innocently for me: a game of quarters with cousins and a bottle of champagne at eleven. Like Bella, when that initial buzz hit, I felt like I was home. I could talk and be funny. The world smoothed out in impossibly velvety ways. My anxiety lessened. Like Bella, I became an expert self-medicator and felt like as long as I was doing what I was supposed to be doing (school, work, all the things that are supposed to make a life) and doing it reasonably well . . . well, what was the problem?

The problem is when you have a *problem* and that problem becomes an even bigger problem: where to get alcohol, how much to get, how to hide it, how to recover from it, how to keep doing it. It's amazing to me now (and sometimes quite funny; people in recovery develop extremely dark senses of humor) the lengths to which I was willing to go to make sure I could keep doing that thing that I thought was helping me function in the world but was actually erasing me, bit by bit. (The anecdote in *The Glass Girl* about a kid duct-taping alcohol to their body to sneak into rehab? Let's have coffee sometime and I'll tell you a story about underage me, a trip to Juàrez, duct tape, and rum.)

I've always been fascinated by how addictions begin (a side note here: some studies suggest alcohol addiction is 50 percent inherited; the percentage rises for other addictions). For Bella, it was a bonding moment with her grandmother and an immediate salve for her anxiety, which increased with her parents' divorce, her grandmother's death, the pressures of school, and a bad breakup with her boyfriend. But lots of kids go through those things and don't abuse drugs or alcohol.

But also . . . lots of kids do. Those are the kids Bella meets in rehab. Kids reeling from trauma. Kids neglected or abused by their parents. Kids with anxiety. Like most of them, Bella doesn't think she has a problem; she's just trying to survive. After all, who's an alcoholic at fifteen? Drinking is everywhere. Everyone does it; or at least, everyone does *something*. There are plenty of people who are responsible drinkers throughout their lives.

And lots of people who aren't, or can't be. They deserve our support when they need help, not judgment. Recovery is not a straight line. Recovery can take years and require many efforts. Relapse happens. Like Fran says in this book, you can have years of sobriety and suddenly the littlest thing will trigger that buried need; something inside you will take over, something you thought you'd successfully outrun.

Oh, let's talk about Fran and Sonoran Sunrise. Bella ends up in a rehab center in the desert. Sonoran Sunrise is run by a team of addicts in recovery doing their best to teach kids to value themselves, confront their fears, earn some successes, believe in themselves. (If you're reading this and you've been to rehab: Bella's experience might not mirror your own. All rehabs are different. This is a work of fiction.)

Can I tell you how much I loved writing Fran's poem? Because I did. Because that poem encapsulates addiction for me: you can smooth out the edges, you can try to drown whatever's inside you that's eating you alive, you can bury shame and anxiety and trauma by dropping shitloads of pills on them or dousing them in alcohol . . . but in the end, those things are still there. You have to face yourself. And that's the toughest part, like Fran says:

You will still be
You.
You must live in spite of all this.

Bella is at the very beginning of addressing her addiction. I don't know what the future holds for her, but I have hope. By the end of the book, she's trying to commit to a sober life. She has support in friends like Dawn and Amber. She's discovering photography as a way to connect with her grief over her grandmother. She's going to *try.* That's all you can ask of someone, and that's all they can do: try. The other side of addiction is recovery, and sometimes it really, really, really sucks here, but also . . . there are great and shining moments, and believe me, you want to be able to experience them clearly. You want to be able to see yourself, like Fran says, in all your heart-shaped glory.

RESOURCES

Al-Anon and Alateen
al-anon.org

Alcoholics Anonymous (AA)
aa.org

In The Rooms
intherooms.com

Narcotics Anonymous (NA)
na.org

National Alliance on Mental Illness (NAMI)
nami.org

Rape, Abuse & Incest National Network (RAINN)
rainn.org

Smart Recovery: Self-Management and Recovery Training
smartrecovery.org

Substance Abuse and Mental Health Services Administration
samhsa.gov/find-help/national-helpline

The Trevor Project
thetrevorproject.org

ACKNOWLEDGMENTS

I often say that I don't know how to write a novel, even though I have quite a few under my belt now. That's because (for me) each novel begins as a fuzzy, indistinct thing: an idea that brightens and dims, a character emerging at some point, then fluttering away. I never know exactly how to get that idea and character down until I start writing the book. Somewhere around the midway point of the first draft, I get an aha moment from my main character: I know how they should speak, how they see the world, what they want to say. And then the book . . . tells me how to write it. I feel especially tender toward Bella in *The Glass Girl.* When her voice came to me while drafting, it was quieter than those of characters from my other books. She seemed softer, somehow, and more hurt in different ways. I was (and am) very protective of Bella and her story of self-medication, anxiety, broken family, and grief.

I'm lucky that I have an amazing and empathetic team that understands me, my stories, and my characters. Writing can be lonely and is often a deeply solitary act; it's a true balm to rouse from that solitary place and find people rooting for you. I'm exceedingly lucky to have an editor like Krista Marino and an agent like Julie Stevenson, who always encourage me to burrow deeper into a story and somehow do it in a very humorous way, like cool doctors distracting you from unwanted shots with unexpected and hilarious jokes. They both make me laugh through the pain of revision, which is really the best way to doctor me, if you want to know the truth. I owe them both big-time.

The entire team at Delacorte Press, Penguin Random House, and Get Underlined continue to offer incredible support for my stories, and I'm extremely grateful to be a part of their team. Many thanks to Beverly Horowitz, Barbara Marcus, Lydia Gregovic, Jillian Vandall, Kathy Dunn, Dominique Cimina, Liz Dresner, Colleen Fellingham, Tamar Schwartz, Kelly McGauley, John Adamo, and Judith Haut. Thank you so much for taking care of Bella's story (and Holly's and Charlotte's and Brandy's and Billy's).

I'm a pretty quiet person who watches a lot of television and listens to music and can spend hours just watching the world go by, but when I do venture out of my cave, I have a lot of people I make a beeline for, because they are awesome and funny and wonderful and talk to me about writing and nonwriting and politics and pets and everything under the sun: Lygia Day Peñaflor, Jeff Giles, Erin Hahn, Karen McManus, Janet McNally, Bonnie-Sue Hitchcock, Liz Lawson, April Henry, Hayley Krischer, Beth Wankel, Holly Vanderhaar, Elizabeth Noll.

I'm often asked about my writing process, and while it's a bit chaotic to describe succinctly here, it does involve writing with the television on in the background, and so I'd like to also thank *Better Call Saul, The Gilmore Girls, Euphoria,* and *House Hunters* for keeping me company during the writing of *The Glass Girl.*

A DISCUSSION GUIDE FOR THE GLASS GIRL

1. The passage before part 1 sets the mood for this book. What do you know or assume about the speaker? What textual evidence supports your thinking?

2. Amber has witnessed Bella in low moments. She is frustrated with Bella's drinking and the behavior that it elicits (getting sick, blacking out, late-night/early-morning phone calls, and deception). What is Amber's breaking point?

3. Reflect on the following passages.
   - "'Stop *saying* that. If you were sorry, you'd *stop* with all this,' [Amber] says. Her voice is sharp." (p. 73)
   - "I made so many tree branches in my sketch because I don't want anyone to see me. I am a watercolor, I wash off." (p. 127)
   - "'Everybody has a story, right?' Laura asks the table, and everyone nods. . . . 'Own it. And move on from there. There's really no other option at this point.'" (p. 224)
   - "'I believe if you can walk into the darkness,' Fran says quietly, 'then you have the strength to walk back out.'" (p. 290)

4. Threads of grief, deception, and guilt bind this narrative. Give examples of how each is manifested in the book.

5. Describe Bella's family dynamic. How do Bella's relationships with her mother and father, Ricci, and Vanessa ebb and flow throughout the narrative? What is life like when Bella returns home?

6. What happens on Thanksgiving night when Bella lies to her father to meet up with Kristen? Where do she and Kristen go? What happens when Bella blacks out?

7. The perils of social media are evident in this book. In what ways does social media impact Bella at home, at school, and at the rehab clinic?

8. Part 2 opens with Bella in the hospital. What caused to her to be there? What did her "friends" do to her? Was an intervention with Amber and Bella's family necessary?

9. What is Sonoran Sunrise? Describe the young people (Billy, Holly, and Brandy) who are there with Bella. Who are Tracy, Fran, and Chuck? What are their roles?

10. How do the letters that Bella writes advance the narrative? What new insights do they give you about Bella's character? How do these letters illustrate who she is as a person and the place she holds in her family?

11. How does Holly and Bella's conversation on page 284 foreshadow what happens to Holly?

12. What happens during visiting day at the clinic? Why doesn't Brandy's family come? What do readers discover about Gideon's visit with her cousin? How does Holly act throughout this day? What do the residents later learn about Holly?

13. Bella is led astray by some people she meets at Sonoran Sunrise. Charlotte convinces her to sneak out and go to the goat pen. What happens while they are out there? What are the consequences of Bella's actions on Day 29? Josh invites her on a date, but he engages in familiar behaviors. How does Bella respond to his actions?

This guide was written by Dr. Shanetia P. Clark, who teaches courses in children's and young adult literature at Salisbury University.

Turn the page to start reading another glorious and heartbreaking novel by Kathleen Glasgow.

MY SISTER, MADDIE, IS crying, her pretty face damp and frightened. One of my legs is heavier than the other and I don't understand and I want to ask her why, but I can't form words, because there's an ocean inside me, warm and sweet, and I'm bobbing along the waves, just like the ones that carried me and Joey all those years ago in San Diego, when everything was perfect or as close to it as we could get. That was a nice time, when I was twelve and Joey was thirteen, letting the waves carry us, Maddie stretched out on the beach in her purple bikini and floppy-brimmed hat. Far away from Mill Haven, we were in a different world, where no one knew who we were.

I try to ask Maddie where Joey is, but she can't understand me. She thinks I'm saying something else, because she leans forward and says, "Do you need more? Do you need me to press the button?"

And her finger presses a button on the side of the bed and the largest wave I've ever known billows over me, like the parachute game we played in the gymnasium in kindergarten, all of us laughing as the fabric gently overtook us and blocked out the world.

My mother's voice is trembling. "This is not normal. This is not something that happens to people like us."

My father sounds weary. He has been weary for years now. Joey makes people weary.

He says, "There is no normal, Abigail. Nothing has ever been normal. Why can't you see that? He has a problem."

My finger stretches out for the button to make the waves come again. My parents make me tired, years and years of fighting about Joey.

My mother's hand touches my head. Like a kitten, I respond, leaning into it. I can't remember the last time she touched me, stroked my hair. Everything has always been about Joey.

"There was *heroin* in his system, Abigail. How did we miss that?"

The word floats in the air before me, something eerie and frightening.

There was vomit spattered on his hoodie at the party. When we found him in the bedroom. He was woozy and floppy and strange and made no sense and I thought . . .

I thought he was just drunk. Stoned, maybe.

"I will fix this," she says to my father. "He'll go to rehab, he'll get better, he'll come home."

She says rehab in a clipped way, like it hurts to have the word in her mouth.

"That's not a magic wand you can wave and make it all go away, Abigail. He could have died. Emory could have died. A girl *did* die."

The ocean inside me, the one that was warm and wavy, freezes.

"What did you say?" I whisper. My voice feels thick. Can they understand me? I speak louder. "What did you just say?"

"Emory," my father says. "Oh, Emory."

My mother's eyes are wet blue pools. She curls her fingers in my hair.

"You're alive," she tells me. "I'm so grateful you're alive."

Her face is blurry from the waves carrying me. I'm struggling inside them, struggling to understand.

"But she just had a headache," I say. "Candy just had a headache. She can't be dead."

My father frowns. "You aren't making any sense, Emmy."

She had a headache. That's why she was in the car. She had a headache at the party, and she wanted a ride home and it can't be right that a person has a headache and gets in a car and dies and everyone else lives. It can't be right.

"Joey," I say, crying now, the tears warm and salty on my face. "I want Joey. Please, get me Joey."

WHEN I OPEN MY eyes, he's there.

I've seen my brother cry only once before, the afternoon he and Luther Leonard decided to dive from the roof of our house into the pool. Luther made it; Joey didn't, and the sound of his sobs as he writhed on the brick patio echoed in my head for days.

But his crying is quieter now.

"I'm so sorry," he says. His voice is croaky, and he looks sick, pale and shaky. There are stitches above his left eye. His right arm is in a sling.

"I thought you were drunk," I say. "I thought you were just drunk."

Joey's dark eyes search my face.

"I messed up. I messed up so bad, Emmy."

Girls swoon over those dark eyes. Or they did. Before he became trouble.

Joey Ward used to be cool, a girl said in the bathroom at Heywood High last year. She didn't know I was in the stall. Sometimes I stayed in there longer than I needed to, just for some peace. It's hard all the time. Pretending.

Not anymore, another girl answered. *Just another druggie loser.*

I cried in the stall, because I knew Joey was more than that. Joey was the one who taught me to ride a bike, because our parents worked all the time. Joey was the one who let me read aloud to him for hours in a bedsheet fort in my father's den, long after he probably should have been ignoring me in favor of his friends, like most older siblings do. He taught me how to make scrambled eggs and let me stay with him in his attic bedroom while he drew.

Until he didn't. Until the day I knocked and he told me to go away.

He stands up, wiping his face with his good hand. His beautiful dark hair is in tangles, hanging over his eyes.

"I have to go," he says. "Mom's waiting."

Rehab. It floats back to me from when Mom said it. Was that yesterday? Or this morning? It's hard to tell. I don't know how long I've been here. Things are bleeding together.

"Joey, why did you do . . . it?"

I wish I could get out of this bed. I wish my leg wasn't hanging from some damn pulley in the air and that my body wasn't heavy with the ocean of drugs inside me.

At the door to my hospital room, Joey turns back, but he doesn't look at me. He looks at the floor.

"I love you, Emmy, but you have no idea what it's like to be me."

And then he's gone.